Biographical Publishing Corporation

Book of Biographies

Biographical Sketches of Leading Citizens of Beaver County, Pennsylvania

Biographical Publishing Corporation

Book of Biographies
Biographical Sketches of Leading Citizens of Beaver County, Pennsylvania

ISBN/EAN: 9783337098537

Printed in Europe, USA, Canada, Australia, Japan

Cover: Foto ©Raphael Reischuk / pixelio.de

More available books at **www.hansebooks.com**

BOOK OF BIOGRAPHIES

THIS VOLUME CONTAINS

Biographical Sketches

— OF —

LEADING CITIZENS

— OF —

BEAVER COUNTY,

PENNSYLVANIA.

"Biography is the only true history."—Emerson.

BIOGRAPHICAL PUBLISHING COMPANY,
GEORGE RICHMOND, Pres.;   S. HARMER NEFF, Sec'y.;   C. R. ARNOLD, Treas.
BUFFALO, N. Y., CHICAGO, ILL.
1899.

PREFACE

AVING brought to a successful termination our labors in Beaver County in compiling and editing the sketches herein contained, we desire, in presenting this Book of Biographies to our patrons, to make a few remarks necessarily brief, in regard to the value and importance of local works of this nature. We agree with Ralph Waldo Emerson that "Biography is the only true History," and also are of the opinion that a collection of the biographies of the leading men of a nation would give a more interesting, as well as authentic, history of their country than any other that could be written. The value of such a production as this cannot be too highly estimated. With each succeeding year the haze of Obscurity removes more and more from our view the fast disappearing landmarks of the past. Oblivion sprinkles her dust of forgetfulness on men and their deeds, effectually concealing them from the public eye, and because of the many living objects which claim our attention, few of those who have been removed from the busy world linger long in our memory. Even the glorious achievements of the present age may not insure it from being lost in the glare of greater things to come, and so it is manifestly a duty to posterity for the men of the present time to preserve a record of their lives and a story of their progress from low and humble beginnings to great and noble deeds, in order that future generations may read the account of their successful struggles, and profit by their example. A local history affords the best means of preserving ancestral history, and it also becomes, immediately upon its publication, a ready book of reference for those who have occasion to seek biographical data of the leading and early settled families. Names, dates, and events are not easily remembered by the average man, so it behooves the generations now living, who wish to live in the memory of their descendants, to write their own records, making them full and broad in scope, and minute in detail, and insure their preservation by having them put in printed form. We firmly believe that in these collated personal memoirs will be found as true and as faithful a record of Beaver County as may be obtained anywhere, for the very sufficient reason that its growth and development are identified with that of the men who have made her what she is to-day—the representative leading men, whose personal sketches it has been a pleasure to us to write and give a place in this volume. From the time when the hand of civilized man had not yet violated the virgin soil with desecrating plough, nor with the ever-ready frontiersman's ax felled the noble, almost limitless forests, to the present period of activity in all branches of industry, we may read in the histories of the country's leading men, and of their ancestors, the steady growth and development which has been going on here for a century and a half, and bids fair to continue for centuries to come. A hundred years from now, whatever records of the present time are then extant, having withstood the ravages of time and the ceaseless war of the elements, will be viewed with an absorbing interest, equalling, if not surpassing, that which is taken to-day in the history of the early settlements of America.

It has been our purpose in the preparation of this work to pass over no phase or portion of it slightingly, but to give attention to the smallest points, and thus invest it with an air of accuracy, to be obtained in no other way. The result has amply justified the care that has been taken, for it is our honest belief that no more reliable production, under the circumstances, could have been compiled.

One feature of this work, to which we have given special prominence, and which we are sure will prove of extraordinary interest, is the collection of portraits of the representative and leading citizens, which appear throughout the volume. We have tried to represent the different spheres of industrial and professional activity as well as we might. To those who have been so uniformly obliging and have kindly interested themselves in the success of this work, volunteering information and data, which have been very helpful to us in preparing this Book of Biographies of Beaver County, we desire to express our grateful and profound acknowledgment of their valued services.

                                                        THE PUBLISHERS.

CHICAGO, ILL., November. 1899.

—————NOTE—————

ALL the biographical sketches published in this volume were submitted to their respective subjects, or to the subscribers, from whom the facts were primarily obtained, for their approval or correction before going to press; and a reasonable time was allowed in each case for the return of the type-written copies. Most of them were returned to us within the time allotted, or before the work was printed, after being corrected or revised; and these may therefore be regarded as reasonably accurate.

A few, however, were not returned to us; and, as we have no means of knowing whether they contain errors or not, we cannot vouch for their accuracy. In justice to our readers, and to render this work more valuable for reference purposes, we have indicated these uncorrected sketches by a small asterisk (*), placed immediately after the name of the subject. They will all be found on the last pages of the book.

BIOGRAPHICAL PUBLISHING CO.

Book of Biographies

BEAVER COUNTY,

PENNSYLVANIA.

CAPT. CHARLES C. TOWNSEND.

Book of Biographies

BEAVER COUNTY

APT. CHARLES C. TOWNSEND, whose portrait we take pleasure in presenting on the opposite page, is senior member of the well-known firm of C. C. & E. P. Townsend, manufacturers of wire, rivets, and wire nails. This is one of the oldest enterprises in Beaver county, and was established by the grandfather of Charles C., in 1828. The plant is located on the west side of the Beaver River in the village of Fallston, and it has been gradually enlarged from time to time until it is recognized as one of the largest enterprises of its kind west of the Alleghanies. Capt. Townsend is a son of William P., a grandson of Robert, and a great-grandson of Benjamin Townsend, and was born in Allegheny, Pa., although he has been a resident of New Brighton since he was ten years of age.

Robert Townsend was born on a farm near Brownsville, Washington county, Pa., April 9, 1790. He was engaged in the wire busi-

ness at Baltimore, Md., until 1816, and then established a similar business on Market street, between First and Second avenues, Pittsburg. In 1828, he started the first wire plant west of the Alleghanies, at Fallston, Pa., —it also being the first iron business in Beaver county. The machinery of this plant was run by water, though a large part of the work was done by hand. In his latter years, he retired from active business, and erected a handsome residence on Third avenue, New Brighton; this property is now owned by his grandson, Edward P. Townsend. Mr. Townsend was of Quaker stock,—a very liberal and charitable man,—and enjoyed the friendship of a host of acquaintances. He passed from this life at the age of seventy-seven years. His wife was Deborah Colman, who was born in England, and came to the United States when a girl of sixteen years; she died aged eighty-five years. They were the parents of eight children: William P.; Mary; Sabina; Eliza-

11

beth; John M.; Caroline; Lydia, and George.

William Penn Townsend, the father of the subject hereof, received his education in the schools at Pittsburg, and at an early age entered the employ of his father,—beginning as a clerk. In 1840, he and his cousin were taken in as partners, the firm name becoming R. Townsend & Company; in 1864, he became sole proprietor. He enlarged the plant, gave employment to many more hands, and put in new and improved machinery. Mr. Townsend delighted in traveling and spent many years in journeying throughout the United States and Europe. He entered the haven of rest at the age of seventy-eight years. He was joined in marriage with Sarah A. Champlin, a daughter of Matthew F. Champlin, of New York State; she still resides in New Brighton, has passed the eightieth year of her life, and is surrounded by many old friends and neighbors, who hold her in tender esteem. She is the mother of five children: Charles C.; Edward P.; Amelia; Elizabeth, and Helen. Although Mr. Townsend was reared a Quaker, he and his wife became members of the Presbyterian church.

Charles C. Townsend attended Pittsburg University, and at the age of fifteen years became a clerk in his father's office. When the War of the Rebellion broke out, he enlisted as a private in the Ninth Regiment, Pennsylvania Volunteers, but was shortly afterward transferred to the First Pennsylvania Cavalry, with the rank of adjutant. After serving two years in the Army of the Potomac, he was discharged on account of poor health. Re-

turning home, he and his brother, Edward P., were taken in as partners with their father, and in 1894 the sons became sole proprietors of the establishment, the firm name being changed to C. C. & E. P. Townsend. They have enlarged the plant, have added the manufacture of wire nails of all sizes, and give employment to about one hundred hands. This is one of the largest enterprises in Beaver county, as well as one of the first. Captain Charles C. Townsend's sons, who now assist in running the plant, are the fourth generation of Townsends who have been interested in this factory. Mr. Townsend is very enterprising, gives his hearty support to those measures which tend to promote the general welfare and bring prosperity to the community, and is recognized by his many friends and acquaintances as a good neighbor and loyal citizen. He resides in the old Bradford residence in New Brighton. He has served as vice-president of the National Bank of New Brighton since 1896, and has also represented this district in the Fifty-first Congress, from 1889 to 1891.

Capt. C. C. Townsend was married to Miss Juliet Bradford, a daughter of Benjamin Rush Bradford, and they are the parents of the following children: Juliette; Gertrude, who died aged twenty-two years; William P., Jr., superintendent of the company warehouse; Vincent Bradford, clerk for the company; Charles C., Jr., of the mechanical department; Benjamin Rush, and John M., an assistant clerk in the company's office. Religiously, Mr. Townsend is a member of the Presbyterian church, in which he is ruling elder. Socially, he belongs to Edwin M. Stanton Post, No. 208, G. A. R., of which he is past commander. In his political affiliations, he is a stanch Republican.

———◆—◆◆———

FRED N. BEEGLE, secretary and treasurer of the Union Drawn Steel Co., of Beaver Falls, Pa., is a thorough business man and understands all the details of the steel business. Largely through his energy, the business has increased to its present volume. The firm now enjoys a splendid foreign, as well as a large domestic, trade. The subject of this sketch was born at Millersburg, Ohio, May 21, 1863, and received his scholastic training in the public schools of his native town, taking a finishing course at the High School of North Manchester, Indiana. At the age of sixteen, he began life for himself, and in April, 1880, located in Beaver Falls, where he was clerk in a grocery store for a few months, subsequently entering the employ of the Western Union File Works, of the same place. He remained with the latter company about five months, as "tester" of files, and then began business on his own account. Opening a wholesale and retail produce business, he continued that very successfully for a couple of years, then sold out to excellent advantage, and spent the following year traveling in the West. Returning to Beaver Falls, Mr. Beegle became manager of a grocery store for B. B. Todd for about two and a half years. He then accepted a posi-tion as order clerk for the Hartman Steel Co. of the same place; during his three years' service with that company he worked himself up to the position of assistant chief clerk.

At the close of that time, the Hartman plant was purchased by Carnegie, Fipps & Company, and Mr. Beegle became chief shipping clerk. One year later he was transferred to their Thirty-third street mill in Pittsburg. This change, however, did not prove a satisfactory one to Mr. Beegle, and he resigned after a few months' service. Very soon afterwards, on November 16, 1899, he entered the employ of the Union Drawn Steel Co., of Beaver Falls, as assistant superintendent. About one year later the company was re-organized, and Mr. Beegle became a stockholder, being also elected secretary and treasurer of the concern. When our subject first became associated with the company, the capacity of the plant was only 2,000 tons per year, of cold drawn steel. Under Mr. Beegle's able management of the business end the output has constantly increased, and every second year a new building has been added and the capacity of the plant at the present time is 30,000 tons annually.

In 1880, Mr. Beegle was united in marriage with Nellie Heath, a daughter of Rev. Mr. Heath, of Oberlin, Ohio. They have one son, Clifford, in whom all their hopes are centered. In his political views, the subject of this record is a Republican, and takes great interest in party successes, but is too busy a man to take an active part in politics or to have political aspirations. He is a son of

Benjamin and Lucinda (Corns) Beegle.

Benjamin Beegle was born in Bedford county, Pa., and was a cabinet maker by trade. He went to Millersburg, Holmes county, Ohio, in 1846, and lived there the remainder of his days. His death occurred in 1882, at the age of seventy-two years. Lucinda Corns, a charming lady and a native of Lancaster county, Pa., became his wife, but laid down the burden of life at the early age of thirty-six. She left the following children to mourn her demise: Benjamin F.; Joseph; Thomas (deceased); Rollin A.; John; Edward; Lucy M. (Brady), deceased; and Fred N., the subject of this brief sketch. The elder Mr. Beegle was a firm believer in the Jacksonian principles of Democracy. He was a true gentleman, intelligent, courteous, and refined, just the kind of a man to make a lasting impression of good on all societies, which were fortunate enough to number him among their members. He favored the Lutheran church.

Fred N. Beegle is a live, enterprising business man, and merits the success which he is meeting in all his endeavors. He is an honest and straightforward citizen and has made many friends both in private and commercial life.

⁂

WILLIAM G. ALGEO, Sr., of Beaver Falls, enjoys the distinction of being the oldest undertaker of Beaver county, Pennsylvania. He was born in Allegheny City, Pa., May 14, 1830, and is a son of Gregg Algeo, who was also born in Allegheny City, where he was reared and received his intellectual training. He embarked in mercantile pursuits at Pittsburg, Pa., and followed that occupation until cut off by death at the age of fifty years. He was joined in marriage with Susanna Gibson, a daughter of Rev. Robert Gibson. Mrs. Algeo was a native of New Jersey and departed this life at the age of forty-five years. They were Covenanters in their religious views, and reared six children, all of whom are now deceased except William G., the subject of this sketch. The following are their names: Rebecca; William G.; Margaret (Pasco); Sarah J. (Robinson); William G., subject of this sketch; and Elizabeth.

William G. Algeo, Sr., obtained his education in the institutions of his native city. After leaving school, he began to learn the cabinet maker's trade with T. B. Young & Co., in 1846, remaining with that company until 1850. After working at his trade as a journeyman for a brief period, Mr. Algeo began business on his own account as a furniture dealer in Pittsburg, Pennsylvania. He continued in that business with a great deal of success until 1860, when he became associated with Robert Fairman in the undertaking business. In 1864, they established the first coffin factory west of the Alleghany Mountains, and manufactured for the trade exclusively. The firm was then known as the Excelsior Coffin & Casket Works and was composed of Hamilton, Algeo, Arnold & Co. That firm

HON. JAMES SHARP WILSON.

continued to do business until 1870, when it was dissolved and Mr. Algeo formed a new company, locating a factory for the manufacture of coffins at Rochester, Pa., and operating under the firm name of Algeo, Scott & Co. This company continued in business until 1875, and was sold out. Mr. Algeo went to Beaver Falls and established a coffin factory there, having his son, William G., Junior, as a partner. In 1876, they closed out the manufacturing department, and embarked in the undertaking business, which Mr. Algeo still follows, being the only man in the county who has continued for so long in that business.

In 1853, our subject was joined in the holy bonds of matrimony with Sarah A. Huff, a daughter of Mrs. Rosanna Huff, of Pittsburg. Mrs. Algeo passed to the world beyond in 1894 aged fifty-three years, leaving three children as a legacy to her husband. Their names are: William G., Jr., who is master mechanic of the Union Drawn Steel Co., of Beaver Falls, and who was joined in marriage with Nora Clayton, a charming lady of Beaver Falls; Mary E.; and Fairman, who led Anna Latham to the altar, and now has two daughters, Viola and Sarah.

Mr. Algeo has, by strict principles of integrity and honor, built up a splendid reputation as a man of push and energy, and has amassed a comfortable fortune that is now of service to him in his declining years. He is a member of Lodge No. 45, F. & A. M. of Pittsburg; of Zerubbabel Chapter, No. 162, R. A. M.; of the A. O. U. W. and the Royal Arcanum. In his political attachments Mr. Algeo was first a Whig but is now a Republican, and, although he has never sought political distinction, he served as burgess of Beaver Falls in 1886-1887. The subject of our sketch is an earnest and zealous worker in the Episcopalian church and is very charitable. He is a very prominent man, and one universally liked by all who have the pleasure of his acquaintance.

HON. JAMES SHARP WILSON, the highly esteemed president judge of the Thirty-sixth Judicial District of Pennsylvania, whose portrait appears on the opposite page, is an honored and talented attorney and a respected citizen of Beaver. Rarely do we find in the state or even in the United States, a man so young as Judge Wilson occupying so important a position, or one so mature in his profession. Judge Wilson has not yet reached his thirty-seventh milestone in age, but he comes from a distinguished family, and has inherited the power of leadership to a marked degree. It is said by some, that he is now the youngest member of the Pennsylvania judiciary.

Like many of our best men, he was born on a farm. His birth occurred in Franklin township, Beaver county, November 10, 1862. Early in life, he displayed his ambition for knowledge, and soon matured not only mentally, but physically. As a student in the public schools, he was ambitious, and at the early age of fifteen years, he began teaching a district school, and was very successful in this task. While teaching he was also a student, preparing for a college course. He entered Geneva College at Beaver Falls, from which he graduated in 1885, receiving the degree of A. B. Since then the degree of A. M. has been conferred upon him by the same institution. After his graduation, he became a law student under Hon. Henry Hice, of Beaver, and while pursuing that study, he taught at intervals in the academy at Harmony, Pennsylvania. Judge Wilson was admitted to the bar of Beaver county, June 4, 1888, and with his active brain and ambitious spirit, he rapidly became a leader in the political organization of his favorite party, which was the Republican.

In 1895, he received the nomination for president judge of the Thirty-sixth Judicial District, and although the conflict was a close one, he was victorious, and as usual, carried off the honors. He fills the chair with dignity and his numerous friends predict for him as brilliant a career on the bench as he has had in political leadership. By his ability and success he proves himself to be a worthy scion of the Wilson family, so noted for its prominent men. Judge Wilson is genial, cheerful, kind-hearted, and obliging, and ever ready to do a charitable act. In his religious views, he was reared a Presbyterian, and steadfastly adheres to its faith, being a member of the church of that denomination.

Judge Wilson was united in marriage with Sarah I. Hazen on December 25, 1888. Mrs. Wilson is a daughter of Nathan Hazen, whose sketch is found elsewhere in this volume, and a granddaughter of Samuel Hazen, of both of whom mention is made in the sketch of Christopher C. Hazen. Judge and Mrs. Wilson have a handsome modern home, with the Judge's private office adjoining it, on the corner of Market and Second streets. This fine residence was built in 1890, and is surrounded by spacious lawns, broad walks, and handsome and ornamental shade trees. This home is rendered truly happy by the presence of the following little ones who surround the fireside: John Howard, born February 1, 1890; James Sharp, Jr., born June 5, 1894; Hugh Hazen, born March 9, 1898, and Mary Elizabeth, born June 5, 1899. The Judge is included among the membership of many fraternal societies, is past master of the F. & A. M.; past grand of the I. O. O. F.; the Elks, and others. Judge Wilson is a son of the late John H. Wilson, grandson of Thomas Wilson, Jr., great-grandson of Thomas Wilson, Sr., and great-great-grandson of Hugh Wilson.

Hugh Wilson was born in County Cavan, Ireland, in 1689, and was a son of Hugh Wilson, who was an officer in King William's army, and was one of the three men who crossed the River Boyne, July 1, 1690,—facing great danger. For this act of heroism, he was rewarded with a tract of land containing one hundred and sixty acres at Cootehill, County Cavan, Ireland, where he established a country seat. His son, Hugh, married Sarah Craig, and in 1728 came to America (history says), to escape religious persecution, settling near Bethlehem in Northampton county, Pa., in what was known as the "Irish Settlement," and was composed entirely of Old School Presbyterians. Hugh Wilson was one of the commissioners selected to locate a site for the court house and jail, which was built at Easton. He was also one of the first justices of the peace, and assisted in holding the first court held in Northampton county, Pennsylvania. He purchased seven hundred and thirty acres of land, and received his title for the purchase in March, 1737. With his son Thomas, he was interested in flouring mills. On retiring from active business, he settled with his sons in Buffalo Valley, Pa., where he spent the last days of his life dying in 1773, and being buried in the churchyard at Lewisburg. The following are his children's names: William, who was born in Ireland, and became a merchant at Philadelphia, but was later located in the West Indies; Mary Ann, wife of Francis McHenry; Elizabeth, wife of Captain William Craig; Thomas, who married Elizabeth Hayes; Charles, who married Margaret McNair; Samuel; James; Margaret, wife of William McNair; and Francis, who returned to Ireland, became an Episcopal minister, and was later appointed tutor for the family of General Lee, of Virginia.

Thomas Wilson, great-grandfather of the subject hereof, was the next in line, and was born in Allen township, Northampton county, Pa., in 1724. When he attained the age of twenty-one years, he erected a flouring mill, with his father, and, by contract, furnished flour for the continental army; he received his pay in continental money, and in doing so lost almost his entire property. Selling what little remained, he took the proceeds and, with his family, located in Buffalo Valley, Union county, in 1792. There he purchased a tract of forest land, and cleared some in order to cultivate the soil. This was about one mile from Lewisburg, where the county-fair grounds and buildings are now situated. Thomas died in 1799, at the age of seventy-four years. He married Elizabeth Hayes, a daughter of John and Jane (Love) Hayes. Mrs. Wilson, in 1803, some years after her husband's death, sold the property, and with her sons, William and Thomas, removed to Beaver county, Pa., where her death occurred, in 1812. Their children were: Hugh, born October 21, 1761, and married to Catherine Irwin; Sarah, wife of Richard Fruit; Elizabeth, wife of James Dunken; William, who married Ann White; Thomas, Jr., grandfather of the subject hereof, who will be mentioned later herein; Mary, wife of Jonathan Coulter; Jane, who was unfortunately drowned while young; James; and Margaret, wife of John Thomas.

Thomas Wilson, Jr., grandfather of James Sharp, was born June 17, 1765, and settled in Beaver county, in 1803. He purchased a tract of land in Franklin township, built a log cabin and engaged in clearing the land. In those early days, as there was little or no chance to market the timber, the first clearing was done by felling and burning the trees, so that a place might be prepared in which to raise grain and vegetables for household subsistence. The chief aim of the pioneers and settlers of that period was to establish a home and rear a family. They were happy with children around the old and spacious fireside. Game was plentiful, the creeks were alive with fish, and wild animals abounded. Here Thomas Wilson, Jr., spent the remainder of his days, and saw much of the forest of his youth, turned into blossoming fields under a good state of cultivation.

He was an active, energetic man, proud of spirit, and austere in business relations, yet kind and charitable to his neighbors. He was united in marriage with Agnes Hemphill, October 7, 1806, and reared a family whose names are as follows: James, born September 19, 1807, and married to Margaret Morton; Nancy B., born December 25, 1808, and joined in wedlock with David Frew; Jane, born March 31, 1810, unmarried; Eliza, born June 5, 1812, who became the wife of Robert Fullerton; Thomas, born November 26, 1813, whose life partner was Mary Davidson; Mary A., born February 6, 1816, who died single; William, born May 7, 1818, who is also single; Col. Joseph H., who was born May 16, 1820, and died May 30, 1862; John, father of the subject hereof, whose career will be mentioned later; Francis S., born July 2, 1824, and wedded to Caroline Wallace; and Craig B., born December 24, 1827, and joined in matrimony with Elizabeth Pontius. The old homestead formerly owned by Thomas Wilson, Jr., grandfather of James Sharp, is now owned by the heirs of Francis S. Wilson.

John H. Wilson, father of the subject hereof, was born May 22, 1822. He was reared a farmer, and chose that vocation for his life work. He was a man of sterling qualities, and of a notably energetic disposition. From the very start, his life was successful; little by little he accumulated property. His home was in Franklin township, where he passed the closing years of his life. Mr. Wilson was looked upon as one of the leading men of his vicinity; a man who was not only thorough in his agricultural operations, but in all his actions as well,—taking great pride in improving and beautifying his place. He served one and one half years as county commissioner. At the time of his death, June 16, 1892, Mr. Wilson owned several farms in the eastern part of the county.

March 18, 1849, the elder Mr. Wilson led to the hymeneal altar, Mary E. Mehard, daughter of James Mehard, who came from Ireland to America and located near Wurtemburg, Pennsylvania. Mrs. Wilson was of Scotch-Irish descent. She preceded her husband to the grave more than three years,—passing away to her final rest on April 28, 1889, at the age of fifty-nine years. This highly respected couple reared a family of six children, viz.: Nancy Jane; Christiana Orr; William L.; Omar T.; James Sharp; and Loyal W. Nancy Jane was born December 26, 1849, and was twice married, her first husband being Dr. J. M. Withrow, and the second being James A. Jackson; she now resides in North Sewickley township, Beaver county, Pennsylvania. Christiana Orr, wife of J. G. McAulis, of Lawrence county, Pa., was born February 17, 1852. William L. was born May 2, 1854;

he wedded Anna Hilman, and resides on the homestead farm. Omar T. was born March 4, 1857; he was joined in matrimony with Virginia West. Hon. James Sharp is the subject of this review. Loyal W., M. D., was born March 25, 1866. He chose for his wife, Emma Weitz, and now practices medicine in New Castle, Pennsylvania.

———— ◆ ◆ ————

HON. JAMES J. DAVIDSON, deceased. It is a matter of profound regret that death should intervene to cut short a life in its very dawn of great promise, a life so efficiently equipped for usefulness to the community in which that life unfolded from childhood to noble manhood—a life gemmed with rare acquirements and high capacities,—full of encouragement to the many, who in their weakness, lean upon others. Such was the life of the most worthy subject of this memoir, Hon. James J. Davidson, who, although he lived but a few short years, did not live in vain. It is a sacred pleasure for those who mourn, to cherish the memory of his manly virtues and beneficent deeds. Eminent lives, independent of years, command the homage of mind and heart.

James J. Davidson was born in Connellsville, Fayette county, Pa., November 5, 1861. He was a son of the late Col. Daniel R. Davidson, and grandson of Hon. William Davidson. Birth and environment are the supreme forces that mainly determine the success or failure of human beings. These forces acting in concert as uplifting factors, success is almost assured; if operating adversely, life often ends in failure. The influences, which give them direction and potency, date far back in ancestral history. These elements, in their most helpful form, as character builders, gave to James J. Davidson his high standing in business circles and his initial success in political affairs.

The grandfather of our subject hereof, William Davidson, was favored with large practical ability, and was a noted iron master in the infancy of that great industry. He was several times a member of the Pennsylvania Legislature, and served as senator and as speaker of the House. He was appropriately looked upon as one of the foremost men of the county of his adoption.

Colonel Daniel R. Davidson, father of the subject of these memoirs, was richly endowed with mental capabilities that would have secured eminence in any of the learned professions, had the bent of his mind led in that direction, but he chose to deal with great commercial enterprises. His keen foresight and power of analysis secured for him large wealth, and constituted him a leader in developing the vast mineral resources, which have made the county of Fayette famous in the industrial world. The mother of James J. Davidson belonged to a family which ranked among the best of Western Pennsylvania, and was a woman of rare intellectual attainments and cultivated taste, who made home life a school of moral and mental training. Such were the marked and conspicuous antecedents of that life which it is the aim of these brief lines to record.

In the sixth year of Mr. Davidson's life, he removed with the family to Beaver county, his future home, and the theater of those early and brilliant achievements which gave such prominence to his short life. His preparatory education was obtained at the Beaver public schools and at Beaver Seminary. In 1878, he entered Bethany College, West Virginia, and afterward spent three years at the University of Lexington, Kentucky, graduating therefrom, in 1883. He returned to Beaver and spent the following two years in the study of law in the office of Hon. John J. Wickham, now of the Supreme Court of Pennsylvania. This fitted Mr. Davidson for the subsequent activities which made him a power in the political and industrial movements of the county and state, as it was not his intention to engage in the practice of the legal profession, but to qualify himself with most thorough business acquirements. This was the height of his ambition, and he made a study of practical matters among his first mercantile enterprises.

In 1886, Mr. Davidson commenced his business career by entering the oil trade as a new member of the firm of Darrah, Watson & Co., oil producers; he was subsequently interested in several kinds of enterprises. In the course of a few years, he became president of the Union Drawn Steel Works, of Beaver Falls, Pa., one of the most prosperous manufacturing plants of the Beaver Valley. Mr. Davidson was one of the largest stockholders of that organization, and was its president at the time of his death. Early in life the subject of this biography became actively engaged in politics, and was soon recognized as an influential leader in the Republican party, supervising partisan policies and giving direction to local and national campaigns. He served seven years as a member of the Beaver Council and was an ardent supporter of the public improvements, which in these later years have made Beaver so attractive for family residences.

In 1894, Mr. Davidson received the unanimous nomination of Beaver county, for Congress, but at the congressional conference held at Beaver Falls, he withdrew in favor of T. W. Phillips, of Lawrence county. In 1896, Mr. Davidson was again the unanimous choice of Beaver county, and at the congressional conference held in Butler, he was nominated on the first ballot. The nomination of so young a man in a district composed of four counties, with numerous aspirants, is proof of a phenomenal ability to control political forces, and was prophetic of a successful future, paralleled by but few in the history of our nation. After his election to Congress in 1896, Mr. Davidson went west to regain his health, but death prevented him from taking the oath of office, and his first year's salary was paid to his bereaved widow.

Toward the close of 1895, Mr. Davidson suffered an attack of "la grippe," which in after months developed into lung disease.

His ambitions were beyond his constitution, and his energetic disposition kept him from taking much needed rest. The failure of medical skill to master this lung ailment, finally induced him to seek relief in change of climate. In July, 1896, he left his home in Beaver, and accompanied by his wife and two children, went to Salt Lake City. A month's sojourn in that city failing to bring any special relief, he changed his location to Colorado Springs. After a six weeks' stay there he removed to Phoenix, Arizona; but change of climate and the most careful nursing and loving attention were powerless to arrest the waste of physical forces, and he succumbed to quick consumption. On January 2, 1897, at the age of thirty-five years, the struggle ended, leaving a grief-stricken wife, two interesting children, and a host of friends to mourn his departure.

Mr. Davidson was a thirty-second degree Mason and was past officer of that fraternity; he was a member of the Tancred Commandery, Knights Templar, and of Syria Temple. A. A. O. N. M. S. His Masonic brethren met his remains at the home depot, and had charge of the memorial services, which were very imposing. Mr. Davidson was also a member of the I. O. O. F. lodge, the Knights of Pythias, the American Mechanics, and the Americus Club of Pittsburg, whose members came in a body to his funeral.

January 31, 1889, James J. Davidson was united by the holy bands of matrimony with Emma Eakin, an accomplished daughter of John R. Eakin, noted as one of the solid men of Beaver county. This most happy union resulted in the birth of three little ones: Philip James; Margaret, who died when only three months old; and Sarah Norton. It was the most earnest desire of Mr. Davidson to build a handsome home for his beloved ones in some attractive spot, and to surround them with every convenience and comfort. But his unusually busy life left him no time to attend to this matter before being cut off by death, with this wish unfulfilled.

Mrs. Davidson and her two children are now residing in a pleasant home located on the south side of Park street, and it is her desire to rear and educate her little son and daughter in a fitting manner, that they may in the future add other laurels to the honored name of their father, a further account of whose ancestors may be found in the sketch of Frederick Davidson, of Beaver Fal's, to be found in this volume.

The publishers of this work take pleasure in announcing that a portrait of Mr. Davidson accompanies this work, being presented on a preceding page.

ALEXANDER DUFF, Esq., justice of the peace of New Brighton, Pa., has in his life time covered a wide range of experience, and has known much of men and affairs in many fields of progress. He has been directly and indirectly connected with several lines of business which have called forth the most earnest effort and steady industry. In every one of these interests which have claimed his time and attention he has manifested the qualities that lead to success. At the present writing, he is enjoying the results of his own thrift, and the rewards of a life well and usefully spent. Our subject was born in Mercer, now Lawrence, county, Pa., July 21, 1832, is a son of James and Jane (Boies) Duff, and grandson of William Duff.

William Duff was a native of County Down, Ireland. His parents died when he was very young, and he accompanied his step-mother to America, and settled at Turt'e Creek, where he lived until he reached manhood. Sarah Duff, a cousin of his, became his wife, and the young folks settled in Mercer, now Lawrence, county, Pa., where they purchased a tract of land, for the most part heavily timbered. When he decided to build a house, he could not get a team in the county with which to move the logs, so the house was built by carrying the logs, by main strength, to the place desired. Later, Mr. Duff built a large log barn, which is still standing. He owned about 400 acres of land, about 200 of which, together with the homestead, is now the property of his grandson, D. G. Duff. "Grandpa" Duff died at the age of about eighty-five years and his good wife passed away at the age of eighty-seven. Their children's names are: James; Oliver; Alexander; William; Mrs. Kildoo; Mrs. Small; Mrs. Struthers; and Mrs. Caldwell,—all now deceased.

James Duff, the eldest of the children, was the father of the subject of this sketch. James was born in Turtle Creek, Allegheny county, Pa., in 1792, and his wife was born the same year. Mrs. Duff's maiden name was Jane Boies. She was the daughter of James and Elizabeth (Wilson) Boies. Her grandfather, Col. Wilson, served in the Revolutionary War. James Duff received 80 acres of land from his father, and after building a log house and barn upon it, and clearing a portion of the land, he sold his farm, and purchased another one, again engaging in farming, which was his sole occupation during life. He was an active, enterprising man, and served in township offices, also rendering valued services to our country in the War of 1812, especially in connection with the struggle on Lake Erie. He died in 1876, at the age of eighty-five years, his death occurring only a few miles from his birthplace. The beloved mother only lacked two months of being ninety-nine years old at the time of her death, and was quite active up to the time of her last illness. On her ninety-eighth birthday her son, Alexander, and his sister gave a re-union for her benefit. That day she rode six miles and back. She loved company, and everybody loved her. Her home was always a pleasant place to all,—her disposition always happy. Hundreds of relatives and friends accepted the invitation and attended the reunion,—the first of its kind ever held in Lawrence county,—and a most joyous occasion.

This worthy and highly honored old couple were Associate Reformed Presbyterians, and reared the following children: William, who was twice married,—his first wife being Hannah Sherrer, and his second wife Jane McClellan; Eliza, who was also twice married,—

her first husband being Cyrus Williams, and her second husband James Kildoo; James, who wedded Lucinda Brown; Sarah, wife of John Poak; Jane, wife of Calvin Reed; John, who was also twice married,—his first wife being Eunice Sherrer, and his second wife Mrs. Small; Matthew, who married Eliza Clark; Mary, wife of B. F. Junkin; Alexander, the subject of this sketch; Lydia, wife of Cyrus Field; and Samuel, who was killed at the Battle of Fredericksburg. He was a private in Cooper's Battery.

Alexander Duff received his intellectual training in the public schools, and started out in life as a farmer. He bought a part of his father's farm, which was partly improved, built a new house upon it, and otherwise enhanced its value, and then sold out to excellent advantage. This occurred in 1863; Mr. Duff then purchased a better and more desirable farm in North Beaver township, Lawrence county, Pa., and carried on farming and threshing,—following the latter business fully twenty years. He enjoyed the distinction of owning and operating the first Massillon thresher in Lawrence county. Later in life, our subject entered the mercantile world by conducting a general merchandise store at Moravia, where he also became station agent. As his farm was located near by, he was enabled to oversee it and also give his personal attention to his store. In addition to all this, he began dealing in grain, which he continued for five years, during which he handled over 100,000 bushels each year.

In 1891, Mr. Duff sold his store to his son, C. W. Duff, and, renting his farm, he removed to New Brighton, where he purchased a handsome residence on Fifth avenue. On his farm, Mr. Duff not only made many improvements but rebuilt the house and barns, and carries on a stock and poultry business. He has 14 fine grade and full bred Jerseys, and a hennery 64x20 feet. He makes a specialty of fancy stock, and eggs, having all his eggs stamped with date of laying, thus insuring a fancy price. He rents his farm on shares and practically conducts it himself. From 1872 to 1877, Mr. Duff served as justice of the peace, and has also served as school director and in other offices of his township. In 1895 he was elected justice of the peace of New Brighton, and for the sake of having some light business to attend to, he handles a fine line of wall papers.

Mr. Duff was united in marriage with Alkey S. Fulkerson, an attractive daughter of Richard Fulkerson, of Lawrence county. She died at the age of fifty-nine years, after having reared the following children: William O., who is a coal dealer at New Castle, Pa., and wedded Rhoda Witherspoon, who bore her husband one child, Iva, whom they lost; Alice C., wife of James Young, of New Castle; Richard H., a graduate of the Cleveland Medical College, and now a practicing physician of Erie county, Pa., who married Ella Burwell, and has two children, Harold and Gail; Ella A., wife of Dodds Campbell, a farmer of Lawrence county, Pa.; Edwin E., a prominent druggist of New Castle, who married Annetta McCreary, — one child, Dorothy, having blessed their union; Charles W., a shoe merchant of New Castle, Pa., who married Laura Gwin, and has three children — Mabel, Fred, and Florence; Robert Frank, who was killed in 1887, at the age of twenty years, by falling from a wagon; and Harry G., a druggist of New Castle, who married Maree Jeckel, of Buffalo, New York. After the death of his first wife, our subject contracted a second matrimonial alliance, this time with Maggie E. Stuart, a daughter of John Stuart, of Lawrence county. No issue resulted from this marriage.

Mr. Duff, since his residence in New Brighton, has identified himself with the town's progress and development. He is a member of the First Presbyterian church of that place, and is also an elder. In 1891, Mr. Duff took a trip across the continent, visiting all the principal places of interest, and spending about four months on the journey.

———— • • ————

MILTON TOWNSEND, real estate dealer and retired merchant, is one of New Brighton's most esteemed citizens. He is spending the sunset of life, in his beautiful home, upon the knoll at the lower end of Third avenue, enjoying every convenience and comfort that could be desired. His residence is one of the finest sights in Beaver county, Pa., being surrounded by spacious lawns, lovely driveways and walks overlooking the valley below, and overshadowed by towering mountains, sublime in their grandeur. The subject of this sketch was born in Jefferson county, Ohio, November 3, 1820, and can trace his ancestors back to the sixth generation, the family being of English origin. He is a son of Talbot and Edith (Ware) Townsend, and grandson of Francis and Rachel (Fallett) Townsend.

Francis Townsend was born on April 15, 1740, was a son of Joseph Townsend, Jr., grandson of Joseph Townsend, Sr., and great-grandson of William Townsend, a native of Berks county, England. Francis Townsend wedded Rachel Fallett on July 8, 1762. They belonged to that good old class of people, the Quakers, who were such important factors in the settlement and early history of Pennsylvania. In 1786, Francis Townsend and his family entered the western part of Pennsylvania, settling at Brighton, which is now known as Beaver Falls. Mr. Townsend at once engaged in business by establishing an iron foundry and blast furnace for the manufacture of pig iron. He was so successful in this venture for many years, that in time he became the owner of considerable land and much valuable property in that vicinity. Like most of his creed, he was a fine old man, actuated by just and upright principles, and lived a life worthy of imitation by his sons. In the year 1800, he retired from active business pursuits and removed to Fallston, where he spent his last years with his sons, who had erected mills there. His death occurred at Fallston. He and his good wife were parents of the following children: David; Benjamin J.; Isaac;

Francis; Talbot; Lydia, wife of Evan Pugh; and one more daughter whose name cannot be recalled.

Talbot Townsend, father of Milton, was born in Chester county, Pa., and accompanied his parents west to Beaver county. In 1816, he went down the Yellow Creek to Jefferson county, Ohio, and engaged in the manufacture of salt for some time. In 1837, he located at New Brighton, Pa., where he built a stone flouring mill, and carried on quite an extensive business for those days. His mill was run by a splendid water power. In dry seasons, people came twenty-five or thirty miles to have their grain ground at his mill, coming, also, many miles by canoe. Much of their flour was shipped to the Pittsburg market, and further down the Ohio River. Mr. Townsend was a very successful miller, and acquired much property in the vicinity of New Brighton. He lived to the advanced age of eighty-seven years, and his most worthy wife lived to be seventy-seven years old. She was, before marriage, Edith Ware, a daughter of Asa Ware, of Salem, Ohio. Both Mr. and Mrs. Townsend belonged to the Society of Friends. Their children were: Milo, who married Elizabeth Walker; Eliza, wife of John Gammal; Milton, subject of this sketch; Alfred, who died unmarried; Lydia, wife of Edwin Morlan; Caroline, wife of Ebenezer Rhodes; and Alice, wife of Samuel Junkins.

Milton Townsend succeeded his father in the milling business for several years, until the mill burned. He then went into the trans-portation business, owning some boats and leasing others, and doing a large freight business up and down the canal for years, until the railroads became so numerous that boating was done away with. He next became agent for the Pittsburg & Cleveland R. R., after which he was clerk of the post office in Pittsburg for a period of two years. Returning to New Brighton, he conducted a shoe store very successfully for years, after which he retired, and built a handsome brick business block on Third avenue, where his father formerly resided. Mr. Townsend then began dealing in real estate,—buying and selling. He purchased the Abel Townsend estate, which consisted of a fine orchard called "Knob Lot," a round knoll at the lower end of Third avenue. He first built a round tenement house in the center of an orchard which contained the finest and largest variety of fruit in that vicinity. Later he had the house remodeled into a handsome dwelling, which he now occupies.

The subject of this sketch was united in marriage with Lavinia Oakley. Mrs. Townsend was a daughter of John M. Oakley, of Brighton, formerly of Baltimore, Maryland. She was born in 1823, and passed to her final rest in 1892. She bore her husband three children, two of whom were sons who died in infancy. The daughter, Emily O., became the wife of Ernest Mayer, one of the two owners of the Mayer Pottery Company, of New Brighton, Pennsylvania. In his political opinions, Mr. Townsend first belonged to the old line Whigs, was later an anti-slavery man and now votes the Republican ticket. In his younger days, he was connected with both the Masonic fraternity and the Odd Fellows.

Mr. Townsend has closed a long career of toil and is now enjoying that calm that comes after the struggle, untroubled by anxious thoughts of what the future may bring forth. His age has already gone far beyond that allotted to the average man, and he is fast approaching the octogenarian mark, but he still retains much of his youthful vigor. He has been identified with every enterprise worthy of note since his residence in New Brighton, and justly deserves the esteem of all.

EDGAR FREDERICK HOPE has been interested in the advancement and prosperity of Beaver Falls since the year 1890, in which year he established himself in mercantile business, and is now recognized as one of the leading and substantial merchants of that borough. His native town is Manchester, England, and his ancestors have resided for many generations in Preston, England. He is a son of Isaac and grandson of Thomas Hope.

Thomas Hope was a life-long resident of Preston, England, and was an expert machinist, conducting a machine-shop and foundry many years. He was called from earth when eighty-three years old. Isaac Hope was also born in Preston, and there also received his mental training; he was also a mechanic by trade and followed the same business that occupied his father's attention for so long a period. Mr. Hope was joined in marriage with Miss Easterby of Benthem, England, and they reared a family of four children: Daniel, who wedded a Miss Bradley; Joseph; Edgar Frederick, the subject hereof; and Eleanor. The father of Edgar Frederick Hope died, aged seventy-two years. The subject of this sketch obtained his primary education in the public schools of his native town, and early in life began to learn the trade of an ironmolder; desiring to seek a home and fortune in the new world, he decided to come to the United States, and accordingly sailed for New York City in 1880; upon his arrival there he found employment on the foundry work of the great Brooklyn Bridge. In 1890, he became a resident of Beaver Falls, Pa., and there established a general store, which he still conducts. Mr. Hope began at the bottom of the ladder, and, with meager advantages for education and no material assistance, has gradually worked his way up to the status of a substantial business man. His business interests are not confined to Beaver Falls alone, for he also has three stores in New Brighton. Our subject's store in Beaver Falls is located on the principal business thoroughfare, and he pays special attention to the lines of stoves and tin ware, glass and queensware and furniture. Mr. Hope by his wonderful determination and energy, coupled with good judgment, has made a decided success in all his business undertakings; he is popular and esteemed in both business and social circles, and is an intelligent and well-to-do citizen.

COL. JACOB WEYAND.

Mr. Hope formed a matrimonial alliance with Miss Frances Bailey, and their home has been blessed with three children: Charles J.; Harry, and Olive. Politically, he is a Republican, whilst in religious views he favors the Methodist church.

———— • • ————

COL. JACOB WEYAND, a retired publisher of Beaver, Pa., whose portrait is shown on the opposite page, enjoys the distinction of being the only living member of the convention that participated in the formation of the Republican party at Lafayette Hall, Pittsburg, Pa., February 22, 1856. He first saw the light of day on March 22, 1828, near Mount Jackson, Lawrence county, then a part of Beaver county. He worked on a farm until he attained manhood, and then attended Beaver Academy. In 1854 he became part owner of the Argus, and assisted in editing and publishing that paper until the winter of 1857 and 1858. Selling his interest in the Argus, he purchased the Free Press, at Carrollton, Ohio, where he was busily engaged at the breaking out of the Civil War. Catching the martial spirit of the times, Mr. Weyand sold the Free Press, and raised a company of volunteers. He was chosen captain, and marched the company to Camp Mingo, near Steubenville, Ohio, where it was at once attached to the 126th Reg., Ohio Vol. Inf., and mustered into service in 1862. During his service, Capt. Weyand was noted for sturdy courage and coolness in the midst of great danger, and although twice wounded in battle, he had no fears for his personal safety, but thought rather of the duty to be performed. He participated in nearly all the battles of the Potomac campaign. In the battle of Monocacy, Md., fought July 9, 1864, Capt. Weyand was placed in command of his regiment, and an officer on the staff of the commanding general that day, in writing a history of the battle, made use of the following language:

"Capt. Weyand, who was commanding the 126th Ohio Vol., was on the extreme right of the line, with the right of his regiment resting near the Monocacy bridge. After the battle had progressed a short time, he was directed by General Wallace to set fire to the bridge, then face the regiment to the left, double quick it to the extreme left of the line, throw it across the pike, and hold the position as long as he could. The bridge was fired and the regiment started off on its perilous movement. It had almost reached the desired destination, when, as it came abreast of the line of the 'hundred day men,' it met a most unexpected obstruction. Immediately in its front was a farm ditch about six feet wide and the same depth, through which a sluggish stream of water was running. A few feet further was a board fence five or six feet high—both running at right angles with the line of battle. Just beyond the ditch and fence was the Washington pike. The ditch was literally alive with 'hundred day men,' who, totally unused to the sort of treatment they were receiving at the hands of the enemy, had taken shelter there from the raking fire which the Confederates had opened on the pike. With the view of keeping that thoroughfare open, the enemy were in line of battle on an elevation of about four hundred yards in our front, and every missile known to warfare seemed to be coming down that hard, dusty road; plowing shot, screeching shells, rattling grape and canister were hurled out, with sharp volleys of musketry, sending up puffs of dust, or tearing up great rifts of the highway. No one could command calmness enough to considerately behold the scene, yet this had to be done; the General had ordered it. Here Captain Weyand leaped the ditch, climbed to the top of the fence, and pointed forward. In an instant every file was moving after him, led by the gallant McPeck. Under the galling fire the men were falling like leaves before an autumn blast, and, realizing the dreadful havoc that was being made in the ranks, Capt. Weyand broke the battle line, and hurriedly moved his regiment some seventy-five yards forward, where a rise in the ground partly sheltered the men from the merciless storm they had just passed. Every officer came out of the conflict bleeding, and every man not hit or killed had his clothes riddled with bullets."

In the eleven preceding battles in which the regiment had borne an honorable part, its splendid discipline and fighting qualities had never shown to greater advantage than in this field. Its brilliant conduct was the theme of officers and men who had no connection with it, and Captain Weyand, who had already

been complimented highly by his superior officers for gallantry at Cold Harbor, was now honored with a recommendation to the Secretary of War for promotion as major and brevet lieutenant-colonel.,Col. Fox, in his book, entitled, "The Three Hundred Fighting Regiments of the War," includes the 126th Ohio Vol. Infantry (Col. Weyand's) regiment as one of that number. After the war, our subject returned to Beaver, Pa., repurchased the Argus, and conducted it until 1874, when he consolidated it with the Radical, publishing both under the firm of Weyand & Rutan. From that time Col. Weyand practically retired from business, with the exception of dealing in real estate to some extent. He purchased the David Hall property of fifteen acres at Beaver, but just within the line of Bridgewater borough, and built a handsome residence. In 1893, Col. Weyand was elected to the legislature; two years later he was re-elected, and the duties of a legislator were performed by him in a very creditable and capable manner.

The subject of this sketch was twice married. In 1857, Victoria Adams, a charming young lady of Beaver county, became his wife, and shared his joys and sorrows until 1892, when he was deprived of her pleasant companionship by death. She was born in 1837, and bore her husband the following children: Emma; Romulus and Remus, twins; Milo Adams; Edwin Stanton; Blanche, and Paul. Emma is the wife of Harry W. Reeves, of Beaver; Romulus and Remus died in infancy; Milo Adams is deceased; Edwin

Stanton is an attorney-at-law in Beaver. He was a law student under ex-Judge Wickham, now deceased, and was admitted to the bar in 1895; he married Wilhelmina Thompson, of Marion, Ohio, who has borne him two children, Dorothy, and "baby," not yet named. Blanche is a stenographer, and Paul is a Methodist minister. He was educated at the Beaver High School and at Allegheny College, Meadville, Pennsylvania. He is now Superintendent of City Missions, at Pittsburg, Pa.

Some time after the death of his first wife, Col. Weyand formed a second matrimonial alliance—this time with Mary E. Cooke, a daughter of Maj. William Cooke. Col. Weyand is a member of the U. V. L. and the G. A. R. He worships at the M. E. church. He is a son of Henry and Mary M. (Ginder) Weyand, and a grandson of Jacob Weyand, who was born in Alsace, Germany, and came to America about the year 1738, settling at Somerset, Pennsylvania, where he and his good wife both lived to a good old age. So far as is known, their children were as follows: Michael; Jacob; John, and Henry, father of the subject of this memoir.

Henry Weyand was born July 31, 1791, in Somerset county, Pa., and there his marriage occurred. He wedded Mary Magdalena Ginder, a daughter of George Ginder. The young folks settled near Mount Jackson, and purchased a farm now known as the William Patterson farm. In his younger day, Henry Weyand taught schools during winters—teaching both German and English—and devoted his summers to working his farm. He was a man of prominence in his community, and served many years as constable. His death occurred at the age of fifty-two years, three months, and nine days. His devoted wife died in August, 1863, aged seventy-three years and eight months. Their family consisted of the following children: Agabus; Mary Ann; Michael; Jacob, and Elizabeth. Agabus died young; Mary Ann is the wife of Jacob Bender; this worthy couple recently celebrated their fiftieth wedding anniversary, at Mahoningtown, Pa.; Michael is the editor of the Beaver Times; Jacob is the subject of this biography, and Elizabeth is the wife of Joseph Strouck.

JOHN ELLIS, a highly respected and enterprising citizen of Beaver Falls, enjoys the distinction of being director of the Co-operative Flint Glass Co. of that place and was one of the organizers of that company in 1879, at which time he located in Beaver Falls. Ever since the organization of the company, Mr. Ellis has been in its employ; he is careful, shrewd, and trustworthy. His work is always done in a way that will stand the closest scrutiny. The subject of this sketch was born January 9, 1852, and obtained his education in Pittsburg. He subsequently served an apprenticeship with Bryce Brothers, and went to Beaver Falls in 1879.

In 1887, Annie Davis, a daughter of John Davis of Pittsburg, agreed to share the fortunes of Mr. Ellis by becoming his wife. This union was blessed with three children: Howard; Mabel; and Clifford B. Mr. Ellis and his family are willing workers of the Presbyterian church. In politics, Mr. Ellis has always been a Republican, but has refrained from accepting official positions. He is a member of the I. O. O. F. organization, and also of the Royal Arcanum. He has been a director of the Flint Glass Co. of Beaver Falls since 1896. He is a son of William and Jane (Owen) Ellis.

William Ellis was born in Cardiganshire, Wales, February 8, 1815, and was reared and educated at that place. He learned the trade of a hatter, which occupation he continued to follow until July 4, 1846, when he started for America. After a five weeks' voyage on board a sailing vessel, he landed at New York, going to Pittsburg by way of Utica, Buffalo, and the canal. After his arrival in Pittsburg, Mr. Ellis engaged in mining for a number of years, then began working in a glass factory, where he found employment for a period of twenty years, the last eight years of which were spent in Beaver Falls, where he died February 25, 1888. He chose for his life partner, Jane Owen, a daughter of Stephen Owen, of Wales. Mrs. Ellis departed this life September 10, 1897, at the age of seventy-nine years. This worthy couple favored the Welsh Calvinistic Methodist church. Mr. Ellis was an ardent Republican, fearless in his ideas, and in the expression of them. He took a deep interest in church affairs, and was very generous and kind hearted, often visiting the sick and poor and needy, relieving their wants or ameliorating their suffering whenever he could. He was a valued member of the Odd Fellows organization. He was also a member of the Ivorites, a Welsh order.

Our subject was one of four children. James, the eldest, died at the tender age of seven years. John is the subject of this sketch. Mary J., born February 14, 1854, became the wife of David D. Evans, of Pittsburg, and has six children, namely: Blanche; William, now deceased; Howard; Elmer; Ethel; and Iris. David Ellis, the youngest of the family, and only surviving brother of the subject of this sketch, was born September 26, 1856, at Pittsburg, Pa. He is one of the prominent and hard working members of the American Flint Glass Workers' Union, No. 38. David commenced his trade of flint glass worker in the factory of Bryce, Walker & Co.; he afterwards worked for Campbell, Jones & Co. He has been a resident of Beaver Falls since 1879, being employed in the Co-operative Works. David Ellis joined the Union of his trade in 1876, when the "Flints" were affiliated with the K. of L., and remained a member of that organization until the American Flint Glass Workers' Union of North America was organized, when he joined the latter body. Besides being a staunch union man, he is very prominent in the ranks of the Odd Fellows, having served as district deputy of the order in Beaver county, and district deputy grand patriarch of the Encampment in the same county. He is, also, a member of Beaver Valley Lodge

CHRISTOPHER C HAZEN,

No. 478, F. & A. M., Beaver Falls, Pa.

Mr. Ellis is a self-made man; having learned self-reliance and habits of industry in his youth, he was not slow to make the best of every opportunity offered. He has won his way to an enviable position, and is esteemed for his many excellent traits and his well-known rectitude of character.

———— • • ————

CHRISTOPHER C. HAZEN, the popular secretary for S. Barnes & Co. (Limited), manufacturers of all kinds of fire brick, of Rochester, Pa., is a resident of New Brighton, Pa., and besides following the occupations of teaching, farming, and stock-raising, for, perhaps, a quarter of a century, he has occupied important positions of trust in Beaver county—such as county auditor and county treasurer. Our subject boasts of English origin, and can trace his ancestors back for two hundred and fifty years; he is a descendant of Edward Hassen, which was the original family name.

Edward Hassen was born in England, September 18, 1649, and with his wife, Elizabeth, came to America, settling at Rowley, Massachusetts. There he served as selectman, overseer, and as judge of delinquents; he owned a large quantity of real estate, including seven gates, or cattle rights, which was considered an extensive ownership. His estate at death was valued at £404 7s. 8d. He was twice married. Little is known of his first wife, Elizabeth. His second wife was Hannah Grant, a daughter of Thomas and

Hugh Grant. Edward Hassen died at Rowley, Mass., in 1663, leaving the following children: Elizabeth; Hannah; John; Thomas; Edward; Isabella; Priscilla; Edna; Richard; Hepzibah; and Sarah.

Thomas Hassen, from whom the subject of this sketch is descended, was born February 29, 1657 or 1658, and died at Norwich, Conn., April 12, 1735. He was a farmer by occupation, and settled upon what was known as the Westfarms, and with his sons was among the petitioners for its incorporation as a parish, in 1716. This tract is now known as Franklin. Thomas was united in marriage, January 1, 1682, with Mary Howlet, a daughter of Thomas Howlet. Their children were as follows: John; Hannah; Alice; Edna; Thomas; Jacob; Mary; Lydia; Hepzibah; Ruth; and Jeremiah.

John Hazen was born March 23, 1683, and was twice married. His first wife was Mercy Bradstreet, daughter of John and Sarah (Perkins) Bradstreet. Mrs Hazen laid down the burden of life in 1725. John Hazen chose for his second wife, Elizabeth Dart. He reared the following offspring: John; Samuel; Simon; Margaret; Caleb; Sarah; Daniel; Elizabeth; Mary; Hannah, the first, and Hannah, the second.

John Hazen, Jr., was born February 21, 1711 or 1712. He was joined in matrimony with Deborah Peck, of Lyme, Connecticut, who bore him nine children, namely: Mary; John; Mary, second; Deborah; Nathaniel; Eunice; Joseph; Lydia; and Samuel.

Nathaniel Hazen was born March 17, 1745,

and was joined in marriage with Mary Bell. History says that Nathaniel was first located in the state of New Jersey, from which he removed to Washington county, Pa., and shortly afterward went to North Sewickley, now Franklin, township, Beaver county, and settled upon a tract of land where S. M. Hazen now resides. A patent for this land, issued from the Government to the eldest son of Nathaniel Hazen, bears date 1790. Nathaniel possessed considerable means, owning two hundred acres of land, and becoming a man of prominence in his day. Having very fertile land, he made a specialty of raising timothy seed, which he carried over the mountains on horseback, and exchanged for salt and merchandise. He conducted a small store, and was the proud owner of the first buggy ever seen in these parts. The house occupied by him as a residence was built of logs, as was the barn—the former containing only one door and one window. Nathaniel Hazen set out an orchard, a portion of which is yet bearing. Among the children reared by him and his excellent wife were the following: Samuel; Nathan; and James. They also reared others, whose names are not remembered.

Samuel Hazen, grandfather of the subject hereof, was born at Peter's Creek, Washington county (now Allegheny county) Pa., August 27, 1791. He wedded Eliza McDaniel, a daughter of Jethro McDaniel. "Grandma" Hazen was born in 1798, and passed away at the age of forty-nine years. Samuel Hazen began his career by working on his father's farm. He subsequently built a woolen mill at Wurtemberg, and carried on the manufacture of woolen goods in connection with farming. So successfully did he manage this enterprise that before his death he became the owner of several farms. He assisted in organizing the Baptist society, of which he was a member. His homestead farm was early known as the "Leverance Farm." His death occurred September 7, 1855, having been previously deprived of his beloved companion, in 1847. Their most happy union was blessed with the following children: Nathaniel; Mary Ann, wife of H. K. Alter; Rebecca, wife of A. Cavin; Hannah, wife of J. C. Thompson; Margaret, wife of John Thomas: Nathan, father of the subject hereof; Samuel, who died at the age of twenty-two years; and Smith M., who married Mary A. Ney. After the death of his first wife, Samuel Hazen contracted a second matrimonial alliance, in this instance with Elizabeth Ann Thompson, who bore him one daughter, Ruth, and who died September 7, 1855, the same day upon which her husband died.

Nathan Hazen, father of Christopher C., was born in North Sewickley, now Franklin, township, December 15, 1829. He won for his wife, Mary Judith Zeigler, a daughter of Abraham Zeigler. Mrs Hazen still survives her husband, whose death occurred July 29, 1898, at the age of sixty-eight years. Christopher C.'s father purchased a farm, that upon which Thomas J. Powell now resides, which he afterwards sold, and purchased another in North Sewickley township. This latter farm was only partially improved, and is still a portion of the estate. Upon this farm the elder Mr. Hazen replaced the old log house and barns with convenient and substantial buildings, in 1851, and six years later he built a handsome, large house. After clearing the land, he was occupied in farming until about 1875, when he purchased the Dr. Withrow property, in North Sewickley township. He then practically retired from active labor, with the exception of keeping a store and officiating as postmaster. He also served as supervisor and as auditor. He was a very active, energetic man, accumulating a fine property, and upon his death left a large estate for distribution among his children, who are as follows: Christopher C., the subject hereof; Elizabeth Eliza, who became the wife of Stewart Thompson, and is now deceased; Mary, wife of Dr. W. O. Morrison, of Struthers, Ohio; Maggie H., wife of Dr. C. H. Knoblett, of Ohio; Ida, wife of Hon. J. Sharp Wilson, of Beaver; and F. Lily, who is devoting her life to her aged mother.

Christopher C. Hazen was born in North Sewickley township, Beaver county, Pa., December 20, 1851. After attending public school he took a course at North Sewickley Academy. He graduated from Lewisburg University, now known as Bucknell College, in 1874. He assisted in working his way through college by teaching a part of the time, which profession occupied his attention before and after his graduation. After his marriage, the subject of this record conducted his father's farm for some time, making a specialty of

stock-raising, breeding some very fine horses, and keeping a choice dairy. Mr. Hazen began his public life in 1885, when he was elected county auditor of Beaver county, serving six years. In 1891, he was elected county treasurer of the same county, serving in that capacity for three years. In 1897, Mr. Hazen became a stockholder in, and secretary for, the S. Barnes Manufacturing Company, which responsible and lucrative position he still retains and seems especially fitted for.

Mr. Hazen engaged in farming for a period of twenty-one years, discontinuing it in 1896, when he purchased a fine residence in New Brighton. This residence was known as the Judge Andrew Duff place, having been built by that gentleman. It is a fine, modern house, surrounded by beautiful, spacious lawns, and is picturesquely situated on the heights overlooking the business portion of the city. Our subject was joined in wedlock with Laura H. De Frain. Mrs. Hazen is a daughter of Jacob and Susan (Boon) De Frain, and formerly resided in Lewisburg, Union county, Pennsylvania, being a graduate of a young ladies' grammar school of that place. Mr. and Mrs Hazen are rearing a large and exceedingly interesting family, of whom they are very proud. Their children's names are as follows: Edith Irene, born November 13, 1875, who served as assistant to her father while he filled the office of county treasurer; Mabel Edna, born March 12, 1877; Edna Blanche, born June 6, 1879; Clara Floy, born June 7, 1881; Amy Anna, born July 10, 1883;

Harry Wilford, born October 19, 1885; Frank Harrison, born November 23, 1887; Nathan De Frain, born December 5, 1889; Harold Herbert, born October 20, 1872, and whose little life flickered out on July 21, 1873; and Thomas Ross Hennon, born June 18, 1898.

Christopher C. Hazen and his family are active members of the Baptist church, of which denomination Mr. Hazen has served as deacon. Socially, our subject is a member of St. James Lodge, No. 457, F. & A. M., is past chancellor of the Knights of Pythias, and attended the Grand Lodge sessions for two years; he is also a member of the Junior Order of United American Mechanics. Mr. Hazen is a most pleasant and agreeable gentleman, numbering his friends by the score, and it is with pleasure that we are able to announce that his portrait accompanies the foregoing outline of his life.

— ◆•◆ —

JOHN WYLIE FORBES. The family of which the gentleman whose name heads this biography is a worthy representative, have resided in Beaver county for more than a century and have contributed their share toward the building up and maintenance of its present flourishing condition. Mr. Forbes is well known throughout this vicinity as a man of high business principles, a dutiful citizen, and enjoys the confidence and esteem of a host of acquaintances. He was born near Moravia, Lawrence county, then Beaver county,—the date of his birth being December 29, 1835,—and he is a son of David and Elizabeth (Wylie) Forbes.

On the paternal side of Mr. Forbes' ancestors, the family was of Scotch-Irish extraction, and William Forbes, his grandfather, was the first of the Forbes family to locate in this vicinity, which he did about 1798. He took up a large tract of land and pursued the vocation of a farmer. The father of the subject of this sketch was born in 1798, and was but six months old when his parents moved to this county. He at first carried on farming but later began dealing in grain, his field of operation being along the old Erie canal. He died in February, 1861. In politics, he was a Democrat of the Jeffersonian type and took an active part in local affairs. He was a member of the United Presbyterian Church, of which he was also an elder. His union with Elizabeth Wylie resulted in the birth of nine children: William, deceased; John W., Rebecca, Elizabeth, Benjamin, Nancy, Robert and Alice, all deceased; and Amanda. On the maternal side of the family, the ancestors of John Wylie Forbes were Scotch, and his grandfather was John Wylie.

The subject of this narrative was elementarily trained in the schools of his native district and further pursued his studies at Westminster College, after which he spent a year and one-half teaching school in the state of Kentucky. Owing to his father's illness, he returned home and took charge of his business. His mother died in 1861. In 1870 he settled in Beaver Falls, where he worked at different vocations. He embarked in mercan-

HON. IRA F. MANSFIELD.

tile pursuits, and in 1888 sold out, and operated a foundry. The latter enterprise he continued until 1892, when the Standard Gauge Steel Company was organized and he was made vice-president of the plant, a position he occupies at the present time. Mr. Forbes is a director and treasurer of the Champion Saw and Gas Engine Company of Beaver Falls. In February, 1865, the subject of our sketch enlisted in the cause of the Union in Company G, 78th Reg., Pa. Vol. Inf., and served throughout the remainder of that terrible struggle.

Socially, Mr. Forbes is a prominent member of Post No. 164, G. A. R.

HON. IRA F. MANSFIELD, an extensive owner of coal mining interests about Cannelton, Pa., whose active furtherance of many well-known enterprises places him among the foremost of the prominent and progressive business men of Beaver county, resides in a handsome home in Beaver, at the corner of Elk and First streets. He is a son of Kirtland and Lois (Morse) Mansfield, and was born in Poland, Ohio, June 27, 1842.

He is descended from Revolutionary stock, being a great-grandson of Captain Jack Mansfield, who served through that war as a captain, and after its close lived in retirement, —having served sixty years in the Second, Fourth and Sixth Connecticut regiments. His son, Ira Mansfield, was the grandfather of the gentleman whose name appears at the head of this sketch.

Kirtland Mansfield, the father of Ira F., was born in Wallingford, Conn., and early in life went to Poland, Ohio, where for many years he was engaged in mercantile pursuits. Later he removed to Philadelphia, Pa., where he lived the remainder of his life. He was joined in the bonds of wedlock with Lois Morse, a daughter of Elkanah Morse, an early settler of Poland, Ohio, where he built the first oil, woolen and grist mills. In 1849, he moved to California, where he died. After the demise of her husband, Mrs. Mansfield returned to Poland, Ohio, with her son, where he was reared under the influence of a kind mother's love.

Ira F. Mansfield received a good mental training in the common schools of his native place, and in Poland College, where he was a schoolmate of President William McKinley. At the early age of fifteen years he went to Pittsburg and learned the trade of a molder, but returned to Poland, and in August, 1862, enlisted in Company H, 105th Reg., Ohio Vol. Inf.,—being the first to sign the roll. He was promoted to be orderly sergeant, then 1st lieutenant, and for conspicuous bravery at the battles of Lookout Mountain and Missionary Ridge he was breveted captain and was assigned as a quartermaster of the Fourteenth Army Corps. He was with Sherman in his memorable March to the Sea and up through the Carolinas, and participated in the grand review at Washington, in May of 1865. He is a man of very methodical ways and of a very observing nature, and during his service kept a diary, and a record of his many interesting and exciting experiences. This he has written out, and, being an artist of superior talent, he has finely illustrated it with pen pictures, and also with many fine photographs, taken in recent years,—all of which make a beautiful and valuable volume. In October, 1865, he leased of Mrs. Edwin Morse, the Cannel coal mines of Cannelton, Beaver county, Pa., and in 1870 bought them outright. He has since owned and operated them, and now owns 357 acres, through which veins run which are from ten to fifteen feet thick. The daily output varies from one hundred to two hundred and fifty tons, and the facilities for shipping are of the best,—the mines being located on a branch of the Pennsylvania railroad. Mr. Mansfield also built a general store there and operated it for a number of years, but it is now managed by C. W. Inman and known as the Cash Store. He also erected a fine opera house and furnished it in elegant style. The postoffice, which was established in the town in 1872, is located on the first floor of his building, and for many years he served in the capacity of postmaster. He bought and rebuilt the Morse homestead, and possesses a very fine farm, one hundred and eighty acres of which is devoted to fruit raising; he has 5,000 peach trees and a large number of pear, cherry and quince trees. He is also interested in the Gulf Company, the Bituminous Company, and the Captain A. Hicks Company,—coal operators. He is a man of wonderful energy and general business ability and his many ventures have resulted in great financial success. In 1887, he moved to Beaver, purchasing the Hum and Singleton property at the corner of Elk and First streets, and there he has erected a very handsome modern brick home, which overlooks the beautiful valley and the Ohio River.

Mr. Mansfield has traveled extensively throughout the United States and is well versed in the current events of the day. He has a fine collection of mounted speciments in botany, especially ferns and orchids—from Beaver county,—and all are illustrated on separate pages, in natural colors,—this being the work of his mother. In politics, Mr. Mansfield is a stanch Republican, and was elected a member of the state legislature from Beaver county in 1880, 1893, 1895, and 1897.— serving his constituents faithfully and well. He was a school director of Cannelton and Beaver, and takes an earnest interest in all matters of an educational nature. He is vice-president of Beaver College, and Beaver Musical Institute, and is president of the board of trustees of Greers College of Darlington. He is vice-president of the First National Bank of Rochester, is a stockholder and director of three building and loan associations, and of several bridge and street railway companies; he is a director of the P., L. & W. R. R., of the Pennsylvania Railroad, and of the Valley Electric Plant.

The subject of this memoir was united in marriage with Lucy E. Mygatt, a daughter of Dr. E. Mygatt, who was born in Danbury, Conn., and was a practicing physician and surgeon of Poland, Ohio, when Mr. Mansfield was married, in 1872. Three children have blessed this union, as follows: Kirtland My-gatt, Mary Lois, and Henry Beauchamp. Socially, he is a member, and commander of, Post No. 473, G. A. R.; past master of the following lodges of the Masonic order, being a thirty-second degree Mason; F. & A. M., R. A. M., and K. T.; is past grand of the Odd Fellows Lodge; and past commander of the Knights of Pythias; he served as aide-de-camp on Gen. H. H. Cummings' staff. In a religious connection, he is a member and elder of the Presbyterian church. and has served as superintendent of the Sunday School. A portrait of Mr. Mansfield is presented, in connection with this sketch.

MRS. MOLLIE F. RANDOLPH, who sprang from a very prominent family of Beaver county, is the widow of George F. Randolph, who, it will be remembered, was drowned in the disastrous flood at Johnstown in 1889, whither he had gone upon a visit. He was one of the most highly respected men of Beaver Falls, and his sad death came as a severe shock not only to his family but to the citizens of the borough, among whom he had a large circle of friends.

Mrs. Randolph was born in Allegheny, Pa., February 14, 1863. and is a daughter of Major F. and Sally K. (Smith) Scott. Major Scott, who during his life was probably one of the best known men of the country, was born near Uniontown, Fayette county, Pa., September 21, 1832, and after receiving an education, he learned the trade of a saddler and harness maker. In 1856, he removed to Allegheny, Pa., and accepted a position as passenger conductor on the Fort Wayne R. R., where he remained for many years, thus becoming acquainted with nearly all the prominent business men of Western Pennsylvania. Discontinuing the railroad business, he bought the St. Charles Hotel in Pittsburg and conducted it for one year, but finally disposed of it and bought the Sourbeck Hotel in New Brighton. Later he retired from the hotel business, and engaged in the wholesale candy business in Beaver Falls, being very successful. When the Fort Wayne R. R. Company built their new depot in Beaver Falls, he was offered the position of passenger agent to take effect upon the completion of the building. This he accepted and was so arranging his business affairs that he might take charge, when he was taken sick and died, just one week prior to the opening of the new depot. Major Scott married Sally K. Smith, who was born in Uniontown, Pa., October 27, 1832, and five children blessed their union, Mrs. Randolph being the only child now living.

Mollie F. Scott was one year old when in 1864, her parents moved to New Brighton, and five years old when they located at Beaver Falls, where she was given a good education. She has always taken an active interest in educational and church matters, and was a member of the church—the choir, and organist, for nine years. She is an entertaining conversationalist and an accomplished musician and singer, and has always been popular in social circles. She possesses exceptional business qualifications and very cleverly manages the property in which she and her mother live on Ninth street, and the brick residence adjoining, these being the estate left to her care by her father. On the maternal side of the family, she is descended in the fourth generation from General Douglas, who attained fame in the Revolutionary War. Her father was a Democrat in politics and served as school director. He was a member of the Methodist Protestant church, and fraternally belonged to the Franklin Lodge, F. & A. M.

George F. Randolph, the deceased husband of the subject of this sketch, was born in Johnstown, Pa., and was a son of Richard Fitz and Emma A. (Boggs) Randolph. He was descended from Edward Randolph, captain in the Revolutionary War, who was a farmer in the heart of Philadelphia. His land was situated on Fifth and Randolph streets, the latter street being given his name because it cut through his farm. He was a strict adherent to the Quaker faith. He reared thirteen children.

George F. Randolph, a son of Edward, was born in Philadelphia and during his active business career operated a general store there, but in his latter days, lived in retirement. He was the father of Edward Randolph, the grandfather of our subject, who was a graduate of Harvard University. For a time he devoted himself to the practice of medicine, but at a later date read law and was a successful attorney. He was united in marriage with Frances McShane, a daughter of a prominent Philadelphia merchant and they reared three children: George Fitz; Richard Fitz; and Charles Fitz.

Richard Fitz Randolph, the father of our subject's husband, was educated at a private academy in Chester county, Pa., but when seventeen years old, he went to Cambria county, to learn the steel trade with the Cambria Steel Company. He remained with them until 1884, when he moved to Beaver Falls and accepted a position in the steel and wire nail mill, a part of the time being assistant manager. He subsequently accepted a position with the Beaver Falls Saw Company, with whom he continued for six years. He was united in marriage with Emma A. Boggs, a daughter of Senator Boggs of Hollidaysburg, Blair county, where she was born, and they reared five children, as follows: George F.; Francis Fitz; Harry Fitz; Richard Fitz; and Charles Fitz. Mr. Randolph is a Republican, and in religious faith is an Episcopalian.

George F. Randolph, deceased, was educated in the public schools of Johnstown, and also took a course of study in a private institution. After completing his education, he went to work in the offices of the Cambria Iron Company and gave satisfaction to his employers. Resigning in 1883, he was offered and accepted a position in Beaver Falls, with the Carnegie Company, and was given entire charge of the nine-inch mill, including the rollers and men. In 1889, while still in their employ, he paid a visit to his birth place, and it was while there that the calamity occurred which startled the whole world, in which he with hundreds of others lost their lives. He was a loving husband and a fond father, and it was indeed a sad bereavement to his devoted wife and their children. His union with Mollie F. Scott resulted in the birth of two children: Mary F., born November 17, 1885; and Helen F., born December 1, 1886. Politically, he was a supporter of the Republican party. In a religious connection he was an attendant of the Methodist Protestant church.

R OGER COPE is one of the persevering, enterprising and successful lawyers at the bar of Beaver county. He has, by virtue of his energy and ability, impressed himself upon the borough of Beaver Falls, and has achieved marked success for a young man. He was admitted to the bar in 1881 and took up his permanent residence in Beaver Falls, where he opened an office for the practice of law. He was born in Fairfield township, Columbiana county, Ohio, December 8, 1850, and is a son of Samuel D., grandson of Jesse, great-grandson of John, great-great-grandson of John, who was a son of Oliver Cope, the first representative of the family in this country, he having emigrated from England.

Jesse Cope was born in Fayette county, Pa., and in 1802 located in Columbiana county, Ohio, where he followed farming. He was a Quaker. His wife was Margaret Dixon, and they became the parents of eight children: Ellis; Samuel; Hiram; Elizabeth (Irwin); Mary (Taylor); Ann; Hannah, and Lucinda. Jesse died aged fifty-six years. Samuel D. Cope was born in Fairfield township, Columbiana county, Ohio, May 5, 1815, and was reared and trained to agricultural pursuits, which he followed throughout his active career. In 1878, he retired to Leetonia, Ohio, where he has since resided. He was joined in marriage with Alice Rogers, a daughter of John and Phoebe Rogers of Columbiana county, and she passed from this earth in 1864 aged forty-eight years. Their children were named as follows: Rufus is practicing law in Chicago, Ill.; Mary Etta (Piersol), deceased; E. Cyrena (Rogers); F. Eudora, who resides at Leetonia, Ohio; Roger; Emma A., deceased; Jeanette, deceased; Amanda F., who lives at Oakland, Cal.; and Alice, who also resides at Leetonia, Ohio. Roger Cope's father was formerly a Republican, but is now a Prohibitionist; during the Civil War he was a strong anti-slavery man.

Roger Cope attended the public school of his native town and Mt. Union College, Ohio; he then taught one year in his native county and one term at Georgetown, Illinois. Having a desire to fit himself for the bar, he began studying with his brother Rufus, who was practicing in that town; subsequently he took a course of lectures at the University of Michigan, from which institution he was graduated in 1881. During his legal studies he applied himself with intelligence, vigor and energy, and thoroughly familarized himself with the theory and practice of law, as his subsequent progress well testifies. Upon graduation, Mr. Cope immediately established himself in business at Beaver Falls, and he has many influential and valuable clients, whose interests are looked after with fidelity and a great amount of success.

Mr. Cope was wedded June 28, 1894, to Mary C. Mercer, a native of Columbiana county, Ohio, and they have one child,— Rue Alice. In politics, the subject of our sketch is a stanch Republican; socially, he is a K. of P.

———— • • ————

JAMES H. WELCH, proprietor and general manager of the Welch Fire Brick Company of Monaca, Pa., one of the oldest, best equipped and busiest of the manufacturing plants in Beaver county, is a man of great energy and enterprise. His career has been one of the greatest activity, having worked his way from a lowly station in life to a position among the most prominent business men of this section of the state.

In 1878, Mr. Welch started the Welch Fire Brick Company at Monaca, soon after the opening of the P. & L. E. R. R., and began the manufacture of the celebrated "W" fire brick, fire bricks of all kinds for mills, furnaces, locomotive tile, cupolas, and buff-building brick,—being the first in the vicinity to turn out that style of brick. He ships the product to every section of the country, and the buff brick used in Madison Square Garden in New York City, was procured from this establishment. He has also owned works at Vanport, Pa., and is a member of the firm of Welch, Gloninger & Maxwell of Welch, Pennsylvania.

James H. Welch was born in Red Brook, Monmouth, Eng., in 1846, on the 7th of June, and received his intellectual training in the public schools of Monmouth, which he attended until he reached the age of twelve years. He then went to work in a grocery store and continued until he was seventeen years old. Being an intelligent appearing youth of fine physique, he was appointed platform inspector and ticket collector at Ross Station, and later joined the Cheltenham police force. This comprised his occupation until within two days before he left England, in 1867, when he came to America settling in Pittsburg, Pa., where he secured a position as assistant yardmaster on the Baltimore & Ohio Railroad. He subsequently entered the employ of the Pittsburg Gas Company and worked in the retort house for three months, when he was appointed weighmaster. After a time, he resigned, bought a team of horses and engaged in contracting. He worked very hard, and his business was flourishing, when he sold out to Minesinger Brothers eighteen years later. In the meantime he had become interested in the brick works at Vanport, and he continued there until he removed to Monaca and, in partnership with his brother, operated the Welch Fire Brick Company. His brother, however, disposed of his interest and was succeeded by Mr. J. H. Gloninger. He started with the old square kilns, but he has made improvements and added modern appliances until the concern outclasses all others in the locality. He was the first in the county to possess one of the celebrated English continuous kilns, having 16 chambers and a capacity of 500,000 bricks. It is a great saving and is distinguished from all others in that while one part is under full heat, the others can be cooled off, emptied and filled. In connection with the works are 135 acres of clay land, to which an incline leads by way of a side entry. A new engine has just been put in to operate the incline, and the heavy grinding and crushing machines for manufacture. This firm makes a specialty in shapes, one contract calling for as many as forty different shapes. Besides the extensive grounds which they have under cover, there is a building 175x90 feet, another three-story building 112x60 feet, with dry tunnels carrying 90,000 bricks in the dry room, and having a capacity of 25,000 per day. The office at the works is located near the railroad, and the general offices and salesroom are located at Pittsburg. Fifty men are in the employ of the company, and when the capacity of the works is doubled as is contemplated, the force of workmen will be largely increased. Mr. Welch is also a member of the firm of Welch, Gloninger & Maxwell of Welch, Pa., the town, which is named after our subject, being supported by the works.

He owns a fine residence in Monaca, which stands upon an elevation above the town and is called Welchmont. It is a very handsome home, being constructed of buff brick after the owner's own plans, and it commands an excellent view of the surrounding country. Mr. Welch also owns a fine dairy farm of 354 acres in Borie township, containing 40 head of good Jerseys and registered Holsteins, and sells milk in Beaver Falls. He raises considerable grain and hay, but it is all fed to the stock. Politically, Mr. Welch is a strong Republican, but has never had the time to devote much attention to party affairs. In religious attachments he is a Baptist, and, socially, is a Royal Arch Mason.

BENJAMIN FRANKLIN, the subject of this sketch, is a prominent educator of Beaver county, Pa., and has grown gray in the active service of that noble profession. He is a son of George and Jane (West) Franklin, and was born August 25, 1831, in Sherburne, Chenango county, New York. His mother died when he was very young, and the young lad was reared by a Connecticut family. The name of his foster-father was Orrin Harmon, who removed to Ohio when Benjamin was still very young. Mr. Harmon was a surveyor by trade and was in the employ of the Connecticut Land Company. Upon going west to Ohio, he settled at Ravenna, where the subject of our sketch obtained his primary education. This was supplemented by a three years' course at the academy at Ashtabula, Ohio, after which young Franklin completed the high school course at Ravenna, and then took a finishing course at Tappan Seminary, his foster-father having a scholarship in that institution.

Mr. Franklin then began his life work for which he had spent many years in diligent preparation. He taught school two years, and then went to Beaver county, Pa., in 1856. After locating permanently in Industry township, where he purchased property, he has followed his chosen calling almost uninterruptedly ever since. After teaching in Industry township for four years, he taught one year in Ohio township. In 1860, he was elected principal of the Fallston schools, where he remained four years by contract. At the close of that time, he was offered a larger salary at North Bridgewater and remained there four years. The people of Fallston then came forward and desiring his services, persuaded Mr. Franklin to return to Fallston by giving him a very substantial increase in salary over that received at North Bridgewater. So he returned to Fallston, and remained there for six years, but as it was his intention to be a candidate for county superintendent of Beaver County the following year, he did not accept the Fallston school, but taught one term in Brighton township as involved a period of effort which would terminate before election time.

In May, 1875, Mr. Franklin was elected county superintendent over M. L. Knight, the incumbent at that time. At the close of his first term of three years, he was elected again to the same position. After his second term had closed, Mr. Franklin did not teach for some time, but purchased a store in Fallston, and engaged in mercantile pursuits, with the assistance of his sons, for a period of five years. At the end of that time, Mr. Franklin accepted a school at Smith's Ferry, being offered special inducements to take it and discipline it. After spending one year there, he taught at Freedom for a year, at College Hill near Geneva College, for two years, at West Bridgewater for two years, in a graded school at Pulaski, in an independent school district for two years, and then returned to West Bridgewater for two terms. Subsequently he retired to his farm in Brighton township and superintended its affairs until 1898. In the autumn of that year he accepted the charge of the school which he is now teaching in Brighton township. For thirteen years, Mr. Franklin served on the board of examiners, and assisted in examining applicants for teacher's certificates. In 1876, he conducted the examination of the Phillipsburg Soldiers' Orphan's School for the state. He also made a creditable showing of school work at the Centennial Exposition at Philadelphia in 1876, receiving the strong commendation of the authorities who passed upon the work. Mr. Franklin has assisted in examinations at the State Normal, at Edinboro, and also at Indiana State Normal Schools. Politically, our subject is a Republican and has always followed that party to victory or defeat.

Mr. Franklin chose for his life partner, Martha Reed, a lady of rare intellectual attainments, who bore him two sons, Orrin H., a successful dentist, a sketch of whose life is

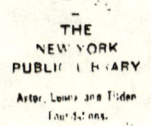

also found in this publication; and Milo O., a machinist in the employ of the Union Drawn Steel Works. The subject of this narrative and his wife are devout worshippers in the Presbyterian church. Mr. Franklin has been elder and trustee of that denomination for fifteen years. He is still serving in that official capacity, and for nine years was superintendent of the Sabbath School.

———— ·•·—— ——

JOHN C. BATES, a gentleman who has, for years, been one of the most enterprising citizens of Rochester, Beaver county, Pa., has for a long period been identified with the Rochester Tumbler Works. He is a son of William and Mary Jane (Thompson) Bates, and was born in Steubenville, Ohio, in 1848.

William Bates, the father of John C., was also born at Steubenville, Ohio, and throughout his entire life was engaged as a brick contractor. He died in his native town at the age of sixty-five years. His union with Mary Jane Thompson, who was born at West Brownsville, and is now living at the advanced age of seventy-four years, resulted in the birth of three children: John C., whose name heads these lines; William, and George.

John C. Bates, the subject hereof, learned the trade of glass making when a boy, at Steubenville, and from there he went to Wheeling, West Virginia, where he continued at that occupation until he removed to Pittsburg. He plied his trade in the latter city until 1877, when he came to Rochester, which has since

been his home. He assisted in the Rochester Tumbler Works, and still efficiently serves in that capacity. He is a man of excellent judgment, and has so conducted his affairs that he is rated among the prosperous citizens of the community. He bought a vacant lot on Penn street, known as the Lloyd property, and upon this he erected a handsome, modern house. In this he resided for years, but he now makes his home with his daughter, Mrs. S. M. Kane, whose residence is on the opposite side of the same street.

John C. Bates was united in marriage with Ida Cotton, of Pittsburg, and four children blessed their home, namely: Virginia, the widow of Samuel M. Kane, a record of whose life follows this paragraph; Bertha, deceased; John Emmett, and Georgella. Mr. Bates is liberal in his religious views. Socially, he is a member of the Odd Fellows' Lodge and Encampment, and the A. O. of M.

SAMUEL M. KANE, deceased, who was a man of sterling worth, and one of the influential citizens of Beaver county, was an organizer of the Rochester Tumbler Works, and general manager thereof up to the time of his demise. He was born May 1, 1839, in Steubenville, Ohio, and as his father died when he was a child, Samuel was thrown upon the world to battle for himself at an early age. Being of an energetic disposition, he grasped what opportunities were his to obtain an education, at the same time finding employment at glass manufacturing. He was ambitious and industrious, and progressed rapidly, acquiring great skill as a workman. Early in life he went to Pittsburg, as many of his associates did, and accepted a larger and more profitable position. He availed himself of every opportunity for advancement, with foresight and sound judgment, and became one of the organizers of the company which built and operated the Rochester Tumbler plant, of Rochester, Beaver county, Pennsylvania. Mr. Kane became its general manager, and under his skillful guidance, the business increased to a wonderful extent, and the works were soon shipping to every state in the Union, and to foreign markets. Today this concern is the largest establishment of its kind in the world —for which development much credit is due to Mr. Kane. He possessed a keen insight in business affairs, and identified himself with numerous enterprises which not only benefited him in a financial way, but were of material advantage to the borough and county. He was a director of the First National Bank of Rochester, president of the Rochester Improvement Company, a stockholder and director of the Rochester Electric Light Plant, and a supporter of other business ventures. He erected an attractive home on Pennsylvania street in Rochester, overlooking the beautiful Ohio Valley, and being one of the finest in that locality. It is well arranged and chastely furnished, and its interior appointments reflect much credit upon the refined taste of Mrs. Kane.

On January 17, 1895, while crossing the railroad near the factory, Mr. Kane was run down by an engine and killed. It was the saddest accident that ever befell the borough of Rochester, and cast a heavy gloom over the entire community. Every citizen mourned as for a brother, and there was universal commiseration. He had been a kind, loving husband, and a true and faithful friend.

Fraternally, Samuel M. Kane was a thirty-second degree Mason; a member of the Knights Templar and Scottish Rites lodges of Pittsburg; the R. A. M. of Rochester; a charter member and past grand master of the Lodge and Encampment, I. O. O. F.; a Woodman of the World; Royal Templar; he belonged to the Junior Order of United American Mechanics, of which he was an honorary member. He was also the organizer of the Order of Rebecca, at Rochester. Religiously, he was a devout member, and trustee, of the Baptist church. A portrait of Mr. Kane precedes this sketch.

———— • • ← ————

STEPHEN MOLTHRUP, an organizer of the Standard Gauge Steel Works, one of the most prosperous and important of the industries of Beaver Falls, is efficiently serving as superintendent of the plant. He was born in Loudonville, Ohio, December 10, 1863, and is a son of James C. and Rosanna (Rust) Molthrup, and grandson of William Molthrup.

William Molthrup was of Scotch-French descent and was born in Vermont, where he lived for some years, having acquired an education and a knowledge of the trade of shoemaking there. He removed to Erie, Pa., where he followed his trade for some time, and then went to Ohio where he spent the balance of his life. He married a Scotch lady and they had two children: Amanda, who was single; and James C., the father of Stephen.

James C. Molthrup was born in Vermont, April 4, 1822, and received his education in the public schools there and at Erie, Pa., where he was taken by his parents when very young. He learned the trade of a founder and machinist and worked for many years in the shops of the Pennsylvania R. R. at Alliance and Crestline, Ohio, continuing in their employ until after the close of the War, when he went into business for himself at Loudonville. Remaining there until 1887, he moved to Beaver Falls and after following the business of a pattern maker for some little time, he went to live a retired life at the home of our subject until his death. He was married to Rosanna Rust, who was born in Onondaga county, N. Y., March 30, 1829, and was a daughter of Stephen Rust. The following children blessed this union: Amanda; Stephen, who died in infancy; Helen (Beavers); Ida (Underwood); Mary (Chapel); Stephen, the subject hereof; James, who died young; and William, whose trade is that of a machinist. Before the War Mr. Molthrup was a Democrat, but at that time joined the ranks of the Republican party, of which he was an unswerving supporter until his death. Religiously, he was a Methodist and was a trustee of the church.

Stephen Molthrup received his educational training in the public schools of Loudonville and Perrysville, Ohio, after which he entered the shops of his father and learned the trade of a machinist. He moved to Beaver Falls in 1886, to accept a position in the shops of the Carnegie Steel Company, and for six years he continued in their employ, after which he was employed by the Union Drawn Steel Company. One year later he went to Pittsburg, Pa., but after a short stay returned to Beaver Falls and re-entered the service of the Carnegie Steel Company. In company with nine others, he was active in the incorporation of the Standard Gauge Steel Company and became a charter member of the concern. He was chosen as one of the directors and accepted a position as machinist. Being a man of many years' experience and possessed of excellent business qualifications, he was the man above all others to superintend the work of this plant, and he was soon placed in charge. The firm has an established reputation for the excellency of its work, for which much credit is due Mr. Molthrup, and it ranks to-day among the leading business enterprises of Beaver Falls. The works covers an area of 300x100 feet, and they employ a large force of men. The officers are as follows: A. Rasner, president; and J. W. Forbes, vice-president; and the directors are: Messrs. Stephen Molthrup, Raymer, Dinger, Gilland, Bevin, Forbes, Reed, and William Molthrup.

Mr. Molthrup was joined in marriage with Ellen M. Miller, a daughter of Philip Miller, and they have a daughter, Helen. Politically,

Mr. Miller is a Republican. He is a member of the Methodist Church. Fraternally, he is a member of the Odd Fellows' Lodge.

———◆◆———

MRS. MARY ANN BALDWN is the esteemed widow of the late Marcus M. Baldwin, who was for several years one of the prominent business men of Beaver Falls. He was born in New York City in 1821, and was the son of Gabriel Baldwin, whose parents came to this country, from England.

Marcus M. Baldwin received his education in New York City, and learned the trade of a ship carpenter. He moved to Pittsburg, and went to work at his trade on the river, remaining there for some years, when he moved to Fallston, Beaver county, Pennsylvania. There he took up the carpenter trade, working as a journeyman for some time. In partnership with another man, he accepted a contract, and after they had completed the work, found that there was a profit of forty dollars to each. With this small capital of $80, they decided to continue, and with hard work, good business ability, and untiring energy, they at last worked themselves to the top, and were known as reliable business men. Their first office was on Sixth street, and the partnership beginning under such peculiar circumstances lasted until the death of Mr. Baldwin, which occurred in 1886. He was a man of splendid abilities and of sterling integrity, and was highly respected by all who knew him. He served in the Civil War,

answering to the call for volunteers, and was a member of Battery B, Pittsburg Artillery. He was a firm Republican, and took an active interest in the party, serving as a member of the council, and as school director. He was one of the first business men in the county, and a member of the Presbyterian church.

The subject hereof, Mary Ann Baldwin, is a daughter of Henry and Harriet Mortley. Henry Mortley was born in Kent, England, in 1812, and learned the trade of a marble cutter, following this until his marriage, when he came to America, in 1834. He settled in New York City, and remained there for several years. He was a very good workman, having served seven years' apprenticeship in England, where he was always given a high grade of work. During his later life, he moved to Ohio and continued working for some time, when he met death in a very sad manner, accidentally drowning in the Hocking River. His wife, Harriet Mortley was born in Hastings, Sussex County, England, and came of a good English family. She was married when but nineteen years old, and although she lived to be eighty-one years of age, she never ceased to mourn her husband's untimely death.

Mrs. Baldwin, the subject of this biography, was mentally trained in the public schools and later learned the trade of dress-making, an occupation which she followed until her marriage. She became the mother of eight children, as follows: Harriet (Pratt); Victoria (Pritchard); Bessie; Caroline; Charles, a con-

1908

HON. HARTFORD PERRY BROWN.

tractor; Ralph Vernon, a contractor; Dorothy; and Marcus R., a clerk. She is greatly loved by all and has hosts of warm friends. She is a member of the Episcopal church, and is ever willing to lend aid to any worthy cause.

HON. HARTFORD PERRY BROWN, whose portrait is shown on the opposite page, is one of the most prominent and enterprising citizens of the town of Rochester, and takes an unusual amount of interest in the growth and prosperity of his adopted town. He is interested in many local enterprises, being president and general manager of the People's Electric Street Railway, secretary and general manager of the Beaver Valley Traction Company, and secretary and treasurer of the Rochester Heat & Light Company; he is also identified with several other important undertakings. He was born on a farm in Raccoon township, Beaver county, Pa., August 7, 1851, and is a son of Oliver Hazard Perry Brown, and a grandson of Amasa Brown.

The original emigrant of the Brown family was Peter Brown, who was of English origin, and who came to America on the Mayflower in 1620. His grandson, George Brown, was born in 1696, and was a farmer by occupation; he died in Colchester, Conn., February 5, 1765. He married Elizabeth Wells, April 12, 1730, and they reared the following children: Elizabeth, born in 1731; Darius, born in 1733; Charles, born in 1734; Lydia, born

in 1736; Hannah, born in 1738; two who died in their infancy; Ezra, born in 1744; Jesse, born in 1746; Oliver, born in 1748; and Amasa, born in 1750. The next in line was Jesse Brown, who was born in Colchester, Conn., February 2, 1746, but in early life went to Utica, N. Y., where he owned and operated a saw-mill; he was also a builder of boats. In 1770 he was first married to Abigail Parke, a native of Norwich, Conn., and to them were born nine children, namely: Bernice, born in 1772; Levi, born in 1773; Nathaniel, born in 1775; Amasa, the grandfather of Hartford Perry; Jeremiah, born in 1780; one who died in infancy; Jesse, born in 1784; Parke, born in 1786, and George, born in 1792. His second union was with Mrs. Marion Drew, by whom he reared two children, Abigail, born in 1808, and John, born in 1812. Amasa Brown was also born in Colchester, Conn., the date of his birth being September 12, 1777. He worked with his father, learning the trade of a boat builder, in which he became a skilled mechanic. As an agent of Aaron Burr, he went to Beaver county, and, in 1806, was made master builder at Bridgewater. Large flatboats were built, which were used to convey produce down the Ohio and Mississippi rivers. Amasa Brown was killed, in 1829, while launching one of these boats. He wedded Eleanor Vankirk, and to them were born six children: Milton; John; Hannah; Oliver H. P.; Mary; and Jesse.

Oliver Hazard Perry Brown was born in Phillipsburg, Pa., now called Monaca, June

10, 1820. He learned the boat building trade, which he followed for many years, and after accumulating wealth, he moved to Raccoon township, Beaver county, where he began the life of a farmer. This latter occupation he continued for eighteen months, and then returned to boat building, settling at Freedom, Pennsylvania. He built three large boats; the first was named Commodore Perry, which was at that time the best boat on the river; the second was Parthenia; and the third was known as Hardtimes, which, singularly, earned more money than any boat which plied the river at that time. The latter vessel was used in conveying cotton from the valley of the Chattahoochee River to Apalachicola Bay. In 1865, he gave up boating, and, in 1866, he bought the property of J. Ranson, on the corner of Vermont and West Adams streets, Rochester, Pa. There he resided, until his death, on November 18, 1892. His wife was Mary McCombs, who was born July 9, 1820, and whose death occurred June 20, 1889. The following children were born to this happy union: Hartson Philmore, born in 1840, and died in 1841; Amanda Eleanor, born in 1842, and married to Samuel R. Campbell, of Beaver Falls; Mary, born in 1844, and died in 1846; Amasa, born in 1848, and died in 1849; Hartford Perry; and Parthenia, born in 1856, and died in 1863. Captain O. H. Perry Brown was one of the founders of the banking house of John Conway & Co., in 1871; he was a charter member of the Rochester Heat & Light Company, and one of its directors until his death.

The subject of this memoir was born in Freedom, Pa., and received his early mental training in the schools of that town, and at Rochester Academy, and Beaver Seminary. He prepared himself for Yale College under the private instruction of Drs. C. C. Riggs and J. W. Scott—the latter having been president of Jefferson College, Washington, Pennsylvania. In 1872, Mr. Brown accepted a position as bookkeeper in the Second National Bank at Pittsburg, and was subsequently promoted to be teller; resigning his position in the bank, however, he entered West Point Military Academy as a cadet from that district. He afterward became a partner in the general mercantile business of Hon. Samuel J. Cross—the firm name being known as S. J. Cross & Co. In 1878, Mr. Brown sold his interest therein to John Davis. Then, in company with James Rees and Simpson Homer, he built the steam boat called Carrier, but in 1884, sold his interest in this boat, and embarked in mercantile pursuits alone. In 1886, he was elected to the legislature from this district, and consequently relinquished his store. In 1888, he was re-elected to the legislature; in 1888, and while a member of the House, he introduced the Ship Canal bill, secured its passage and an appropriation of $10,000, with a commission, which made a survey of the Lake Erie and Ohio River Ship Canal, in 1889. In May, 1887, he assisted in the organization of the Rochester Heat & Light Company, of which he was made secretary, and, later, treasurer. The gas of this company is nearly all produced in Beaver county, and during the winter of 1898, a million cubic feet per day was used. Mr. Brown was one of the promoters of the People's Electric Railway, which was opened to the public in August, 1892; the line is four miles in length, extending from the Rochester junction of the Traction Company to Freedom and St. Clair, and running four cars daily. He was elected president of this enterprise, and, July 1, 1897, he was made manager. He is a stockholder in the Beaver Valley Traction Company Railway, and in 1892, was made secretary and general manager, a position which he resigned in 1895, but was re-elected in 1899. He is also a stockholder in the Sharon Bridge Company, the People's Insurance Company of Pittsburg, and was formerly a stockholder in the J. Conway banking house.

Mr. Brown was joined in marriage to Miss Sue T. Cross, a daughter of Samuel J. and Frances E. (Wells) Cross. Hon. S. J. Cross was born in Washington township, Rhode Island, January 6, 1828, and came to Beaver county in 1855. For twenty years he was the leading merchant of Rochester. He passed from this life September 27, 1875. His wife now resides with the subject of this sketch. Their children were named as follows: Sue Thurston, the wife of Hartford Perry Brown; Julia Frances; Samuel Joseph; Emma Wells; George Herbert; Thomas Wells; and May, who died in her infancy. Mr. and Mrs. Brown are the parents of six children: Hartford Perry, Jr., who was born

February 5, 1875, and died in 1889; Frances Mary, born October 19, 1876; Emily Edna, born November 11, 1878; Sue Thurston, born October 27, 1880, and died in 1893; Julia Parthenia, born March 27, 1887; and Stanley Quay, born February 17, 1889. Mr. Brown and family are members of the Baptist church. In 1880, Mr. Brown erected a handsome brick residence on West Adams street, which he makes his home.

WILLIAM G. ALGEO, Jr., master mechanic of the Union Drawn Steel Works, has won an enviable reputation as master of his craft and is a highly esteemed and respected citizen of Beaver Falls, Pa., being also well-known through Beaver county. He was born February 4, 1854, in Pittsburg, Pa., where he was also reared and schooled; his educational advantages, however, were extremely limited, and he obtained only a slight knowledge of the common branches. At the age of fifteen years, he quit school to learn the trade of a machinist in Pittsburg. After completing his trade, he went to Rochester, Pa., where he learned the trade of a cabinet maker with his father, and remained in that line of business until 1878. Entering the service of the Western File Works of Beaver Falls he remained with them two years, as a journeyman. At the end of that time, Mr. Algeo was employed by the Love Sewing Machine Co., at Rochester, Pa., and was occupied in the manufacture of sewing machines for the next three years. He was subsequently engaged by the Standard Horse Shoe Nail Works at Fallston, then by the Great Western File Works, and then by the Hartman Steel Company, where he remained four years, three of which found him in charge of the machine department. Later, Mr. Algeo entered the service of the Union Drawn Steel Company, being the first man hired by the company. The plant, though small at first, has gradually been improved, and enlarged until it has become one of the largest and most substantial enterprises of the town. Mr. Algeo's position is that of master mechanic and there is hardly a detail in the whole range of the plant but what he can attend to with accuracy and skill. When work has passed his expert and trained hand and eye, it is sure to have been done right.

Our subject is a stanch Republican, but has never sought nor held office. He was at one time a member of the Knights of Pythias, the Jr. O. U. A. M., the I. O. of H., and the Maccabees. Like his honored father, William G. Algeo, Sr., whose sketch also appears in this publication, he is a member of the Episcopal church. Our subject was joined in marriage by the beautiful and impressive Episcopal service, with Nora Clayton, a lady of rare accomplishments. Two children, Mabel and Alice, blessed their home for a short time, but were taken away by the "grim reaper."

Our subject is a prominent citizen, public-spirited, generous, and liberal, and has ever labored zealously to promote the welfare and prosperity of his town and county. In his business sphere, he is everywhere known as a man of indomitable spirit, extreme integrity, and correct method. The growing and valuable interests he directs show the impress of a master mind. They are of the utmost importance not only to the people of Beaver Falls, but to the manufacturing world as well. Mr. Algeo is recognized as a moving spirit of the business and is accordingly esteemed and respected.

JOHN MARTIN, a young man who has always been engaged in the manufacture of bricks, holds the important position of foreman of the Pennsylvania Clay Manufacturing Company, of Monaca, Pa., in which capacity he has efficiently served since 1897.

This is one of the six large plants controlled by Park Brothers, with general offices at Rochester, Pa., and it is one of their best. It is known as "No. 4," and is devoted to the manufacture of paving brick exclusively, the output being 25,000 finished bricks per day. This yard was established many years ago, but did not come into possession of the present firm until 1895. There are forty acres of clay of a superior quality, and the mine is a 12 ft. vein sunk through a 72 ft. shaft, the material being conveyed from the mines to the works on a train road. It is dumped into a set of rolls and crushed, then carried by an automatic elevator into a mill where it is ground and mixed for the brick machine. When it comes from the brick machine which has a

capacity of 35,000 per day, it is ready for the dry kilns, a double deck affair with a capacity of 100,000, and from there it is taken to the kiln. Of these they have ten of the round, down draught variety, each one of them holding from 47,000 to 70,000 bricks. Facilities for shipping are of the best, being located on the P. & L. E. R. R. The firm have a Columbia engine of 125 horse power, and ship all of the product to local, Western Pennsylvania and Eastern Ohio markets. Mr. Martin has complete charge of the operation of these works, and as he has been engaged in that line of work all his life, he conducts them in the most efficient manner. He has 35 men in his employ, with whom he is exceedingly popular and they, one and all, accord him the greatest respect.

John Martin was born in Clarion county, Pa., July 29, 1869, and attended the public schools until he was thirteen years old, when he accepted a position in a brick yard. His first engagement was with the Climax Fire Clay Company, with which he remained for ten years, learning his trade in the most thorough manner. He then moved to Beaver county, and for five years faithfully performed similar duties in the employ of Barnes & Company. In 1897, he resigned his position to accept that of foreman of the plant he now operates, one of the substantial concerns of Monaca. He has taken a deep interest in the progress of this little borough, and has made many friends since locating there.

On July 4th, 1895, Mr. Martin was united in marriage with Lillie Mennall, a native of Beaver county, and a daughter of Richard Mennall, and they are the parents of two children: William, who was born in 1896; and Melvin, who was born in 1898. Mr. Martin has dealt some in real estate, but has now discontinued that business; he bought his present residence in 1899. He is a member and steward of the Methodist Episcopal church. Politically, he is a sturdy supporter of the Republican party. He is a member of the Woodmen of the World.

DR. SAMUEL DIXON STURGEON, a leading physician of New Galilee, Pa., whose portrait appears on the opposite page, has been located in that thriving little town since 1891. He enjoys quite an extensive practice, considering the short time he has been there, and is frequently obliged to take long drives in the country on professional duty. He is patronized by many well-to-do citizens, and owns a fine modern residence. Shortly after purchasing this home, Dr. Sturgeon built a large and convenient barn to comfortably shelter his driving horses. Dr. Sturgeon was born at Noblestown, Allegheny county, Pa., July 7, 1851. He is a son of Henry P. and Miriam L. (Ewing) Sturgeon. When Samuel was five years old, his parents removed to Ashland county, Ohio, where he lived until he had attained the age of sixteen years. His academic schooling was received at Greersburg Academy and Beaver College. He taught school eight years in Beaver county, first at Oakdale, one term, then at Brush Run, one term, South Beaver, one term, Brighton township, three terms, Bridgewater, one term and at Darlington public school, one term.

He then decided upon a professional career, and entered the Western Reserve University of Cleveland, Ohio, where he pursued a course of medicine. He graduated from that institution with a degree of M. D., in the class of 1884. In May of the same year, Dr. Sturgeon opened an office as general practitioner at Darlington. His pleasant, courteous manner and agreeable ways soon made a favorable impression on the people, and brought him patients. He remained in Darlington for seven years and then sold out, locating next at New Galilee, where he still remains.

Dr. Sturgeon married Fanny K. Tyler, an accomplished daughter of Moses W. Tyler. Mrs. Sturgeon was born in Brattleboro, Vt., and moved to Erie, Pa., with her parents, when quite young. It was there that she obtained her primary education. Her classical training was received in Boston, Massachusetts.

Besides his property in New Galilee, the Doctor has several outside investments. Politically, he affiliates with the Republican party, and has served a number of years as a member of the county executive committee. In addition to this, he has held all the township offices. He takes a keen interest in local affairs,—being on the school board and in the borough council. The church relations of Dr.

and Mrs. Sturgeon are with the Presbyterian denomination, of which church the Doctor has been a trustee for many years. Socially, our subject is a valued member and past master of Meridian Lodge, No. 411, F. & A. M.

———◆•◆———

ROBERT S. IMBRIE, real estate dealer and insurance agent of Beaver, Pennsylvania, is a gentleman whose, life has been spent wholly in Beaver county, Pa., with the exception of three years passed in Franklin county, in the same state, and, although he appears to be a man of middle age, is to-day in his seventy-first year. He obtained his elementary education in the public schools of his native place, taking a finishing course at Beaver Academy, and afterwards following the profession of teaching for a period of five years. He next engaged in mercantile pursuits by conducting a branch store with his brother at Mercersburg, Franklin county, Pa., for about two and one-half years. Later he went into the same business alone, keeping a general store at Loudon, Franklin county, until 1861, when he sold out and started a new store at Darlington, Beaver county. Upon the death of his father, in 1864, he again sold out his business and went upon the homestead farm, which he conducted and managed for his mother until it was sold a year later. Mr. Imbrie then accepted a position with the Wheeler & Wilson Sewing Machine Co., at Beaver, and continued as their general agent for a period of nine years, being very successful at that business, and selling hundreds. of sewing machines. He subsequently severed h's connection with that firm and dealt for some time in agricultural implements, that he might have occupation at home where he could share domestic pleasures and companionships. But the machine companies sought his services again, and he was finally induced to enter that sphere once more, engaging with the White Sewing Machine Co. for one year, and with the American for three years.

Our subject then abandoned that business entirely, and turned his attention to fire insurance, associating with the firm of Hurst & Imbrie. Later, at the death of Mr. Hurst, fire insurance was dropped and life insurance was taken up in its stead. Since then Mr. Imbrie has been connected with the "Mutual Life, of New York," the "Manhattan" and the "Equitable." The latter is the one in which he is now mainly interested. Some years ago, our subject built a residence on Third street, which is now owned by Mr. Shoemaker, but later, purchased his present residence on North Park street. This is a large, handsome structure of brick, built by his brother Delorme, in 1859; it is a beautiful place, and is finely located, making an ideal homestead.

In 1859, Nancy E. Scott, a favorite daughter of William Scott, a highly respected resident of New Brighton, Beaver county, became the wife of Mr. Imbrie, and is said to be a very attractive and entertaining lady. To them were born the following children: Mary, who died in her fourth year; J. Maurice, a molder, deceased at the age of thirty years, who wedded Ella Morgan and had three children, Martha, Robert, and Paul; Nannie S., wife of Joseph Irons, of Beaver Falls, who has two children, Lorain and Helen; Nettie, a stenographer, of Pittsburg; Mabel, a music teacher, of Pittsburg; Grace, who is still at home, and is a fine musician; and Jessie, also a stenographer, of Pittsburg.

In his political views our subject has ever been a Republican, and although he has never sought office or political distinction, he has served as school director and as member of the borough council. In business he is careful, shrewd, and trustworthy. Enjoying the patronage of the best class of people, his work is executed with facility and dispatch. As a neighbor, he is kind and obliging, and his enterprising spirit has been felt in all movements to advance the welfare of his community. In his religious convictions, Mr. Imbrie is a devout Christian and a member of the United Presbyterian church; he has served many years as elder and as superintendent of Sunday School.

Robert S. Imbrie was born in Big Beaver township, Beaver county, Pa., August 12, 1829. He is a son of John and Nancy (Rankin) Imbrie, and grandson of David and Mary Imbrie. David Imbrie was a native of Scotland, and while still a single man came to the United States. He was a tanner by trade. He became the owner of a tannery in Westmoreland county, Pa., and conducted it for many years. Late in life he retired from that business and spent his closing years upon a farm previously purchased by him. Both he and his good wife Mary lived to a good old age. Their children were: David; Robert; James; John, father of Robert S.; George; Mrs. Catherine Slone; Mrs. Mary Fleck; and Mrs. Jane Maloney.

John Imbrie was born in Westmoreland county, Pa., where he early learned the trade of a tanner in his father's tannery. Some years after arriving at manhood, he removed to Big Beaver township, Beaver county, Pa., and purchased a farm of 106 acres, heavily timbered. Erecting a tannery upon his land, he carried on that business for several years, but later turned his attention to farming. He bought 50 acres quite near his former purchase, and upon it passed the remainder of his life. This farm was commonly known as the Economite farm, and upon it his death occurred at the age of seventy-three years. He was joined in wedlock with Nancy Rankin, daughter of James Rankin. She survived her husband until she reached her eighty-eighth year.

John Imbrie rendered eminent services to our country during the War of 1812, being stationed at Fort Erie. He was looked upon as an influential citizen, and above all a man who could be trusted, and enjoyed the love and esteem of all who knew him. Possessed of good judgment, and richly endowed with perseverance, he carried through to a successful termination his every undertaking. He served as justice of the peace, and as county commissioner, many years. He was a Seceder, and later, a United Presbyterian. He and his much beloved wife reared the follow-

ing family (all of whom are now deceased except Robert S. Imbrie and his brother John): Addison; Delorme; Mary, wife of J. P. Martin, whose life history is found elsewhere in this volume; Nancy, wife of James L. Ansley; Robert S., subject of this biography; Minerva, who died at the age of eighteen years; John, still single; Jeremiah R.; and David. The last two served in the Civil War in the 10th Reg. Pa. Reserves, and both died from the effects of the exposure and hardships of campaigning.

The subject of our sketch is a gentleman who is intelligent, courteous, and refined,—just the kind of a man to make a lasting impression for good on all societies, who are so fortunate as to number him among their members.

———◆•◆———

JOHN F. FERGUSON has been a prominent citizen of the borough of Beaver Falls for the past ten years and is the proprietor of one of its leading livery stables. He has been engaged in various enterprises in this locality, all of which have proved successful, and he is a popular and well-to-do citizen. He was born in this county. December 8, 1850, and is a son of John and Janiza (Elliott) Ferguson.

John F. Ferguson's great-grandfather was a life-long resident of his native country, Ireland. John Ferguson, the grandfather of John F., was also a native of Ireland, and was a tallow-candle maker by trade; he was the sole member of the family who came to this country. He settled in Beaver county, where he spent his remaining days in carrying on agricultural pursuits. He built a house, which still stands on the premises. He was the father of a son and four daughters,—John, Mary, Maria, Ann, and Sarah, all of whom are deceased with the exception of Mary.

John Ferguson was born on the homestead March 31, 1814, and resided there all his life, pursuing the vocation of a farmer. As a result of his marriage with Janiza Elliott, a family of two sons and three daughters was reared, as follows: Agnes, who is the wife of Henry Sloan of New Brighton, Pa.; John F.; Sarah Jane, who is the wife of Elisha Baxter of Beaver Falls; Mary E., who was united in marriage with Abram Berry and resides in New Brighton; and Thomas B., who has charge of the old homestead.

John F. Ferguson possesses a common school education and spent his boyhood days assisting his father at home; he continued to remain on the home farm until thirty-five years of age, when he decided to go into business on his own account; he began contracting and teaming in Beaver Falls and New Brighton, and followed that occupation until 1888. In that year he opened a livery business in Beaver Falls, and has successfully conducted it up to the present time. He has established a fine trade and is well worthy of the large patronage he receives. For many years he was engaged in the ice business, but sold out in 1893. He is an enterprising and progressive citizen, and possesses the esteem and good-will of his many acquaintances.

Mr. Ferguson formed a matrimonial alliance with Miss Jeannetta L. Anderson, a daughter of Frank Anderson, of Beaver Falls, the nuptials occurring August 31, 1896. In religious belief he favors the Methodist denomination. In politics, he is a Republican.

DR. WILLIAM S. COOK is a young dentist who has built up a large practice in the short time he has resided in Beaver Falls, and is likely to become one of the most prominent and successful dentists of his time. Dr. Cook was born in Darlington, Beaver county, May 31, 1868, and was educated at Greersburg Academy, an institution of learning established in Darlington, in 1802. Immediately after his graduation therefrom, June 11, 1886, young Cook entered upon the noble profession of teaching, following that calling for a period of three years in his native county. At the close of that time, he began the study of dentistry, and in 1889 entered the Philadelphia Dental College, from which he graduated February 26, 1891. Immediately after his graduation, Dr. Cook located in Beaver Falls, where he established an office and engaged in the practice of his profession. He has been located since October 1st, 1898, at the corner of Sixth avenue and Twelfth street, where his many patrons seek him both early and late.

Dr. Cook is a member of the Odontological Society of Western Pennsylvania and Eastern Ohio. The doctor has a rare literary talent which, coupled with a thorough knowledge of his profession, has given him a chance to distinguish himself. He has read papers, prepared in an intelligent and able manner, before the above mentioned society. Among his most noted papers are "The Cleft Palate," "The Repair of the Cleft Palate by Means of the Obturator." He has also written and read other papers of less importance than those above noted. Dr. Cook is an enthusiastic Republican, and never fails to do his duty toward that party when election day arrives. He has served as a member of the council from the third ward of Beaver Falls and, fraternally, is a member of the Woodmen of the World.

Miss Jane E. Anderson became the Doctor's bride on December 27, 1893. Although he and his accomplished wife have no family of their own, they greatly delight in and admire the little "fairies of light." They are both willing members and workers of the United Presbyterian Church and are known throughout the community as kind hearted, charitable people. Dr. Cook is a son of Thomas and Margaret (Duff) Cook, and grandson of James Cook.

James Cook was a native of Ireland and was of Scotch-Irish descent. He came to America when young and shortly afterward located in Darlington, Beaver county, Pa., where he purchased a farm and engaged in clearing it for the purpose of utilizing the rich soil. He lived upon that farm the remainder of his life, engaged in agricultural pursuits. Upon this old homestead near Darlington, Thomas Cook, the father of William S., was born, January 16, 1845, and was reared and educated in the same locality, remaining there until 1861, at the breaking out of the Civil War. He enlisted in the Union Army as a member of Company D, 100th Reg. Pa. Vol., known as "The Round Head" regiment. Mr. Cook served with that regiment until his discharge, the latter part of November, 1862. The most important battles in which he participated were, James' Island, Hilton Head, S. C., and Chantilly, Va., in which last engagement he was wounded, and was taken to a hospital at Point Lookout, Md., where he was confined from the first of September until he received his discharge in November.

Returning from the war, he learned the blacksmith's trade, completing his apprenticeship in 1865. He then began working as a blacksmith in Darlington, where he also engaged in the manufacture of carriages and wagons in connection with his trade. He remained in Darlington until 1889, when he went to Beaver Falls, and has since followed the same line of business. In his political views, Mr. Cook is a Republican, and has always taken an active interest in the success of that party, although he has never sought political distinction. He is a member of Beaver Falls Lodge, F. & A. M., also of Harmony Chapter, No. 206, R. A. M., at Beaver Falls, and is a past colonel of the Union Veteran Legion, No. 4, of Beaver Falls. He is also a member of the L. A. W. and a charter member of Beaver Valley Cycling League No. 88, which was organized in the early part of 1893, with fourteen members and, at the present writing, has a membership of one hundred and twenty-six, and occupies the entire second story of the Martsolf building, on Seventh avenue. He has been one of the board of directors since its organization, and is now serving as its president; he has been twice a delegate.

Dr. Cook is known to be a conscientious and honorable man; by his pleasant manner and courteous bearing, he at once gained the good will of the citizens of Beaver Falls, while his close application to his profession and the painstaking care he exercises in the cases that have fallen to his share, have won him the confidence of the entire community. The marvelous rapidity with which he has built up his present practice is almost incredible to one unacquainted with the doctor's push and energy.

JOHN B. WILSON. Among the enterprising and reliable business men of Beaver, Pa., is the gentleman whose name appears at the opening of this biography, who is the senior member of the well known firm of J. B. Wilson & Son, the largest hardware merchants in the community. Mr. Wilson also deals largely in real estate, owning several houses and lots out in the east end of Third avenue, which is now considered the most beautiful residence portion of Beaver. His ancestors were of Scotch-Irish descent, and his grandfather was pioneer of the family in this country. Industry township, Beaver county, Pa., is the birthplace of our subject, his birth occurring on February 2, 1839. He is a son of Thomas and Jane (Burnsides) Wilson.

George Wilson, grandfather of John B., was a native of the northern part of Ireland and was of Scotch ancestry; in 1819, he came to this country with his family of five children, and took up a tract of fifty acres in Industry township. He sold this property, which is now the James Jackson farm, and then bought two hundred and forty acres of timber land. He erected a log house and had resided upon his newly purchased land but a short time when death claimed him; he was then about sixty years of age. He was married to Elizabeth Lindsey, also a native of Ireland, and their children were as follows: Thomas; James, settled in Hannibal, Mo.; George, deceased; Margaret, wife of William Sutherland of Hannibal, Mo.; and Catherine, who was wedded to William Humphrey. George Wilson and his wife were buried in the old Beaver cemetery.

Thomas Wilson was born in Ireland in 1808, but was reared to manhood on his father's farm in Beaver county, and upon his father's death he took charge of the homestead; after attaining an advanced age, his son, George Wilson, took charge of the farm, and is still in possession of it. He was wedded to Jane Burnsides, also a native of Ireland, and a daughter of John Burnsides, who came to this country and located in Dresden, Ohio, where he carried on farming. Mr. Wilson died when eighty-three years old, while his wife departed this life in 1872, aged fifty-five years. They reared the following four children: George, who has the homestead; John B.; Margaret, the wife of C. A. Bowers of Beaver; and Eliza. Religiously, the family were Presbyterians; politically, Mr. Wilson was a Republican.

John B. Wilson was reared on the old homestead and received his mental training in the public schools of that district; after teaching school two years, he went to Beaver to learn the plasterers' trade; he then engaged in contracting for about eight years, after which he located in Youngstown, Ohio, where he embarked in the grocery business for a period of ten years; on disposing of this he returned to Beaver and began the sale of agricultural implements; this was in 1875. The continual increase of his patronage made it necessary to seek large accommodations, and accordingly, in 1883, he bought the old Clark Hotel property, which is located on Third street. He turned the old building around and rebuilt it, putting on an additional story, and also building barns and a large warehouse. He stocked the concern with a complete line of hardware goods, and the business progressed satisfactorily until March 2, 1888, when the entire building was destroyed by fire. Mr. Wilson immediately built a brick building 30 by 100 feet, and also erected a warehouse. The other half of the lot he sold to Mr. Anderson. An extensive stock of hardware goods and implements was then put into the new structure and Mr. Wilson conducted the largest and best equipped store of its kind in the county. In 1897, the subject of our sketch took in his son as a partner, and the firm name was afterwards known as J. B. Wilson & Son; the capital stock of the firm has been increased to $10,000. Mr. Wilson purchased a square on Third and Wilson avenues, and on the corner lot erected a handsome brick residence; he has also built a double-house adjoining his home, and has sold many lots in the block. He is a progressive and loyal citizen; intelligent and well-read; and he has a host of acquaintances in the vicinity.

Mr. Wilson and Matilda Eakin, a daughter of J. R. Eakin, were united in marriage, and they are parents of three children: Mary E.; Genevieve C.; and Royal Q.; the latter is connected with his father in the hardware business, and is one of the most promising young business men in Beaver; like his father, he has won the esteem and confidence of all. Mr. Wilson and family are all members of the Presbyterian church, the former having been a trustee of the church for the past twenty years; politically, he is a Republican.

———— ◄ • ► ————

WILLIAM G. HARKER. One of the prominent and successful industries of Beaver Falls, Pa., is that of Knott, Harker & Company,—manufacturers of fire-grates, hardware novelties and castings of all kinds; the gentleman whose name appears at the opening of this biography is the superintendent of the above enterprise and much of the success of the plant is due to his

EDWARD JAMES ALLISON.

good judgment and untiring efforts. He was born on the Conoquenessing Creek, Beaver county, April 15, 1851, and is a son of William and Mary Ann (Peatling) Harker.

Wi liam G. Harker's parents were both born in Lancastershire, England, and shortly after their marriage they came to the United States, in 1846, and located on a farm in Beaver county; until 1854 he was engaged in farming, but in that year he settled in New Brighton, and worked in a saw-mill. He afterwards entered the employ of W. P. Townsend & Co., remaining in their employ until death claimed him. He was a Republican in politics; religiously, he was an active and consistent member of the Methodist Protestant church. He was married in his native country and became the father of the following children: Mary Ann, the wife of J. W. Graham of New Brighton; Charlotte, the deceased wife of W. H. Elverson of the New Brighton Pottery Works; William G.; Lizzie, wedded to J. H. Rice, a farmer in Michigan; Charles E., a machinist residing in New Brighton; Carrie, wedded to Sheldon Roat, a farmer living in Michigan; and Albert P., a machinist, of New Brighton.

William G. Harker attended the common schools of New Brighton and at an early age served an apprenticeship to the molders' trade; he then accepted the superintendency of the Beaver Falls Car Works Foundry, in which capacity he continued to serve for a period of eight years. Upon the organization of the Knott, Harker & Company enterprise, the subject of our sketch was made superintendent,—a position he has faithfully filled up to the present time. The company is engaged in the manufacture of fireplace-grates, hardware novelties, and all kinds of castings; it a'so operates a machine shop and gives employment to some 60 skilled hands. Mr. Harker is an expert mechanic and is greatly respected by the employees under his charge; he is an intelligent and loyal citizen, commanding the good-will of all who know him.

Politically, Mr. Harker is a Republican, although in local matters, he always supports the one whom he considers best qualified for the position. He is a member and trustee of the Methodist Protestant church of New Brighton; socially, he is a member of the K. of P., and a director of the Y. M. C. A. of New Brighton. On October 26, 1875, Mr. Harker was joined in matrimonial bonds with Miss Irene Wilson, a daughter of Joseph Wilson of New Brighton, and they are the parents of the following children: Joseph, deceased; Ernest Ira, deceased; Clyde; and Elsie.

——————

EDWARD JAMES ALLISON, whose portrait is shown on the preceding page, is cashier of the First National Bank of Beaver, Beaver county, Pa., and is one of the most enterprising and highly esteemed citizens of the county He has distinguished himself in business circles as a shrewd, practical and conservative man, whose judgment has not failed him in critical moments. His record has been honorable, and his integrity is unquestioned. He has ever been quick to see the main chance in business, and has accumulated a handsome competency by the most open methods. Mr. Allison, who is a descendant of one of Beaver county's most noted men, was born at Bridgewater, in February, 1852, and is a son of Thomas and Emily (Logan) Allison, and grandson of Hon. James Allison.

Hon. James Allison, attorney-at-law, of Beaver, was born in Virginia or Maryland, where his father, James Allison Sr., owned a very large plantation and numerous slaves. Hon. James Allison chose the profession of a lawyer, and was educated at a law school at Washington, D. C. About 1794, he located in Beaver, Pa., and engaged in the practice of his profession. As there were few lawyers there at that early date, he had more business at times than he could attend to; he was considered one of the ablest lawyers of his day, making a specialty of clearing up land titles. After he succeeded in establishing a large and well-paying practice, he was twice elected to Congress, but resigned during his second term, to resume his practice, which was far more remunerative. He accumulated a handsome competency, and was esteemed by all who knew him. He lived to the good old age of eighty-three years, and his companion departed from his side in her sixty-seventh year. His wife, who was a Miss Bradford, bore her husband the following children: John; Samuel; William; James; Thomas; Sarah; Margaret; Juliette; and two who died in early childhood.

Thomas Allison, the father of Edward James, was a pupil in Beaver Academy, and early in life began a mercantile career at Bridgewater, conducting a store for a period of twenty-two years, at the same stand now occupied by R. S. Ranger. Mr. Allison subsequently removed his business to Beaver, where he was similarly engaged for fourteen years, on the corner of Third street and College avenue. In 1892, Mr. Allison retired from business pursuits, and one year later his death occurred, at the age of seventy-six years. He was united in marriage with Emily Logan, a daughter of Joshua and Sabina (Swift) Logan, respected citizens of Beaver county. The maternal grandmother of Mr. Allison, Sabina Swift, was a granddaughter of Lucy Eliot, a lineal descendant of Rev. John Eliot, "the apostle to the Indians." In 1646, the legislature of Massachusetts passed an act for the propagation of the gospel among the Indians, and in the same year John Eliot began his labors at Nonantum, of forming churches and translating the Bible and other Christian books. The beloved mother of the subject of this record is still living, and resides at Beaver.

Edward James Allison was the only child of his parents, and received his finishing education at Beaver Academy. He began his career by working in his father's store, where he continued until he was appointed teller of the First National Bank of Rochester, Pennsylvania. This position he occupied for five years, resigning to become cashier of the First National Bank of Beaver, Pa., his present responsible position.

The First National Bank was established March 31, 1888, with a capital of $50,000, Edward B. Daugherty being president, Hon. John M. Buchanan, vice-president, and Edward J. Allison, cashier. At the death of E. B. Daugherty, in 1897, Hon. J. M. Buchanan became president, and Dr. J. H. Wilson, vice-president. The bank is located in the Anderson block, and is one of the handsomest and best ordered business places in Beaver Valley. The building is centrally located, and its rooms are well lighted by one of the finest plate glass fronts in the county. Its interior is newly decorated, and its construction and arrangement are thoroughly adapted for the purpose for which it was intended. It contains a beautiful office, finely decorated, and private offices for the president and directors. It is heated throughout with steam, and contains one of the best vaults of modern date, with time-lock, etc. The bank is considered not only proof against fire and burglars, but is conducted on safe lines. In evidence of the careful and conservative management of its business, is the fact that within the ten years since it was chartered, it has placed to the credit of the surplus account the sum of $50,000, or an amount equal to its capital, and has paid dividends at the rate of six per cent., since April 1, 1888. The average deposits are $225,000; the average loans are $265,000. This bank has recently placed in its building one of the largest and best constructed safety vaults, with deposit boxes, in Western Pennsylvania. It is not necessary to say that the First National Bank embraces in its management and directorship some of the best and most substantial citizens of Beaver Valley, that it is considered one of the finest banking houses in Western Pennsylvania. Its present officials are: John M. Buchanan, president; Jefferson H. Wilson, vice-president; Edward J. Allison, cashier, and Robert F. Patterson, teller. Its board of directors are: John M. Buchanan, Jefferson H. Wilson, Alfred S. Moore, David A. Nelson, Alfred C. Hurst, Samuel Moody, John I. Martin, John T. Taylor, and Joseph L. Holmes.

Edward James Allison, whose name heads this biography, was united in marriage with Margaret McCaughey, a daughter of the late Rev. Alexander McCaughey, who during life was a much beloved pastor of Salem, Pennsylvania. Mr. and Mrs. Allison have a handsome modern residence on Beaver street, built in 1889. This home is rendered much happier by the presence of two little sons and one daughter, whose names are as follows: Dwight M., born in February, 1891; Margaret M., born September 12, 1895; and James, born September 11, 1898. Mr. Allison also owns considerable other valuable real-estate in Beaver. Like his honored ancestors, he is a Republican in politics. He worships in the Presbyterian church, of which he is a member and a trustee. He has held minor offices in the borough and takes a lively interest in the promotion and progress of Beaver. He is a gentleman with a wide range of experience in the financial field, where he is an important factor, and his thoroughness and methodical ways stand him in good stead. The subject of this biography is a member of the Masonic fraternity of high standing, and easily ranks as one of the best citizens of Beaver county.

———•◆•———

R. GEORGE S. BOYD, a popular and successful physician of Beaver Falls, Pa., is one of the most prominent Homeopathic practitioners in Beaver county. He has been practicing at his present location for nearly twenty years, and controls a large business. Dr. Boyd has worked hard and earnestly for his success, and deserves the reputation and confidence with which he has been rewarded.

Dr. Boyd was born at New Sheffield, Pa., on May 6, 1850. He received his primary mental training in both public and select schools, afterwards taking a collegiate course at Curry Institute in Pittsburg. After receiving special tuition in that school, he followed the profession of teaching for a period of nine years, chiefly in Beaver county. He decided to fit himself for the medical profession, and with that object in view, he studied medicine with his brother, John S. Boyd, after which he took the required course of lectures at the Cleveland Homeopathic Hospital College, and graduated with the class of 1880. Dr. Boyd immediately established himself in Beaver Falls and has remained ever since, even occupying the same office, refitted, however, from time to time, with the most modern appliances used by the most progressive medical men of to-day. His practice, small at

first, has increased with each succeeding year until now the Doctor has all he can attend to.

In 1881, Dr. Boyd was united in marriage with Emma J. Laird, an affable daughter of Alexander Laird of New Scottsville, Pennsylvania. Dr. Boyd is an influential member of the State Medical Association, and also of the Homeopathic Medical Society of Beaver county. He was one of the organizers of the Beaver Falls Board of Health in 1893, and has been president and secretary of that organization. His interest in educational matters is not lacking, and is proved by his having served on the school board. In politics, the subject of this sketch is a Republican, but his practice is not confined to his Republican friends and their families; indeed, the Doctor never allows politics to interfere with his professional duties whatever. He is also a member of the medical and surgical staff of the Beaver Valley General Hospital. Dr. Boyd is a son of Samuel and Martha (Maratta) Boyd, and grandson of John Boyd.

John Boyd was a native of Ireland, coming to America and settling in Allegheny township, Allegheny county, Pa., where his son Samuel was born. Samuel Boyd was reared and educated in his native county, and learned the trade of a cabinet maker. After living a number of years in Bridgewater borough, he removed to New Sheffield, Beaver county, where he followed farming in connection with the undertaking business. His last years were spent in Beaver Falls, where he died, aged seventy-nine years. His widow, the beloved mother of our subject, still survives her hus-

LEWIS W. REID.

band and resides in Beaver Falls. Mrs. Boyd was, before marriage, Miss Martha Maratta. She was born in 1820 in Hopewell township, Beaver county, Pennsylvania. The Doctor's brothers and sisters are John S., of New Brighton; Sarah (Todd), of Washington, Iowa; and Frank, of Beaver Falls. The highly respected father was an earnest Republican, and took a decided interest in the success of his party. He was honored by the confidence of the people, and served as postmaster before and during the Civil War.

Dr. Boyd is, at this writing, a very active man. His constitution has been of that sort that has enabled him to go through all kinds of weather to attend to his practice, without any bad effect upon himself. His affluent circumstances are due to thrift and careful attention to his professional duties, and his standing in the community is certainly well merited.

—————

LEWIS W. REED, the efficient and accommodating postmaster of Beaver, Pa., where he is also an active attorney, is one of the most enthusiastic Democrats in the whole of Beaver county. Ever since arriving at maturity, he has been particularly zealous in the interests of his favorite party, and has officiated as chairman of the Democratic committee for several years, having long been a member of that organization and having served for seven years as its secretary. Although he never sought office, he has been repeatedly offered political prefer-

ment. Mr. Reed was born in Raccoon township, Beaver county, Pa., and after attending the public schools of New Sheffield, took an academic course at Woodlawn Academy. He then became assistant editor of the "Beaver Star," and while engaged in that capacity, also studied law under the preceptorship of Hon. J. M. Buchanan. He was admitted to the bar February 4, 1889, and, opening an office in Beaver, he engaged in the practice of his profession for two years. At the close of that time, he became associated with J. M. Buchanan and continued to be a law partner of that noted attorney for five years. On account of failing health, Mr. Reed was obliged to discontinue his professional duties, having already had several hemorrhages. Although reluctant to do so, he gave up his practice, intending to make his home in a warmer climate, but after a few months of exercise in the open air, his health rapidly improved, and he was able to resume his work. His office is now located in the Buchanan Block, at rooms 214 and 216.

Mr. Reed is secretary and a stockholder of the Star Publishing Co., a director of the Farmer's National Bank of Beaver Falls, and has served as school director of the borough, for three years. He was appointed postmaster of Beaver, February 8, 1896, and immediately appointed Miss Lizzie J. Hepting, assistant, and Miss Martha H. Morgan as clerk. The office, which is also located in the Buchanan block, is a handsome one, and is fitted up in the most modern style. The postoffice of Beaver was established as early as

1802, and was called Beaver Town, until 1829, since which time it has been known as Beaver postoffice. The first postmaster was James Alexander, who was appointed January 1, 1802; he was succeeded by the following: Joseph Hemphill, July 1, 1803; James Alexander, August 9, 1804; James C. Weiser, January 1, 1816; James Alexander, January 11, 1818; Andrew Logan, April 29, 1832; Charles Carter, May 28, 1838; James Lyon, June 1, 1841; Miss E. D. Carter, December 27, 1855; Miss Margaret J. Anderson, July 23, 1861; Mrs. S. J. McGaffick, November 1, 1866; Miss May McGaffick, January 23, 1867; Mrs. Sophia C. Hayes, February 12, 1868; Miss May McGaffick, February 15, 1869; Miss N. B. Imbrie, March 19, 1875; Miss Mary E. Imbrie, January 29, 1883; Daniel M. Donehoo, March 17, 1887; A. G. White, December 23, 1891; and Lewis W. Reed, February 8, 1896.

Lewis W. Reed was united in marriage with Lizzie Hall, a daughter of William B. Hall, a prominent farmer of Raccoon township. William B. Hall was a descendant of Robert Hall, of English and Scotch descent. Robert Hall was born in Lancaster county, Pa., and went to Beaver county, where he purchased four hundred acres of land, and engaged in agricultural pursuits. His last days, however, were spent in Freedom. The worthy subject of this sketch and his amiable wife find it a pleasant duty to rear and educate their family, which consists of one son and two daughters, as follows: Lewis G., born January 10, 1883; Vera, born November 26, 1887; and Helen, born June 29, 1891.

Mr. Reed built a fine modern residence, in 1890, on Beaver street, his present handsome home. In 1892, he also built a residence for his beloved mother on Laura street, and in addition to these, he owns two attractive tenement houses. He has always taken a lively interest in the development and progress of Beaver, and, like his forefathers, is an active member of the Presbyterian church. Mr. Reed is also a valued member of the Masonic fraternity.

Thomas Reed, great-grandfather of the subject of this record, was a native of Scotland, whence he came to America, settling near Baltimore, Maryland. He left two sons, one whose name was James and another whose name has not been preserved. James Reed, grandfather of Lewis W., was born near Baltimore, Md., and in early manhood went to Beaver county, settling first in Raccoon township, where he purchased a farm, in 1837. This farm is, today, owned by his son, John Reed. Upon this farm, James Reed pursued the calling of an agriculturist until cut off by death at the age of sixty-seven years. He was joined in marriage with Agnes Baker, a daughter of Michael Baker. Mrs. Reed lived to attain the age of sixty-nine years, and with her husband, belonged to the Old School Presbyterian denomination. James Reed was known as a very progressive farmer, and the old homestead, built by him in 1837, is still standing as a monument to his thrift and economy. To him and his beloved companion were born the following children:

Harriet, wife of Daniel Baker; Jane, wife of Cornelius Weigrandt; Washington B., (father of Lewis W.), who will be mentioned later; John, who wedded Ruth Allen; Rosanna, wife of Robert Potter; Elizabeth, wife of Dr. John Bryan; and Jesse, who wedded Martha Kennedy.

Washington Baker Reed, father of the subject of this biography, was born on the old homestead, January 14, 1820. He received a good scholastic training, for those days, and began life as a farmer. Upon the death of his father in 1868, he bought out the other heirs of the homestead of two hundred acres. Later, he sold fifty acres, and had one hundred acres under a state of high cultivation. He was a public-spirited man and a stanch Democrat,—serving in many township offices. He was a trustee of the Presbyterian church, and was highly esteemed by all who knew him. He died July 20, 1890, aged sixty-five years. He led Eliza Kerr to the altar, in 1851, and she bore him the following children: Lizzie, wife of Sheridan Knowles, of Beaver; John A., who married Mary Deming, of Beaver; Lewis W., the subject of these lines; Cornelius W., who was united in marriage with Ella Shoemaker, and resided at McKeesport; Sampson K., who wedded Sarah Baker, of Beaver; Harriet, wife of David G. Hood, of McKeesport; and Agnes, wife of Hugh Orr, of Beaver.

Sampson Kerr, the maternal grandfather of Lewis W., was born in Raccoon township, and was a son of John Kerr, a surveyor by trade, who was granted a tract of land containing four hundred and four and two-thirds acres,—obtaining a patent for the same. This tract bordered along the Ohio River in Raccoon township, Beaver county, Pa., and upon it John Kerr settled prior to the year 1800. He built a house, where George Fox now lives, and here his two sons were born. Their names were,—Sampson and James. In 1836, the homestead, containing two hundred and ninety-eight acres, was deeded to Sampson. John Kerr was one of the founders and elders of the Presbyterian church, which stood at the same place where Bethlehem Church is now located. He was a justice of the peace for many years, the office at that time being a much more important one than at the present day. After filling this station in a most acceptable and capable manner, he passed to his final rest at about the age of eighty years. Sampson Kerr was looked upon as a well-to-do man, of his day. After selling the homestead, he went to Beaver, and conducted a hotel on Third street for many years, where the Wade building now is. Later he kept the Keystone hotel of Pittsburg. After retiring, he died in Allegheny City at the age of seventy-seven years. He was twice married. His first wife was Agnes Reed, a daughter of John Reed, who was a settler adjacent to the Kerrs, where he owned four hundred acres of the finest land bordering on the Ohio River. Their home was built on the rear end of the Samuel Clear farm. Mrs. Kerr died in 1842, at the age of thirty-four years, leaving one daughter, Eliza, the mother of Lewis W., who was then twelve years old. Her father was married again, his second wife being Maria Blackburn. Of this union were born the following seven children: Morris, Harriet, Frank, James, Albert, Josephine, and William.

Sampson Kerr led an exemplary life, and was a leading figure in many avenues of business, where his cheery presence is now missed. He belonged to the Old School Presbyterian denomination, and was a devout Christian man.

The publishers of this work take pleasure in announcing that a portrait of Mr. Reed accompanies this sketch, being presented on a preceding page.

C. EDGAR MYERS, an energetic and prominent young business man of Beaver county, has charge of the Singer sewing machine business in this county, and makes his headquarters at Beaver Falls. He is a native of Forest county, Pa., and is a son of R. W. Myers.

R. W. Myers was born and educated at Youngstown, Ohio, and is a graduate from Raines Grammar School. At Franklin, Pa., he learned the trade of a jeweler, and after working in the bank of Wick Brothers a short time, he became associated with his father-in-law, Willard Lindsey, in the wholesale and retail jewelry business. After being in the jewelry business several years, he accepted a position with the Singer Sewing Machine Company which he retained until recently, when he became traveling salesman for the Consolidated Lamp and Glass Company. Mr. Myers introduced the Singer sewing machines in Beaver county and had his office at 1017, Seventh avenue, Beaver Falls; he was among the first to locate in his present business vicinity, and added a jewelry department to his establishment. He was joined in marriage with Miss Olive D. Lindsey, and their home has been blessed by the birth of two children, namely: C. Edgar; and Mary S., born at Clear Lake, Wis., December 25, 1880. She was educated in Beaver Falls, Pa., and is now assisting our subject in the machine business. Politically, R. W. Myers is a strong Republican; socially, he is a member of the K. of P., and a chartered member of the A. O. U. W. Religiously, he is a Presbyterian.

C. Edgar Myers was but a child when his parents moved to Beaver Falls, Pa., and his primary education was obtained in the schools at that place. He also graduated from a business college, and then accepted a position as clerk in his father's office; he was afterwards appointed collector of this county by the Singer Sewing Machine Company, a position he held but a short time when he was transferred to the central office at Pittsburg. Two years later, he was promoted to the responsible position of traveling auditor, and was said to be the youngest man who ever held that position. Mr. Myers, in the fall of 1898, resigned his position to accept the vacancy left by his father; he has handsome office rooms, located on Seventh avenue, and the great success of the Singer Sewing Machine agency in this vicinity is due largely to his energetic

F. EDWARD BEHMAN

efforts. Mr. Myers is a very courteous and affable gentleman, and has won for himself the esteem and good-will of hosts of acquaintances throughout the country. He is a well-read, popular and good business man. Religiously, he is a member of the Methodist church; politically, he is a supporter of the Republican party. On June 28, 1899, Mr. Myers was united in marriage with Miss Blanche R. Shuster, a daughter of Henry Shuster, of Beaver Falls.

F. EDWARD BEILMAN. Beaver county numbers among its citizens many men who started life under the most discouraging circumstances, but who, through their own persevering industry, struggled on to better things and finally attained positions of prominence. Such, briefly told, are the conditions which existed in the life of the gentleman above-mentioned, who is today reckoned as the foremost business man of this section of the state,—being owner and proprietor of a large department store at Beaver Falls. Twelve years was the age at which he set out to do battle with the world at large, as cash boy in the large department store then known as that of Barnes, Hengerer & Co., of Buffalo, New York. His action was contrary to the wish of his parents. Ambitious by nature, bright of intellect, and situated as many another boy was, he won favor in the eyes of his employers, who were seemingly cold and austere men of business. Having gained their good will by taking every oppor-

tunity to serve them as best he could, he was from time to time advanced until he was their trusted head cashier at the age of twenty-four years,—a very young man for a position of such responsibility. This was the only firm by whom he was ever employed, and in 1889, he severed his connection with them and removed to Beaver Falls, Pa., where he has since been one of the most active and prosperous citizens.

F. Edward Beilman was born in Buffalo, Erie County, N. Y., June 21, 1860, and is a son of Jacob and Catherine (Speiser) Beilman. Jacob, the father of our subject, was born in Bavaria, Germany, and came to this country with his parents at the age of seven years, first settling in New York City. When the Erie Canal was opened, they traveled by that route to Buffalo, N. Y., which was then an unimportant place. The union of Jacob Beilman with Catherine Speiser was blessed with eleven children, as follows: Anthony; Mary; Josephine (Lechleiter); James; Adeline; Edward; Catherine; F. Edward; Helen (Schneider); Frank, and Elizabeth (Triller). Anthony is a resident of Chicago. Mary, James, Adaline and Edward are deceased. Catherine married E. G. Burns, who is charity agent in Buffalo, and about whom there is an interesting bit of history. He was one of seven pair of brothers who enlisted in the Civil War, all being in the same company and the best of friends. Singular to relate, one of each pair of brothers fell in battle. F. Edward is the gentleman to whom this record pertains. Helen's husband has held a responsible position with the water works for the past fifteen years. Frank is a civil engineer.

The subject of the present writing received his early mental instruction in the parochial schools of Buffalo, and, in 1872 (as before stated), entered the employ of Barnes, Hengerer & Co. as cash boy, and, by native shrewdness and perseverance, worked his way up to the place of office boy, and then to that of assistant cashier, which he held for six years. He had gained the entire confidence of his employers and they offered him the position of head cashier. It was by no means a small undertaking for one so young, but possessing unlimited confidence in his ability he accepted it and performed its duties with credit,—justifying the faith reposed in him. Alive to the fact that his future depended upon himself, he saved his money and invested it in real estate in Buffalo, which he subsequently sold at a good round profit. This he repeated several times and in a few years was the fortunate possessor of a respectable bank account, and some very valuable realty. At this time he began to deal more extensively in lands, forming companies, which bought up tracts and laid them out into building lots, which they put upon the market. In this manner he was largely instrumental in building up the suburban districts of the city, and realized largely on his investments. That he is shrewd and gifted beyond the ordinary, is evidenced by the fact that he has never lost on any of these transactions. He was seemingly gifted with the Midas touch, and having once acquired property its value increased with wonderful rapidity. Upon one occasion he bought a lot in one of the residence districts, and before eight o'clock the next morning, disposed of it at a profit of $350. At another time he bought a tract of land in an obscure part of the town for $700, and shortly after sold it for $1.500. Soon after the year 1880, his attention was attracted to the oil business, and journeying to McKean county, near Bradford, he invested in oil to good advantage. He began to look for other investments, and in 1889 he resigned his position with Barnes, Hengerer & Co., and, removing to Beaver Falls, formed a five years' partnership with William Rowan, starting a large dry goods business. Disposing of his interest in this firm to his partner, in 1894, he built his present store, the largest and finest in the borough; it is a two-story, iron-front building and covers a lot 100x40 feet in dimensions. It has steel, sixteen feet high ceilings. The large assortment of stock is carefully systematized and arranged in orderly fashion. The basement is the salesroom for carpets, linoleum, lace curtains, mattings and oil cloths, and also contains the carpet workshop. Upstairs is carried a comprehensive line of general dry goods, notions, ladies' suits and cloaks, millinery, gentlemen's furnishings, and the thousand and one other things which go to make up a department store. Mr. Beilman is a man who through his great enterprise has attracted public attention, and is universally held in high esteem. He has identified himself with many paying ventures, being an organizer, the principal stockholder, and a director, of the Keystone Store Service Company, manufacturers of a computing scale, an invention far superior to any other on the market. This company have had considerable litigation with a Dayton concern, but have beaten them at every point. Mr. Beilman is a prominent stockholder in the People's Water Company; a stockholder and director of the Riverview Electric Street Railway Company; and is a member of the executive committee of the Beaver Falls Improvement Company, in which he has been an indefatigable worker. He was one of the most faithful workers in securing $50,000 required, and was made a special representative, to bring the Eclipse Bicycle Company to Beaver Falls. He is an earnest advocate for free bridges, a city charter and a "Greater Beaver Falls." Politically, he is independent and although frequently importuned to accept office, he has always declined.

Mr. Beilman was united in marriage with Matilda M. Doll, who was born in Buffalo, N. Y., in May, 1865, the nuptials occurring September 19, 1887; they have two children: Louise, born August 9, 1889, and Norman A., born in February, 1892. Mrs. Beilman was called to her reward on February 20, 1892, just eight days subsequent to the birth of her second child, and was interred at Buffalo. The subject of this biography formed a second union, with Margaret McDunn, who was born March 30, 1870, and is the daughter of Patrick B. and Margaret McDunn of Cambria county, Pa., their union being blessed with three children: Homer J., born in August, 1893, and died in January, 1894; Melvin J., born December 25, 1895; and Martha, born April 1, 1897. In a religious connection Mr. Beilman is a member of the Catholic church. He is also a member of the order of the R. A. For many years he was a member of the Buffalo City Guard Cadet Corps, one of the crack organizations of Buffalo, from which came many brave officers of the late war. Mr. Beilman's portrait, executed from a photograph, taken in the fall of 1899, is shown in connection with the above account of his successful career.

———— • • ————

DR. WALTER F. RAYLE, a leading dentist of Beaver Falls, Pa., where he is recognized as a man well versed in his profession, is a scholarly, refined gentleman and has never been known to neglect his duty. It is characteristic of the man, that when he takes up a project or advocates new procedures in his profession or in business, he throws his who'e soul into the affair in hand, and does all that can be done to bring matters to a successful conclusion. This very characteristic has won for him a host of patients and loyal friends whom he serves faithfully. Dr. Rayle was born July 31, 1849, in South Beaver township, Beaver county, Pennsylvania, is a son of John and Jane (Wells) Rayle and grandson of William Rayle. Receiving quite an ordinary education in the common schools, he then took a most thorough course at the Worcester High School, in

Ohio. After choosing the profession of dentistry as his life work, he endeavored to fit himself by studying in the office of Dr. Jones of Worcester, a leading practitioner in that profession.

Walter F. Rayle passed the examination, in 1867, successfully, and at once located in Darlington, where he established an office and by his pleasant, courteous manner and good habits, won the respect of the people in general, who soon began to need his professional services. Leaving quite a nice little practice in Darlington in 1870, Dr. Rayle removed to New Wilmington, where he pursued the same calling for six years. In 1876, he located in Beaver Falls, where he is still to be found. In his political views, he is a Republican, and steadfastly supports the measures and men of his party through victory or defeat. Dr. Rayle is a member of the McKinley Pioneer Club of Beaver Falls, and is chairman of the executive committee. The Doctor is also a school director, elected by the first ward, and has served in other local offices. He is responsive to charitable appeals, and occupies an important position as a man of standing in the community. He has been a faithful member of the Presbyterian church ever since he attained the age of eighteen years, and has led an industrious, useful and eminently successful life, unsullied by deeds of wrong.

Dr. Rayle was joined in marriage with Josephine Murray, who has borne him three children, namely: Amy Pearl, who is still at home; Bessie Jean, a teacher in the public school; and Charles Clifton. Bessie Jean graduated from the high school with highest honors in a class of 16, and is also a graduate of Slippery Rock Normal School. The Doctor is a prominent member of Walnut Camp No. 2, Woodmen of the World, and has been secretary of the camp for a period of seven years.

William Rayle, the paternal grandfather of our subject, was one of the pioneer settlers of Beaver county, where he pursued the peaceful occupation of a farmer all his active days. He was an old line Whig and served one term as county commissioner; in fact he was filling that office at the time of his death, which occurred at the age of fifty-four years.

John Rayle, the father of Walter F., was born in Beaver county, Pa., December 3, 1805. He spent his entire life as a resident of the same county, and died July 13, 1882. He was also a farmer by occupation and, in conjunction, conducted a blacksmith shop on his farm. In a religious connection he was identified with the Free Presbyterian denomination at Darlington, of which church he was an elder. He chose for his life partner Jane Wells, a daughter of Joseph Wells. She bore her husband seven children, viz: Jane Belinda, widow of John Kerr; Ann Matilda, wife of Josiah Long, who resides on College Hill, where Mr. Long carries on farming; William D., who lives in Columbiana county, Ohio, where he is known as a progressive farmer; Joseph Wells, who lives at Canal Fulton, Stark county, Ohio, and is engaged in mercantile pursuits; John B., who is also a merchant at Beaver Falls; Susanna B., wife of John Barclay, of Alliance, Ohio, also a merchant; and Walter F., the subject of this sketch.

The maternal grandfather of our subject, Joseph Wells, was an old settler of Beaver county, and owned a large farm, which included nearly all of the land now occupied by Patterson Heights. In connection with his agricultural pursuits, Mr. Wells conducted a hotel, and was an enterprising, public-spirited citizen.

———————

JAMES TAYLOR, a mechanical genius, who has brought himself into wide prominence in the western section of Pennsylvania, is well-known as the superintendent of the establishment of Emerson, Smith & Co., of Beaver Falls, Beaver county, Pennsylvania. He was born in Fallston, September 9, 1851, and is a son of Samuel and Nancy (James) Taylor, and grandson of James Taylor.

James Taylor, the grandfather, was born in Sheffield, England, in 1785, and received his mental training in the public schools, after which he engaged in coal mining for some time. Upon coming to America, he bought a large tract of land in an unimproved condition in Galesburg, Illinois, and to this he added until he had acquired some 370 acres. He began the improvement of his tract, erected good, substantial buildings, and lived there until his demise in 1858, aged seventy-three years. He reared seven children, as follows: Joseph, who never came to this country; Samuel, the father of the subject of this personal history; Thomas, a successful coal operator in Washington county, Pa., who is also interested in silver mining; Sarah (Bailey); Martha, deceased; Jonathan, also a coal operator; and John, who now resides upon the old homestead at Galesburg, Illinois. Politically, he was a staunch Democrat. Religiously, he was an Episcopalian.

Samuel Taylor was born in Sheffield, England, July 4, 1821, where he was sent to the public schools, in addition to which he took a special course in geometry and freehand drawing, becoming an expert designer and pattern maker. He came to this country with his parents, and in 1842 accepted a position as cabinet maker with the Kennedy Keg Factory, designing and making patterns for all of the machinery used in the factory. He then engaged in pattern making in Pittsburg and New Brighton. He afterwards became superintendent for Minor & Merrick, New Brighton. He acquired wonderful skill and was unexcelled at his profession, some of the patterns which he made being still in existence. He was connected with the Kennedy Keg Factory many years, but held interests in other firms, and in the latter part of his life was engaged in business for himself at Fallston. He formed a matrimonial alliance with Nancy James, a daughter of Benjamin and Margery (Williams) James, coming of sturdy Quaker stock. Benjamin James served in the War of 1812 with General

Jackson, being under him at the Battle of New Orleans. He was a farmer in early life, but later undertook mercantile pursuits, having a store at what is now Hoytdale, Beaver county. He married Margery Williams, whose father, Thomas Williams, was one of the very first white men to settle in Beaver county, locating there in 1793. Besides farming he did a large distilling business. This union resulted in seven children: Sarah A. (Craven); Joseph J., now in Spokane, Wash.; Nancy, the mother of James Taylor; Howard; Benjamin; Amelia (Murray); and Eliza. Nancy James was a pupil in the district schools, and lived at home until her marriage. Samuel Taylor and his wife were the parents of the following: Joseph, who was first a pattern maker, then a millwright, and is now a farmer in Beaver county; Elizabeth (Bradley); James, the subject hereof; Franklin, who died at the age of three years; John F., a machinist who is assistant to his brother James; Jason R., station agent on the P. & L. E. R. R. at Beaver, Pa.; Thomas W., who died at the age of three years; and Orrin P., a pattern maker, who died at the age of twenty-three years. Mr. Taylor was an active Democrat in politics and filled most of the borough offices, having been burgess, justice of the peace, a member of the town council and president of the school board. Religiously, he was an Episcopalian. He died in 1892, at the age of seventy-one years, and his wife still survives him at the age of seventy-four years.

James Taylor attended the public schools of Fallston and New Brighton, after which he learned the trade of a keg maker with M. T. & C. Kennedy, with whom he remained until 1870, when he learned the trade of a machinist, for which he showed great aptitude. He worked for M. & S. H. Darrah for four years and two months, three years of this period as an apprentice, and the remainder of the time as a journeyman. Upon being offered a position with Emerson, Ford & Company as a journeyman, he accepted and continued for a few months, when he went to New Castle, Pa., to work on large blast-furnace engines. After being thus engaged for three months, he returned to Fallston and worked for Darrah & Company for some years. In January, 1876, he re-entered the employ of Emerson, Ford & Company. That firm dissolved partnership and Mr. Taylor became a dye maker, and was so employed until February of the following year. Then the firm for which he had previously worked was re-organized under the name of Emerson, Smith & Co., and as he was at the time possessed of many years' experience and a wide reputation, he was offered the place of master mechanic and given charge of eighty-five men. He has since been promoted to the office of superintendent, a position he still fills with credit to himself and satisfaction to his employers. This firm was the first to manufacture band-saws in this country, and in addition to this they make cross-cut saws, shingle-saws, metal and stone saws, gang-saws, a specialty of the inserted tooth-saw, knives and other edge tools, odd-shape mold cutters, and other experimental work. Besides being an exceptional mechanic, Mr. Taylor is an inventor of no mean ability and numerous labor and expense saving devices now used by saw manufacturers throughout the country are products of his skill. The plant under his superintendence covers an entire square, is two stories high, and in addition has its offices and engine room. The firm employ 125 men, and although they are under the constant supervision of Mr. Taylor, he still finds time to do a little of the mechanical work himself. He has been awarded several valuable patents, one of the most important being a saw sharpener and setter which will be invaluable to any firm using saws. He is engaged on several other inventions which he expects to have patented. Mr. Taylor has been decidedly successful in life in a business way, and is one of the most substantial citizens of the borough. He owns some real estate on Seventh avenue, in Beaver Falls.

On December 10, 1878, he was joined in wedlock with Maud Kerr, a daughter of Mathew Kerr. She was born in Ireland, being of Scotch-Irish extraction, and received her mental training in the public schools of her native place, and at Butcher's Business College in Beaver Falls, having come to America in 1871. This union resulted in the birth of the following children: Roy; James, who is a sophomore in the High School, took first honors in his class during the year 1899, is a debater of ability, giving promise of future brilliancy, and is preparing himself for admittance to the bar; Stanley B.; and Olive E. In politics, Mr. Taylor is a firm supporter of the principles of Democracy, and for years served on the county committee. Religiously, he is a member of the Presbyterian church. Socially, he is a member of the Royal Arcanum.

WILLIAM A. P. GRAHAM, secretary and treasurer of the American Porcelain Co. of New Brighton, Pa., is one of the leading and most enterprising citizens of that town. The American Porcelain Company, of which he is a member, was incorporated November 24, 1894, by Thomas Craven and Thomas R. Marshall. They purchased the Scott Brothers' Tile Factory, which was located near Allegheny street, and remodeled it for the manufacturing of solid porcelain ware of all kinds, for kitchens and pantries, tubs, sinks, and all porcelain articles. They have built up a reputation for fine quality of work, and have many orders for specialties in porcelain ware. They have four kilns, two of which are 12 feet in diameter, and two, 18 feet in diameter, having a capacity to manufacture the largest tanks and tubs, of natural clay, in western Pennsylvania. The plant covers nearly three acres of ground, which includes kilns, engine house, storage and warehouse, and shipping house. They employ thirty men, most of whom are skilled mechanics. The porcelain enamel, which was Mr. Craven's own conception, is the best on market to-day.

William A. P. Graham, the subject of this biography, was born in Allegheny City, Pa., January 29, 1860, is a son of Nathan, and grandson of Charles, Graham, who was of Scotch-Irish ancestry. Nathan Graham was born in Chambersburg, Franklin county, Pa., and early in life learned the trade of coach building. In 1845 he moved to Allegheny City, where he became connected with the firm of Park & Phelps, wagon and coach manufacturers. He remained with that firm until 1872, when he retired. He was elected alderman and justice of the peace of the second ward of Allegheny, and later was notary public. He dealt quite extensively in real estate during his active life, but retired from business a few years before his death, which occurred in 1897, at the age of seventy-seven years. He married Elizabeth Doubler, a native of Chambersburg, Pa., and she died in 1895, at the age of seventy-five years. The children which resulted from this union were: Emma, who married Matthew Eyster; Amelia, who married William Duval; Mary L., who married A. B. Hay; Ida, who married Thomas E. Marshall, and has one child, Etta; Etta H., deceased, who was the wife of William Righter; and William A. P., the subject of this sketch. Thomas E. Marshall, who is president of the American Porcelain Co. is very popular, and a thorough business man. He was for several years the leading merchant of New Brighton, but in February, 1898, his store, which was located in the Opera House Block, burned, and since that time he has devoted his entire attention to the American Porcelain Company. Nathan Graham was a Republican, and a member of the Lutheran church.

William A. P. Graham attended the high school of Allegheny City, and then pursued the study of photography for three years, but as his eyes failed him, he was ob'iged to abandon it. He accepted the clerkship at Raymond Bros.' wholesale house in Allegheny, and remained with them until 1889, when he went to New Brighton, and became clerk and bookkeeper for the Pittsburg Clay Manufacturing Company. When the American Porcelain Co. was incorporated, he became one of the stockholders, as well as secretary and treasurer. He married Lillie M. Farmer, a daughter of Thomas Farmer.

Thomas Farmer was born in Birmingham, England, a son of William Farmer, who was a skilled mechanic in wire drawing, especially in silver and gold metal. His services were sought by New England manufacturers, and he came to this country, but soon went back to England. There for many years he manufactured iron screws for wood work. Later in life, after retiring, he came to America in 1857, and died at his son's home in Wheeling, West Virginia, at the age of ninety years. He was married twice, first to Miss Coleman, who died early in life. Their children were as follows: Ann; Edward; William; Mary A.; and Thomas. His second marriage was with Ann Platt, and she bore him three children, namely: John P.; David J.; and Samuel. Thomas Farmer early in life became a portrait painter, and came to America in 1855, locat-

ing in Pittsburg. His brother came to this country in 1857, and Thomas gave up painting, and went into business with his brother, John P., at Philadelphia. They manufactured carriage bolts, and after a few years moved to Newark, N. J., and later, to Wheeling, West Va. After selling out there, they moved to Canton, Ohio, and two years later, located at New Brighton, Pa., where they carried on a general machine shop for a few years. They then began the manufacture of rivets at Penyan, New York. Here Mr. Farmer retired from business and moved once more to New Brighton, Pa., where he still resides. He married Jane Chivers, a daughter of Joshua Chivers, and their children are as follows: Agnes; Howard; Ella; and Lillie, the wife of the subject of this sketch.

Mr. and Mrs. Graham have one child, William A. Mr. Graham is a firm Republican, and is a member of the Royal Arcanum and of the Woodmen of the World; he belongs to the Episcopal church. He is highly respected in the community, and is always willing to give aid to anything which is for the good of the people of his town.

———— ◆ ◆ ————

HENRY ENGLEHART COOK, the superintendent and general manager of the Beaver Valley Electric Light & Power Co., of Beaver Falls, Pa., a highly esteemed citizen and ex-sheriff of Beaver county, was born in Bridgewater, Pa., July 31, 1843, and is a son of Henry and Margaret (Reiter) Cook.

Henry Cook was born in Weingarten, Germany, January 15, 1807. He was joined in marriage, in March, 1831, with Margaret Reiter, who was also born at the same place. Mrs. Cook is a daughter of Ferdinand and Margaret (Hurst) Reiter, and is still living at Beaver, Pa., enjoying the best of health. Much valuable information, data, etc., for this sketch were generously and cheerfully furnished by her, and were obtained from a Bible she carried to school when a child, being inscribed on the pages reserved for family records, in a well written German hand. She was born August 13, 1810.

Henry Cook had a brother in Johnstown, Pa., who persuaded him to come to America. With his wife and three eldest sons, he started from the old country in June, 1838, taking passage on a sailing vessel; meeting with much bad weather, they did not arrive at New York until the following September. After landing, they proceeded by wagon and stage to Philadelphia, Pa., thence by canal to Harrisburg and Johnstown. Arriving there, they learned of a great boom in the Beaver Valley, where a canal was in operation and villages were built. They left Johnstown for Pittsburg, and traveled in wagons to Monaca, Beaver county, which was then called Phillipsburg. At that place, Mr. Cook followed the trade of a stone mason for some time, removing later to Bridgewater, and still later settling in Beaver, Pa., where he built a fine residence on Fourth street, now owned by his widow. While working upon this residence, he was taken ill with cholera, caused by drinking cold water, while overheated from work. This illness terminated in death July 14, 1845. He was a man who possessed a strong constitution and was unfortunately cut off in the very prime of life, and did not live to enjoy what he had planned, a haven of earthly rest.

Mr. Cook built much of the masonry of his day, in and around Beaver. He also built the reservoir now standing back of Henry E. Cook's residence. He was born and christened with the name of Koch, as the family formerly spelled their name. Upon getting his naturalization papers made out, he was asked his name, and omitted to tell the authorities how it should be spelled. Upon the completion of the papers, he accepted them, supposing them to be correct. Later, upon discovering the mistake, he thought it would make no material difference and did not have them changed; this course he afterward regretted very much as, by voting under the name of Cook, he soon became known by that name, until the family finally adopted that method of spelling it. He built his home on Fourth street in 1844, and there his death occurred. His good wife was left to rear and educate the family, which she did as few mothers have done,—devoting her whole life to that task. She is now esteemed by all and revered by her children, whose names are as follows: Jacob Frederick, born in Germany, January 19, 1832, died February 14, 1847, and lies buried in the Lutheran burial ground of Pittsburg; John Francis, who was born in Germany, February 23, 1834, and died October 18, 1855; Christian Frederick, who was born in Germany, January 10, 1838, and was killed May 12, 1864, in the battle of the Wilderness, being a member of Company F, 140th Reg., Pa. Vol. Inf.; Christine Louise, born August 10, 1841, who became the wife of D. M. Miller of Beaver, and is the mother of five children; and Henry Englehart, the subject of these lines.

Henry Englehart Cook attended the public schools, and with a careful mother's training grew to be a boy who was respected and trusted by all who knew him. At the age of thirteen years (in 1856), he was appointed under James Buchanan, to carry mail on horseback from Beaver to New Lisbon, Ohio; this duty occupied two days every week, in all kinds of weather, and involved a trip of 28 miles. In addition to this, he carried the mail, four days each week, from Beaver to Rochester, Pennsylvania. In accomplishing this task he never failed, and his reliability and punctual habits won him a reputation which determined his future. At the age of eighteen years, he enlisted in the Union Army, October 9, 1861, on the first call for volunteers. He was a private in Company F, 101st Reg., Pa. Vol. Inf., and served three years. In the battle of Plymouth, N. C., he was taken prisoner and confined in the Andersonville prison, in Georgia, being removed thence to Charleston, and then to Florence, S. C., where he was exchanged December 13, 1864. Returning to parole camp at Annapolis, Md., he was granted a thirty days' furlough on account of his poor health, and went home to recuperate, and relieve an anxious mother's fears. He went back to his regiment and received an honorable discharge March 18, 1865, although his papers bore date of December, 1864.

On the termination of the war, Mr. Cook returned to his home, and, after following the carpenter trade for a short time, he became interested in the lightning-rod business. Subsequently he was elected constable of Beaver, serving three consecutive years, until 1881, when he was elected sheriff by the Democratic party by over two hundred majority. He served three years as sheriff, during which the great riot at Beaver Falls took place, in which some twenty rioters were placed in his custody, four of whom were convicted,—sentence being suspended. At the close of his term, Mr. Cook was appointed deputy revenue collector of the twenty-third district of Pennsylvania, serving four years and three months. He then became superintendent and manager of the Beaver Valley Electric Light & Power Co., of Beaver Falls, which position he is still filling in an eminently satisfactory manner. In 1873, he purchased about one acre of land on Fifth street, and built a fine residence thereon, grading the lawns surrounding it, and setting out an abundance of small fruit and shade trees. In addition to this he rebuilt his mother's residence, adding another story; he also owns a fine tenement house on Fourth street, built by his uncle, Jacob, in 1844. His possessions include a number of choice building lots, he having purchased, in 1890, a tract of land 120 by 300 feet. This tract is known as the Mark estate, and is situated on Beaver street. Mr. Cook divided a portion of it into five fine lots, one of which he sold to each of the following persons: E. J. Allison, James Reed, Lewis Reed, and the purchaser of the premises where J. I. Martin now lives. These are among the best residents of Beaver.

The subject of this writing has been twice married. His first wife was Sarah K. Sheldrake, a daughter of Joshua and Elizabeth (Shoemaker) Sheldrake. She was born in 1845, and passed to her final rest, leaving five children, namely: Frederick H., a contractor and carpenter of Beaver; Carrie Louise, still unmarried; Charles O., an electrician of Beaver Falls, who married Ollie Miller, and had two children, Lloyd and Henry; Henry W., a carpenter; and Mary E., also enjoying single blessedness.

Mr. Cook contracted a second matrimonial alliance, this time with Mary E. Matheny, a daughter of John and Caroline (Shoemaker) Matheny. No issue resulted from this union. The family worship with the Presbyterians, and contribute liberally toward the support of that denomination. Mr. Cook's portrait accompanies this sketch.

JOSEPH W. KNOTT, the secretary and treasurer of the firm of Knott, Harker & Co., of Beaver Falls, Pa., has lived a varied and useful life, every act of which has been marked by some innate honesty of purpose, and by such strict adherence to the highest principles of probity, that his name is honored and his influence is felt throughout his chosen community. Mr. Knott has occupied his present responsible position ever since the organization of the firm of Knott, Harker & Co., in 1884. The company was formed for the purpose of manufacturing fireplace grates, and hardware novelties, but quite recently, extensions have been made, machine shops added, etc., and castings of all descriptions are now manufactured. When the plant is running full time, about 60 men are employed.

Mr. Knott is also a director in the First National Bank of Beaver Falls and takes a fitting and appropriate interest in the progress of the town, being classed among its most progressive citizens. The subject of our sketch was born near Manchester, England, April 4, 1844, and is a son of Moses and Ann (Whitworth) Knott. His parents came to America in 1849, when he was only five years old. They crossed the Alleghany Mountains by way of the Ohio Canal and the Pittsburg R. R. going first to Lawrence county, and later to Beaver county. His father had learned the trade of a cotton spinner while living in England, and followed that business in this country for many years. In 1853, he located in Fallston, Pa., where he secured a situation in a cotton mill, but subsequently went to the town of Brighton, now Beaver Falls. Some time after locating at the latter place, he embarked in the grocery business, keeping a little store stocked with staple groceries; and at same time holding the position of postmaster of Brighton. The office was

discontinued while he was in charge, under Buchanan's administration, and the place was without a postoffice until about the year 1865, when the town took new life under the name of Beaver Falls.

Moses Knott was a man of quiet, unassuming manner and gentle disposition. He was for many years a member of the Methodist church. His death occurred in August, 1894, at the age of eighty-five years. His sterling qualities secured for him the esteem and love of a large circle of friends, and made his name honored throughout his locality.

Joseph W. Knott was primarily educated in the public schools of New Brighton. After leaving school, he accepted a position in a dry goods store at that place, where he remained from 1865 to 1870. In 1870 he held a position with an iron firm in Sharpsville, Mercer county, after which he was employed as bookkeeper and cashier for the Beaver Falls Cutlery Works until 1884, covering a period of fourteen years. In 1834, he became a member of the firm of Knott, Harker & Co., and was chosen secretary and treasurer of the same,—his present position,—which he has filled in a highly creditable manner, satisfactory to all concerned.

The subject of our sketch chose for his wife and life partner, Martha Brierly. Mr. and Mrs. Knott have only one child now living, and that is Lois, who is a prominent teacher in the schools of the state of New York, and of whom they are exceedingly proud. Mr. Knott is a gentleman who has traveled life's road, attending strictly to the matters which

DR. ORRIN H. FRANKLIN

have confronted him along his path. His experience is filled with a record of labors well done. Wherever his duties have led him, all branches of service have received his attention, and he has tried to discharge all the obligations of his citizenship with a fidelity which has borne to him the merited good will of his fellow men.

— ◄ • ►—

DR. ORRIN H. FRANKLIN, whose portrait is presented on the opposite page, is a leading and successful dentist of Beaver Falls, where he has been engaged in the practice of his profession for many years; he is a practical man and has a shrewd eye for improvements and new adaptations in his profession. Almost his entire time not devoted to practice, is spent in study, and his friends and admirers are satisfied that he will yet win a name that will rank high in the world of science; even the few that are slow to take up with any new thing, no matter how meritorious, concede that his success is something wonderful. Dr. Franklin is a son of Benjamin and Martha (Reed) Franklin, and was born in Industry township, Beaver county, Pa., February 3, 1859. He received a good common school training; after leaving school he learned the trade of a cooper and keg maker, commencing at about the age of fifteen years, with the firm of M. T. & U. S. Kennedy.

Young Franklin was quick and handy with tools, having much natural ability in that direction, and soon became an expert keg maker; he worked at that trade for four or five years, receiving at first but 30 cents per day. It was his amibition to fit himself for something better, and to this end he applied himself with an ardor that has been followed by very successful results. By strict attention to business and by economy, he saved enough money while in the cooper business to carry him through college. After studying for two years with Dr. A. M. Whisler, of New Brighton, one of the oldest practitioners of the county, he entered the Pennsylvania Dental College of Philadelphia, completing the course February 25, 1882. Immediately after his graduation, Dr. Franklin located in New Brighton and practiced dentistry there for four years, securing a liberal patronage. In the meantime, Dr. Franklin had opened up a branch office at Beaver Falls, where he also practiced dentistry a part of his time. At the end of his fourth year he had opportunity to sell the business at New Brighton for a satisfactory consideration, and was induced to dispose of his interests at that place and devote his whole attention and time to the practice of his profession in Beaver Falls, which, by that time, had increased to extensive proportions.

Dr. Franklin is a conscientious gentleman and is very highly regarded wherever he is known. His professional ability is recognized and the high position he occupies in the estimation of the citizens of Beaver Falls is well merited. He is a member of the Odontological Society of Pittsburg.

Dr. Franklin was married to Lucy Thornley, an accomplished lady, September 30, 1885. One son, Benjamin, resulted from this union.

Benjamin Franklin, father of the subject of these lines, was a native of the state of New York, and was reared and educated in Ohio, whither he had been taken. He subsequently located in Beaver county, Pa., and adopted the profession of teaching, to which he has devoted his energies since that time; he now has the distinction of being the oldest teacher in Beaver county. He is spending his declining years at New Brighton, in charge of a school. He ranks high among the ablest instructors in Western Pennsylvania and has served two terms of three years each, as superintendent of schools of Beaver county. He has always taken a leading part in the educational development of the county, being an advocate of good schools and competent teachers as the best means of suppressing lawlessness, and making honorable citizens, and true men and women. He and his good wife were blessed with two children, the elder of whom is the subject of this biography, and the younger, Milan O., resides with his father, in New Brighton, and occupies a position in the Union Drawn Steel Works.

———— • • ————

THOMAS L. MINESINGER is a prominent and well-to-do resident of Beaver Pa., and is one of the successful oil producers of the county. He is a native of Ohio township, Beaver county, Pa., his birth occurring April 12, 1844; he is a son of Godfrey and Sarah (Laughlin) Minesinger, and grandson of Jacob Minesinger.

Jacob Minesinger was born in Wurtemberg, Germany, though his parents were originally from Italy. Jacob learned the stonemason trade in his native country, and in 1798 came to the United States; he bought four hundred acres of timber land in Green township, Beaver county, which is now the home of Mr. Robert Sweney. He made many improvements upon the farm, besides clearing a large portion of it, he and his sons built a large stone house. Jacob and his wife Catherine were buried in the family ground on the homestead farm. He and his family were members and regular attendants of the Presbyterian church. His children were: David; Jacob; James; John; Joseph; Godfrey; and Elsie.

Godfrey Minesinger was born on his father's farm and his boyhood days were spent in learning the masonry trade and aiding his father in cultivating the farm; he bought one hundred and fifty-five acres of new land, upon which he built a fine set of buildings; as his boys grew up they operated the farm while he worked at his trade as a mason. He built the stone abutment for the suspension bridge at Wheeling, West Virginia, and contracted for railroad masonry for many years. His farm is now the property of Charles Brooker. He owned a considerable amount of other property in this county, including the George Brown estate. He died in the latter part of 1874, aged sixty-eight years. His wife was Sarah Laughlin, a daughter of Thomas

Laughlin; she was born in 1800 and died in 1886; their children were three: John and Joseph, deceased; and Thomas L., the subject hereof. Mr. Minesinger was well-read, intelligent, and public-spirited; he was a man who delighted in debates and for the sake of an argument he would often support the side of a question contrary to that which he really believed; being a man of superior judgment, he was often called upon for advice in various business transactions. He was a consistent Presbyterian.

Thomas L. Minesinger attended the district school and assisted his father during his youthful days, and at seventeen years of age he was apprenticed to the blacksmith trade; after three years of that labor he sought the river life and in 1862 he started as striker's engineer on the Ohio River, but the last four years of his river life were spent as engineer. Returning home, with his brother John he followed farming five years, when he accepted a position as station agent at Smith's Ferry; he afterwards spent twelve years as a merchant, and was also postmaster of the village. Selling out to S. J. Fair in 1894, he settled in Beaver and became associated with S. P. & D. H. Stone, also of Beaver, in the production of oil,—working in Ohio township and other places in the county. Mr. Minesinger owns a neat residence on the corner of Bank and Commercial avenues, which he makes his home.

The subject of this sketch was first united in marriage with Narcisse B. Smith, a daughter of Jesse Smith of Smith's Ferry; she died aged thirty years; three children were born to their union: John L., a graduate from Western Pennsylvania Medical College of Pittsburg, now practicing at Bellaire, Ohio; Jesse, deceased; and Eddie S., who is now in his second year in the above named medical school. Mr. Minesinger's second wife is Mary Ecoff, a daughter of J. Ralph Ecoff of Rochester, Pa., and they have one child, Thomas L., who is now attending school in Beaver. Mr. Minesinger is a Republican in politics; socially, for the past twenty years he has been a member of the Glasgow Lodge, No. 485, F. & A. M., of which he has also been past master; and of the I. O. O. F. In religious views, he is a prominent member, and a trustee, of the Presbyterian church of Bridgewater.

———————

EDWARD L. DAWES, whose pronounced success as a member of the firm of Dawes & Myler has brought him into wide prominence, is a man gifted with extraordinary ability. He is a young man in the prime of life, but in all his transactions, he has displayed shrewdness and foresight far beyond his years. He is a son of John L. and Charlotta Jemima (League) Dawes, grandson of Jonathan Dawes, and was born in Allegheny City, Pennsylvania.

His father, John L. Dawes, was born in Nottingham, England, and came to America a single man. He followed the trade of a painter in Trenton, N. J., and afterward in Pittsburg and Allegheny City. In the last named city he was engaged in contracting for painting and continued thus until he began the manufacture of glass in the line of drug supplies and sundries. He conducted a wholesale house in that line until his demise at the age of sixty-one years. He was united in marriage with Charlotta Jemima League, who was born in Virginia but is now living in Allegheny, and their union resulted in the following offspring: Harriet; Mary; Martha, deceased; Edward L., the subject of this biographical record; and John L.

Edward L. Dawes was reared and educated in Allegheny City, and at the age of thirteen years entered into active employment as truing boy for his father. Upon reaching man's estate he became a partner in his father's business, continuing as such with good results until he was twenty-seven years of age. He then became bookkeeper of the Standard Manufacturing Co. of Pittsburg, and ten months later was chosen as manager of that concern, remaining in that capacity until 1888. Having gained largely in practical business experience, he was qualified to enter into business on his own behalf, and in that year he removed to New Brighton and formed a partnership with W. Albert Myler, under the firm name of Dawes & Myler. This firm is now proprietor of one of the largest establishments in this section of the state.

Messrs. Dawes and Myler, both men in the prime of life and possessed of considerable experience, located at New Brighton, Beaver county, in 1887, and purchased four acres of land at Allegheny street and Block House Run, on which they built a brick plant and engaged in the manufacture of porcelain lined bath-tubs and sanitary specialties, and also of plumbers' supplies. They employed about eighty men of experience during the first year, and in March, 1889, placed their product on the market. Being of a superior quality, no difficulty was experienced in selling all that could be produced, and in time it was seen that the plant must be enlarged to meet the requirements of the demand. In 1892, an additional three acres of land was purchased, and now six acres are covered with buildings, all of which are of brick but the foundry, which is a substantial frame building. It is heated by hot air and lighted by electricity from their own plant. The works are run by steam and are in operation day and night, as many as 425 men being employed daily, and the pay roll per day being not less than $1,000. It is a fact worthy of mention that ever since the firm was first organized the plant has been in full operation and has not missed a single pay day. It can readily be seen that in addition to bringing industrious men and establishing new homes in the town, the large amount of money put in circulation by the employees has resulted in material benefit to the borough of New Brighton. The goods of their manufacture have a wide reputation and are sold in the markets of all the countries of Europe, in Australia, Japan, Cuba, and the Hawaiian Islands, as well as in every state in the Union.

Mr. Dawes bought a desirable lot, a part of the Bradford estate, in New Brighton, and in

WENZEL A. MIKSCH

1887, erected an elegant modern brick home at No. 1332 Third avenue, which is complete in every detail and convenience. He was joined in hymeneal bonds with Katherine Torrance, a daughter of Francis Torrance, of Allegheny City, and she died young, leaving two children: Frances L.; and Martha, deceased. Mr. Dawes formed a second alliance with Jean Waddell, a daughter of Thomas Waddell, of Jacksonville, Illinois. In religious belief he is a conscientious member of the Presbyterian church. He takes a deep interest in the affairs of New Brighton and has been identified with a number of worthy enterprises, being at the present time a director of a bank, and vice-president and director of the Beaver Valley Hospital. He is a man of pleasing personality and possesses a large circle of friends throughout the community.

ENZEL A. MIKSCH, a member of the American Glass Specialty Company, and a prominent citizen of Monaca, Beaver county, Pa., is a glass decorator of wide reputation, and has in recent years invented a new process which promises in time to revolutionize the art of glass decorating.

Mr. Miksch is a native of Bohemia, and received a good mental training in the public schools of that country. That being the greatest glass manufacturing center of Europe, he adopted the trade of a glass worker, and learned every detail of the business in the most thorough manner. At the age of twenty-one years, he came to America, in 1881, stopping first at East Liverpool, Ohio, for two months, and then removing to Pittsburg, Pennsylvania. After remaining there for a period of eight months, he located at Monaca, and followed his trade there for three years. In 1885, he returned to Pittsburg, and for thirteen years was foreman of the Thomas Evans Company, in the glass decorating department. In the meantime, in 1889, he purchased ten acres of land in Monaca, Beaver county, and erected what is probably the finest house in that section, reflecting great credit upon his good judgment and artistic taste. Since that time he has made his home there, although for some years his work was in Pittsburg. It was while working on paper weights that he made a remarkable discovery, and for a considerable period was engaged in developing it. In 1897, having perfected his invention for the decoration of glassware, he became one of the organizers of the Metropolitan Glass Company of Monaca, manufacturers of advertising specialties— a concern with which he was connected until 1898. He then severed his connection with that firm and started his present venture, the American Glass Specialty Company, in partnership with his brother, Charles Miksch. It is a novel invention, and marks a decided advance in the art of decorating glass. As yet the invention is but two years old, and is meeting with great success. There are but two firms of this character in this country and our subject has the proud distinction of having started both. The building he now occupies was completed in 1898; it is a two-story affair, 26x90 feet, and embraces the main works, the furnace room, printing room, transfer room, and enamel room. The articles which they make require most painstaking effort, and Mr. Miksch has attained a skill which approaches perfection. They have two kilns operated by natural gas, and a small test oven. Their goods find a ready market all over the world, and bid fair to supersede the old style of glass decorating. They have no trouble in disposing of their product, and have sales agents in all the large cities. Mr. Miksch is possessed of excellent business qualifications and has been very successful, owning his present location, the building occupied by the Metropolitan Glass Company, and the house in which he lives.

Politically, the subject of this writing is an aggressive Democrat, and has been president of the council for the past six years, but has now retired from active politics. He is a member of Germania Blue Lodge, No. 509, and Duquesne Chapter, F. & A. M., both of Pittsburg. A portrait of Mr. Miksch accompanies this sketch of his life, being presented on a preceding page.

WILLIAM R. GALEY, of the firm of Galey Brothers, extensive oil producers, is a highly respected citizen of Beaver, Pa., and is well and favorably known throughout Beaver county. He was born in Porter township, Clarion county, December 5, 1848, receiving in his youth an ex-ceptionally thorough mental training in the public school. He began his career by working upon his father's farm until he attained the age of twenty years, when he became an oil driller at Pleasantville, Pennsylvania. He has spent his entire life in the oil and gas business, being now quite extensively engaged in that capacity. He has operated oil wells in many counties not only in Pennsylvania, but also in Ohio, sometimes alone, and sometimes in partnership with others. He drilled the gas wells for, and helped to establish the Bridgewater Gas Co., in the Sheffield district, but subsequently sold his interest therein. He is one of the stockholders of the Beaver National Bank and was one of the prime factors in its organization. In 1891, Mr. Galey settled in Beaver, where he purchased a brick dwelling from A. Moore, and has since made his residence there, taking an active interest in the progress of his adopted town.

Mr. Galey was joined in matrimony with Ida Nicholas, an accomplished lady of great force and sweetness of character. Mrs. Galey is a daughter of Charles and Isadore (Howard) Nicholas. Her father was born in Ohio, and died in early manhood, leaving a widow and one little daughter, Ida, to mourn his untimely death. Mrs. Nicholas contracted a second matrimonial alliance, this time with Obi Olds, by whom she had one son, Herbert, now deceased. A second time she was deprived of her companion and after a suitable period, married a third time, becoming the wife of William Fenton, to whom she bore three daughters: Minnie M.; Miranda I.; and

Lydia A. Mrs. Fenton departed this life at the age of fifty-eight years.

To our subject and his estimable wife have been born two sons and two daughters, whose names are: Herbert Edgar; Willie; Etta Irene; and Charlana Mabel. The two sons died in infancy, and Etta Irene became the wife of Howard Atha, of Allegheny, Pennsylvania. Charlana Mabel is the darling of the household, which she rules at will. She was born as recently as July 24, 1897. Mr. and Mrs. Galey are active members of the Methodist Episcopal church. The subject of this sketch is a son of Robert and Margaret (Rogers) Galey, and grandson of Daniel and Margaret (Fulton) Galey. Daniel Galey was a native of Ireland and came to America in 1819, landing at Philadelphia, Pa., and settling in Maryland, along the Chesapeake Bay. There he accepted a position as manager of an extensive plantation, and was overseer of a large number of slaves. He continued to work in that capacity until cut off by death at about forty years of age. He was joined in matrimony with Margaret Fulton, who survived him until she attained the advanced age of seventy-eight years. After the death of her husband Mrs. Galey and her children removed to Belle Vernon, Fayette county, Pennsylvania. Their son, Robert, is the father of the subject of this sketch.

Robert Galey was born in the Province of Connaught, Ireland, in 1811, and accompanied his parents to America, when only eight years old. At the age of fourteen years, he was apprenticed to learn the blacksmith's trade, which he mastered in all its details, serving a full apprenticeship. He became quite skilled as a workman, made axes by hand and was considered an expert pattern maker. He started a small shop for himself, and by strict attention to his business accumulated quite a sum of money for those days. In 1835, he removed to Cherry Run, Clarion county, Pa., and purchased 100 acres of new land, which he cleared into fields for farming purposes. Later he sold out and purchased a larger tract of timber land at Red Bank, in the same county. He busied himself cutting his timber, which he sold to the operators of a charcoal furnace. Iron ore was also discovered on his land, in such paying quantities that by its sale, he not only paid off all his indebtedness, but was enabled to purchase three good farms along the Allegheny River in Perry township, Clarion county, Pennsylvania. During the Civil War, Mr. Galey was largely interested in raising sheep upon these farms; at one time he and his sons owned as many as 800 fine specimens. In 1867, oil was discovered on his farm, after which, for several years, he was largely interested in numerous oil wells. In company with his son John, he purchased Kink's Island, and put down a well that yielded an average of 75 barrels of crude oil per day for a period of four years. Another deal which was considered among his best investments, was the purchase of the Captain Clark farm in Washington county, for $17,-000. Four years later he sold it for manufacturing purposes, for the round sum of $40,000.

Since then the place was sold for $100,000.

Robert Galey possessed a strong constitution and was an active, energetic man with nerves of iron. He was a self-made man in the truest sense of the word, not only accumulating a large fortune but loaning considerable amounts of money and being very charitable. He was highly esteemed by all who knew him, and spent his last days at Belle Vernon, where his death occurred in June, 1895. He was twice married. His first wife, whose maiden name was Rachel Sparr, a daughter of John Sparr, died at the early age of thirty-two years, leaving three sons as a legacy to her husband. Their names are: John H., who is a member of the firm of Guffey & Galey at East End, Pittsburg, Pa.; Thomas F., of Beaver; and Robert, also of Beaver. Some time after the death of his first wife, Mr. Galey married again. This time he was wedded to Margaret Rogers, who is still living. She is a daughter of Samuel and Margaret (Cook) Rogers, and was born December 25, 1822. Her father was born in Donegal, Ireland, was a son of George Rogers, and grandson of Oliver Rogers, who was born in England, but settled in Ireland, and, in his day, was said to be the tallest man in Europe. His son George visited America, but stayed only a short time, returning to Ireland, where he died. The latter's son, George Rogers, came to America in 1832, settling in Clarion county, Pa., where he engaged in agricultural pursuits, near Parker's Landing. His life was terminated by death at the age of sixty-six years, while his wife lived to be seventy-two years of age. Their children were: Elizabeth; Jane; Sally; Margaret, mother of William R.; Rebecca; Letitia; William; and Mary.

Robert Galey's second marriage resulted in the birth of the following offspring: William R., subject of this sketch; Samuel, a dealer in oil at East End, Pittsburg; Daniel, also a dealer in oil, residing at Parker, Pa.; Rachel, wife of Thomas Grant; James G., of Beaver, also in the oil business; David H., superintendent of the Sewickley Gas Co.; and Laura G., wife of Lieut. Charles Farnsworth,—Mrs. Farnsworth is now deceased, and left one son, Robert.

Our subject is a man of sterling worth, of upright dealings, and is a useful member of the community, who has contributed his share to the enterprise and thrift of Beaver. He gives liberally of his means to worthy charities, and assists in many ways to elevate the moral and social life of his community.

FRANCIS L. BANKS, deceased, was well known in Beaver Falls as a valuable and enterprising citizen, and he was worthy the respect and esteem accorded him by the residents of that borough. He was a machinist by trade, and for many years served in the capacity of superintendent of the hardening department of the Great Western File Works of Beaver Falls. He was a son of Francis and Maria (Barton) Banks, and was born in New York City, July 19, 1825.

On the Banks side, the family is of English

origin, and the grandfather, William Banks, was a native of London, England. His son Francis resided in New York City and was there engaged in business all his life. On the maternal side, the great-grandfather was Henry Barton of Hol'andish extraction, and he was a soldier in the War of Independence, lived in Hackensack, N. J., and owned a number of slaves.

Francis L. Banks was reared in New York City and there also obtained his elementary training; in his younger days he was engaged in the book-binding business in that city, but subsequently drifted into the file business. Upon coming to Beaver Falls he was tendered the position of superintendent of the hardening department of the Great Western File Works, which position he accepted and faithfully performed the duties of that responsible office until his retirement about the year 1891. Mr. Banks was prominently connected with different fraternities; he was at one time grand templar of Pennsylvania, was a member and secretary of the Ancient Order of United Workmen, and was also a member and secretary of the Royal Arcanum. Politically, Mr. Banks took an energetic part in the organization of the Republican party in this vicinity, but though active in party affairs, he never sought political distinction. In his religious action he was a consistent member of the Episcopal church, and was also a senior warden many years; he was also a great worker in the Brotherhood of St. Andrews. His demise took place at his home in Beaver Falls, February 18, 1899, and his death was deeply deplored by his family and his friends, who knew him as a dutiful citizen and friend, a kind neighbor, and a loving father and husband.

Mr. Banks was joined in marriage with Miss Mary Culver; she was born April 3, 1827, and died January 20, 1889. She was a daughter of Daniel Culver, a native of New York City, and he traces his ancestral history back to 1632; the Culver family is one of the oldest families in New England, and her grandfather was in the Revolutionary War. Mr. and Mrs. Banks were the parents of one daughter, Gertrude Kendall, the wife of William H. Chandley. Mr. Chandley is engaged in plumbing, gas and steam fitting, and also contracts for the laying of water works systems. He is located in Beaver Falls, where he has already established a large patronage. To Mr. and Mrs. Chandley have been born a family of seven children: Henry Banks; Gertrude May; Sarah Winifred; Mary Ivy; Anna Drusilla; Georgia Caroline; and George Francis, deceased.

HEZEKIAH HULME is the efficient and well-known sexton of Grove Cemetery, New Brighton, Pa., and he has been in charge of the same for the past score of years. He was born in Lancastershire, England, February 23, 1844, and is a son of Mark and Mary (Flindle) Hulme.

Mark Hulme was born in England, and there he continued to reside until his death in 1863, pursuing his vocation as a hat maker, which he had learned during his boyhood days.

Hezekiah Hulme also learned the hatter's trade, and upon his arrival in the United States in 1868, he remained in Lewiston, Maine, a short time, and there took up his former occupation. He then made a trip to Denver, Colo., and after prospecting in the West, he returned East and first located in Mercer county, Pa., and later, in Beaver county, where he has ever since continued to reside. He first settled in Beaver Falls, where he worked at cutlery, but in 1879, he was given charge of his present position. The Grove Cemetery was incorporated March 19, 1859, and the grounds were dedicated to the purpose of burial October 13, 1859; thirty-two acres were first purchased adjoining Block House Run, and later, twenty-seven acres were added thereto. The cemetery is located on the east side of New Brighton, near Braeburn Hillside stream, and is commonly known as Oak Hill; beautiful drives and walks are laid out through the grounds, which contains many fine oak, hickory, ash, and elm trees. There is also an attractive variety of shrubbery, which is always kept in excellent trim by Mr. Hulme and his assistants; there are two entrances to the cemetery, one on Grove avenue and the other on Nineteenth avenue, better known as the north entrance. Mr. Hulme occupies a neat cottage near the Grove street entrance, and his assistant also resides near that entrance. By the faithful performance of his duties the subject of this sketch has gained for himself the esteem and good-will of not only the members of the corporation, but of the citizens of New Brighton and vicinity.

Mr. Hulme was first united in marriage with Sarah Chadwick, a daughter of George Chadwick, and a native of England; she died at the age of twenty-five years, leaving one son, George, who is also deceased. His second wife is Matilda Swift, a daughter of James Swift, of Liverpool, England, a contractor and builder, who died at the age of fifty-five years, in Cheshire, England. Mr. Hulme is a faithful member of the I. O. O. F., of which he is also past grand; and a member and past chief patriarch of the Encampment. In religious views, he is inclined to favor the Episcopal church. In politics, he is a Republican.

———— • • ————

RICHARD SMITH HOLT, a leading attorney-at-law of Beaver, Pa., and one of the ablest lawyers in Beaver county, is a member of the law firm of Wilson & Holt. Mr. Holt was a pupil in the public school and in Peirsol's Academy at West Bridgewater, after which he attended the State Normal course at Edinboro, Pa., working his way through college by teaching, which profession he followed for some time after his graduation. After teaching for six years, he began to study law under the late Samuel B. Wilson, Esq. After his admission to the bar in 1888, he entered upon the practice of his profession, and after the death of his preceptor he became a law partner of George Wilson, the son of Samuel B. Wilson.

Since then the firm has been Wilson & Holt.

For a man whose life has been as busy as his, Mr. Holt has done much outside of his regular duties. He is now serving his sixth year as a member of the city council. He is deeply interested in educational matters, and has served as a member of the school board. He is a prominent and active member of the American Mechanics.

Mr. Holt purchased a vacant lot near the corner of Fourth and Market streets upon which he built a handsome residence in 1892 and 1893. When his day's work is done, and he retires to his home, he is pleasantly greeted by his accomplished wife, and five unusually bright and interesting little ones, of whom both Mr. and Mrs. Holt are extremely proud. Mrs. Holt was, before her marriage, Sarah Eveline Brunton, a daughter of William A. Brunton, a sketch of whose life will be included as a part of this narrative. Their children's names and ages are as follows: Beulah G., born January 20, 1886; Mary Jane, born January 19, 1888; Elizabeth Wilson, born April 6, 1890; Margaret Anna, born September 22, 1892; and Sarah Eveline, born in May, 1898.

Richard Smith Holt is a son of Samuel J. and Mary Ann (Taylor) Holt, a grandson of William Holt, a great-grandson of Thomas Holt, Jr., and a great-great-grandson of Thomas Holt, Sr. The family is of English origin.

Thomas Holt, Sr., removed from the eastern part of Pennsylvania to Mifflin county, Pa., settling at McVeytown, Oliver township, where he owned 600 acres of land. He was joined in wedlock with Elizabeth Mitchell, a daughter of John and Jane (Ross) Mitchell. Their union was blessed with numerous offspring, namely: Thomas, Jr., who married Elizabeth Walker; John, who married Sarah Mellikin; William; Elizabeth, wife of John Magee; Mary, wife of Jacob Yost; Jane, wife of John McClintock; Dorcas, wife of Mr. Stackpole; Eleanor, wife of Francis Windell; and James, who was killed by the Indians.

Thomas Holt, Jr., was a farmer, and lost his beloved wife not many years after their marriage. He went to Trumbull county, Ohio, where his death is supposed to have occurred, as all trace of him was lost. Only two children were born to him and his wife, and they were twins: William Humphrey and Dorcas,—born in 1806. Dorcas became the wife of James Critchlow.

William Humphrey Holt located in Brighton township, Beaver county, Pa., about 1833, as the tax receipts of 1834 show that he paid taxes on a farm previously purchased by him. This farm is now the property of S. R. Workman. Later, Mr. Holt sold that farm and bought one which Samuel Johnson now owns. Still later, he purchased a farm just west of the Samuel Johnson farm, and upon it he spent his closing years. Upon all his farms he made improvements, and the last one purchased by him is still owned by his heirs. He laid down the burden of life in 1877, while his wife lived until 1896, when, at the age of ninety-three years and two months, she passed away. Mr. Holt was a very public-spirited man and served as supervisor of his township and as school director, and was elder and class leader of the M. E. church. Six children were born to him and his worthy wife, namely: Mary, who first became the wife of Socrates Small, and after his death wedded George Triess; Thomas Fritz, who married Margaret J. Fritz; John Wesley, who died in infancy; Samuel Jacob, the father of our subject; Dorcas, who also died in infancy; and Rachel Ann, wife of John Hogue.

Samuel Jacob Holt, father of our subject, was born in Brighton township, Beaver county, and was reared on a farm. When grown, he followed the occupation of teaming until he purchased a farm in Brighton township, upon which he lived until 1898, when he abandoned farming and retired to Beaver, Pennsylvania. His whole life has been spent in agricultural pursuits, in which he has been successful to such a marked degree that he not only still owns his farm, but also property in Beaver and Vanport. In his political views, the elder Mr. Holt follows the leadership of the Republican party. He was united in marriage with Mary Ann Taylor, whose life was terminated by death in 1898, at the age of sixty years. Their children were: William H., who married Carrie R. Hamilton, and is a prosperous farmer of Brighton township; Richard Smith, the subject of this life-review; Thomas Fritz, who was twice married, —Annie Merton being his first wife, and Rebecca McCollough the second one, and who is a stone mason at New Castle; Elizabeth Jane, and Jefferson, were the next two, who

both died in infancy; Mary, wife of Dr. James H. Shoemaker of East Liverpool, Ohio; Frank R., D. D. S., a successful dentist of Beaver, Pa.; and Clyde, a teacher and law student of Beaver.

Richard Smith Holt first saw the light of day in Borough township, Beaver county, Pa., on December 15, 1860. He is still a young man and his friends predict great things for him in the future.

William A. Brunton, father-in-law of our subject, was born in Green township, Beaver county, Pa. He is a son of John and Margaret (Alexander) Brunton, and grandson of William Brunton. William Brunton was of German nationality, and was a farmer by occupation. Little is known of him except that he located in Green township, and lived to be about seventy-five years of age. His wife, Barbara, lived to be about eighty-five years old, and bore her husband eleven children, as follows: John; Joseph; Thomas; Henry; William; Elizabeth; Sarah; Rachel; Rebecca; Nancy; and Mary Ann.

John Brunton, father of William A., inherited a part of the homestead farm, and followed the quiet and peaceful life of a farmer all his days. He died at about fifty years of age, but his wife, who was a daughter of Stephen Alexander, lived about seventy-seven years. Their children were: Mary; William, father of Mrs. Holt; Elizabeth; Sarah; and Barbara.

William A. Brunton bought out all the heirs and became owner of the homestead, which he sold later and embarked in the gro-

JACOB PFLUG.

cery business at Shippingport. This he conducted for twelve years, and then returned to farming, which he continued until 1887, when he removed to Beaver, Pennsylvania. Since then he has been interested in other pursuits. He was joined in marriage with Mary J. Vazey, a daughter of Francis Vazey. One son and six daughters blessed their union. They were named: John; Sarah E., wife of Richard Smith Holt; Margaret; Lalla Belle; Estella E.; Daisy F.; and Barbara E.

William A. Brunton enlisted in 1862 in Company II, 140th Reg., Pa. Vol., as a private. The principal battles in which he took part were: Fredericksburg and Gettysburg. At the latter he was wounded in the knee and leg, which prevented his walking for three years. He now draws a pension from the U. S. Government, and is a valued member, of the G. A. R., Post No. 47; he also belongs to the I. O. O. F. Few men so completely have the confidence of the public as has Mr. Brunton, and his standing is certainly well merited.

———— ◆ • ◆ ————

JACOB PFLUG, a gentleman who for many years has been a prominent and influential farmer of Marion township, Beaver county, Pa., is now living on his farm of one hundred and forty acres, which is known as the old Pflug homestead, and enjoying the benefits of his early toil. He is a son of George and Dorothy (Martzolf) Pflug, and was born on May 28, 1817, in Germany, about ten miles from where the first battle of the Franco-Prussian War was fought.

George Pflug, the father of Jacob, came to America on March 16, 1830, with his entire family, and after a voyage of sixty-four days landed in Baltimore, Md., on the 9th of June following. They next moved to Pittsburg by means of a six-horse team, arriving on July 4th, and there George Pflug obtained employment in a nail factory, although his trade was that of a carpenter. When he landed in that city he had but $100, but by hard and conscientious work, in September of the year 1830, he was enabled to buy forty acres of wild land at a cost of $135. In the fall he moved his family to Marion township, Beaver county, where the property was located, and there he built a log house. The next year, leaving his family at home, he went to Phillipsburg, Pa., and worked at boat building for a man named Phillips, continuing thus for three years. In 1833, he erected a small house at Freedom, Pa., it being the first one built in that town, and sold his first purchase at a price of $1,100. He then bought the land on which the house of Jacob Pflug is now located; at that time it was all timber land, but prior to his death it was mostly cleared. He lived upon this property the remainder of his life and at the time of his death in July, 1850, owned one hundred and forty acres. Late in life he replaced the original log cabin with a handsome residence now occupied by his son Jacob. He married Dorothy Martzolf, and they had the following children: Dorothy (Dedrick), deceased; Magdaline (Repe), deceased; Salama (Scheny); Jacob, the subject hereof; Mary, who first married Abraham Burry, and is now the wife of Frederick Householder; Frederick, a farmer in Butler county, who first married a Miss Garvich, and later wedded Catherine Klein; Barbara, the wife of Michael Veiock; and Philip, deceased.

Jacob Pflug was thirteen years of age when he came to this country with his parents, and after arriving in Pittsburg he worked in a hotel at the corner of Wood and Fourth streets, as porter. When his father bought his first tract of forty acres, he moved to Marion with him, and he and his mother cleared four acres the first year. His mother was a very industrious woman and an excellent help-meet to her husband. Before coming to this country she worked upon a farm and was accustomed to plowing with two cows. Jacob Pflug always remained at home, but was at times engaged at working out at the carpenter's trade with his father. He also made shingles and took contracts for roofing houses. After coming into possession of the old homestead he made many improvements, and has since made additions to the house and erected a fine barn. He also greatly added to the property, increasing it to about three hundred and ninety acres, but all excepting the original tract of one hundred and forty acres he has given to his son. He is now engaged in general farming and his advancing years are being spent in the peace and quiet of farm life. He is a well read man, takes a sensible view of all subjects coming to his attention, and is deeply interested in the progress being made by his fellow workmen. He is highly thought of and has friends far and near.

In 1840, Mr. Pflug was joined in wedlock with Salama Householder, by whom he had the following issue: Jacob, the husband of Caroline Herrman; Salama, the wife of Henry Schramm; Caroline, the wife of John Geohring; Frederick, deceased; Henry, whose wife is Caroline Miller; Mary, the wife of Henry France; George, deceased; Elizabeth, the wife of Frederick Harmon; Amelia, the wife of William Caterrer; Daniel, who married Elizabeth Gettman; and Matilda, whose first husband was Elmer Geohring, and who was married a second time to Albert Hartzel. The subject of this sketch after the death of his first wife, was united in marriage with Vernelia Geohring, and they have one son, Albert, who resides at home. Politically, he is a Democrat and has held all of the township offices excepting those of justice of the peace and constable. Religiously, he is a devout Lutheran. His portrait is presented on a preceding page, in proximity to this.

— — —•• •—

W ALBERT MYLER, a gentleman who has made his home in Beaver county for little more than a decade, has established a reputation for general business ability which entitles him to be ranked among the leading men of Western Pennsylvania. His start in life was an inauspicious one, but with a degree of energy such as but few possess, he strove for success, and to-day is a member of the firm of Dawes & Myler, owners and proprietors of one of the largest manufacturing establishments in the county.

Messrs. Dawes and Myler, both men in the prime of life and possessed of considerable experience, located in New Brighton, Beaver county, in 1888, and purchased four acres of land at Allegheny street and Block House Run, on which they built a brick plant and engaged in the manufacture of porcelain lined bath-tubs and sanitary specialties, and also of plumbers' supplies. They employed about eighty men of experience during the first year, and in March, 1889, placed their product on the market. Being of a superior quality, no difficulty was experienced in selling all that could be produced, and in time it was seen that the plant must be enlarged to meet the requirements of the demand. In 1892, an additional three acres of land was purchased, and now six acres are covered with buildings, all of which are of brick but the foundry, which is a substantial frame building. It is heated by hot air and lighted by electricity from their own light plant. The works are run by steam and are in operation day and night,—as many as 425 men being employed daily,—and the pay roll per day being not less than $1,000. It is a fact worthy of mention that ever since the firm was first organized, the plant has been in full operation and has not missed a single pay day. It can readily be seen that in addition to bringing industrious men and establishing new homes in the town, the large amount of money put in circulation by the employees has resulted in material benefit to the borough of New Brighton. The goods of their manufacture have a wide reputation and are sold in the markets of all the countries of Europe, in Australia, Japan. Cuba, and the Hawaiian Islands, as well as in every state in the Union.

Mr. Myler was born in Pittsburg, Pa., and is a son of John A. Myler, who during his early life was engaged at merchant tailoring and attained a high degree of success. He retired from that line of business and became president of the National Bank for Savings. For eighteen years he served as postmaster of Allegheny with credit. W. Albert Myler was reared in his native city and obtained a good intellectual training in the schools there. Energetic and ambitious as a boy, he early sought employment and was engaged in the wholesale mercantile business until 1878, when he became bookkeeper for the Standard Manufacturing Company of Pittsburg. He remained in that connection until 1888, when he removed to New Brighton, and engaged in business for himself as a member of the firm of Dawes & Myler. He has since evinced an earnest interest in all that pertains to the growth and development of the borough, and is one of its most dutiful citizens. He purchased a fine lot which was a part of the old Metz orchard at one time, and in 1897 built thereon an elegant brick residence, modern in design and in all its conveniences. Surrounded on every side by a beautiful and well-graded lawn, with its drives and walks, it presents a very attractive appearance and is always greatly admired.

W. Albert Myler was united in marriage with Mary I. K. Dennison, a daughter of Prof. David Dennison of Youngstown, Ohio. Prof.

Dennison was one of the early academy teachers in New Brighton, Allegheny City, and Pittsburg. This union was blessed with two children; Mary Gertrude and Jean Hay.

———— ◆ ► ————

DR. ADDISON S. MOON. Preeminent among the young physicians and surgeons of note, so numerous in Beaver county, Pa., stands the subject of this sketch. There is no cause more noble than that of relieving suffering humanity, no life more nobly spent than in faithfully fulfilling the duties incident to the life of a physician and surgeon. Dr. Moon was born at Hookstown, Beaver county, Pa., on October 25, 1859. He is a son of Robert Allison and Sarah (Sterling) Moon, and grandson of William Sterling, of Ireland.

William Sterling came to America from his native land, locating in Green township, Beaver county, where he finally settled permanently and followed the peaceful occupation of a farmer. He thought little of the dangers which were to be met and overcome in a new and undeveloped country, and it is largely due to the bravery of such men as he, that the Keystone State owes her prosperity today. He lived to a good old age, passing away in the same community where he had spent so many happy years.

Robert Moon, father of Addison S., was born in Rensselaer county, N. Y., where he was also reared and educated. After reaching manhood, he desired to fit himself for something better than an ordinary life, and decided in favor of the profession of medicine as his future sphere of effort. Accordingly he went west and studied medicine with his brother, Arnold C. Moon, of Knoxville, Ohio. After completing his studies and taking the required course of medical lectures, he went to Hookstown, Pa., in 1845, and opened an office. His genial and pleasant manners won many favorable comments among the residents of that place. Soon fortune smiled on his endeavors, and his practice, small at first, increased to great proportions, during the thirty years of his stay there. But there came a time when he desired a change of location, and April 6, 1875, he removed to Beaver Falls, where he spent his closing years, actively engaged in the duties of his profession, and being looked upon as a very skillful physician. He crossed the river of death to the light beyond, on October 26, 1892. More than half a century was passed by him in doing good to others. Who shall say that he has not received his just reward? In early life he led pretty Sarah Sterling to the hymeneal altar, and she proved to be a most tender and solicitous companion; when returning from some long, tiresome journey, weary and exhausted, he was greatly cheered and refreshed by her sweet companionship. Mrs. Moon was born February 2, 1829. Two children blessed their happy union, Helen M. and Addison S., the subject of this sketch. Helen M. was twice married; her first husband was Rev. James S. Brandon, a minister of the United Presbyterian church. She is

JOHN IMBRIE MARTIN.

now the wife of William A. McCormick, an attorney-at-law, of Mercer, Pennsylvania.

Addison S. Moon received his primary education in the schools of Hookstown and Beaver Falls. Later, he attended Beaver Seminary, and spent two years at Westminster College. In addition to this, he took private instruction for some time, being ambitious to obtain the best possible education. He then studied medicine in the office of his father, who was desirous of leaving his large practice to his only son. After studying diligently for some time, young Moon took a three years' course in the medical department of the Western Reserve College at Cleveland, Ohio, from which he graduated with high honors in 1884. On February 27th of that year, he returned to Beaver Falls, and practiced his chosen profession, but after two years, being ambitious to become more thorough in his calling, he went to New York City, where he took a special course in the College of Physicians and Surgeons. He also took a course in Polyclinics in New York. Returning again to Beaver Falls, he has practiced there ever since, with even greater success than he anticipated.

Dr. Moon is a member of the American Medical Association and is secretary of the Beaver County Medical Society of which he has been a member since locating in Beaver Falls. Politically, he is a Republican, but never sought nor desired office. The Doctor is also a member of numerous beneficiary societies; being examiner for the Prudential Life Insurance Company and also for the Western Mutual Life Association of Chicago. On May 17, 1888, Lulo A. Perrott became his bride and this union has augmented his pleasures and soothed his sorrows. Their home was brightened by two children, but the grim messenger, Death, recalled one precious treasure. The names of their children are: Merl P., born March 4, 1891, and Alta Sterling, born June 1, 1894, and died July 12, 1894, being deprived of life by a sad accident.

Dr. Moon is a self-made man according to the common significance of the term. As a physician, he is well and favorably known throughout a large circle of patrons, a reputation he has won by a degree of energy, determination, and skill, that have secured for him an extensive field of practice and have fairly given him a place among the leading men of his profession.

———————

JOHN IMBRIE MARTIN, whose portrait is shown on the opposite page, is a substantial and capable citizen of the town of Beaver, with which community he has been prominently identified for many years. He has served as deputy sheriff, and as sheriff, of Beaver county, but is now engaged in the real estate business. He was born on the old homestead in Darlington township, Beaver county, and is a son of James Powers Martin, and a grandson of James Martin.

Major Hugh Martin was the great-grandfather of the subject hereof, and although born in the North of Ireland, he was of Scotch-French extraction; he came to this country in 1770, and was an Indian scout and captain of a reconnoitering party during the War of Independence; he met with many thrilling adventures while in that capacity, which he was wont to relate with pleasure. Before the close of the war he was commissioned a major. About the year 1798, he took up a tract of fifteen hundred acres of land, a portion of which was near Greensburg, Westmoreland county, Pa., and the rest extended into Darlington township, Beaver county. His three sons, William, John, and James inherited the estate upon his death.

Mr. Martin's grandfather received the homestead and one hundred and seventy-five acres, as his portion of the estate; he greatly improved the property by supplanting the old set of log buildings with a new set of brick and stone buildings, which are still in use by the heirs of his son, James P. He reared a family of children, and those who grew to maturity were: Hugh, Daniel, Leasure, Jesse, Robert, John, James P., Eliza J., and Maria. He died aged seventy-two years, and his wife, Elizabeth Leasure, also attained an advanced age.

James Powers Martin was born in 1828, on the homestead, and upon the death of his father, bought out the interests of the heirs to the homestead; the greater part of his life was devoted to farming, in which he was very successful. He was at one time connected with an oil refinery, which was built on his farm, the oil being manufactured from cannel coal. From January 1, 1876, to 1879, he served as sheriff of this county, being elected on the Republican ticket. At about seven o'clock on Christmas Eve of 1892, he was struck by an engine while walking down the railroad track, from the result of which he died the next day at one o'clock. He had just left the railway station after accompanying his daughter there, and was on his return home, when the accident occurred. His death was deeply lamented both by his family and relatives, and by his host of friends. He was married, in 1850, to Mary Imbrie, a daughter of John Imbrie, a prominent farmer of Big Beaver township, Beaver county, and they were the parents of the following children: James R., a lawyer of Beaver; John I., the subject hereof; Rose, the wife of A. Duff, of Beaver Falls; Mary I., the wife of Isaac Hall; William H., a real estate dealer of Beaver Falls; De Lorma E.; Lilla J., the wife of Dr. J. R. McQuaid, of Leetsdale, Pa.; and Jere C.

John Imbrie Martin was reared on the farm and attended the Darlington Academy; he continued to work on the homestead until he became associated with A. Duff in the dry goods business at Beaver Falls. Four years later he sold out and returned to farming, which he followed four years. He was then deputy sheriff under Sheriff A. J. Welsh, for one term, and in 1890 he was elected sheriff, —his term beginning January 1, 1891, and ending January 1, 1894. During this period, he erected dwelling houses on Fourth street, also one on Beaver street, in which he made his home; in 1898, he erected his present handsome residence opposite the college, on College street. Mr. Martin devotes much of his time to real estate; he is also interested in other enterprises in the borough.

Mr. Martin was joined in matrimonial bonds with Griselda Best, a daughter of Charles L. Best of Lawrence county, and one child has blessed their home,—Norman I., born June 28, 1894. Politically, the subject of this biography is an active Republican; he has been elected a director of the schools for several terms. Religiously, he is a Presbyterian. Fraternally, he is a member and past master of St. James Lodge, No. 457, F. & A. M. Mr. Martin is a prominent member of the Beaver County Agricultural Society, of which he has been treasurer for the past three years.

———— • •————

ꝺERE C. MARTIN is conspicuous among the prominent and influential members of the Beaver County Bar,— being a partner of his brother, J. R. Martin, with the firm name as Martin & Martin. His popularity and executive ability have been appreciated by the citizens of Beaver, to the extent that he has been honored with the office of chief burgess of his adopted town, and he is at present officiating in that capacity. He was born in Darlington township, Beaver county, April 11, 1867, and his ancestors have been residents of this county for more than a century. He is a son of ex-Sheriff James Powers Martin, grandson of James Martin, and great-grandson of Hugh Martin.

Major Hugh Martin was born in the north of Ireland and was of Scotch-French origin; he came to America in 1770 and served during the Revolutionary War as an Indian scout and captain of a reconnoitering party, in which capacity he met with many thrilling adventures, which he often related with pleasure. He was commissioned major during the latter part of the war. About the year 1798, he settled in Westmoreland county, Pa., near Greensburg, and there he took up a tract of fifteen hundred acres of land; the larger part of it extended into Beaver county, Darlington township. Upon his death his estate was divided among his three sons, William, John and James.

James Martin received the homestead and one hundred and seventy-five acres of choice land; the first set of buildings was made of logs, but James Martin built large brick and stone buildings, all of which are still in constant use, and are owned by the heirs of his son, James P. Martin. James Powers Martin was one of a family of twelve children; those who grew to maturity were Hugh, Daniel, Leasure, Jesse, Robert, John, James P., Eliza J., and Maria. James Martin died aged seventy-two years, leaving a large estate; his wife, Elizabeth Leasure, also died at an advanced age.

The father of Jere C. Martin was born on the homestead in 1828, and bought out the heirs of his father's estate upon the latter's death; his entire life was principally devoted to agricultural pursuits, but he was at one time associated with an oil refinery built on his farm,—the oil being manufactured from cannel coal. He was elected sheriff of Beaver county on the Republican ticket and served from January 1, 1876 to 1879. On the evening of December 24, 1892, Mr. Martin accompanied his daughter, Mrs. A. Duff, and family, to the railway station in a conveyance, and, upon their departure, he started on his way home, walking down the track, but just before leaving the track he was struck by an engine. This occurred about seven o'clock in the evening, and on the next day at one o'clock he departed from this world. He was popular, widely known throughout the county, a good citizen and friend, and his many excellent qualities and courteous bearing gained for him the esteem and respect of all who knew him. He was married in 1850 to Mary Imbrie, a daughter of John Imbrie, a prominent farmer of Big Beaver township, this county. She was born in 1831, and died in 1877. They were the parents of the following children: James Rankin, a partner in the law firm of Martin & Martin; John Imbrie, ex-sheriff of this county; Rose, the wife of A. Duff of Beaver Falls; Mary I., the wife of Isaac Hall; William H., a prominent real estate dealer of Beaver Falls; De Lorma E.; Lilla J., the wife of Dr. J. R. McQuaid, of Leetsdale, Pa.; and Jere C.

The subject of this sketch was intellectually trained in the public schools, in Greersburg Academy, and in Washington and Jefferson College at Washington, Pa.; from 1891 to 1893 he served as deputy sheriff under Sheriff John Imbrie Martin, his brother, and during this period he devoted his spare time in the study of law, having access to his brother's law library. September 19, 1894, he was admitted to the bar and immediately became a partner with his brother, J. R. Martin. Since January 1, 1897, he has served as chief burgess of Beaver, being elected on the Republican ticket. The borough of Beaver is located on the north bank of the Ohio River and near the mouth of Beaver River. Under the administration of Hon. Thomas Martin, then Governor of Pennsylvania, in 1791, the town was surveyed and laid out. Martin & Martin, attorneys-at-law, have a fine office in the Dawson Block on Third street, and also one in Beaver Falls. Jere C. Martin has only been practicing a little over four years, but is recognized as exceedingly bright, of excellent address, quick to see the point and application of law, of unusually good judgment, accurate in the preparation of legal papers or causes for trial, and as having a clear legal mind and giving promise of standing high in the ranks of his profession. His partner, J. R. Martin, is a hard and conscientious worker, thoroughly equipped for his profession, and he has merited the confidence reposed in him, his progress having been deservedly rapid.

Jere C. Martin was wedded in 1894 to Miss Rose Best, a daughter of Charles L. Best of Enon, Lawrence county, Pa., and two children have been born to them, Dorothea and Griselda. He is the owner of a fine home in Beaver. Socially, he is a member and past

1508

master of St. James Lodge, F. &. A. M.; and is also a member of the Elks; and the K. of P.

———— • • ► ————

JOSEPH T. PUGH, whose portrait appears on the opposite page, is, perhaps, the oldest living resident in Beaver county, Pa., his birth occurring at Fallston, January 6, 1809; he has for many years made his home in New Brighton. He has the appearance of a man of sixty years, being still strong and active, with mind unimpaired; he has fine eye-sight,—as he still reads without glasses,—and he may be considered an authority on the early history of this county. His father, John Pugh, was a son of Jonathan Pugh, and a grandson of John Pugh.

John Pugh was of Welsh origin, and was among the early Quaker settlers of Philadelphia. Jonathan was born in Limerick township, Philadelphia county, Pa., and his wedding with Naomi Evans was solemnized at a meeting held at Gwynedd, in that county, September 27, 1759; our subject has the certificate of the marriage framed and in good condition; it was signed by thirty-two witnesses. They settled in Chester county, Pa., where he bought two plantations. His death occurred March 8, 1798. His children were: Elihu, Evan, Jesse, John, Ruth, Sarah, Jesse, (2), and Mary.

John Pugh was born near Pughtown, Chester county, August 20, 1779; his brother Evan was also born there November 13, 1765. In May, 1804, John and Evan Pugh came to Beaver county, and as both had learned the milling trade, they erected mills at Fallston. Their mill was not only patronized by the farmers of the neighborhood, but many came from distant points to have their wheat ground. They shipped extensively to Pittsburg,—the flour and feed being taken to that city on boats. Later a carding and cloth dressing factory was added, and still later they began to manufacture cotton goods. Evan Pugh withdrew from the business a number of years later and the father of Joseph T. continued alone until 1858, when he rented the mills. He also conducted a grocery store at Fallston and operated a linseed oil mill. His mills were all destroyed by fire, in which he suffered heavy losses. He built the handsome brick residence now occupied by Mr. McKibben, and resided there until death claimed him in May, 1860. He married Sarah Townsend; she was born January 13, 1777, and died July 16, 1826. They were the parents of the following children: Jonathan; Caroline; Mary Ann; and Joseph T., the subject hereof. Jonathan died young; Caroline died in 1831,—she was the wife of John Minor, and the mother of one daughter, Caroline, who married David Critchlow; Mary Ann, who died in 1881, was first married to Warren Seely, M. D., and later, to John Minor,—she is the mother of Henry. John F., and Henrietta. John Pugh, father of our subject, formed a second union, with Mrs. Ann Peck. He was president of the branch of the United States Bank, located at New Brighton.

The subject of this record attended such

schools as were held in his native district, and early in life learned the machinists' trade at Fallston; he did not pursue his chosen occupation to any great extent, however, as he began the manufacture of barrels and window sashes, which he continued until he retired from active business life. He also became interested in various other enterprises in the village.

Mr. Pugh wedded Nancy, a daughter of Robert and Nancy McCreary of Fayette county, Pa., and she died aged fifty-six years. They reared the following children: John; Sarah Ann; Evan; Mary; Caroline Cecelia; Irene Ida; and Henry. John is a dentist of Philadelphia, and wedded Amelia Blanchard. Evan, deceased, was married to Catherine Price, by whom he had two children. Mary first married H. C. Torrey, and, secondly, was wedded to George Post. Caroline Cecelia married Eugene Pierce, and one child, Mary E., was born to them. Henry married Fannette Line and they have three children: Harry, Fred, and Helen. Mr. Pugh was reared a Friend and has always adhered to that faith. He has taken a prominent part in promoting the growth and prosperity of the town and county, and his kind and genial disposition has made him a popular and much respected citizen; he has proved himself a good neighbor, and a kind and loving husband and father; now while passing through the sunset of life, and enjoying the fruits of a laborious past, he is surrounded by a host of warm friends who will always cherish and honor his name.

LEWIS GRAHAM, the efficient sheriff of Beaver county. Pa., who was elected to that office in 1897 by over 1,200 majority (the largest majority ever received by any candidate in the history of Beaver county), is a large, splendidly built and well-proportioned man, and an ideal sheriff. He was born in Freedom, Beaver county, June 26, 1850, is a son of John and Sarah (Feazell) Graham, and grandson of Adam and Nancy (Bell) Graham.

After attending public school at Freedom, Lewis was a pupil in the New Brighton school. While still a lad, he became messenger boy for the Western Union Telegraph Co., at New Brighton. Being an ambitious boy, he sought a position where he could do manual labor and earn money. Next he accepted a job as water boy on the railroad a short time, after which he enlisted as an orderly during the Civil War, serving in the construction corps and being engaged in rebuilding railroads. He thus spent seven months in the states of Tennessee, Georgia, and Alabama. He next obtained a position as cabin boy on a steamer plying on the Ohio River from Pittsburg to Omaha, Nebraska. He proved to be so capable and worthy a lad that he was offered a better position with Kensley & Whisler of New Brighton, as clerk, and worked later in the same capacity for William Kennedy. He then accepted the appointment of first baggage master for the Fort Wayne R. R., and occupied that position for two years, serving as a clerk in Pittsburg the following eight years. But, longing for his home surroundings and friends, he returned and engaged in the cutlery business for two years. He then became connected with the Singer Sewing Machine Co., remaining in their employ for ten years. Accepting a more lucrative position as clerk in the Lake Erie depot at Beaver Falls, he worked there for some time, and then took charge of the Bridge Station for a period of six years. He served three years and then became a candidate for the office of sheriff. He resigned to become deputy sheriff and the result was most gratifying to him, as he simply exchanged places with his former employer by becoming sheriff, while ex-Sheriff Molter now occupies the position of deputy.

Mr. Graham built a handsome residence on Patterson Heights, which he still owns. He moved his family to Beaver when elected, however, and resides in the residence portion of the Beaver county jail. This is a model structure, beautifully located on the south side of the public park on the corner of Market street, and nearly facing the court house. The county jail is built of sandstone from Beaver county, and was constructed in 1856. It contains thirty-six cells, fourteen of which were added in 1898. It is of modern construction throughout, being heated by a hot air furnace, and is kept in the best of order by Sheriff Graham and his able wife and assistants. The sheriff also has an office in the court house.

Adam Graham, grandfather of our subject, followed the occupation of boat building nearly all his life, constructing many steamboats for the Ohio River and also for the canal. His life was practically spent in Freedom, where both he and his wife died. He married Nancy Bell, an attractive lady, and they reared the following children: John, now deceased, who was the father of Lewis; Addison, who settled in Kentucky, and is also deceased; Theodora, who resides in Freedom; Minerva (Cooper); May (Marcus); and Emily (Hooper).

John Graham, father of the subject of this sketch, was born in Freedom, Beaver county, Pa., and spent his early life in assisting his father in boat-building. He was cut off by death just in the prime of life, dying in 1855 at the age of about forty years. His widow, who was Miss Sarah Feazell before her marriage, still survives him and resides at Beaver Falls. Their children are: John B., a carpenter of New Brighton; Lewis, the subject of this sketch; William, also a carpenter by trade, and residing in New Brighton; Helen, wife of T. M. Elliott of Beaver Falls; Zetta, wife of John Webster of New Brighton; and one daughter who died in early childhood. Our subject wooed and won for his life companion Elizabeth Carter, an accomplished daughter of William Carter. Mr. and Mrs. Graham have been blessed with a family of seven children, namely: Adelaide Victoria Carter; Orin Palmer, who died young; Margaret Carter; Lewis Edward; Sarah Elizabeth; Oscar Lawrence Jackson; and John Reeves.

William Carter, father-in-law of our subject, was born at Morristown, Westmoreland county, Pa., is a son of Charles and Jane

(Anderson) Carter, grandson of London Carter, and great-grandson of King Carter, who was given a large grant of land in Virginia. London Carter rendered valuable services to our country during the Revolutionary War.

Charles Carter was born in the eastern part of Virginia, and was engaged in the manufacture of iron, locating in Westmoreland county, where he conducted a furnace. Later, he removed to Butler county, and later still, to old Brighton, now Beaver Falls, where he also owned a furnace. He was united in marriage with Jane Anderson, who bore him the following children: Charles; William; James; George; Charlotte; Jane; and Elizabeth. William Carter in early life followed the profession of teaching. Subsequently he was an engineer, after which he worked in the cutlery business at Beaver Falls, and owned an interest in the paper mills there. His death occurred in his seventy-fifth year. At the time of his death, he owned valuable property. Mr. Carter was joined in matrimony with Valeria Reeves, a daughter of Daniel Reeves. Mrs. Carter died at the age of fifty-two years, leaving the following six children as a legacy to her husband: Charles, who resides in the West; Celesta, now deceased; Adelaide, widow of John Scott; Margaret, wife of T. R. Galton; John, also deceased; and Elizabeth, wife of the subject of this review.

Sheriff Graham has always taken a deep interest in educational affairs, and has served as a member of the school board for three years. Socially, he is a member of the K. of

P., and is a charter member of Social Lodge of New Brighton. Mr. Graham has truly been the architect of his own fortune. Starting out with an humble beginning, by steady perseverance and strict adherence to his purpose, he has risen step by step, to a position where he is conspicuous in the public gaze. Sheriff Graham is a general favorite and performs the duties of his office in a highly capable manner. He is a member of the Elks. In religious feeling the family favors the Methodist church.

———— ◆ ◆ ————

HON. JOHN FLEMING DRAVO, of Beaver, Pa., ex-member of the legislature, and surveyor and revenue collector for years in Pittsburg, Pa., was also prominently connected for a long period with the coal and coke interests of that place. He was at various times president of the coal exchange. No man has held more positions of trust and more completely won the confidence of the people, or done more to develop the commercial interests of that busy city, than Mr. Dravo. He has been a director in the Tradesmen's National Bank, and the People's Insurance Company, and has been variously connected with other corporations of note. He was one of the prime organizers of the Pittsburg & Lake Erie R. R., and took an active part in the construction of this line, which has paid satisfactory dividends to the original stockholders from the first year of its existence. In educational work our subject has always taken a deep and fitting interest, and, as trustee of the Allegheny College at Meadville, and as president of the Beaver Female College, he has won distinction by his earnest and intelligent labors. For four years he rendered valuable services as president of the State Reform School, and for eight years served as director of the Allegheny County Home, one of the most worthy of local charities. It is said that Mr. Dravo is honest to a fault, and no citizen of Allegheny or Beaver county stands higher in the estimation of the people. Every position held by him has been faithfully and honestly guarded, and upon retiring, he has left no stain or suspicion attached to his good name.

John Fleming Dravo was born in the village of West Newton, Westmoreland county, Pa., October 29, 1819, and was reared in Allegheny, attending the public schools, and afterward entering Allegheny College, where, after two years of diligent study, his health failed and he was compelled to cut short his college career. He assisted in the office of his father, who was an extensive and successful coal merchant, and thereby gained a practical knowledge of business methods. Upon arriving at manhood's state, young Dravo went to McKeesport, Allegheny county, Pa., and engaged in mining and shipping coal, in which venture he acquired prominence and fortune and became the owner of a large amount of real estate. He planned and founded the town of Dravosburg, on the Monongahela River, less than a dozen miles from Pittsburg. In 1868, Mr. Dravo disposed of his extensive coal interests and engaged in the manufacture of coke. After establishing large plants at Connellsville, Pa., he organized the Pittsburg Gas, Coal & Coke Company, of which he became general manager and treasurer, and, later, executive head. This latter corporation began operations with 40 ovens and upon the resignation of Mr. Dravo in 1883, its plant comprised 300 ovens, and its monthly output was almost half a million bushels. A man of strict integrity and high character, with a gentle and considerate regard for the interests of the large force kept constantly employed under him, our subject made many friends among the laboring classes, among whom he is extremely popular.

In 1860, he was elected to the presidency of the Pittsburg Coal Exchange, and held that conspicuous position until his resignation in 1870. In 1884, he was chosen president of the Chamber of Commerce of Pittsburg, succeeding Hon. J. K. Moorehead, whose lamented death created a vacancy in this position. Mr. Dravo labored with a single eye to the advancement of the commercial interests of the city. With a solicitude born of a thorough knowledge of the subject, he labored incessantly for years to secure needed improvements in the Monongahela Valley, and along the Ohio River. He wrote and spoke in favor of the work on any and all occasions. His letters and speeches referring to this subject alone, if published, would make a good sized volume. No small share of his efforts was put forth at the national capital, whither he was repeatedly sent to represent and defend the cause of his fellow citizens. Master of the situation, and arguing his favorite measure with great earnestness, he made a profound impression on the House Committee on Rivers and Harbors, and secured substantial recognition of his claims and demands, gaining many advantages which a less enthusiastic advocate might have failed to obtain.

Mr. Dravo's earlier political efforts were in opposition to slavery; this institution he opposed on principle, and he loudly denounced it, in season and out of season, in accordance with the manner of the anti-slavery advocates of those days. He polled his first vote as a "Henry Clay" Whig, and an avowed enemy of slavery. In 1848, he was nominated in Allegheny county as a candidate for the state legislature by the supporters of the Buffalo platform adopted at Utica, N. Y., June 22, 1848, who had for their motto "Free Men." Prominent and active among clear seeing and resolute citizens who radically severed their connections with the old parties for the sake of principle, Mr. Dravo stood, and worked in harmony with the movement which culminated, in his state, in the virtual organization of the Republican party, at the Lafayette Hall convention in Pittsburg, February 22, 1854. When the party sprang full-fledged into the field in 1856, Mr. Dravo was at once acknowledged a leader, and has since never forsaken its cause. In that and all subsequent political campaigns his splendid oratorical powers have assisted materially in the support of the party's principles, and the vigor with which he has carried on his work, together with his unflinching adherence to the men and measures of the party, have earned for him the title of "Stalwart."

Few political orators equal Mr. Dravo in the open discussion of the finance or tariff question of our nation, and although these are his chief themes of late, he has abundant information and an eloquent vocabulary always on hand to suit any occasion. A beautiful illustration of this was afforded in his address on the death of General Grant, pronounced July 25, 1885, at the memorial services held at Beaver Falls, and also at a special meeting of the Pittsburg Chamber of Commerce, held July 23, 1885, for the express purpose of taking suitable action in view of the nation's great loss. Calling the meeting to order, President Dravo said: "The sad intelligence of General Grant's death has made it necessary that this Chamber should be convened that appropriate action may be had, touching an event of national import. I do not use extravagant language when I say the most eminent citizen of the Republic has passed away, and the people are moved to the expression of sorrow at the death of him who, when living, they delighted so much to honor. General Grant's record is emblazoned on every page of our country's history for the past quarter of a century. In health, on the battlefield, he proved himself the greatest commander of the age; in civil life he was crowned by a grateful people, with the highest honors; and as president of the United States, he displayed the sterling virtues of integrity and unswerving devotion to the best interests of the nation he did so much to serve; in sickness, long continued and marked by extreme suffering, he evinced a patience and charity befitting the closing scenes of an illustrious life. It is for this Chamber to take such action as you in your wisdom may deem most appropriate."

One of the secrets of Mr. Dravo's power of oratory is that he speaks from the heart, and by his own earnestness and enthusiasm sways the emotions of his hearers and seldom fails to carry conviction. Although a hearty advocate and supporter of his favorite cause, he declined to appear as a candidate for office. Notwithstanding this fact, in 1886, he was made the Republican nominee for the state legislature to represent Beaver county, Pa., in which he resides, and having almost universal indorsement, he was elected. His talents and abilities found immediate recognition at Harrisburg by his appointment on the committees of "ways and means" and "constitutional reforms," two of the most important committees of the legislature. Serving as secretary of both, and as a warm friend of temperance reform, he introduced the "Constitutional Prohibitory Amendment," which was successfully passed. He likewise made an eloquent speech nominating Col. Matthew Stanley Quay for U. S. Senator.

In 1881, our subject's name was brought forward by his party friends as a candidate for the office of collector of customs, and surveyor of the port of Pittsburg, and he was appointed to that office by President Garfield. At that time, the senate was not unanimous in the matter of appointments, and there was some delay in confirming his nomination. At this juncture, the political strength and great popularity of Mr. Dravo were emphatically demonstrated by unanimous voice. The business men of Pittsburg, without regard to party views, demanded his confirmation, and the entire press of Beaver county supported the demand, and was loud in its praise of his fitness and qualifications for the position. On all sides and frequently from the most unexpected sources, came warm advocacy of his claims. These appeals were sufficiently powerful to overcome all opposition, and his appointment was confirmed by the senate May 20, 1881, when he was duly commissioned. His services as collector covered a period of four years, which was marked by a most efficient and capable administration of that office. Upon the accession of a Democratic administration, Mr. Dravo resigned. In the business life of Pittsburg, he has been for many years a conspicuous and honored factor, and has frequently lent his personal and material aid towards building up the city institutions. Our subject is a descendant of Anthony Dravo, whose original name was Anthony Dreaveau.

Anthony Dravo, grandfather of our subject, was one of the early settlers of Pittsburg. He came from France over a century ago under the following interesting circumstances. In 1789, the year the Bastile fell, the Marquis De Lussiere was the owner of a beautiful estate in one of the suburbs of the city of Paris. There lived with him a young florist, who had so gained his confidence, that he was looked upon as a confidential friend and companion. At the beginning of that terrible chapter of history known as the French Revolution, the Marquis and his young friend whose name was Dreaveau, sought refuge in America. In the Monongahela Valley opposite the mouth of Turtle Creek, and in full view of the scenes where Washington had won his fame as a soldier, De Lussiere, with the aid of his faithful friend, made for himself a home and surrounded it with things of beauty, a faint reminder of the loved estate from which a cruel fate had driven them. This home, built by the French marquis, is known as Hamilton Hall, and has since been the property of the Von Bonnhorsts, Swartwelders, Riddles, and others.

The young friend who stood by the Marquis in the great crisis of his life, and accompanied him over the sea in 1794, located in the village of Pittsburg, Pa., and is now called the pioneer florist. The garden of Anthony Dravo just outside of Fort Pitt, purchased from Gen. O'Hara, quarter-master of that fort, occupied one-half of the square of what is now the central business portion of the city. There for many years, our subject's grandfather pursued his calling, for which both training and taste had peculiarly fitted him. When this country was in its "teens" there was no other spot in Pittsburg so pretty and attractive as Dravo's flower and fruit garden on Hay street, extending from Pennsylvania to Liberty streets. In those early days, Anthony Dravo was authority on all things pertaining to flower or fruit culture. The florist was never happier than when entertaining visitors from his native France. Many noblemen from that country were entertained in the Dravo home, bringing letters of introduction from the Marquis De Lussiere to his Pittsburg friend. When Lafayette visited the city, he went to greet the friend of his friend, and talk over with him the scenes both had witnessed in Paris, a generation before.

With the growth of Pittsburg industries called for the grounds he occupied in Liberty street. Anthony Dravo purchased larger grounds at East Liberty, and there his business flourished until his death, nearly half a century ago. Michael Dravo, father of our subject, was the eldest son of Anthony Dravo. He was born at Pittsburg and was united in marriage with Mary Fleming, a daughter of John Fleming, Sr. After marriage, the young folks settled in Westmoreland county, Pa., where our subject was born, but later in life they returned to Pittsburg and lived to a good old age.

In 1868, our subject went to Beaver county and purchased a home on First street, overlooking the Ohio River, and its beautiful scenery. In 1891, this home was destroyed by fire, but was replaced by a handsome modern home of stone and brick. November 23, 1843, Mr. Dravo was united in marriage with Eliza Jane Clark, an accomplished daughter of Robert and Margaret Clark of Allegheny county, with whom he has spent over half a century. Ten children have been born to them, namely: Cassius M. Clay, born in 1844,

STEPHEN F. STONE.

DAN H. STONE.

and died in 1845; Margaret J., born January 2, 1846, who is the widow of Robert Wilson and resides with her parents; Josephine M., born June 5, 1848, who was joined in marriage with J. H. McCreery, a prominent attorney of Beaver, and is the parent of the following children,—John D., Thomas, Mary, Caryl, and Vankirk; Mary Emma, born in 1851, and died in 1869; Annie Maria, born 1854, and died the same year; Ida Clark, born 1858, and died in 1861; John S., who was born March 9, 1861, is a prominent oil dealer, and wedded Sadie McClerg, who bore him one child, Eliza J.; Lida, who is at home; and Etta S., who was born March 30, 1865, and died in 1888.

John S. Dravo and his family are consistent and active members of the M. E. church, of which denomination Mr. Dravo has been a member since he attained the age of eighteen years. He was also Sabbath School superintendent, and has been a local preacher for many years. He is beloved and respected by all who know him and his relations in and out of the family are what all good and honest men endeavor to sustain, in order to make their lives above reproach or criticism.

———— • •————

STEPHEN P. and DAN H. STONE, Jr., prominent and progressive business men of Beaver, Pa., whose portraits accompany this sketch, are scions of one of the pioneer families of Beaver county. The family was established here when this section of the state was little more than a wilderness, principally inhabited by the Indian race, and infested by beasts of the forest. This region has furnished good, substantial men to the community, who have zealously promoted the rapid growth and development of the country.

Stephen P. Stone, grandfather of the gentlemen named above, was born in Derby, Conn., April 21, 1759, and was for some years a sea captain. In 1804, he went to Western Pennsylvania where he purchased twenty-four hundred acres of land for $1,200, it being located in Franklin and Marion townships, Beaver county. He returned to his native state for his family, and incidentally disposed of one-half of his purchase at $1 per acre,—thus paying for the whole. He established a home in Marion township and erected a set of log buildings, which included a house, store and barn. It became known as the "Stone place," and is now owned by J. D. Boots. He next built a large eight-room brick house, with spacious and convenient rooms, and this was considered the finest residence in the township. It is still standing and in good condition,—being owned by Mrs. Mary A. Leyda. He subsequently purchased a large tract of land where Harmony is now situated, and in 1805 bought the point of land lying north of the Beaver and Ohio rivers, known since as Stone's Point. He built a residence there, now belonging to August Myers, and established a landing and warehouse for supply boats,—both being swept away in the flood of 1832. He also kept a tavern there, mainly for the accommodation of boatmen. He purchased pig iron from the Bassenhem furnace,—it being delivered by wagon and shipped on keel boats, for it was before the day of railroads and steamboats. These boats were "poled" up the river by men, or drawn by horse where they could be, and were carried down the river by the current to the different ports. Upon reaching their destination many of the boats were sold, and the men, who had received fifty cents per day for their work, were compelled to walk home. The boats not sold were stocked with various kinds of goods, and "poled" up stream again. Mr. Stone continued at this branch of work all of his life, and was a very prosperous man. He died in the last residence which he built (now owned by the heirs of Margaret Davidson), on October 2, 1839. Religiously, he was a member of the Episcopal church. He was first joined in wedlock with Caty Hull, January 5, 1795, and they had nine children, namely: Stephen; Eliza, who married Elihu Evans; Mary J., the wife of Joseph McCombs; Dan H.; Sherlock; Charles; Catherine, the wife of Henry W. Smith; Adelia; and Henry L., who died at the age of two months and one day. Mrs. Stone died September 18, 1825. Mr. Stone formed a second marital union with Sarah Fuller, November 4, 1829, after he had attained the advanced age of seventy years. His widow was again married, to Samuel Colter; as a result of her second union three children were born: George H., Marshal P., and William E.

Dan H. Stone, Sr., the father of Stephen P. and Dan H., Jr., was born in Derby, Conn., September 27, 1802, but was very young when his parents removed to Pennsylvania. During his younger days he assisted his father and was charged with many duties of a very responsible nature. When but eighteen years of age, he was sent on horseback to Columbus, Ohio, to collect a bill for his father, amounting to $2,000. His first day's work for himself was in assisting to pole a boat eighteen miles, working from sunrise to the first star of evening and then walking home,—his salary being fifty cents per day. Like his ancestors he was very fond of the water, and as this was one of the principal employments of the day, he followed it for many years. Later, in connection with his brothers, Stephen and Charles, he owned and operated several steamboats, which ran to Pittsburg, Cincinnati, Louisville, and New Orleans. They had the contract for carrying the United States mail, and this yielded them large profits. Mr. Stone was very successful and accumulated considerable wealth; before the war he disposed of his interest in the business. Having inherited a portion of the old homestead in Marion township, he built saw mills and engaged very extensively in lumbering. His business was injured largely by the panic of 1873, and as he was of a generous nature, he gave assistance to others, which almost resulted in his financial ruin, and left him again a poor man. His health failed and he died on March 25, 1879. July 14, 1853 was the date of his marriage to Mary Patterson, a daughter of James Patterson, who was an early settler of Beaver county and a resident of Beaver Falls,—then known as Brighton. She was born November 5, 1830, and is still living at Beaver, and enjoying the best of health. Their union resulted in the birth of seven children, as follows: Stephen P.; Elizabeth, the widow of D. F. Robinson; Dan H., Jr.; James P., who is engaged in the real estate business in Beaver Falls; Mary J.; Charles H.; and Sally P., a resident of Beaver.

Stephen P. Stone was born in Beaver, Beaver county, Pa., September 17, 1854, and attended the public schools and Beaver Academy, but as his father had met with reverses, he was obliged to seek work at an early age. He entered a saw mill when fourteen years old, and from then until 1877 he did whatever work he happened to find. He was very ambitious and applied himself with a will, and in 1877 he received the appointment of deputy prothonotary of Beaver county. He gave satisfaction, and was elected prothonotary of the Court of Common Pleas in 1879, serving in that capacity for six years, when he was made assistant cashier of the Beaver Deposit Bank. He was subsequently promoted to be cashier, and now discharges the duties of that responsible position. He is a man of tried business ability, is progressive and enterprising, and is held in the highest esteem by his employers and his townsmen. The Beaver Deposit Bank was established in 1871 by M. S. Quay; J. S. Rutan; D. McKinney. M. D.; and J. R. Harrah. Mr. Quay was president, and upon his retirement, was succeeded by S. P. Wilson. Business was first transacted in the Barkley Building, where the Buchanan Block now stands, but in July, 1887, the bank was removed to the James Allison building, where it has since been located. The subject of this sketch is one of the stockholders, and was an organizer, of the Bridgewater Gas Company of which he became treasurer; he is treasurer of the Beaver Valley Traction Company, of which he was one of the organizers, and is financially interested in the People's Electric Street Railroad Company.

On May 12, 1887, Stephen P. Stone was married to Louise M. Knox, a daughter of George W. Knox of Carlisle, Pa., a prominent, retired lawyer, of Philadelphia, and they are the parents of three children: Joseph K., born March 5, 1888; Stella Louise, born October 22, 1889; and Virginia K., born August 24, 1894. Politically, Mr. Stone is a Republican and has served as a delegate to the state convention, and on the county committee. He is a member of the Odd Fellows' lodge, of which he is a past grand; of the Masonic order, from F. & A. M. to K. T.; of the Junior Order United American Mechanics; and of the Elks. In 1887, he built a very fine residence opposite the depot, graded the lawn and set out shrubbery and fruit, making it one of the most desirable homes in the borough. It is excellently located and commands a beautiful view of the villages and mountains along the Beaver and Ohio rivers.

Dan H. Stone, Jr., was born in Beaver,

Pa., September 1, 1860. He attended the public schools and the U. P. Seminary until 1875, and in January, 1880, received the appointment of deputy prothonotary under his brother, Stephen P. Stone, continuing thus for two terms of three years each. In 1885, he was elected prothonotary of the Court of Common Pleas (assuming his trust in January, 1886), and was re-elected in 1888. He discharged his duties to the complete satisfaction of his constituents. During his incumbency of the office, he became desirous of entering the legal profession, and as a result, he studied law with Hon. J. M. Buchanan and Hon. M. F. Mecklem,—being admitted to the bar on September 19, 1892. Immediately after he began practicing, and by dint of hard and conscientious labor, he has established a good reputation and a large clientage. Intuitively, he applies the theoretic principles of law to the common affairs of every day life, and it is to his practical faculty that his success is mainly due. He is a stanch Republican and has been an active worker in party affairs. He has taken great interest in the progress of Beaver, and has been identified with the Beaver Valley Traction Company; was an incorporator, and, formerly, attorney, of the High River Bridge Company; and of the People's Electric Street Railroad Company. He has been attorney for several railroads in Western Pennsylvania. He is a member of the Masonic lodge, and of the Odd Fellows' lodge, of which he is past grand. He owns some valuable real estate in Beaver, and is one of its most substantial citizens.

Charles H. Stone, the youngest son of Dan H. and Mary (Patterson) Stone, was born in Beaver, Pa., where he attended the public schools. He became assistant to his brother, Dan H., when the latter was prothonotary, and also studied law with him,—being admitted to the bar on December 6, 1896. He also served as assistant clerk under his brother, Stephen P., in the Beaver Deposit Bank. He is a very popular young man in the borough, and has worked up quite a lucrative practice. Fraternally, he is a member of the Knights of Pythias.

———— ◆◆ ————

CHARLES RUNYON, manager of the Keystone Tumbler Co., of Rochester, Pa., is one of the enterprising and energetic men of that borough, and is well known throughout the county as fully worthy of the esteem in which he is held. He was born in Jefferson county, Ohio, and is a son of Philip Runyon. He came to Rochester, in 1875, and started a grocery store on New York street; this business he continued with much success for three years. He then entered the employ of the Rochester Tumbler Co., and so won the confidence of the firm that he soon worked himself up to the position of assistant manager of the plant. When the Keystone Tumbler Co. was organized, he was one of its promoters and stockholders, and was made general manager of that company. The company was organized, in 1897, and the plant was built on the site of the old Agnes brick

OLIVER MOLTER.

yard on Railroad avenue. It is a three-story building, 360x110 feet, with basement, and the company employ upwards of three hundred men. They manufacture blown and pressed glass tumblers, plain and decorated. Their work is of a superior quality, and they ship direct to jobbers throughout the United States, South America, Cuba, Mexico, and Europe. Since the company's organization, they have run a night and day force, and the work has gone on steadily.

Mr. Runyon married Mary Wickham, a daughter of Jarvis Wickham, of Rochester, Pa., and they are the happy parents of three children, namely: Ethel; Laura Belle; and Charles Edwin. The subject of this sketch has been a member of the borough council for six years; and he is also a member of the I. O. O. F. He has always been a faithful attendant of the Episcopal church. Mr. Runyon has a bright future before him, as he is a young man with great determination and energy, and will make a success of anything which he undertakes.

———— • • ————

OLIVER MOLTER, ex-sheriff, and now deputy sheriff, of Beaver county, Pa., is one of the popular and respected citizens of Beaver, where he has resided all his life. He was born in Beaver, October 15, 1841, and is a son of Jonas Christopher and Fanny (Kemp) Molter, and grandson of John Molter, who was the family emigrant from his native country. He re-sided in Beaver many years, but, in the "forties," he settled in Stark county, Ohio, where he spent his remaining days,—dying at the age of eighty years. He was the father of a large family of children, of whom the following grew to maturity: John; Peter; Jonas C.; Margaret, and Elizabeth.

Oliver Molter's father was a brick-maker by trade and followed that occupation during his early days, but afterward engaged in coal mining, which he continued until he was elected justice of the peace of West Bridge-water, and faithfully discharged this trust until death claimed him. His wife was Fanny Kemp, a daughter of John Kemp, of Beaver, Pa., and she died at the age of sixty-nine years. Their children were named as follows: Henry, who is now a resident of Missouri; Peter J., deceased; Christopher, who resides in Chicago, Ill.; Oliver, whose name heads this brief memoir; Margaret, who is the wife of Thornton Harn, of Bridgewater, Pa.; Fanny, who is deceased; Mary, who was wedded to J. Kaszer, of Rochester; Eliza, who is the wife of James Olcott; and Martin L., who is a prominent citizen of New Brighton.

Oliver Molter was intellectually trained in the public schools, and in the academy at Beaver; starting out in life, he was employed at coaling and canaling, which occupations he continued until August, 1864, when he enlisted in Company B, 204th Reg., Pa. Vol. Inf. On the termination of the war, he returned home and became the owner of several mines, which he operated for several years; in 1877, he opened a fine livery stable in New

Brighton; he has since greatly enlarged this until it is now one of the best and most completely equipped in the county. His son is now in charge of the stable.

Mr. Molter first wedded Margaret B. Parris, a daughter of J. P. Parris, and she passed from this life aged fifty-six years. This union resulted in the birth of four children: William, deceased; Nora and Ida,—twins,— the former being the wife of E. O. Lindsey of New Brighton, and the latter, of Dr. Z. C. Laberge; and Frank, who married Edith Smith. The second union of Mr. Molter was with Ada Laney, daughter of Samuel and Elizabeth Laney, and they were blessed by the following children: James, who married Christina Hair; Grace, who is the wife of Harry Lockhart; Bertha; Herbert; and Ralph. Mr. Molter is a strong Republican and has served as school director, assessor, and in the town council. He is president of the Beaver Signal Manufacturing Company. Socially, he is a member of the F. & A. M.; K. of P.; Elks; A. O. U. W., and the Senior Order of United American Mechanics. In religious views, he is a Methodist. His portrait accompanies the foregoing account of his life.

————◦•◦————

ULYSSES S. STROUSS, M. D., one of the most active and energetic physicians and surgeons of Beaver, Pa., where his name is identified with many enterprises of magnitude and note, has been ac-

tively engaged in his profession at that place alone since 1884. Dr. Strouss was born in Hanover township, June 5, 1848, and was reared on a farm, thoroughly learning what constitutes a day's work. In gaining an education, he was ably assisted by his father, who, after sending him to the public school, considered him able to "hoe his own row." Later, Ulysses took a finishing course at Mansfield Academy, and after graduating therefrom, he engaged in teaching school, being then only seventeen years of age.

But our subject was not content with that profession, but had higher aspirations in life. He desired to fit himself for the medical profession, and studied medicine under the preceptorship of Dr. R. L. Walker of Mansfield, while teaching school at that place. Later, he continued his studies in the office of Dr. C. McConnell of Service, and afterward entered the medical department of the Western Reserve College of Cleveland, Ohio. Entering this college in 1870, he graduated therefrom in the class of 1872, and began the practice of his chosen profession with Dr. R. A. Moon at Hookstown, continuing there until 1874. At that time, he made a change of location, by going to Fairview, where he succeeded in building up a large and remunerative practice. He remained there until 1884, when he sold out his business interests in that place to Dr. J. S. Louthan. Dr. Strouss had gained more confidence in his own ability and skill by this time, and now looked about for a larger field. He found his heart's desire at Beaver, one of the most beautiful boroughs of Western Pennsylvania, and located there shortly after leaving Fairview. From the beginning of his practice in Beaver, his knowledge and skill, his promptness and strict attention to business gained for him the respect and confidence of the people in general. His patronage has increased to such dimensions that its requirements can only be met by working early and late. Upon locating in Beaver in 1884, Dr. Strouss purchased a residence and office at the corner of Third and Beaver streets, also buying the land and building adjoining on Beaver street. In 1892, he purchased his present residence on the corner of Beaver and Turnpike streets. He built a business block on Third street, which he rented, and has at different times sold lots from his land, until now that portion of the borough is covered with beautiful residences occupied and owned by some of the best people of Beaver. He has also built other houses in different parts of the town.

Although Dr. Strouss is a close student and keeps himself up-to-date in his profession, he has not been indifferent or idle as to the progress of his adopted home. Rather it may be said that he has been actively and financially interested in many enterprises worthy of note during the last fifteen years in Beaver. He was one of the original stockholders of the Beaver National Bank, and is one of its directors; he is also a stockholder of the Rochester Electric Light Company; a stockholder and director of the Beaver Loan Association, and a stockholder in various other enterprises. He served as U. S. pension examiner under

Cleveland's administration, and is a valued member of the Beaver County Medical Society. Socially, he is a member and past master of St. James Lodge, No. 457, F. & A. M.; of Eureka Chapter, No. 167, R. A. M.; Pittsburg Commandery No. 1, K. T.; Syria Temple, A. A. O. N. M. S., besides which he is district deputy grand master of the Thirty-seventh District, and also a member of the Royal Arcanum.

In 1870, Dr. Strouss was united in marriage with Esther M. Hartford, a daughter of James M. Hartford of South Beaver township, Beaver county, where he was known as a leading and progressive farmer. Two children, both daughters, have been born to our subject and his wife: Jane M., a graduate of Millersville State Normal School, and Martha E. Both are accomplished young ladies, and are still at home, where they entertain their many friends frequently in a truly hospitable manner. In the beginning of the present year, Dr. Strouss enlarged his residence, adding a fine commodious office and an attractive reception room. Previous to this improvement the Doctor's office was on the corner of Third and Beaver streets. Dr. Strouss is a son of the late David and Emily (Woodrough) Strouss and grandson of John Strouss.

John Strouss was born in Germany and with his two brothers came to America, where they all became American citizens. John Strouss settled in Lancaster county, Pa., but subsequently purchased a farm near Clinton, in Allegheny county, where he lived until the time of his death. He was known as a very progressive farmer, and owned considerable property. John Strouss erected a flouring or grist mill upon a farm known as the Potato Garden. He was a practical farmer and went west in search of wheat land; instead of buying near Allegheny City, which was then only a small village, he sought land on a higher elevation and away from the river and fog. Here upon this farm, he lived happily and attained the advanced age of ninety-six years. He was thrice married. The name of his first wife is not known, but her children were: Jonas, John, David, Simon, Hannah, Martha, Elizabeth, and Mary. Sometime after the death of his first wife, Mr. Strouss wedded Mrs. McCoy, who bore him three sons: William, James, and Henry. After the death of his second wife, Mr. Strouss again felt the need of a companion, and was joined in wedlock with Ann Cloud,—there being no issue to this union.

David Strouss, father of our subject, was born in Allegheny county, Pa., and when grown to manhood, conducted his father's mill and also learned the tanner's trade, which was one of the best trades in practical use in his day. He leased Hood's tannery in Allegheny county, which he operated for some time, but, later, leased a tannery in Washington county. After running that very successfully for years, and accumulating some capital, Mr. Strouss discontinued working at his trade, and invested some of his surplus cash in a farm situated in Hanover township, Beaver county, Pennsylvania. This farm is today owned by his sons, William and David

M. Besides this farm, David Strouss owned other farming property. He was a man of sterling qualities and knew the value of every cent; he arose at break of day and all his children were on hand, also, to accomplish a good day's work. His motto was "strike while the iron is hot,"—and everything was done by rule and in due time. In this way, progress was the natural result. Although he was ambitious, Mr. Strouss was also kind and charitable, and he was respected and looked upon as an exceedingly careful, prudent, industrious, and worthy man, whose life is quite worthy of imitation. At the age of sixty-six years, he took down the gun which always hung over the door, with the intention of cleaning it for the purpose of protecting his sheep from the ravages of dogs. As the gun had not been used in a long time, it was not supposed to be loaded. Mr. Strouss raised the hammer and blew in the gun, when it was discharged into his face, causing his death,—a sad ending to a noble life. How many sad accidents occur in exactly the same way!

His life companion was Emily Woodrough, of English ancestry. She survives her husband, having attained the advanced age of four score years and six. They reared eleven children, viz.: John W., now deceased; Elizabeth, widow of J. R. McKinzie; Josiah, also deceased; William J., residing on the homestead farm; Jane, deceased; Junius, who was killed in the Civil War while fighting for our country; Martha (deceased), wife of William Keefer; Melissa, wife of C. Swearengen; Ulysses S., subject of this sketch; Mary, wife

of George Henderson; and David, also residing on the homestead.

The subject of our sketch and his family are consistent and valued members of the Presbyterian church, working willingly in behalf of its interests, and ever giving liberally of their means. In business circles, the name of Dr. Strouss stands exceedingly high all over the county. At home as a citizen, no one is more popular or has more friends.

———— • • ————

GEORGE DAVIDSON, a recent portrait of whom appears on the foregoing page, is a man of much prominence in the borough of New Brighton, Pa., and since February, 1888, he has been cashier of the National Bank, of that place. This institution is one of the most progressive and substantial banks in Western Pennsylvania, having been organized October 29, 1884, to succeed the old National Bank of Beaver County, which had its origin November 12, 1864, as the successor of the Bank of Beaver County, a state institution established in 1857. The last named concern occupied the quarters of the late United States Bank, and its offices were situated where Dr. Simpson's are now located. Its officers were: S. Merrick, president and E. Hoops, cashier. On November 12, 1864, the National Bank of Beaver County was chartered with a capital of $200,-000; a fine brick block was erected, the front of which was of pressed brick, purchased in Philadelphia at $100 per thousand, it being the first brick of the kind ever used in the Beaver Valley. The building was of three stories; on the first floor were the bank offices; while on the second and third floors were dwelling rooms. The banking apartments were finished in the best of material, and had two large safes. S. Merrick, who was its first president, was later succeeded by John Miner, and upon the organization of the National Bank of New Brighton, M. T. Kennedy was made president, serving until his death, in November, 1884, when John Reeves became his successor. In August, 1893, Robert S. Kennedy was chosen president and C. C. Townsend, vice-president, to succeed Robert S. Kennedy. From the time the bank was organized until April 6, 1883, Mr. Edward Hoops served as cashier; he was succeeded by C. M. Merrick, who in turn was succeeded by the subject hereof. H. R. Ross is teller, and Clarence E. Kennedy is bookkeeper. The officers of this organization are among the most prominent and capable men in this part of the state, possessing high business ability, and being fully competent to fill the important positions they hold.

George Davidson was born in Fayette county, Pa., October 13, 1859, and is a son of Daniel R. Davidson. At the age of eight years, his parents moved to Beaver, Beaver county, Pa., and there he obtained his primary education; he afterwards attended college in West Virginia from 1877 to 1880. Owing to ill-health, he spent several years in traveling through the western states, and, upon his return to Beaver county, became deputy prothonotary under Dan H. Stone. On leaving this position, he entered the National Bank of New Brighton, as cashier, which office he now holds. Mr. Davidson is greatly interested in the progress of his adopted borough and county, and is ever ready to give his support to those measures which, in his opinion, tend to promote the welfare of the community. His popularity and sterling worth are shown by the fact that he is now serving his sixth term as treasurer of New Brighton, and is manager of the clearing house of the associated banks of Beaver county, which association he helped to form.

The subject of this record married Mary Wilson, daughter of Samuel B. Wilson, a prominent resident of Beaver, and this union has been blessed by the birth of the following children: Daniel R.; Samuel K.; Elizabeth; Margaret; William, and Mary,—the two last named being deceased. Mr. Davidson owns a beautiful home on the corner of Third avenue and Fifteenth street.

———— ◆ •• ————

OHN BURTON ARMSTRONG, M. D., ranks among the leading physicians and surgeons of Beaver county, Pa., having been actively engaged in the practice of medicine in Beaver since 1893. His strict attention to his professional duties, as well as his peculiar success in treating many difficult cases, have brought him into prominence in the best families of the vicinity, in addition to which he has many patients in the surrounding counties. Being a man of iron nerve and ambitious spirit, he delights in keeping abreast of the times in his profession, and thus is prepared to grasp the most complicated cases and treat them according to the best and most modern methods. It is said that some very critical cases have been attended by Dr. Armstrong with marked success.

The Doctor also has quite a large office practice. His office, which is in close proximity to his residence on West Third street, is often filled to overflowing with patients awaiting their turn in the consultation room. Dr. Armstrong is of Scotch ancestry, and was born in Brighton township, Beaver county, within one mile of Beaver, on January 15, 1868. After attending the district school, he completed a high school course at Beaver, chose medicine as his profession, and endeavored to fit himself by becoming a medical student under Dr. Jas. McCann of Pittsburg. He then attended the Western Pennsylvania University (now known as the Medical Department of Western University), from which he graduated in March, 1891. Soon after graduation, he practiced his profession for a year at Allegheny City, for a short time at New Kensington, Westmoreland county, and at Rochester, Pa., for one year. Although his success was encouraging considering the short duration of his stay in each of the above places, neither location suited him, and he looked about for another locality where he could settle permanently. His thoughts naturally reverted to the home of his youth, in close proximity to which was the beautiful little borough of Beaver, which he always admired and where he had many acquaintances and friends. After deliberating for some time, he decided to locate in Beaver, and his success has been even greater than he anticipated, thus proving the wisdom of his selection.

Dr. Armstrong wooed and won for his wife, Anna Mary Fraser, an accomplished daughter of Alexander Fraser. The Doctor and his estimable spouse have one son, a bright little boy, born January 6, 1895, and named John Alexander, in honor of both his maternal and paternal grandfathers. The subject of our sketch is a zealous Republican and has served as school director in the borough. He is also a member of the F. & A. M. lodge, and of the Knights of Pythias. Both he and Mrs. Armstrong are active communicants of the M. E. church, of which the Doctor is now steward.

Dr. Armstrong is a son of John and Isabella Margaret (Adams) Armstrong, grandson of John and Nellie (Dillon) Armstrong, and great-grandson of John Armstrong, who was born in the eastern part of the Keystone State, probably in Chester county, or in Philadelphia. Tradition tells us that the family originated in Scotland, and belonged to the old Scotch Presbyterians. The founder of the American branch of the family came to America from the north of Scotland previous to the year 1800. The grandfather of Dr. Armstrong crossed the mountains of Central Pennsylvania and settled in Allegheny county, in 1805. In addition to this information little is known of him except that he followed the occupation of a farmer, and his remains lie buried in the Concord churchyard near Baden, Beaver county, Pennsylvania. He was one of four sons, whose names are: John; Samuel and James, who both died single; and Robert.

John Armstrong, the grandfather of our subject, was born in Chester county, Pa., in the year 1800; when but five years of age, he was brought by his parents to Beaver county, Pennsylvania. He was reared on a farm, and spent his life following that occupation on farms near Darlington and Baden, where his death occurred at about the age of fifty years. His wife, whose maiden name was Nellie Dillon, lived until she had passed her eightieth mile-stone. Their children were: John, the Doctor's father; Samuel, now deceased; Ruth, wife of Daniel Emerick of Ogle, Pa.; Esther, deceased; and Mary, also deceased.

John Armstrong, father of the subject of our narrative, was born August 27, 1831, near Greersburg (now Darlington) Beaver county, Pennsylvania. Early in life, he learned the shoemaker's trade, and began working at it on the old homestead. But that occupation was not congenial to him; his active mind and equally active body required the broader field of business pursuits. He abandoned shoemaking and went to Warren county, near Tidioute, where for seven years he was interested in the lumber business. During that time, he accumulated a small capital, which he desired to invest wisely. With keen foresight he purchased a tract of land along the Allegheny River, at Henry's Bend, near Oil City, paying for the tract $450 of hard-earned cash. Upon this land he carried on farming until oil was discovered in that vicinity. The first oil well drilled on the banks of the Allegheny River was on his farm, and, while the excitement was at its height, Mr. Armstrong sold the farm for the fabulous price of $31,000. After dealing in oil for some time, he retired to Rochester, Pa., and, soon after, purchased the Jackson farm, near Beaver, containing 105 acres of choice farming land, upon which he has enjoyed a happy life as one of Beaver county's prominent farmers. He has made many improvements on his land, and has built handsome and substantial buildings. In 1898, his large barn, with contents, was completely destroyed by fire, but it was re-built as soon as possible.

Mr. Armstrong is a public-spirited man, a stanch Republican, and has served as supervisor and school director. He was joined in wedlock with Isabella Margaret Adams, a daughter of John and Jeannette Adams, who formerly resided in Northumberland county, Pa., and removed later to Parkersburg. Mrs. Armstrong was born March 26, 1841; she bore her husband the following children: Calantha Abigail, still single; Jeannette, wife of Dr. J. J. Allen of Monaca, Pa.; Annie M., deceased; John Burton, to whom this sketch pertains and who is commonly known as "J. Burt Armstrong"; and Vienna Isabella.

Alexander Fraser, father-in-law of our sub-ject, was born January 1, 1840, near Inverness, Scotland. He is a son of Alexander Fraser, who was descended from Scotch nobility, and came to America with his wife, Mary, and his family, in 1845,—settling in the Scotch settlement near Wellsville, Ohio. There he followed, for many years, the occupation of a farmer, and is now enjoying the ripe old age of eighty-seven years. He was deprived of his wife and beloved companion, however, who died at about the age of seventy years. They came to America on a sailing vessel which was six weeks in crossing the ocean; they landed at New York City, taking the tedious route to Ohio by way of Hudson River, Erie Canal, and Lake Erie. Although a true Scotchman, "Grandpa" Fraser loves America. To him and his worthy consort were born ten children, seven of whom grew to maturity, namely: Alexander, Jr.; William; Margaret; Isabella; Hannah; Mary; and Jeannette.

Alexander Fraser, Jr., arrived at manhood just in time to respond to our country's call for brave men during the Civil War. He enlisted from Wellsville, Ohio, in the 3rd Reg., Ohio Vol. Inf. and, later, re-enlisted in the navy and went down the river from Pittsburg, serving until the close of the war, and receiving an honorable discharge at New York City. After the war, for a period of twenty-five years, Mr. Fraser served as baggage master on the Pennsylvania Railroad. During the repair of that road, his train was sent over the Fort Wayne R. R. through Alliance, and at Wellsville, Ohio, his home, a terrible collision occurred, in which Mr. Fraser was so badly injured that he died the same evening, October 17, 1893. He left a wife and six children to mourn his unfortunate demise; Mrs. Fraser was, before marriage, Miss Emma Hayes, a daughter of Thomas C. Hayes. She was born in old Brighton, now Beaver Falls. The names of their children are: Annie M., wife of our subject; Margaret H., now deceased; Charles W.; Chauncey M.; Grace E., deceased; and Alexander D.

———◆·◆———

GEORGE M. HEMPHILL. The gentleman whose name heads this sketch is the efficient and well-known postmaster of Bridgewater, Beaver county, Pennsylvania. He was born in Rochester, Beaver county, and is a son of Captain Sharp and Abbie (Bloss) Hemphill.

The great-grandfather, Moses Hemphill, was born in Northampton county, Pa., of English ancestry. His life was spent in his native county, and he reared: Joseph, James, Thomas, Mrs. Kerr, and Mrs. Nogle. The grandfather of George M., Joseph Hemphill, was born in Northampton county, and became a civil engineer and surveyor. Before the year 1800, he went to Beaver county, Pa., and became one of the commissioners to form Beaver county. He served as associate judge, county treasurer, and county commissioner, and the first surveys and deeds of Beaver county were signed by him. He kept a general store in Beaver county, and was well known throughout its limits. His death occurred in 1834, at the age of sixty-two, and his wife, who was formerly Jean Hay, died at the age of seventy-seven. They were both buried in Beaver county. Their children were as follows: James W.; Cynthia, who married Dr. Smith Cunningham; Jane, who married John English; Nancy, who married Samuel R. Dunlap; Thomas; Ellen, who married Alex Scott; Mary, who married Joseph Moorehead; Margaret, who married Thomas Cunningham; and Captain Sharp, the father of the subject of this sketch.

Captain Sharp Hemphill was born in Beaver county, in the town of Beaver, and was educated in the old Beaver Academy. For a short time, he was interested in mercantile business, and then he went on the Ohio River as a steamboat clerk. He continued work on the river for forty-five years, and was, for many years, captain of steamboats running from Pittsburg to New Orleans, and also from St. Louis to Fort Benton. Often, in the pioneer days, when he was on the Missouri River, the boats were shot at by Indians. He served in the 101st Reg. of Pa. Vol., in the reserve corps, and was a Mason. He became paralyzed in his later life, and died at his home in Bridgewater, Pa., at the age of seventy-two. He married Abbie Bloss, a daughter of Chester W. Bloss, of Peacham, Vt., and she is still living at the age of seventy-two. The children which resulted from this union are as follows: Emma, who married John Coleman, of Bridgewater, Pa.; George M., the subject of this sketch; Clarence, a glass worker at

Rochester, Pa.; Jean, deputy postmistress of Bridgewater, Pa.; Mary; Joseph, who married Annie Brunell, and lives in Pittsburg,—having two children,—Grace and Edith; Alice, who married John Thornely, of Beaver Falls, and has two children,—Arthur and Mildred; and Edith, who married H. B. Twitmyer, of Pittsburg.

George Hemphill, the subject of this biography, attended the schools of Rochester, Pa., and was employed at glass houses in Rochester and Monaca for nineteen years. He also spent several years on the river, and has been engaged in various occupations. He settled in Bridgewater, and June 1, 1897, was selected as postmaster to succeed L. F. Weyman. Mr. Hemphill is a member of the K. of P. He is well known in the vicinity, and takes an active interest in all affairs which are for the good of the community.

—————— • • —— — — —

ROBERT B. ROSE. It is always of great interest to trace various industries from their beginning to the status existing at the present day. This is true of transportation on the rivers, for, before railroads came into existence, this was the principal means of carrying produce from the fields of operation to the points of disposition. In the first instance, rudely constructed boats served the purpose of the pioneer settlers of Western Pennsylvania, as it was the only way in which they could send the lumber cleared from their lands to a market. Next in use were the flat and keel boats, which, laden with produce, were floated down the river. Up to this time all transportation had been attended with great difficulties, but soon the invention of Robert Fulton, which excited the wonder of the entire civilized world, was put to a practical test on the Ohio River. Steam barges were built and also steam packets, which pushed boats up stream, that formerly being done by hand, with long poles. When the steamboat plied up and down the river, it was thought that facilities for traffic were complete, but this, in turn, has been partially superseded by the iron horse, owing to its great expedition. Nevertheless the steamboats are still extensively used for the transportation of freight, for they have attained a high rate of speed and are enabled to transport material at a much less cost than railroads. Among the prominent residents of Western Pennsylvania is an interesting and influential class of people, composed of men who have spent years of their lives as boatmen on the river. Robert B. Rose, one of the most enterprising business men of Rochester, Beaver county, Pa., is one of these. He is the proprietor of the Rochester wharfboat, and also deals largely in eggs, poultry, grain, etc.

Mr. Rose was born in Adams county, Ohio, and is a son of Smith Rose, who was at one time a merchant, but later became a steamboat agent at Rome, Ohio, continuing thus until his death. The subject of our sketch passed his early life in his native state, and at an early age was employed at work on the river, which he has always followed. He first found   employment   at   Rome,   Ohio, when he purchased his first wharfboat; disposing of that, he moved to Vanceburg, Ky., where he purchased another. He gained a wide knowledge of the boat business, and, being of an industrious nature, continued to better his condition. He removed to Rochester, Beaver county, Pa., and there bought the property and wharfboat of George Lukens. This was the first boat operated at Rochester, being originally owned and run by John McDowell, who disposed of it to Mr. Lukens and his son. When Mr. Rose purchased the business of George Lukens, the boat had become too old to use and he sold it; he then bought another which he continued to use until 1891, when he built one of the finest wharfboats on the Ohio River. It is 158 feet long, 32 feet wide, and has a capacity of about 500 tons. On the second floor is a suite of seven fine rooms, and on the first floor is a large office and waiting room and the storage space. The borough of Rochester has never made any effort to improve the landing there, and much could be done to further the enterprise of river shipments, which would result in much benefit to the borough itself. Our subject has his boat so arranged that it moves with the rise and fall of the river, which varies over thirty feet,—the landing being on Water street at the foot of James street. Mr. Rose is prepared to give shipping rates to all points south and west, and to many points east. A large proportion of the products of the manufacturers of Rochester and other Beaver valley towns is shipped from his wharf, and it is a frequent sight to see a long string of teams and dray wagons, waiting to unload their goods. One of the most delightful trips in the central portion of the United States is on the steamers of the Ohio River, going down that river to the Mississippi, thence to New Orleans, and back. Mr. Rose is a man of pleasing personality, and his friends are almost without number.

He was united in wedlock with Elizabeth H. Blair, a daughter of William D. Blair, of Stout, Ohio, as the postoffice is called, though the river designation of the place is Rome. This union resulted in the birth of two children; Luella W.; and Eva Marie, who died at the age of two years.

DR. JOHN C. McCAULEY. The borough of Rochester, as regards her practitioners of medicine, is unsurpassed by any other in the state of Pennsylvania. There are located within its limits, men who have practiced for many years and who have attained far more than local distinction, being classified with the leading men of the district. Standing prominently to the front is the gentleman whose name heads these lines, a representative of the younger generation of physicians. He is young in years, but hard and continued study in a renowned medical institution, combined with a natural bent for the profession, has given him that skill which ordinarily requires years of experience to acquire. He is in high standing in Rochester, and among his large number of patients are numbered men of prominence throughout this section of the state. He is a native of Rochester, and is a son of Leander and Martha M. (Andrews) McCauley.

David McCauley, the great-grandfather of our subject, was born in County Armagh, Ireland, and lived there until his death. His wife, Jane (Corran), with her son Robert and her other children, came to America in 1819, settling in Pittsburg, Pennsylvania. Robert McCauley, who was the grandfather of the subject hereof, was twenty-one years of age when he came to this country. He possessed a superior education, and his vocation in life was that of an instructor, teaching in Pittsburg and in Sewickley township, Beaver county, Pennsylvania. In 1825, he purchased a farm of 250 acres in New Sewickley township, which is now owned by his children, and there resided until his death at the age of seventy years. He married Mary Mitchell, a daughter of John and Elizabeth (Patterson) Mitchell, who died at the age of eighty-two, and their children were: John; David C.; Leander; Robert P.; James; Elizabeth, the wife of James Mathews; Mary, who became the wife of Dr. S. H. Andrews; Emiline; and Martha, who married Joseph Briggs. Mr. McCauley was an active Democrat in his day, and served as assessor and in other township offices. Religiously, he was a member of the Presbyterian church.

Leander McCauley attended the public schools and Freedom academy, after which he engaged as a teacher in the schools of Beaver county and also in the state of Ohio. In 1857, he removed to Williams county, Ohio, where he purchased a saw mill, and operated it for a period of five years. He then took up carpentering and pattern making, and later carried on farming on the old homestead for twenty-one years. In 1897, he retired to the town of Rochester, where he erected him a fine home and has since lived. He married Martha M. Andrews, a daughter of John and Elizabeth (Harnit) Andrews, of Enon Valley, Lawrence county, Pa., and four children were born to them, as follows: Wilfred James, who died in infancy; John C., the subject hereof; Mary M., who died at the age of sixteen years; and E. S. H., a physician and surgeon, of Beaver. Religiously, the family are Presbyterians.

Dr. John Corran McCauley, after completing his preliminary education in the public schools, began the study of medicine with J. S. Boyd, M. D., of New Brighton, Pennsylvania. He entered into his work with characteristic energy, and in 1890 was graduated from the Homeopathic Medical College, of Cleveland, fully qualified for his chosen profession. He immediately located at Rochester, where he succeeded to the practice of Dr. G. H. Smith. He has built up an extensive patronage, and enjoys the confidence and good will of his fellow-citizens to the fullest extent. In 1893, he built a fine residence in Rochester, with an office in connection. He is a member of the Beaver County Homeopathic Medical Society; the State Homeopathic Medical Society; and the American

PAULUS T. KOEHLER.

Institute of Homeopathy. He is also a member of the board of censors of the Cleveland Homeopathic Medical College. He is also on the staff of the Beaver Valley Hospital.

Dr. McCauley was united in marriage with Jennie C. Parks, a daughter of Theodore Parks, of New Sewickley township, Beaver county, and they have one child, Mary E., born March 28, 1897.

———————

PAULUS E. KOEHLER, who owns an elegant four-story hotel in Monaca, and also has extensive real estate interests there, is a prosperous citizen of that place, where he has resided for a great many years. A portrait accompanies this biography.

Mr. Koehler was born in Prussia, April 10, 1856, where he attended the public schools. He was also a pupil of the high school, and pursued the study of theology, with the intention of becoming a missionary. He was a brilliant scholar, and gained the honors of his class, but he never took orders, as he preferred a business career. He learned the trade of a decorator of porcelain under the talented E. Schledmich, the celebrated Prussian exporter, and was with that gentleman until 1881, acquiring the highest degree of skill in his art. He then came to America, and located at East Liverpool, Ohio, and took charge of the decorating shop of George Homlichhaus, also doing contract jobs for other firms. One year later, he accepted a very good position with the Phoenix Glass Company of Monaca, Pa., and had the honor of decorating the first piece of work ever turned out by that firm, which is the largest glass firm in the world in that line of business. Mr. Koehler built two kilns, and remained in their employ until 1884, when the factory was burned to the ground, and he then started a shop of his own in Monaca, doing work for various glass firms. He has always been a very fine workman, and some of his productions show a perfection of finish which is hard to surpass. When the Phoenix works were rebuilt, the firm prevailed upon Mr. Koehler to accept his old position, although his business was in a flourishing way. He built the first clay kiln ever constructed for firing decorated glass, those in use previous to that time being of steel. He is a very clever and ingenious man, and made a number of discoveries which have proved of great value to him. Upon returning to the Phoenix Glass Company, he took the work on contract, and with good results. He held this position until 1897, when he gave up the business on account of failing health, after a satisfactory connection of almost twenty years.

In 1883, Mr. Koehler first began to deal in real estate, and since that time he has handled over $100,000 worth of property in Monaca. Being convinced that the borough had a bright future before it, he purchased a piece of property in 1883, and has erected several houses, all of a class which are an improvement to the town. He was one of the organizers of the Citizens' Improvement Company, which has been active in developing the interests of the community. There is a large tract of land on Dorchester Heights for manufacturing and residence sites, all nicely laid out, and in it the subject of this sketch owns twenty-one lots, individually, besides holding an interest in the company. He was also in the business of developing gas, and bought gas lands quite extensively. He owns ten acres of building lots in the borough, and is a director and local representative in the Building & Loan Association. In 1898, he built the Hotel Monaca, a fine four-story building of buff brick, and it is undoubtedly the finest in Beaver county, on the south side of the Ohio River. The interior is in keeping with the beautiful exterior, having fine, lofty rooms and offices, with appointments complete in every particular. It contains fifty large rooms, its dimensions being 86x46 feet, and is a first-class hotel, enjoying the patronage of all the high-grade transient trade. Mr. Koehler's confidence in the future of Monaca remains unshaken, and he contemplates the erection of a business block, similar in style to the hotel, imparting a metropolitan air to the town. He was active in his efforts to secure a bridge across the Ohio River, and is now a stockholder of the bridge company.

In 1876, Mr. Koehler was united in marriage with Marie Schilling, and they have nine children: Anna (Betts); Henry, a graduate of Butcher's Business College, who is a mold-maker by trade; Louisa; Otto M., a decorator, who is also a graduate of Butcher's Business College; Howard; Amelia; Elsie; Edward; and Sophia. They had also four who died in infancy. Religiously, he is a liberal supporter of churches. He is a Republican in politics, and has been a member of the council since 1896 (having been re-elected in 1899), and has served on the county committee. Socially, he is quite prominent, and belongs to a number of orders. He has been grand district deputy of R. A.; past chancellor, K. of P.; a member of the Woodmen of the World; B. P. O. E.; Syria Temple, A. A. O. N. M. S. In the Masonic Order he is a member of Rochester Lodge, No. 229; Record Chapter, No. 167; Ascalon Commandery, No. 59; and the Consistory of the Scottish Rites, No. 320.

———— ••• ————

JOHN M. KELSO, a veteran of the Civil War, is the proprietor of one of the finest general merchandise stores in Beaver county, and resides at New Galilee. He was born in Noblestown, Pa., August 31, 1843, and is a son of Mark and Mary (Borland) Kelso.

John Kelso, the grandfather of John M., was born in Franklin county, Pa., in 1750, and obtained his education in the East. Upon the outbreak of the Revolutionary War, he volunteered his services to the cause of Independence, and, in all, served seven years and six months, holding the rank of sergeant major when he retired from the army. He was a brave soldier and has an honorable war record. At the close of the war he removed to Allegheny county and took up a large tract of wild land, which he cleared, and upon this he erected log buildings. He married Miss McCormick, who was born in Allegheny county, and they reared six children: George; John; Benjamin; Mark, the father of John M.; Jennie (Ormond); and Mary (Cook). Politically, he was a Whig. Religiously, he was a member of the Associate Reformed church. He passed to the world beyond, in the year 1810.

Mark Kelso was born in Allegheny county, Pa., in 1802, and, notwithstanding the many difficulties he encountered, obtained a good education. He assisted his father in cultivating the farm, and upon the latter's death succeeded to the possession of the old homestead. He was a large sheep-raiser and wool-grower, and was proud of the quality of his stock. He was a Whig and later a Republican. He was a faithful member of the United Presbyterian church, and was an elder therein for years. He died in 1865, and his wife survived him many years, dying in 1889, at the age of eighty-one. His union with Mary Borland, a daughter of Matthew Borland, of Allegheny county, Pa., resulted in the following issue: Margaret (Nesbit); Mary A. (Woods); John M., the gentleman whose name heads these lines; Matthew B., who died in infancy; George H., a farmer; and Joseph A., a merchant, who, prior to his death, in 1898, was a partner of the subject of this sketch.

John M. Kelso received his mental training in the public schools of Allegheny county, and was engaged as a teacher until 1883, when he moved to the borough of New Galilee. It was a very small place at that time, there being but three stores located there, but our subject predicted its future growth, and, in partnership with his brother, Joseph A. Kelso, bought out the store of A. F. Reed. There they did business for five years, at the end of which time they bought a building of Mr. Porter. In a very short time they acquired a large and lucrative trade, and at the present time John M. Kelso is the leading merchant of the town. The building in which he is located consists of one story, a basement and a stock room, and is without doubt one of the most completely stocked stores in Beaver county, carrying a full line of dry goods, boots and shoes, hats and caps, clothing, notions, hardware, crockery, house furnishings, jewelry, drugs, confectionery, tobacco and cigars. He is a man of great energy and enterprise, and the manner in which he caters to the wants of his customers has brought him into public favor.

John M. Kelso, fired with the patriotism of an American citizen who loves his country, enlisted, in 1864, in Company I, 112th Reg., Pa. Vol. Inf., near Pittsburg. After doing garrison duty around Washington, D. C., he was sent to the seat of war and took part in some of the hardest-fought battles, such as the battles of the Wilderness, Spottsylvania, North Anna River, Cold Harbor, Petersburg, Weldon Railroad, and Chapin's Farm. He was taken prisoner, and was forced to endure the tortures of Libby Prison, Belle Isle, and Salisbury, being confined in these notorious places for about six months. He was then exchanged, but the harsh treatment to which he had been subjected, and the lack of proper food, had undermined his robust constitution, and he was stricken with typhoid fever, from which he did not recover until after the close of the war.

Mr. Kelso formed a marital union with Caroline H. Imbrie, a daughter of Rev. David R. Imbrie, and a granddaughter of Rev. David Imbrie. Her great-grandfather was a native of Scotland, who came to New York City, where he remained for a short period, and then returned to his fatherland. Upon again sailing for this country, he was shipwrecked and lost most of his valuables and personal effects,—in fact, the proceeds of most of his property. He settled in Service, Pa., buying a large tract of land, which he cleared, and then erected houses and barns. He was a successful stock-raiser. He married Miss Flack, and they had two children: David; and John, who engaged in farming, in Beaver county.

Rev. David Imbrie was educated at Canonsburg, studied for the ministry, and was licensed to preach in the Associate Reformed church. He preached for many years at Bethel, Lawrence county, Pa., and at Darlington. His death came very suddenly and in a very dramatic manner. He died one Sabbath morning as he was entering the pulpit. His son, Rev. David R. Imbrie, received his collegiate or theological education at Canons-

burg. He was pastor of a church at New Wilmington, Pa., for more than twenty-five years, and was held in the highest esteem. He married Nancy R. Johnston, who was born in Franklin county, Pa., and they had eight children, four of whom are now living, namely: Rev. J. J., who was educated at New Wilmington and in Westminster College, is a graduate of the Allegheny Theological Seminary, and now holds two charges in Butler county; Rev. D. R., who received the same educational training as his brother, and is chaplain of the Allegheny County Workhouse; Nannie I., the wife of R. S. Clark, a well-known farmer; and Caroline H., who attended the public schools at Ottawa, Kansas, and Bridgewater Academy, Pa. She taught school for three years and was then united in marriage with the subject of this biography. They are the parents of four children: Frederick L.; George N.; Joseph A.; and Nannie I. Religiously, Mr. Kelso is a member of the U. P. church and has been an elder since 1888. He is a Republican in politics, and held the office of school director for six years.

JAMES T. CONLIN may be classed among the self-made men of Beaver county, having begun at the foot of the ladder and worked up to his present position; he is public-spirited, a man of fine business qualities, and enjoys the respect and good will of a multitude of acquaintances. He was born at Freedom, Pa., June 1, 1855, and is a son of John and Mary (Carroll) Conlin.

HENRY SLPP.

Mr. Conlin's parents were born near Castle Bellingham, County Louth, Ireland, and after their marriage, in 1845, they came to the United States, first locating in Baltimore, remaining there three years, and then moving to Rochester. He worked on the railroad at Freedom, Baden, and Rochester, and passed his latter days in Rochester, dying in 1881, at the age of seventy-six years. His wife died in 1876, aged fifty-five years. To them was born the following family of children: Margaret, who was married to M. Maloney, both of whom are now deceased; Catherine, who is the wife of J. Gildernew, of Pittsburg; Annie, who is the widow of Charles O'Donald; Joseph P., a resident of Alliance, Ohio, who was wedded to Miss Mary Hogan; and James T.

When Mr. Conlin was three years of age, his parents moved to Baden and there he obtained his primary education; at twenty-one years of age, he began railroading as a section man. He was promoted next to tie inspector, then to baggage master, and September 1, 1889, he was appointed assistant ticket agent at Rochester and July 17, 1899, was appointed ticket agent to succeed W. G. Masten,—in which capacity he is at present serving. Mr. Conlin bought a small residence on Washington street, which he later sold, and built a large house on Pinney street; in 1897, he sold the latter place to Benjamin Pfeiffer, and purchased a lot of J. J. Hoffman, on the corner of Hinds and Penn streets, where he erected a handsome dwelling, which he makes his home. Mr. Conlin is secretary of the Central Building & Loan Association; a director of the Keystone Tumbler Co., Limited; a director of the First National Bank of Rochester; and a partner in the S. M. Hervey & Company Insurance Company, the largest insurance agency in the county.

Mr. Conlin has served three terms in the council. Religiously, he is a member of the Catholic church, while socially, he belongs to the Woodmen of the World, is a member and collector of the Royal Arcanum, and has passed through all the chairs of the Elks lodge. The subject of this sketch was joined in marriage with Miss Annie Huering, a daughter of Theodore and Mary Huering, and they are the parents of five children, namely: Elizabeth; Theodore; Theodora; Mary; and James. Mrs. Huering resides in Rochester, Pennsylvania. Mr. Huering died in June, 1898, and at the time of his death, was residing in Rochester.

———————

HENRY SEPP, whose wholesale liquor establishment is the largest and best in Western Pennsylvania, is located in Beaver Falls where he is numbered among the foremost business men. He is a son of Bernard and Martha (Hahn) Sepp, and was born in Hessen, Germany, May 27, 1849. Mr. Sepp's portrait accompanies this sketch.

The grandfather of Henry Sepp was Henry C. Sepp, a prosperous farmer living in Germany, whose father was a man of education and a surveyor by profession. The instruments by which the latter earned a livelihood are treasured heirlooms of the family. Bernard Sepp, the father of the gentleman whose name heads these lines, followed an agricultural life, owning and working a fine farm of sixty-six acres, and making a specialty of cattle raising and dairying. He married Martha Hahn, who was born and schooled in Germany, and they had five children: Conrad, a baker of Braddock; Anna M., who died in infancy; Henry, the subject of this personal history; Lizzie A. (Eppel), whose husband is a butcher at Braddock; Mary (Marx) of Chippewa township; and Adam C., deceased.

Henry Sepp received his schooling in Hessen, Germany, spending his youth on the farm. When sixteen years of age, in 1865, he came to America, locating in Allegheny, Pa., where he learned the trade of an axe polisher, accepting a position with Joseph Graff, doing work by contract. The fact that this is the only firm for which he worked in this country,—continuing with him for twenty-six years,—speaks volumes for the steadiness and perseverance of Mr. Sepp. When the concern was removed to Beaver Falls, in 1871, he accompanied it and continued in its employ until he went into the liquor business at the corner of Fifteenth street and Fourth avenue, renting a building for that purpose. He remained in that store for four years, when he erected his present building, which he has since occupied. He has one of the most complete stores and bottling plants in Western Pennsylvania, it being large and roomy, and equipped with the most approved machinery. The bottling and washing are done by machinery, which is driven by a gas engine, and the capacity is 200 dozen bottles per day. Next to these rooms is the large cooling room, for keeping the liquor in condition for use at all times,—the plans for this room being devised by our subject. It is double-walled, and filled with paper. Next to this is the sale room, in which he has a large line of expensive liquors, including rare old wines of ancient vintage, both domestic and imported. Across the yard is another store room, a wagon shed, and stables. In fact his facilities for this line of business are unexcelled, and the business has grown to such proportions that he finds it necessary to keep three delivery wagons going at all times. Three men are employed in the bottling department, and the cooler has a capacity of two carloads. He has an extensive line of goods for medicinal purposes, in which his trade is very large. Although a man of the greatest enterprise, his honesty and conscientiousness are unquestioned, and he has refused to give credit in all cases in which he thinks it will encourage debt and shiftlessness.

Mr. Sepp was joined in the bonds of wedlock with Elizabeth Theis, who was born in Hessen, Germany, and they reared nine children: Henry, Jr.; Elizabeth, who died at the age of five years; Mary (Roy); William, who is assisting his father; Bertha; Lena; Katie, an accomplished musician; Eddie, who died at the age of five years; and Edna. The four youngest children are students, and contemplate entering college. In political affiliations, Mr. Sepp is a strong Republican, whilst in religious faith and fellowship, he is a member of the German Lutheran church. Fraternally, he is a member and past master of the Ancient Order of United Workmen, past chancellor of the Knights of Pythias, and a member of the German Druids.

Henry Sepp, Jr., the oldest child born to his parents, was born in Beaver county, June 22, 1871, and received his mental instruction in the public schools. He then learned the trade of a glass maker and followed that until his twenty-first year, when, after completing a course in Rand's Business College, he engaged as bookkeeper for his father. He has continued in that capacity up to the present time, and is a man of tried business qualities. When he was but thirteen years old, he began studying music, taking lessons on the violin; he is now an accomplished musician and the leader of Sepp's orchestra, one of the most favorably known musical organizations in this section of Pennsylvania. Mr. Sepp was united in marriage with Clara Stauffer, who was born in Canada and moved with her parents to "Brownstone," Michigan, where she attended school. She later moved to Beaver Falls, Pa., where she was married to the son of Henry Sepp. Henry Sepp, Jr., is an aggressive Republican, and although he has often been urged to accept office in the borough, he has uniformly declined. Religiously, he is a Lutheran. He is a member of the Knights of Pythias; Nonpareil, A. C.; and the Beaver Falls Turnverein. The residence he now occupies is a two-story frame building, adjoining his father's home, which he bought in February, 1897.

ALFRED P. MARSHALL. Among the eminent lawyers of Beaver county, is the gentleman whose name appears at the opening of this brief biography. Slowly, but continuously, from a briefless attorney, he has attained, by conscientious and unremitting labor, a large and lucrative practice. As a lawyer, he is careful, painstaking and of calm, judicial temperament. His ability to grasp large and intricate problems of law, his sound judgment in business matters, and his untiring energy are some of the factors which have made him successful. He was born in Perry township, Lawrence county, Pa., May 17, 1850, and is a son of Joseph A. and grandson of James Kyle Marshall.

The father of James Kyle Marshall was a native of Ireland, and he came to this country and settled in Washington county, Pennsylvania. James Kyle Marshall was supposed to have been born on the vessel while en route for America; he lived on the farm now owned by Josiah Blythe, located in Washington county. He wedded a Miss Andover, and they reared a family of children; those who grew to maturity were: John, James, Joseph, Nancy, Mary, Margaret, and Susanna.

Joseph A. Marshall was a native of Washington county, but spent the greater part of his life in Perry township, Lawrence county, Pa., where he was the owner of a fine farm, which he put under a high state of cultivation. He was married to Delilah Houck, to whom was born a family of twenty children as follows: James Kyle, deceased; Sarah, who was wedded to J. W. Hyde; Jonathan D., who is a farmer in Franklin township, Beaver county; William B., deceased; John C., who is a farmer in Butler county; Rebecca, who is the wife of A. L. Vangorder; Amanda; Lina A., who wedded W. I. Scott; Lucinda, who is the wife of James Duncan; Mary Agnes, who was the wife of Rev. T. L. Scott, and died in India; Alfred P., to whom this sketch relates; Clinton B., who is a farmer of Perry township, Lawrence county, Pa.; Frank B., who is a farmer of Allegheny county; Matilda, deceased, who was the wife of J. M. Scott; Joseph, who is a farmer of Perry township; Margaret, deceased; and four others, who died in infancy. Politically, Mr. Marshall was first a Democrat, but being opposed to slavery, he became a Republican. He was elected to many township offices, which tends to prove his popularity and the esteem in which he was held by his fellow-citizens. He was a member of the United Presbyterian church. He departed from this life in his sixty-seventh year.

Our subject attended the public schools, Westminster College, Pa., and Mount Union College, Ohio, and spent his leisure hours on his father's farm. Being very ambitious to acquire a thorough education, he attended college during the summer months, while in the winter he taught school, and in that way secured ample funds to carry him through an educational course. This he continued for a period of seven years and then he entered the law office of Hon. John G. Hall, of Ridgway, Pennsylvania. He subsequently entered the office of Samuel B. Wilson, of Beaver, Pa., and was admitted to the bar of Beaver county, in April, 1876. He immediately began practicing in Beaver, where he has remained ever since. Later, he took Mr. McCoy as a partner under the name of Marshall & McCoy, but since the latter's death, in 1890, he has continued the practice of his profession alone. Mr. Marshall has won an enviable prominence as a business lawyer and man of affairs; since his admission to the bar he has been actively engaged in the practice of law, meeting with exceptional success. His well-known studious habits, and the conscientious, thorough and exhaustive manner in which he deals with all matters undertaken by him, assures a continuous and ever increasing professional prosperity.

Mr. Marshall was united in the bonds of matrimony with Miss Cora F. Bentel, a daughter of Charles H. Bentel, and granddaughter of Philip and Margaret (Smith) Bentel. Three children have been born to them: Annie B., Charles B., and Lillian C. Philip Bentel, the great-grandfather of Alfred P. Marshall's wife, was a native of Wurtemberg, Germany, and came to Beaver county, Pa., with the Economites, locating in Economy. His wife was Margaret, by whom he had one child, Philip. Philip Bentel, after attaining his manhood, opened a general store in the house he erected in 1832, in the village of

DONALD C. ALLEN.   MRS. DONALD C. ALLEN.
                DONALD C. ALLEN, JR.

Freedom. He conducted the store for a period of thirty years, and in addition, started the bank of Philip Bentel & Company, of which he served as president. This bank is still in existence, and since its establishment, in 1872, it has been known by the above name. Philip Bentel was a very enterprising and successful man, and served in his district as a school director and as a councilman. He was a Lutheran, and a devoted member of that denomination. He was joined in marriage with Margaret Smith, a daughter of Tobias Smith, and she died in 1881, at the age of seventy-five years. Mr. Bentel died in 1883, aged seventy-seven years. They were the parents of the following children: Thalia, the wife of John Conway; Mattie, wedded to Joseph Leadley; John, married to Mary Batey; and Charles H.

Charles H. Bentel was reared and educated in Freedom, and started in life as a store keeper at Alliance, Ohio; one year later, he returned to Freedom, and succeeded his father in the mercantile business, continuing thus for a period of seventeen years. When the bank was established, in 1872, he became cashier, and upon the death of his father, he abandoned the mercantile business; he is president of the bank, as well as owner. Mr. Bentel is a prominent and well-to-do citizen of the village, and possesses the confidence and esteem of a multitude of acquaintances. He is a stanch member of the Presbyterian church, while socially, he has been a member of the Masonic order for the past thirty years.

Mr. Bentel was wedded to Miss Amanda Clark, a daughter of Captain Samuel, and Minerva (Reno) Clark; they are the parents of five children, namely: Annie; Cora F., the wife of the subject of this sketch, who was born in West Virginia, but reared in Pittsburg, Pa.; Thalia; Mattie, who is the wife of J. G. Mitchell, and Philip, who is bookkeeper of the Keystone Lumber Works.

———◆◆———

DONALD C. ALLEN is a dealer in flour and feed in the borough of Beaver Falls, Pa., and is among its most enterprising merchants. He was born near Prospect, Butler county, Pa., August 13, 1860, and is a son of William and Penelope (Lambie) Allen, and grandson of Robert and Jane (Cochran) Allen.

Robert Allen was born in County Down, Ireland, and in 1832, with his wife and family, came to the United States; he settled on a farm in Mercer county, Pa., which had been purchased for him by his son William. There he continued to reside until overtaken by death, which was at the age of eighty-four years. His wife, Jane Cochran, also died at about that age. They were the parents of a family of six children, namely: Margaret (Montgomery); Mary (Stewart); William; Robert; Samuel; and Cochran. William Allen, the father of Donald C., was born in County Down, Ireland, in the year 1815, five years previous to the arrival of his parents in this country, and spent several years on his father's farm in Mercer county. He then went to Pittsburg, Pa., and worked in a wholesale grocery store at No. 196 Liberty street, for a period of ten years. He then engaged in the grocery business in the village of Prospect, Butler county, Pa., successfully continuing thus for ten years; he then sold out his store, bought a saw and grist mill three miles south of that village; rebuilt the mills, and continued in the milling business until death claimed him,—which was in 1879. He was united in the bonds of wedlock with Miss Penelope Lambie, a native of Edinburgh, Scotland, and a daughter of William Lambie; she passed from this earth, in 1897, aged seventy-four years. Their union was blessed by the birth of the following children: Robert, deceased; Agnes, who died aged seventeen years; Marion (McCandless); Jeannette R. (Crabbe); Penelope, the wife of James Balph, a medical missionary, and prominent resident of Latakia, Syria; Margaret, a school teacher; William L., deceased; Donald C., the subject of this brief memoir; and John G., who is in the grocery business in Beaver Falls. Religiously, he was connected with the Reformed Presbyterian church.

Donald C. Allen obtained a good schooling in his native district, and spent his boyhood days in helping his father in the work about the mill; in 1884 he began work at lumbering, but in 1889, he went into the grocery business with his brother, John G. Allen. He continued thus until 1897, when he sold his interests and bought out R. A. Bole, who was engaged in the flour and feed business. Mr.

Allen is well deserving of the large patronage he has already secured, and his genial manners and straightforward business methods have secured for him hosts of friends.

Mr. Allen formed a matrimonial alliance, in 1896, with Miss Mary E. Heiser, a daughter of Daniel Heiser, of Lewisburg, Pa., and their home has been blessed by the birth of one son, Donald C., Jr. Mr. Allen is an active member of the Reformed Presbyterian church; he was the prime mover in establishing the Mission Sunday School at Patterson Heights, and is still a leader in the school. He is a deacon, and a trustee, of the church. On a preceding page is shown the family group, of Donald C. Allen, his wife, and his son, Donald C., Jr.

MARTIN WHITE, one of the successful and popular agriculturists of Darlington township, Beaver county, Pa., is one of the oldest Masons in the district. He is a prominent member of Meridian Lodge, No. 411, F. & A. M., and also of the Chapter and Commandery. Mr. White is a man of considerable intellectual ability. He is not only a sound thinker, but is also an interesting conversationalist, and expresses his views in a clear and concise manner. In politics, he is an ardent Democrat and assumes the aggressive, but could never be prevailed upon to accept office.

Mr. White was born in Allegheny county, Pa., October 28, 1828. He is the eldest son of the late John White, and grandson of

Thomas White. Thomas White was a native of the north of Ireland, where he was reared and educated. He came to America just previous to the breaking out of the Revolutionary War. He took an active part in that long and bloody struggle, and after its successful termination, began trading in Mexico. Upon one of his trips to that country he was captured by bandits. All his earnings were seized, and he was imprisoned for six months. He subsequently purchased land in Kentucky and also along the Monongahela River, in the vicinity of Pittsburg, Pa., the present site of which city was then all farming land. After making some improvements on his land Mr. White sold it, and purchased another tract in Beaver county, whither he removed during the later part of the eighteenth century.

Thomas White was united in marriage with a Miss Martin, and to them were born the following children: James, of Mexico; John, father of the subject hereof; Joseph; Jane (Duncan); Nancy, wife of Judge Caruthers; and Susan (Burns).

John White, father of the gentleman to whom this writing pertains, was born in Allegheny county, Pa., in January, 1802. He attended the public schools of his native county, and, although the opportunities for his mental culture were limited, he made the most of what he could obtain and became a fairly good scholar. He learned the art of tilling the soil and assisted his father for many years. A four-hundred-acre farm fell to him, as his heritage. To this

he added eight hundred acres of land which he purchased in Beaver county. The latter was only partly improved. John White removed to his Beaver county farm in 1850. He further improved his place by building spacious and convenient barns. Besides carrying on general farming, he was a very successful sheep-raiser for many years, and made a great deal of money. But after some years the foot-rot caused much loss among his sheep and that branch of farming was discontinued entirely.

T. Martin White's father was public-spirited and generous. He was one of the men prominent in building railroads from New Galilee to the cannel coal mines. But his efforts in that direction were not appreciated. He failed to receive the support such an enterprise deserved, and lost heavily. He was quite prominent in political and church matters, and his opinions and advice were frequently sought by his neighbors and associates. He served many years as justice of the peace. Five children were born to him and his excellent wife. Their names are: T. Martin, the subject of this biography; John B.; Duncan, who was burned to death; Mary (Waterbury); and James, who died at the age of twenty-one years.

T. Martin White obtained a fair primary education in the public schools, which was supplemented by a thorough course at Hookstown Academy, from which he graduated. Later he worked on the farm for some years, but discontinued that line of work to engage in contracting. He went to New York City ·

and engaged in business quite successfully as a street contractor. He was one of the first men who ever did wood block-paving in that great city. One large contract secured by him was for the paving of Fourteenth street, but he faithfully executed others as large. He did a very successful business. His success was all the more marked from the fact that he had lived most of his life on a farm, and, in a city so important as New York, he was successful in competing with men who had been born and reared there, and possessed the customary shrewdness of city contractors.

Mr. White continued this life for eight years, and was then urged by his parents to return to Beaver county. With a sense of filial duty he gave up fine business prospects and returned home to brighten the declining years of a much-loved father and mother. He at once took charge of the farm, and faithfully fulfilled the obligations devolved upon him until the death of his parents. He and his brother, John B., succeeded to the estate. The subject of our sketch received as his share two hundred and twenty-five acres of the old homestead farm, where he still resides. This is conceded to be one of the best farms in Beaver county. It is almost an assured fact that if crops are poor on this farm there are no good crops in the county.

Mr. White has been twice married. His first union was with Elizabeth Hall, a daughter of Joseph Hall, who was a well known boat builder of Freedom, where the birth of Elizabeth occurred. Her death took place in 1890. Mr. White's second marriage was contracted with Emma Blair, of sturdy Pennsylvania-German stock. She was born in Clarion county, and has presented her husband with one son, T. M., born in 1898. Mr. White is justly regarded as a representative farmer of Darlington township, and liberally supports all religious denominations, having no favorite one.

ON. MILLARD F. MECKLEM. There are but few counties in the state of Pennsylvania that can boast of as many brilliant lawyers as Beaver. They are a class of citizens which, more than any other class, has the power to attract public attention to a community, thus materially aiding in its growth and development. The gentleman, whose name appears above, is one of the most conspicuous members of the bar of the county, and resides at Rochester, where he has an extensive practice. Profound in his knowledge of legal principles and gifted with the power of eloquence, he has long been a prominent figure in the public eye,—serving for some time as president judge of the district.

Mr. Mecklem is a son of Archibald M. and Margaret (Thompson) Mecklem, and was born in Pittsburg, Pa., October 15, 1851. His grandfather was Samuel Mecklem, who, in the year 1800, came from the state of New Jersey to North Sewickley (now Marion) township, Beaver county, Pa., being one of the pioneers of that section, lying in the beautiful valley of Brush Creek. He purchased a tract of land covered with timber, and in the wild state in which it was left by the hand of nature. Stately trees fell before the onslaught of civilization, and a wonderful transformation took place. A log house and barns were erected and the wild lands became fertile fields of pasture and grain. The nearest neighbors were far distant, but there this hardy old pioneer lived in happiness with his wife and children until his death. He married Rachel McDonald, who was of Scotch ancestry, and their children were as follows: Jethro; John; Eli; Samuel; Archibald M.; Gideon; Sarah, the wife of Joseph Wolf; and Eliza, who became the wife of James Jones.

Archibald McDonald Mecklem was born on the old farm in 1806, and as he grew up aided in clearing it. At that early day, money was little used as a medium of exchange, and the produce of the farm was bartered for any article which was desired. It was not easy to obtain an education at that day, and books were very scarce. Ambitious, and not afraid of work, Archibald and his brothers made some splint brooms by taking a green ash tree, pounding the wood, peeling it up from one end, a distance of fifteen inches, and then cutting the balance down to a handle. Happy in the thought of the books these would buy, they made their way to the store, several miles through the snow, and were dismayed to find that their product was rejected, as the market was flooded with just such articles. As the kind merchant noted their disappointment, he asked what it was they wished to buy, and upon being informed that it was books, his

heart went out to them and the exchange was effected. Archibald's diligent search for knowledge led him to abandon the backwoods and seek the culture and refinement of city life. He was yet in his teens, when he went to Pittsburg, and there applied his hand to anything he could find to do. Energetic and saving, he laid by as much of his wages as he could, and in time was enabled to enter the grocery business, which he conducted for many years on Liberty street, near where the Union Station now is. In 1855, he sold out and opened a general merchandise store at Darlington, which he operated for fourteen years, with the best of results. In 1869, feeling the weight of years, he decided to lessen his business cares, and, accordingly, sold out, and kept a small store at North Sewickley. A few years later he died aged sixty-eight years, and was buried in the North Sewickley Cemetery. His first marriage (with Rachel Barris) resulted in the birth of several children, all of whom died in infancy. She died at a very early age, of consumption. Mr. Mecklem formed a second matrimonial alliance with Margaret Thompson, a daughter of Joseph Thompson, a pioneer farmer of North Sewickley, and they had the following issue: Rose, the wife of C. T. Crawford, of Esplin, Pa.; Millard F., the subject of this personal history; Joseph T., a farmer of Franklin township, Beaver county; Jane, the wife of S. S. Bennett, of Rochester; and Ross D., who died in infancy. Mrs. Mecklem died at the age of fifty-nine years. Mr. Mecklem was very strongly opposed to slavery, and assisted in the working of the old "underground railroad." Religiously, he was a faithful adherent to the faith of the Baptist church.

Millard F. Mecklem received a good intellectual training and made the best of his advantages, attending the public schools of Darlington, the North Sewickley Academy, and a private school at the latter place. He taught for several years in the public schools, and then, having decided upon a professional career, registered as a law student in the office of Chamberlain & Pearsol, of New Brighton. He was admitted to the bar on March 10, 1882, and in the fall of that year located at Rochester, where he has since practiced his profession. In 1883, he was elected burgess of Rochester and served with such satisfactory results, that he was five times re-elected. Being a careful and faithful student, and withal, clear minded, he has acquired a fair knowledge of the law, and has secured a large clientage. He rose rapidly in his profession and was chosen district attorney, an office he held for five and one-half years, when he resigned to accept the position of president judge. He succeeded president judge John I. Wickham (who had resigned), and was appointed by Gov. Hastings, being the unanimous choice of the county. Mr. Mecklem then appointed D. M. Twiford, Esq., as his successor as district attorney. He meted out justice in an honest and impartial manner, obtaining favor with the public and the lawyers who practiced in his court. Upon the expiration of his term, before anyone had left the court room he was presented with a beautiful gold-headed cane by W. B. Cuthbertson, Esq., and other well-known attorneys made remarks as to his ability and the esteem in which he was held by all. The Judge accepted in a fitting manner, and with his characteristic, unassuming style. In 1895, he became a director of the First National Bank, of Rochester.

In 1881, Judge Mecklem was united in marriage with Ella Jackson, a daughter of Robert and Eliza (Thompson) Jackson, of North Sewickley township, and their children are: Erle Homer, Norman Jackson, Ella and Margaret Millard. Fraternally, he is a member of the Royal Arcanum and the Order of Elks. He is a member of the Baptist church, and his wife is a consistent member of the Presbyterian church. In 1890, Mr. Mecklem sold the home in which he lived, on Pennsylvania street, and built a handsome residence and office at the corner of Madison and Connecticut streets.

———— ◆ • ◆ ————

WILLIAM CARR, one of the most prosperous and substantial citizens of Rochester, Beaver county, Pa., is the proprietor of a large boot and shoe store in that borough, and is prominently identified with many other business enterprises. He is a son of Robert and Mary (Haw) Carr, and was born in Steubenville, Ohio, October 12, 1848.

Robert Carr, the father of our subject, was born in County Down, Ireland, and after his marriage came to America in 1831, landing in the city of Philadelphia. He moved to Pittsburg, Pa., where he learned the trade of a glass blower, and from there went to Washington county and became a farmer, and several years later moved to Steubenville, Ohio. He took up the trade of a metal worker and followed it with much success until his death, which occurred early in life. His wife was Mary Haw and she attained the ripe old age of ninety-five years, being a hale and hearty woman all her life. Their children were as follows: Jane, the wife of John McCowen; Mary, the wife of Lloyd Parks; Nancy, the wife of Samuel Irvin; John, deceased, whose union with Mahala Campbell resulted in the birth of two children, Thomas and Georgia; Thomas, of Rochester; Robert, also of Rochester; and William, the subject of this writing.

William Carr, the youngest child of the family, attended the public schools, but as his father died leaving a family of small children, he sought employment at an early age. He was an ambitious youth, and while not in school did outside jobs,—at the age of six years acting as firer of glassware. He spent much of his time in the glass factory and acquired such skill that he was later enabled to demand a good position, when he went to Pittsburg. He was employed as finisher for J. B. Lyons, and continued in that capacity until 1872, when the Rochester Tumbler Company was organized. He became a stockholder in this company and helped to build the plant, after which he started the business and continued in it as an active partner until

1895. He then retired from that business, although he is still a stockholder and director, and purchased the store of James Ing in the Darr building. He is one of the leading boot and shoe merchants in Beaver county, and has built up an excellent trade, enjoying the patronage of the leading citizens of the community. He is as honest as he is sagacious in his transactions, and he has made many friends by his upright dealings. He is a stockholder and director of the Rochester Improvement Company, and has built four residences in Rochester, one on Brighton street, and three on Jackson street. His home is on the latter street, and is one of the best in the town.

William Carr was united in marriage at Steubenville, Ohio, with Mary E. Aldridge, who was born in 1848 and died in 1892, and was a daughter of Rodney Aldridge. Their children were: Carrie, deceased, the wife of Henry J. Miller; Edward, who is associated in business with his father; and Nellie, who was united in marriage with Lewis Gillen, of New Brighton. Mr. Carr was again married to Mrs. Annie Newman, who by her first union had five children: Minnie; Eva; William; Frank; and Annie. Mrs. Newman is a daughter of William Boswell. Politically, Mr. Carr is a Republican and served in the borough council three years. He was a delegate to the county convention. He is chairman of the Rochester Centennial to be held in 1900. Fraternally, he is a member of Blue Lodge, No. 229, F. & A. M.; of Eureka Chapter, R. A. M., of Rochester; of Ascalon Commandery, No. 59, K. of T., of Pittsburg; of Pennsylvania Consistory, S. P. R. S., and of Scottish Rites of Pittsburg (being a thirty-second degree Mason); of Rochester Lodge, I. O. O. F.; and of the Elks. Religiously, he is a member of the Episcopal church. He was president of the M. S. Quay club when that organization was in a flourishing condition.

———•••———

DR. WALTER A. ROSE. The gentleman, whose name appears at the opening of this sketch, stands high in his profession, and is known throughout Beaver county as one of the most popular and efficient physicians in the vicinity. A man of commanding appearance and genial presence, he has won for himself many warm friends, and his many excellent qualities of mind, and skill in his profession, have gained for him a large and lucrative practice. He was born in Elgin county, Ontario, Canada, April 17, 1842, and is a son of Alexander and Catherine (Monroe) Rose.

Alexander Rose, the father of our subject, was born near Edinburgh, Scotland, and emigrated to Canada, which was his home the rest of his life. He was a mechanic by trade, but became a speculator. He was among those to start the reformation in Canada, and was closely identified with William Lyon McKenzy and George Lawton. He met death early in life, being drowned in a small lake. He married Catherine Monroe, and their children were as follows: Isabelle, widow of the late John Warburton. living in New York City; Jeannette, deceased, who was married to Elihu Moore; Catherine, who married Colin McDougall, and lives in St. Thomas, Ontario; Margaret, who married Edward Capsey, of Illinois; Rachael, who died in youth; and Walter A., the subject of this biography.

Walter A. Rose attended the public schools of his native town and also the schools at St. Thomas, and registered as a medical student under Dr. Robert L. Sanderson, of Sparta, Ontario. Being of a studious turn of mind, and naturally bright and quick to learn, he made rapid progress, and entered the University of Michigan, remaining there for two years. He then attended the university at Buffalo, N. Y., and graduated from that institution with the class of 1867. He chose Rochester, Pa., for his future home, and began practicing there. It was not long until his fine abilities were recognized, and though he entered the town a complete stranger, he acquired a large practice in a very short time. It is one of the largest in this part of the state, and while it is general, he makes a specialty of the throat and nose. He is spoken of by everyone in the highest terms, and is greatly loved by all in the community. In 1887, he bought a vacant lot, and erected a large and elegant three-story brick building, which is known as the Rose Block, and is on the corner of New York and Brighton streets. The first floor is devoted to his office and reception rooms, and to the First National Bank, and one of the best restaurants in the

town. The second and third floors are finely fitted up for family use. The building is located in the heart of the borough, and is a very handsome and commodious structure.

Dr. Rose is division surgeon for the Pennsylvania R. R. Company. He owns extensive oil interests in Ohio, and has dealt largely in real estate in Rochester. He has done all in his power to further the progress and business interests of Rochester, and we find his name associated with the incorporators of the Rochester Street Railway, the Keystone Tumbler Company, and with the directorship of the Second and Third National Building Associations of Rochester. He is a member and past grand of Rochester lodge, F. & A. M., No. 229, and R. A. M. and Ascalon Commandery, No. 59, K. T., Allegheny, Pa., and of the Scottish Rites Masonic Commandery of Pittsburg, No. 320, and the Syria Temple, Nobles of the Mystic Shrine of Pittsburg. He is examining physician of the Maple Leaf order, Woodmen of the World.

———— • • ————

JOHN B. YOUNG. A history of Beaver county would be quite incomplete without a sketch of the oldest member of the Beaver county bar. Such is the gentleman whose name appears at the head of these lines, whose important legal connections and recognized ability have placed him in the front rank of distinguished lawyers of this county. He is a resident of Beaver, and is at present serving his third term as justice of the peace of that borough. He was born at Achor, Columbiana county, Ohio, August 25, 1834, and is a son of Jacob Young, and a grandson of Baltzer Young.

Baltzer Young was born in Germany, but in his early manhood, he came to the United States, and first settled in Philadelphia; he subsequently traveled west on the Little Beaver River to Columbiana county, Ohio, and there took up a tract of land. He erected saw, grist and (later) carding mills, and the place was known as Young's Mills; these were destroyed by fire, and he built other mills, which have since been removed to Negley by his grandson, and are still in use, although their running power has been changed from water to steam. He also operated a large farm in addition to milling. He passed from this life, aged eighty-five years. His wife was Susanna Boose, by whom he reared a large family of children. Those who grew to maturity were: Jacob; John; Peter; Samuel; George; David; Mary; Elizabeth; Margaret; and Rachel.

Jacob Young was born in Philadelphia, Pa., and succeeded his father in the mills; he also kept a store many years, but in his fondness for the farm, he sold out, bought a large tract of land, and began tilling the soil. He also engaged in sheep raising, and once owned several hundred sheep. At the time of his retirement at Achor, Ohio, he owned eleven hundred acres of land. He died there, aged sixty years. He wedded Susanna Brown, a daughter of George and Alice Brown, and she also died in her sixtieth year. They were the parents of the following children: George; Alice; Jacob Boose; Sarah G.; Rachel; Matilda Jane; Rebecca; Mary Ann; Peter B.; John B.; Caroline A.; and Emily.

John B. Young obtained his elementary education in the public schools, and in Beaver Academy, and in the meantime decided to adopt the profession of a lawyer. In order to pursue his studies in that direction, he entered the law office of Hon. Thomas Cunningham, and was subsequently admitted to the bar, in 1858. He immediately opened an office in Beaver, where he has continuously practiced up to the present time, and the great ability and keen judgment displayed in the handling of his cases have not only made him well known before the Beaver county bar, but have placed him in the ranks of the foremost attorneys in Western Pennsylvania. Since 1861, in addition to the regular practice of the law, he has also served as pension attorney. Besides being prominent as a lawyer, he is equally prominent as a man of affairs; he has been honored with the office of district attorney of Beaver county, trustee of Beaver Academy, chief burgess of Beaver, and is now serving his third term as justice of the peace. In 1864, he enlisted in Company H, 5th Reg., Pa. Heavy Artillery, and was honorably discharged in 1865, at the close of the war.

Mr. Young married Anna Böcking, a daughter of Adolph and Mary Böcking,— both natives of Prussia; her parents came to this country in 1849. Mr. Böcking was a landscape artist of great talent, and many of his pictures have taken the highest awards in New York City, Philadelphia, Pittsburg, and many other large cities. Mr. and Mrs. Young reared the following children: Elma Jennett, who is the wife of G. W. McGraw, of Pittsburg, Pa., and has four children (Ethel, George W., Elizabeth A., and John B.); Louis A., who is a harnessmaker and grocer, at Denver, Colorado, and married Ida Mansfield (by whom he reared John B., and Louis A., Jr.); Annie C.; Maude E., who wedded L. L. Mosher, attorney-at-law, at Indianola, Iowa, and had five children (Lee, Wendell P., Donovan, Edith and Hugh); Amelia B., who wedded Charles L. Sheets, of Beaver Falls, Pa., and has one son (Oliver Byron); William T., who is a harnessmaker living at Mercer, Pa.; Alice; Pearl; and Anna Melinka. The subject of this sketch was a strong antislavery man, and supported the Republican ticket from the holding of the first Republican conference at Pittsburg, Pa., until after President Grant's first election, since which time he has been a radical reformer,—advocating municipal and governmental ownership, cooperation in the production and distribution of wealth as distinguished from competition, the necessity of the initiative and referendum, and the "single tax," as one of the coming reforms. Religiously, he is a member of the Baptist church, while his wife is a member of the Presbyterian denomination. Mr. Young is a man of fine appearance and popular manners, and is a favorite with all who know him; his courteous deportment and genial ways have gained for him the confidence, esteem and good-will of a host of acquaintances. His portrait appears on a preceding page.

———◆◆◆———

ITUS M. WELSH is superintendent of the Union Water Company of Beaver Falls, Pa., in which capacity he has efficiently served since the first of January, 1895. He is a prominent and well-to-do citizen and is always interested in the growth and prosperity of his adopted borough; his birthplace was in Chippewa township, in this county, and he is a son of John W. and Jeannette (Garwood) Welsh, and a grandson of Andrew Welsh.

The great-grandfather of the subject hereof was James Welsh, who was of Welsh extraction. His son, Andrew, the grandfather of Titus M., was the member of the family who came to this country, and he is classed among the old settlers of Chippewa township, Beaver county, Pa., having taken up a large tract of land there; his occupation was farming. Politically, he was an Old Line Whig, and later a Republican; he served as justice of the peace of Chippewa township, and was popularly known as "Squire" Welsh. He was a soldier in the War of 1812, and was at Erie when Commodore Perry overwhelmingly defeated the British squadron. He was married to Keziah Newkirk and they reared a family of children, one of whom was John W.

John W. Welsh was born on his father's farm in Chippewa township, in 1826, and there spent his entire life tilling the soil; he passed from this earth in 1894. In politics, he was a Republican, while religiously, he was a member of the Methodist church. His union with the mother of the subject hereof resulted in the birth of the following children: Titus M.; Moses B., deceased; Franklin P., a resident of Beaver Falls; Ira E., who is a farmer living in Erie county, Pa.; Phoebe, who is the wife of Ollie J. Wallace, of Homewood, Beaver county; Andrew Morris, deceased; Lucius Wright, deceased; Lizzie J., who is the wife of William Wallace of Thompson, Beaver county; Addie K., who was wedded to Chauncey Robinson, of Connellsville, Pa.; Richard W., who resides at Mahoningtown, Pa.; and one who died in its infancy.

Titus M. Welsh obtained a thorough intellectual training in the public schools of Chippewa township and at Beaver Academy, but the practical portion of his education was received through actual business experience. He worked on the homestead until a year after his marriage, in 1867, and then moved to Beaver Falls, where he accepted a position as file hardener in the file works of that borough. After continuing in that capacity for two years, he went to Conneautville, Crawford county, Pa., where he spent one year, as a partner in a carriage wheel factory, which was subsequently destroyed by fire,—Mr. Welsh thus sustaining a severe loss. Returning to Beaver Falls he took up his former position in the file works, but in 1880, he entered the employ of Emerson, Smith & Company as steam engineer; after remaining in their service ten years he lost his position during a strike, but afterwards accepted a like situation with the Carnegie Company. In September, 1894, Mr. Welsh resigned from this connection, and, at the beginning of the following year, entered upon his present work as superintendent of the Union Water Company of Beaver Falls.

In politics, Mr. Welsh is a Republican, and served three years as a member of the council from the sixth ward, and also as a congressional delegate. Socially, he is a member of the I. O. O. F., also of the Encampment of Beaver Falls; and of the Woodmen of the World. His marriage to Miss Lizzie J. Inman, a daughter of Azariah and Jane Inman, was blessed by the birth of five children: Frank I., who is employed in the American Steel Works of Beaver Falls; Albertice A., who died aged two years; Lorena M., who died aged seven years; Clyde W., who works in the same mill as does his brother, Frank I.; and Wilber L., who is engaged with L. D. Clark, wholesale confectioner, Beaver Falls.

--- ⇥ • • ⇤ ---

GEORGE F. WEHR is one of the substantial and prominent citizens of the town of Rochester, Pa. He is president of the borough council, and takes a deep interest in the growth and welfare of his adopted town. Besides being interested in various enterprises in Rochester, he is also superintendent of the etching and cutting department of the Phoenix Glass Company, of Monaca, Pennsylvania. He was born near Lancaster, Butler county, Pa., February 19, 1864, and is a son of Frederick and Elizabeth (Martsolf) Wehr.

George F. Wehr's father was born in Germany, and upon coming to the United States, he located in Butler county, Pa., where he became the owner of a fine farm; he successfully followed farming all his life, and passed away at the age of eighty-four years. His first wife died leaving a family of four children: Andrew; Michael; Lizzie; and Kate. The subject of our sketch was the only child born of the second union, and his mother is now living at Monaca, Pennsylvania.

Mr. Wehr was eleven years of age when he entered school at Allegheny, and remained there until he was fourteen. At that age he began clerking for George Bechtell, at Monaca, but a year later he accepted a position with the Rochester Glass Manufacturing Company, working in the punch department, of which he afterwards became foreman. He later became manager of the coloring department in the Phoenix Glass Company, of Monaca, but at the present time he is superintendent of the etching and cutting department. Mr. Wehr has been a member of the council during the past three years, and, since 1897, has served as president of that body. The council of Rochester was established by an act of the legislature, March 20, 1849, which was signed by Gov. William F. Johnston and town clerk George St. Clair Murry.

September 16, 1884, Mr. Wehr was united in marriage with Miss Emma Stiles, a daughter of Atlas Stiles, of Rochester, and she died

ALFRED M. WHISLER, D.D.S.

leaving two children: Willie Atlas, born June 5, 1885; and Martha Elizabeth, born June 23, 1887. February 13, 1890, he wedded Mrs. Emma R. Marshall, a daughter of George Young, also of Rochester, and from this union the following children have resulted, namely: George Frederick, born July 21, 1894, died January 6, 1895; and Annie Marie and Andrew Howard, twins, born April 7, 1896. The subject of this sketch occupies a neat residence on the corner of Vermont and Jefferson streets, which he erected in 1893. He formerly resided where A. Neidergall now lives on Jefferson street. Mr. Wehr was reared a Lutheran but is a member, trustee and steward of the Methodist church. Socially, he is a member of the I. O. O. F.; Rebecca Lodge; K. of P.; Jr. O. U. A. M.; Elks Lodge; Protective Home Circle; and the Fidelity Mutual Life Association.

———— ◄ • ► ————

ALFRED M. WHISLER, D. D. S., the oldest practicing dentist in New Brighton, Beaver county, Pa., has for many years occupied a high position in the town, and is greatly esteemed by all his fellow-citizens. He was born in Rochester, Pa., October 13, 1839, and is a son of John H. and Agnes (Jackson) Whisler.

Jacob Whisler, the grandfather of our subject, was a son of Christian Whisler. Jacob was born in Virginia, whence he moved to Lancaster county, Pa., about 1814, and after-ward came to the vicinity of Beaver county, where he settled, in Pulaski township. There he bought and cleared up a farm,—a government tract consisting of 160 acres,—which is now owned by Mr. Stuber, and is said to be a very valuable piece of land. Jacob Whisler served in the Revolutionary War, and died when more than seventy years old. His wife, whose maiden name was Catherine Hart, died at the age of eighty. Their children were: Benjamin, Jacob, Andrew, Joseph, and John H. John H. Whisler was born near Carlisle, Cumberland county, Pa., in 1802, and in early manhood taught school during the winter. He apprenticed himself as boat-builder to John Boles, of Bolesville, Beaver county, and later became Mr. Boles' partner in business. He then bought Mr. Boles' share in the business and followed boat building for the remainder of his active life. He made principally cotton and canal boats. In his later years, he was a silent partner of S. Barnes & Co., clay manufacturers. He married Agnes Jackson, a daughter of James Jackson, one of the pioneer settlers of Pulaski township. Agnes Jackson was a relative of General Andrew Jackson, her father being a cousin of the general. Mr. Whisler died at the age of eighty-two, and his wife died at the age of eighty. Their children were as follows: Jackson, deceased; Leander, of Sioux City, Iowa; John H., living in Rochester; Jeremiah; Alfred M., the subect of this biography; Addison W., a reporter, of Rochester, formerly a boat builder, who married Rebecca Q. Brobeck; Amanda J., deceased; Charles

F., deceased; and Mary Ellen, who was the wife of the late R. H. Kerr. Mr. Wheeler's father was an active politician, and held several minor offices. He helped to build the Presbyterian church at Bridgewater, Pa., and was an elder therein. At the time of his death, he was the only living original member.

Alfred M. Whisler became a student of dentistry with James Murray, of Bridgewater, and practiced his profession in Rochester, with T. J. Chandler, from 1862 to 1867. He then moved to New Brighton, and located in the office which he now occupies. He could not stand higher in the profession than he does, and he has worked up a large and lucrative practice. For many years he has made a specialty of gold crown work, bridge work, and the like. His patrons are from the oldest and best families, and his practice is ever increasing. He married Mamie M. Marquis, a daughter of Dr. D. S. Marquis, of Rochester, Pa., and their children are as follows: Gracie S., who died at the age of eight years; Edward B., a clerk in the auditor's office of the P. & L. E. R. R.; Frazier, who married E. Kinney Lowe, of Washington, D. C., and has one child, William R. The subject of our sketch is a Democrat. He attends the Presbyterian church; is a member of Union Lodge, No. 259, F. & A. M., of New Brighton, Pa., and served as worshipful master in 1877, '78, '79 and '86. He was high priest of Harmony Chapter, No. 206, in 1889. Dr. Whisler's portrait accompanies the above account of his life.

RICHARD J. MARLATT, who is a representative of the younger generation of farmers of Beaver county, cultivates a fine farm of one hundred and fifty-two acres located in Chippewa township. He is a man of enterprise, quick to adopt all modern and improved methods of farming, and has attained a degree of success which is surprising in one so young. He is a son of Michael and Abbie (Allison) Marlatt, and was born in Beaver county, September 7, 1875, on the old homestead, where he now lives.

His grandfather was Richard Marlatt, who was born in New Jersey, where he was educated and learned the trade of a carpenter. this he followed there for some years and also after his removal to Sewickley, where he died at an advanced age.

Michael Marlatt, the father of Richard J., was born in New Jersey in 1830, and, although his educational advantages were limited, he acquired a good mental training. The school terms were of but three months' duration, and he was able to attend but a short time. He was an accurate mathematician, a discriminating reader, and a profound thinker, and had he had but the opportunity presented to the student of today, he would undoubtedly have created a name for himself along professional lines. He was obliged to adopt a mechanical career, and it was but natural that he should choose the trade of his father, that of a carpenter. He assisted his father and then followed the business for himself for some time, after which he hired out as a farm hand by the day. He then bought a small farm near Leetsdale, Pa., and did a general market-gardening business, hauling to Pittsburg. He had to haul the produce the entire way, and it was by working and sleeping out of doors that he lost his hearing, a very sad affliction for one of such intelligence. Selling his Leetsdale property, he went to Beaver Falls, bought building lots and worked at his trade; but owing to his wife's poor health, he traded his city property for the farm on which the subject of this record now lives, and in addition gave a money consideration. It is an improved farm of 152 acres, one-half of which is cleared, and has a good house. He erected new barns and did a general gardening business,—retailing in Beaver Falls. He set out three elegant orchards, and engaged in dairying and stock-raising. In 1898, in the sixty-ninth year of his age, he died very suddenly while engaged in work upon his farm. His wife was Abbie Allison, who was born in Allegheny county, in 1836, and they reared the following children: Joseph, a pastor of the M. E. church in Tacoma, Washington, and a graduate of Meadville Academy; Amy (Hendrickson); Charles, superintendent of Morado Park; Sadie (Wells), deceased; Robert, a farmer; Rev. Wesley, a graduate of Geneva College and formerly a successful attorney, who received the degree of D. D. from the University of Michigan, and died while pastor of the M. E. church at Johnstown, Pa.; William, a farmer who now assists the subject hereof; and Richard J., whose name heads these lines. Politically, Mr. Marlatt was a

Republican and served as school director and supervisor. He was a trustee of the M. E. church.

Richard J. Marlatt received a good intellectual training in the district schools, and has lived his entire life upon the old home farm. Upon his father's death, the farm descended to his heirs, and our subject has since had its management. Self-reliant and industrious, he has cultivated the farm in the most approved style, and his efforts have been attended by the greatest success. He follows closely the footsteps of his father, doing a large general market business, and also has the place stocked with good cattle and horses. He has a wide knowledge on the subject of farming, and his opinions are respected to a degree not usually accorded one so young. He is very popular with his fellow-citizens, having a large circle of friends throughout the township. Politically, he is a Republican, but does not aspire to office. He is a faithful member of the Methodist Episcopal church.

ERNST H. SEIPLE, the genial and efficient cashier of the Union National Bank of New Brighton, Pa., has occupied that important position since 1894. The bank is finely located at the corner of Ninth street and Third avenue in the Merrick building, which was purchased and especially fitted up with suitable equipments for the purpose. The interior is finely furnished with a superb set of modern fixtures and contains office, director's and president's rooms, with burglar and fireproof safe of the most modern design. The bank has a capital stock of $50,000, and is doing a substantial business, conducted on safe lines. C. M. Merrick was the first president. The first vice-president was E. Autenreith, who was succeeded by J. F. Miner. E. H. Seiple, cashier, C. C. Keck, assistant cashier, and H. R. Boots, messenger, complete the force.

Ernst H. Seiple was born in New Hamburg, Mercer county, Pa., in 1864. He is a son of Joseph H. and Sarah (Beil) Seiple. Joseph H. Seiple was also a native of Mercer county, Pa., and early in life, engaged in merchandizing at New Hamburg, Pa., and later at Greenville. He subsequently retired from mercantile pursuits to a farm, which he had previously purchased. The remainder of his days was spent in the uneventful quietude of agriculture,—a life which he thoroughly enjoyed until called away by death, at the age of seventy years. His faithful wife was Sarah Beil, a lady of many estimable qualities. She died at the early age of forty-two years, leaving the following children: Elizabeth, wife of Charles T. Bortz, of Kent, Ohio; David A.; Clara A.; Milton S., of Greenville, Pa.; Ernst H., the subject of these lines; Mary, wife of J. W. Long, of Youngstown, Ohio; and Nevin Deha, of New Brighton, Pa. Mr. Seiple attended the public schools, after which he took a finishing course at Tiehl College. He then began his career in life, accepting a position as clerk in the Greenville National

Bank, where he remained from 1882 to 1884; he then was a clerk for four years, at the National Bank of Beaver County. For the following two years, he was teller in the First National Bank at Rochester, Pa. After this he was with the auditor, the treasurer, and the purchasing agent, in the general offices of the Pittsburg & Lake Erie Railroad, at Pittsburg. When the Union National Bank of New Brighton was established, April 20, 1891, Mr. Seiple was elected assistant cashier, which position he filled in a highly capable manner. Since his residence in New Brighton, he has taken a very active interest in the progress and development of that town. He purchased the Merrick homestead at the corner of Fourteenth street and Third avenue, and fitted it up handsomely for his family. He is a stockholder of the Standard Horse Nail Company, the Beaver Valley Traction Company, and is treasurer of the Beaver County and New Brighton Building and Loan Association.

On July 9, 1894, the subject of this sketch was joined in marriage with Charlotta Weber, a daughter of Henry Weber, of Meadville, Pa., and their home is brightened by the presence of one daughter, Elizabeth. Mr. Seiple was reared in accordance with the doctrine of the German Reformed church, but is now a supporter of the Presbyterian denomination. Socially, he is a member of the Union Lodge, No. 259, F. & A. M., and also of the Harmony Chapter, No. 206, of the R. A. M. Mr. Seiple has shown himself in all his experience in life, to be capable of conducting his individual business with equally

as great success as he has served the public interests. It is needless to say, that our subject is justly entitled to the appreciation of his friends. Unaided, when little more than a youth, he began, in this land of equal opportunities, to achieve that success, which energy and perseverance assure, and to exert that influence which ability and fidelity command. He is the advocate of every cause considered worthy, and has the courage to proclaim his convictions.

———— ◆ ◆ ————

HENRY C. FRY, whose portrait is shown on the opposite page, to whom much credit is due as the principal organizer of the Rochester Tumbler Company, the most extensive manufacturers of pressed and blown tumblers in the world, is a man of thorough business qualifications, and, through his connection with numerous enterprises, has attained a wide reputation. He has done much to aid in the progress of Rochester, as the tumbler works, of which he is president, constitute the principal industry of the borough. He was also the chief organizer of the First National Bank, of Rochester, of which he has been president since its incorporation. He has always evinced the deepest interest in the welfare of his fellowmen, alleviating their distress whenever he could do so, and encouraging them by gentle and sympathizing counsel; for these little kindnesses of word and deed, he will be long remembered by the citizens of the community after his demise. He is respected and loved in Rochester as but few of its residents are. Mr. Fry was born in Lexington, Ky., September 17, 1840, and is a son of Thomas C. and Charlotte Fry.

John Fry, his grandfather, was born in the North of Ireland, and, with his brother, William, emigrated from Dublin to New York City, locating at Wilkesbarre, Pa., soon after, and still later in Washington county, Pennsylvania. The brothers were possessed of ample means and invested extensively in real estate. They were descended from a prominent Irish family, and had, each, an excellent education, for that day. In the early part of the nineteenth century, John Fry moved to Lexington, Ky., and bought a large tract of land, upon which he built a handsome brick mansion. There he resided until his death, at the age of almost ninety years, and was buried in a cemetery on a portion of his own land. The city of Lexington is built on his land, with the exception of some two hundred acres, and the old homestead known as the "Elms" is owned by his descendants. He married Elizabeth Miller, a lady of Scotch birth, and they had three children: William, Eliza and Thomas C.

Thomas C. Fry, the father of Henry C., was born in the city of New York, and during his early years was connected with the firm of Curling, Robinson & Co., glass manufacturers, of Pittsburg. He spent the remainder of his life at the "Elms," at Lexington, Ky. He married Charlotte Fry, who died at the age of fifty-six years, and among their large family of children, was Henry C., the subject of this record.

Henry C. Fry, endowed with superior talents, a sturdy constitution, and an ambitious temperament, at an early age sought activity in the business world. He was sixteen years old when he went to Pittsburg, bearing good recommendations, and obtained employment as a shipping clerk for the firm of William Phillips & Co., manufacturers of glass. He continued in their service until 1862, when he enlisted in the 15th Reg., Pa. Vol. Cav., as a private. Upon being mustered out of service in 1864, he became a member of the firm of Lippencott, Fry & Co., manufacturers of glass, which was afterward changed to Fry & Scott, and still later, to Fry, Semple & Reynolds. In the spring of 1872, he, with others, went to Rochester and purchased the Lacock property of ten acres, which had formerly been a beautiful maple grove, and a portion of which was, at a later period, the brickyard of G. Agner. The Rochester Tumbler Company was formed by these gentlemen, and they built a plant on this property,—all of the members of the company taking an active interest in the work. The company comprised the following well-known business men: H. C. Fry, G. W. Fry, S. M. Kane, William Moulds, S. H. Moulds, Thomas Carr, William Carr, Thomas Matthews, John Hayes, J. H. Lippencott, and Richard Welsh. Two years later their establishment was burned to the ground, but was immediately rebuilt, the following men being then added to the firm: George Searles, Robert Carr, and John Carr.

They manufactured both pressed and blown glass tumblers, and their work met with such success that they have been obliged to enlarge the plant and increase their facilities from time to time, so that it is now the leading establishment of its kind in the world. They ship direct to all parts of the United States, England, and other portions of Europe, South America, Africa, Australia, China and Japan, —sending out from three to ten carloads per day. A switch runs through the middle of the plant, and thus the loading is all done under cover. They do not depend upon others for the material they use in the factory, but make their own barrels, boxes and crates for shipping; they grind clay and make pots, and also manufacture their own molds. They have a private electric light plant, using 1,000 incandescent lights daily; they have their own water works, and a tank with a capacity of 3,100 gallons, which is also connected with the city water works; they have an ice house for drinking purposes. They employ a permanent force of twelve hundred men and women, and have an output of 150,000 dozen of blown goods per month, and 150,000 dozen of pressed goods. Each department of the works is kept at a high state of efficiency,— nearing perfection,—as the most skilled men in the business are in their employ. While the best of order is maintained throughout their establishment, each employee, from the skilled cut-glass worker to the apprentice, feels free from constraint, and wears a contented expression upon his countenance. The firm has been considerably changed since it was first organized, and as it exists today, is: H. C. Fry, president; William Moulds, general manager; S. H. Moulds, assistant manager; J. H. Fry, secretary; and Clayton Vance, treasurer.

In June, 1883, Henry C. Fry actively assisted in the organization of the First National Bank, of Rochester, with a capital of $50,000, and it has been a successful institution from the start,—having at the present time a surplus of $40,000. The subject of this writing has served as president since its inception, and his skilful management has been a prime factor in its prosperity. I. T. Mansfield is vice-president, and T. H. Fry is cashier. Henry C. Fry is also a director and stockholder of the Olive Stove Works, and of the Rochester Electric Light Company, of which he was at one time president. In 1876, Mr. Fry built his residence on a part of the original Pinney estate, one of the most desirable locations in the borough, situated on the corner of New York and West Jackson streets. At one time he owned the adjoining lots, having a large and beautiful lawn, and also the corner property opposite his residence, on which there is located a noted spring which furnishes his house with an abundance of pure water. The spring has quite a history, and is well remembered by the early settlers in that vicinity. Indians were wont to camp about it, and it was known as the "Cure All." It is now under cover, and a beautiful lawn and vineyard add to the delightful spot. Mr. Fry is a man of pleasing personality and great strength of character, one of his chief characteristics being to make others happy.

The subject of this biography formed a matrimonial alliance with Emma Matthews, of Pittsburg, a woman attractive in her many virtues, who, by her kindliness of heart, made friends with everyone. She was a loving wife and mother, and their home was one of the greatest happiness until she closed her eyes in final sleep, in 1884. Five children resulted from this union: Harry C., associated with the Rochester Tumbler Company, who married Rachel Power; Clara, the wife of H. J. Sage; Gertrude, who married A. M. Jenkinson; J. Howard, who is also identified with the company; and Mabel, who is attending Vassar College. Mr. Fry formed a second alliance, with Belle McClintock, a woman beloved for her many excellent traits of character. He is a faithful member, and a liberal financial supporter, of the Baptist church, in which he has served as a trustee and deacon. For the past twenty-four years he has served as superintendent of the Sunday School.

———— • • ————

WILLIAM R. HAZEN, who is widely known throughout Western Pennsylvania as superintendent of the Beaver Valley Traction Company, has efficiently served that company since 1885, when horse cars were still used. He is a son of Isaac and Mary (Olinger) Hazen, and was born in North Sewickley township, Beaver county, Pa., in 1862.

James Hazen, the grandfather of William

R., was one of the pioneers of Beaver county, moving here when it was a complete wilderness and settling in North Sewickley township. Clearing a place, he built a log house and barns, and lived there the remainder of his life. Among the children born to him and his wife Jerusha, was Isaac, father of the subject of this writing.

Isaac Hazen was born in North Sewickley township and received his intellectual training in the public schools. He learned the occupation of a farmer and assisted his father upon the farm for some time; he then purchased a tract of eighty acres for himself, clearing it and constructing thereon good substantial buildings. He improved the place, placing it under a high state of cultivation, and lived there throughout his life. His wife's maiden name was Mary Olinger, and by her he had seven children, as follows: Amariah (Fogle); William R.; Laura (Thompson); Nettie (Nye); Violetta (Miller); Lizzie (Smith); and Howard. Politically, Mr. Hazen was a Democrat and served as school director. He was a Baptist in his religious views.

William R. Hazen was given a common school education and spent his younger days in assisting his father upon the farm, but in 1880 he removed to Beaver Falls and adopted a mechanical career. He was naturally adapted to this and acquired a high degree of skill at it. He was first employed in the cutlery works, then in the axe factory, and later in the file factory. He continued in the file works until 1885, when he became interested in the street car company at Beaver Falls, and after being connected with the road for one year he was given charge of the stables. He continued in that capacity until 1892, when the horses were supplanted by electricity, and the road was transformed into an electric road. Until the road was placed in good working order he served as conductor for two months, and as such met with a very serious accident which compelled him to lay off for one year. Upon his return to duty, he was appointed to the post of car dispatcher and served in that position until 1898, when he was promoted to the office of general superintendent of the road. The responsibilities of the position are many and arduous, but he has ever discharged the duties of his trust to the best of his ability, and to the entire satisfaction of the officials of the company. The lines over which he has supervision extend from Morado Park to the lower end of Beaver, Pa., being mostly double track and continuous rails. There are fifty-five men in his employ. The power-house is in Beaver Falls, a one-story brick structure, with dimensions of 120x60 feet, and was built in 1892. It is equipped with two very powerful Buckeye engines of 140 and 125 horse power respectively, with four dynamos of immense power, and is fitted with the Thompson-Houston equipment. It also supplies power for the Patterson Heights Inclined Electric Road, and for the Beaver & Vanport line. The car barn is located in Rochester township in a very pretentious building of vitrified brick, the dimensions being 260x120 feet, and besides storing all of the cars, it contains the superintendent's office, the general offices and the mess room for employees. Mr. Hazen resides in a very desirable home at No. 2715 College avenue, which he owns. He is a man of pleasing character and his nature abounds in good will toward his employees and his fellow-citizens, by whom he is held in the highest esteem.

William R. Hazen was united in marriage with Irene Jackson, who was born in Beaver Falls, where she attended the public schools. She was graduated from the Beaver Falls High School, and then taught school until her marriage. They became the parents of three children, namely: Earle and Lyle, twins, born in 1891; and Fern, who was born in 1892. Politically, Mr. Hazen is a Democrat, and is a member of the council from College Hill Borough, and also a school director. In religious views he is a Baptist. Fraternally, he is a member of the Knights of the Golden Eagle, and the K. of L.

GAWN WARD, a very prominent citizen of Beaver Falls, Beaver county, Pa., was for many years one of the most active business men in that locality, being proprietor of a hardware store just prior to his retirement on January 1, 1899. He came to the borough when its population numbered less than three thousand, but having entire confidence in its future, he bought considerable property in what is now the heart of the town, and conducted the first store in the section. He became a promoter of various industries, and has ever striven for the best interests of Beaver Falls. It is to the efforts of such men that the prosperity of the borough is due.

Mr. Ward is a son of James and Margaret (Cleland) Ward, and was born in County Down, Ireland, in 1836. His grandfather was Robert Ward, who was born in England and moved to the North of Ireland when a young man, buying fifty acres of rich farm land. He engaged in general farming and devoted ten acres to the culture of moss. He was the father of two children by his first marriage, James and Arthur.

James Ward was born in County Down, Ireland, and was instructed in the common schools, after which he bought a small farm of twenty acres. He married Margaret Cleland, a daughter of Gawn and Agnes Cleland, members of an ancient Scottish family which settled in the North of Ireland, and they had ten children, as follows: Robert; Hugh; Arthur; William; John; Agnes; one who died unnamed; Gawn; Thomas; and Matthew. All the boys took to farming and the two girls died in infancy. In 1844, James Ward came to America with his family, locating in New York City, where for sixteen years he conducted a bakery and grocery store with considerable success. In 1860, he removed to Allegheny City, Pa., where he kept a grocery store for the balance of his life. His death occurred in 1887, and in him the city lost a man prominently identified with its business interests, and one who was by everybody highly esteemed. He was a Republican in politics, whilst in religious attachments, he was formerly a Presbyterian, but at the time of his demise, a Methodist.

Gawn Ward was instructed in the public schools of New York City, after which he assisted his father in the store, thus at an early age acquiring a thorough knowledge of business methods. When he moved to Allegheny City with his father, he conducted a store on his own account, and with good results, for a period of nine years. In 1871, he located at Beaver Falls, which was then a flourishing place of about 3,000 inhabitants. With remarkable foresight, Mr. Ward noted the direction in which the town would grow, and purchased a piece of ground in the heart of the present business district, being the first man to open up business there. Merchants in the lower end of the town were accustomed to joke him about being located in the country, but to the intense satisfaction of Mr. Ward, the wisdom of his choice was brought home to them. The men who laughed began to regret that they had not likewise invested, when they saw the center of business gradually move in that direction, and they were reluctant to pay prices much in advance of former valuations. Mr. Ward started in a frame building on Main street, now Seventh avenue, between Tenth and Eleventh streets, and there were only two or three other houses in the vicinity, including the Economy Bank. Almost immediately the town began to build up, new factories were located there, and busi-

ness was enlivened throughout that section of the county. The axe manufacturing establishment was started, also the Emerson, Smith & Co. Saw Works; the P. & L. E. R. R. came through, and numerous other enterprises started. Mr. Ward became a promoter, and was for nine years treasurer, of the Co-operative Stove Foundry, during which time he also kept a general store. The grade of the street was cut down and he erected a brick store building, which he still owns, and which is occupied by a drug store. He then dropped the general store and conducted a grocery store exclusively, but a short time subsequent thereto, he, in partnership with J. D. Perrot and Jacob Ecki, bought the Howard Stove Works. After running that for some years, he sold his interest to his partners and engaged in the hardware business, having a very large trade. He dealt in builders' supplies, house furnishings, hardware and stoves, paints and glass, and for many years was a special agent in the territory, for Baldwin & Graham's supplies, Frankie steel ranges, and Alaska refrigerators. On January 1, 1899, after a most active career, in which he acquired a handsome competency, including considerable valuable property, he retired to spend the remaining years of his life in the enjoyment of a well-earned rest. He therefore sold his stock, rented his store, and took up his residence in his beautiful house located on Eighth avenue, above Twelfth street, which he built in 1896. It is one of the most striking residences in Beaver Falls, and is built from plans of his own. Mr. Ward owns most of the stores on one side of Seventh avenue, between Tenth and Eleventh streets,— among the best known being the offices of the Union Water Company, the Western Union Telegraph office, Schaefer's jewelry store, Nye's barber shop, a drug store and a tailor store. He also owns a corner dwelling with an adjoining office, the hardware store which he conducted for so many years, a building on Twelfth street between Ninth and Tenth avenues, and some very choice building lots in Sewickley borough, Allegheny county, Pennsylvania.

In New York, Mr. Ward was united in matrimonial bonds with Margaret Orr, a daughter of William and Dorothy Orr, who was born and educated in the North of Ireland, and they became the parents of ten children, as follows: Dorothy; Thomas W., who is engaged in business with his father; Margaret (Barnes), now deceased; Charles, a machinist by trade; James G., who is connected with the Heat & Light Company, of Allegheny City; William H., who was also in business with his father; Arthur, who is in the employ of the Union Drawn Steel Company; John E., who follows the trade of a machinist; and Agnes (Walters), whose husband was a prominent jeweler of Beaver Falls, and is now deceased. Politically, our subject is a Republican, and has been a member of the council for seven years, but has declined all other offices. Religiously, he is a member of the Methodist Episcopal church, and is a trustee, steward, and treasurer of the board. He belongs to the A. O. U. W.

WILLIAM M. DONALDSON, one of the foremost business men of Big Beaver township, Beaver county, Pa., has for some years discharged the multitudinous duties of general manager of the firm of H. Donaldson's Sons, manufacturers of white lead kegs, and general coopers, and in this capacity he has displayed unusual ability. He is also a member of the firm and the plant under his control is quite an extensive one, the daily output numbering 700 kegs of various sizes. He is a son of Henry and Ann (Proctor) Donaldson, and was born in Brooklyn, N. Y., January 25, 1849.

His grandfather was Arthur Donaldson, who was of Scotch parentage. He was a cooper by trade and made that his life work. He died at an early age of cholera, when that dread disease was epidemic. He reared four sons: Joseph, a cooper by trade, who was a tank builder for war vessels during the war, but spent his last days in Connecticut in agricultural pursuits, dying in 1890; Henry, who was the father of William M.; George, who was engaged in coopering; and Elisha, also a cooper, in the employ of the Atlantic White Lead Company.

Henry Donaldson was born in New York in 1816, and was educated in the public schools, receiving a good mental training despite the fact that his opportunities were very limited. Like his father and brothers, he undertook coopering and entered the employ of Christopher Tyler, a New York refiner, who established a refinery in Beaver county, having been given entire charge of the cooper plant. He held this position until the company was absorbed by the Standard Oil Company, and in 1878 he started in business for himself as a manufacturer of white lead kegs, which were then made entirely by hand. He was a very progressive man, and as new improvements appeared, he was among the first to adopt them and test their merit. He started a steam plant in 1879, and as his sons grew up they were instructed in the art of his trade, becoming as thorough workmen as himself. He died in 1890, after a long and prosperous life. His wife was Ann Proctor, who was born in England, and accompanied her parents to this country when she was yet a young girl. This union resulted in the following offspring: Henry M.; Edwin Miller; Jane A.; William M., the subject hereof; Emma F. (Piper); Theresa E.; Marcus W.; and Edgar; the three last named are deceased. Henry M., who is a member of H. Donaldson's Sons, was born in Brooklyn, in 1845, and has always been engaged at his present occupation. He is a Prohibitionist, but was formerly a supporter of the Republican party. He is a school director and a member of the borough council. Fraternally, he is a member of the Masonic and Odd Fellows orders, and also of the Knights of Pythias. He married Ella McCowin, a daughter of Thompson McCowin, of Enon Valley, and they have four children: Harry, aged twenty years, who works in the shops; Maud, Ethel, and Hazel. Edwin Miller, another member of the firm of H. Donaldson's Sons, was born in Brooklyn, N. Y., in 1847,

and was instructed in the public schools. He married Mary Davis, and they have three children: Gertrude, Charles, and Byron. Religiously, he is a member of the M. E. church. He is a Republican in politics, and is a member of the Odd Fellows order, and of the Knights of Pythias. Henry Donaldson was a very devout Christian and was connected with the Congregational church until 1873, when he became a member of the Darlington Presbyterian church and so continued until his death. He was an Abolitionist and a Republican, serving as burgess two terms, as school director, and as a member of the borough council. He was a member of the Odd Fellows order.

William M. Donaldson removed to New Galilee in 1861, with his parents, and attended the public schools of New Castle, after which he entered the cooper shops of his father, with whom he was associated until the death of the latter. The works were left to the children, the three sons purchased the interests of their sisters, and the name was changed to H. Donaldson's Sons. William M. attends to the financial affairs of the firm, does the buying and selling, and has entire charge of the affairs of the plant. A great deal of responsibility attaches to the position, but he has been equal to its requirements as the prosperous condition of the establishment indicates. The business was first carried on in a little shop across the street from where the main building is now located, and the work was all done by hand. What a wonderful change has been wrought! The main building is a two-story

CHARLES W. KLEIN.

affair, and is so equipped with machinery that it is a difficult matter to pass through it. Its dimensions are 40x25 feet. On the second floor is the machinery for cutting, planing and manufacturing heads. The kegs for white lead are made of white oak and mostly contain 25, and 100, pounds; the firm also make kegs for cider, pickles and vinegar. The boiler room is an annex to the main building, and contains a 25-horse power boiler; on the first floor are machines for sawing to length, ripping to width, planing and jointing. The kegs are set up by hand and after the hoops are put on, they are taken to the pressing machine for drawing together. They are then put in lathes to be turned smooth, and are headed up and finished. The 100-pound kegs are made in the building across the road, whose dimensions are 26x16 feet. A portion of this building is used as a store house. The firm employs a force of twenty men and turn out 700 kegs per day, shipping mostly to the Sterling White Lead Company, of New Kensington, Pa., and the W. W. Lawrence Paint and Enamel Company, of Pittsburg.

Mr. Donaldson was united in marriage with Jemima Piper, a daughter of Edward and Emma (Proctor) Piper, both of whom were natives of England. Jemima was born in Brooklyn, N. Y., and her union with our subject resulted in the birth of the following children: William H.; Lillie M.; Elsie P.; Nellie P.; and Gladys M. William H. is an accomplished musician, and a graduate of Dana Musical Institute, of Warren, Ohio. He has superior talent in that line, and expects to make music his profession, a field in which he gives promise of attaining prominence as a director and composer. Lillie M. is a student of Darlington Academy, and Gladys M. was born in 1897. Religiously, Mr. Donaldson is a member of Darlington Presbyterian church, of which he was a trustee for six years. He is an independent Republican, and is auditor and also a member of the council and of the school board.

———◆·◆———

CHARLES W. KLEIN, the genial and efficient secretary and treasurer of the Co-operative Flint Glass Company of Beaver Falls, Pa., whose portrait appears on the opposite page, is another notable example of what may be accomplished by perseverance and strict attention to business. The duties that have fallen to his lot during his unusually useful life, have been performed with a cheerfulness and steadiness of purpose that have made his career a source of encouragement to others, an example for imitation. Charles W. Klein was born in Allegheny City, Pa., November 15, 1862, and was educated in the schools of Beaver Falls, and at Iron City College, in Pittsburg. While still attending school, he began to learn the trade of a stove mounter, by working in the evenings, on Saturdays, and during vacations. In 1878, young Klein became bookkeeper for the Howard Stove Company, remaining with that company about three months, when he was offered a better situation as bookkeeper of the Co-operative Flint Glass Company

(Limited), which he at once accepted. He continued thus until the fall of 1886,—accepting at that time a position as business manager for the Columbia Glass Company, of Findlay, Ohio. In 1888 the Findlay Flint Glass Co. was organized, and Mr. Klein was made secretary of the organization. In June, 1891, the factory of that company was destroyed by fire, and was not rebuilt.

After closing up the business of the company, Mr. Klein became secretary and treasurer of the Co-operative Flint Glass Co., of Beaver Falls. That change occurred January 18, 1892, and the position is still retained by him. He has charge of all the business of the company, and manages all their affairs. In business life, Mr. Klein is regarded as a man of extremely good judgment. He realizes fully the many responsibilities which rest upon his shoulders, but performs the many daily duties incumbent upon him with a tact and ease that result only from long experience. November 4, 1886, Marguerite McClelland, a daughter of William McClelland, of Shoustown, Pa., became the wife of Mr. Klein, and their union is blessed with three children, whose names are: Leta, now deceased; Madeline, born January 4, 1893; and Gretchen, also deceased.

Charles G. Klein, father of the subject of this record, was born in Baden, Germany, June 17, 1833. Early in life, he became apprenticed and learned the blacksmith's trade, which occupation he followed for some years. In 1853, Mr. Klein came to America, and located in Pittsburg, where he began working at the trade of stove mounting, in Bradey & Sons Foundry, and remained with them until 1868. He then removed to Beaver Falls, Pa., and engaged with the Howard Stove Company, where he is still busily employed. He was united in marriage with Catherine Kirsch, a native of Wurtemberg, Germany. Six children blessed their union, namely: Catherine, now deceased; Charles W., the subject of this sketch; Louis F.; Elizabeth, wife of Joseph M. Vanderwort, of Beaver Falls; Walter G.; and Lillian.

Charles G. Klein is foreman of the mounting department of the Howard Stove Company. In his political views, he is in accord with the Republicans, but although an active worker for his party, he has never cared to accept office. In a religious connection, he is identified with the German Lutheran church.

For a man whose life has been as busy as his, the subject of this narrative has done much outside the sphere of his regular duties. It is a matter of general knowledge that in his official capacities, he has ever been all that the public could desire. By the corporation which he represents, he is trusted implicitly. On the social side of his nature, he possesses all those traits which win and hold the friendship of all who come within their influence. Mr. Klein is president of the Dime Savings & Loan Association of Beaver Falls, and has been one of the directors ever since its organization; he has been, since 1894, the secretary of the board of directors of the Columbian Building & Loan Association; he is also president of the local board of the Union

Dime Permanent Loan Association of Rochester, New York. Mr. Klein is an active member, and a trustee, of the United Presbyterian church. Fraternally, he belongs to the order of Elks. In politics, he is a stanch Republican. He was elected to the council in 1896, and re-elected in 1899. In 1898, he was chairman of that body.

———— • • ————

JOSEPH H. EVANS. This leading and representative citizen of Beaver, Pa., is well known as one of the most extensive oil producers in Western Pennsylvania, and has built up by energy and strict integrity an excellent reputation, and amassed a handsome fortune. Mr. Evans is truly the architect of his own fortune, and his present enviable position is due wholly to his thrift, foresight, and good business methods. Few men so completely hold the confidence and esteem of the public as he, and his standing is deservedly high. He was born May 16, 1851, in Venango county, Pa., and is a son of John and Mary (Kiser) Evans.

John Evans left Westmoreland county, Pa., while still a young man, and located in Clarion county, where his marriage with Mary Kiser occurred. Mrs. Evans is a daughter of Joseph Kiser and has proved herself a valuable aid to her husband in his various business enterprises. John Evans was a very industrious man and for many years followed lumbering and rafting, becoming an expert river pilot. After amassing a considerable sum of money, he purchased a tract of timber land and engaged in clearing it,—making the most he could from the lumber. This tract was situated along the banks of Paint Creek, Clarion county, where Mr. Evans also built a saw mill and was occupied not only in manufacturing lumber from his own timber, but in doing similar work for his neighbors. His mill was largely patronized and he continued to operate it until 1869, when he sold out and removed to Elk River, Sherburne county, Minn., where he purchased a fine farm and followed agricultural pursuits the remainder of his life. There his death took place at the age of sixty-five years. His widow still survives him, and now resides in Clarion county, Pennsylvania. Mr. Evans in his business ventures prospered even beyond his expectations, and at the time of his death, the large and valuable estate he left insured a competency to the family of loved ones left behind. The following children were born to him and his devoted wife, and they all grew to manhood and womanhood: Mrs. E. A. Clelland; Mrs. Emily Deekey; Mrs. Sarah J. Shaw; Mrs. Susan J. Wallace, deceased; Bradford; John Henry; Joseph H., the subject of this sketch; Charles Wesley, deceased; and Harrison Lincoln, also deceased.

Joseph H. Evans attended public school until he attained the age of sixteen years. Then he began manual labor by drawing oil in barrels, from Shamburg, to Pithole. Subsequently he went to Minnesota with his father, and engaged in the lumber business, as a partner in the firm of Chase & Pillsbury, of Minneapolis. The company contracted for lumber jobs and continued in that line of work until 1876, when Mr. Evans withdrew and returned to the Keystone State, settling in Elk City, where he formed a company, styled Kiser & Evans, leased his grandfather's farm, and began putting down oil wells. His first well yielded 125 barrels per day, bringing $4.25 per barrel, and proved to be one of the best wells in Clarion county. In 1877, Mr. Evans sold his interest in this enterprise and operated oil wells at Bradford, McKean county, Pa., until 1886. The following three years he was associated with Mr. Fitzgibbons; since which period he has been a member of the Devonian Oil Co., which consists of the following men: C. B. Collins; J. R. Leonard; J. D. Downing; and J. H. Evans. The company owns some 300 wells in Ohio, Indiana, West Virginia, and Pennsylvania, all in successful operation. In 1882, Mr. Evans became associated with the Bradford Exchange, and speculated in oil some four years. He is a member of the Victor Oil & Gas Co.; the Superior Oil Co.; he is also a stockholder of the Beaver Mining Company.

Mr. Evans can be found at his office on the corner of Wood and Fourth streets, in Pittsburg, where all his business is transacted. In 1890, he went to Beaver, Pa., and purchased a fine residence on College avenue. This residence was built by Mr. Tallow. After visiting many places in Western Pennsylvania, Mr. Evans wisely decided that the borough of Beaver, with its convenient location, its fine streets and splendid school, was the most suitable location to be found for a permanent home. In 1895, he purchased the corner lot of Wilson avenue and Third street, a very desirable location, and built one of the finest modern brick residences in this part of the state. The brick for this dwelling was manufactured by the Alluma Shell Brick Company, of which company Mr. Evans is a stockholder; it does quite an extensive business in manufacturing all kinds of pressed brick. In addition to the property above described, Mr. Evans owns several lots and tenement houses in Beaver, and has taken an active interest in the progress and development of his adopted town.

The subject of this sketch sought and won for his life partner, Jennie Donaldson, a charming lady, of Knox, Pennsylvania. This happy union was blessed with one son, Harry C., and one daughter, May D., both of whom are students. Mr. Evans is a stanch Republican, but never sought office; he is a Mason of high degree, being a member of Beaver Lodge, F. & A. M.; a R. A. M., of No. 1 Commandery, Knights Templar, of Pittsburg; of the Consistory; and of Syria Temple, A. A. O. N. M. S., of Pittsburg. His beautiful home ever extends a hearty welcome to his many friends, and all his circumstances and surroundings are of the most desirable kind. In personal relations Mr. Evans is exceedingly genial and enjoys the utmost popularity. As a business man, he is broad and liberal, yet shrewd and far-seeing, as well. He is a good financier and manager, as his notable prosperity clearly evidences.

GEORGE W. MACKALL.

GEORGE W. MACKALL, who has acted in the capacity of prothonotary of Beaver county, Pa., for many years, is an active citizen of the borough of Beaver. He is interested in various enterprises in the town, including the well-known Beaver Signal Manufacturing Company, and other concerns of equal note. He is of sturdy Scotch-Irish extraction, and was born in Green township, Beaver county, July 12, 1842,—his parents being James and Mary (Foster) Mackall.

George W. Mackall's grandfather was Benjamin Mackall, a native of northern Ireland, who, at the age of twenty-one years, was commissioned a captain in the Colonial Army, and served throughout the major part of the War of Independence. He came to Georgetown, Beaver county, in 1802, and was there engaged in farming; his wife was Miss Rebecca Dawson, by whom he reared a family of six children, as follows: Jane; James; Thomas; Nellie; John D.; and Samuel. James Mackall was born at Point-of-Rocks, Md., January 16, 1788. In 1817, he bought two hundred and forty-four acres of land and began agricultural pursuits; he made all the present improvements upon this land, and was recognized as an enterprising and progressive farmer. He was a Whig and a Republican in politics, and served as county commissioner. Religiously, he was a member of the Episcopal church. In 1815, he married Mary Foster, a daughter of Thomas Foster; she was born November 7, 1797, and died November 22, 1860,—her husband dying August 20, 1874. Their union was blessed by the following children:

Thomas; Rebecca; Benjamin; Phoebe; Jane; John D.; Mary; Samuel; James; Sarah Ellen; and George Washington. Rebecca married Jesse Kinsey; Benjamin wedded Mary Dolby; Phoebe was the wife of Milton Calhoun: Jane was joined in wedlock with James Mackall; John D. married Harriet A. Cornell; Samuel, a farmer of Green township, Beaver county, married first Sarah Harvey and had three children,—she died and he married Jennie Dawson; James. of Georgetown, Pa., married Sidney A. Miller; Sarah Ellen wedded Harrison Dawson; and George Washington is the subject hereof. He has but two brothers living,—James and Samuel.

George W. Mackall attended the public schools, and at fourteen years of age became a clerk in a store at Hookstown, Beaver county, for John Sterling; he later accepted a like position with Joseph Hall, and then with M. L. Christler. Like many other boys of his day, he was fond of river life, and accepted a position as cabin boy on one of the boats that plied up and down the Ohio River; after several years of this life, he became a second-mate, but becoming tired of that life, he engaged in boating coal down the river, for a period of six years; he then became a contractor for oil drilling in Ohio township and vicinity, after which he conducted a store at Glasgow, Pa., and also served as justice of the peace of that village for five years. In 1887, he went to New Brighton, Pa., and became connected with the publication of the Tribune. In August, 1892, he was elected to the office of prothonotary of Beaver county, which made it necessary for him to come to Beaver, where he has since resided. Mr. Mackall discharged the official duties of that position in such a thorough manner that he was re-elected. Since the closing of his term, he has been living in retirement. He is a stockholder in the Beaver Signal Manufacturing Company; he resides in a fine house, situated at the end of Fourth street. The subject of this sketch participated in the War of the Rebellion, having enlisted, in 1863, in Company H, 56th Reg., Pa. Vol. Inf.; at the expiration of his term he became a member of Company H, 5th Reg., Heavy Artillery; at the close of the war, he had been promoted to be a sergeant.

Mr. Mackall was wedded to Miss Mary Jane Calhoun, who was born in 1845,— a daughter of James and Eliza (Gamble) Calhoun. Her father was a ship carpenter, and was born in Allegheny county, Pa., but spent most of his life in Beaver county, building boats. He was the father of the following children: Seraphina S., the wife of D. S. Hamilton; Nancy Ann, deceased; Ellen, first wedded to J. McKee, and later to D. A. Jolly; Lucinda, the wife of Abner Martin; Priscilla, wedded to John Laughlin; Peggie Ann, deceased; Isabella, deceased, and Elizabeth, twins,—the latter wedded to John Strain; William G., deceased; Mary Jane, the wife of the subject hereof; and Arvilla, the wife of S. L. Dawson. Mr. and Mrs. Mackall are the parents of three children: Howard C.; Mary Eliza; and George Raymond. Howard C. served as deputy prothonotary for his father,

and was married to Roberta Waterson; one child, Mary Addie, has been born to them. Mary Eliza is the wife of Wilbert W. Knowles, clerk for the P. & L. E. R. R., and has a son, Duane M. George Raymond is attending Beaver College. Mr. Mackall is a member of the E. M. Stanton Post, G. A. R., No. 208, of New Brighton; of the Sr. O. U. A. M., No. 301; and of the Elks, of Rochester, No. 283. Religiously, Mr. Mackall and family are members of the Methodist church. Mr. Mackall's portrait is shown on the opposite page.

———◆•◆———

ALEXANDER F. REID, a very prominent merchant of Beaver county, has an excellent store at New Galilee, carrying a complete line of groceries, hardware, boots and shoes, hats and caps, household furnishings, drugs, agricultural implements, and, in fact, almost any article for which there is a demand. He is a man of enterprise, and his continued efforts to accommodate the citizens of the borough, and the courtesy which he extends to his patrons, have won for him public favor. He is a native of Ireland, having been born in Belfast, November 15, 1838, and is a son of William and Maria (Findlay) Reid.

William Reid, the father of Alexander F., was born in Belfast, Ireland, in 1797, and there he received his intellectual training and adopted the occupation of a farmer, which he followed throughout his life. He was joined in the holy bonds of matrimony with Maria

Findlay, a daughter of William Findlay, of Scotch-Irish ancestry, and they reared the following children: Eliza (Reed) deceased; John, whose business was that of a linen shipper; William, who is living a retired life in Pittsburg; Jane (Little), deceased; Anna (Williams); Maria, deceased; Alexander F., the gentleman whose name heads these lines; Charles, who has charge of a department in a linen manufacturing establishment; and Russell, whose death occurred at the early age of ten years. Religiously, Mr. Reid was a Presbyterian. He was called into the unknown world, in 1857, at the age of sixty years.

Alexander F. Reid, after completing his mental training in the public schools of Ireland, served a four years' apprenticeship in a grocery and hardware store. In the year of 1863, he came to America and landed in New York City; but a short time thereafter, he removed to Pittsburg. He subsequently worked in Sharpsburg about two years, and in 1870 located in New Galilee, Beaver county, Pa., where he engaged in business for himself.— renting a place for about eight years. In 1878, he built his present store, a two-story building, with dimensions of 80x24 feet, in addition to which there is a warehouse and a basement. In this he conducted his store in a very successful manner until 1883. His wife's health having failed in that year, Mr. Reid removed with his family to California, and remained there two years, during which time he became a competent druggist and conducted a drug store. Upon returning to New Galilee, in 1885, he resumed business in his former location, and has since conducted one of the neatest and best arranged stores in that section. Being a man of exceptional business qualifications, and having had wide experience in his business, he realizes the wants of his customers and satisfies them in every way consistent with his own interests. He is a stockholder in the Rochester National Bank. He has the respect of his fellow-citizens to a high degree, and they are proud to acknowledge themselves his friends.

In 1865, at Sharpsburg, Alexander F. Reid was united in marriage with Mary E. Henry, a daughter of Wilson and Eliza (Garvin) Henry, and a granddaughter of William Henry. William Henry was born in Ireland, and when a child, came to this country with his parents, where they bought a tract of land in Westmoreland county, Pennsylvania. They cleared this land of its timber, and erected log houses and barns. William acquired property of his own, engaged in lumbering and also worked on the river. He followed that and farming all of his life. He married Miss Borland and they reared five children, of whom Wilson was the second. Wilson Henry, the father of Mrs. Reid, attended the schools of Westmoreland county, Pa., and during his youthful days worked in the mines and on the river. He rented a farm near Sharpsburg for some years, and then bought one of two hundred acres, in 1863. He moved upon it in 1870, and was extensively engaged in dairying, fruit growing and general farming, which he continued throughout his active life, and became a very prosperous man. He was a Republican in politics. Religiously, he was a Presbyterian, and was ruling elder for a number of years. Mr. Henry married Eliza Garvin, a daughter of Joseph Garvin, and they reared eleven children, as follows: Samuel, an insurance agent at Beaver; Joseph G. (deceased), a railroad agent all of his life; William (deceased), a farmer and missionary of West Virginia; Sarah J. (Hodil); Mary E., the wife of the subject hereof; Rev. Benjamin C., D. D., who was graduated at Washington and Jefferson College, and received the degree of D. D. from Princeton University, and who has been a missionary to China for twenty-five years,— returning home but twice; Nancy G. (Wetzig); Eleanor (Brown); Wilson, a fruit grower in California; James S., a journalist in Washington, D. C.; and Anna M., who is now living at home.

Mrs. Reid was born at Turtle Creek, Pa., attended the schools of Sharpsburg, and was a pupil of Sharpsburg Academy. She was married in 1865, and they reared eight children, as follows: Anna M.; Jane E.; William H.; Charles W.; Agnes Eleanor; Alexander R.; James McArthur; and Benjamin Clair. Anna M. (Schueler) was born September 12, 1866, graduated at Geneva College, and finished her education in a private institution in California, under Prof. Conklin. Jane E., born January 29, 1869, attended the public schools and also completed her intellectual training under Prof. Conklin; she married a Mr. Miller. William H. was born April 1, 1871, and died in February, 1877. Charles W. was born August 13, 1874, and died February 9, 1877. Agnes Eleanor was born June 10, 1876, attended the public schools, and then took a course in Slippery Rock Normal School, from which she was graduated, in 1895. She then taught for two years in the borough schools, and entered the School of Designing, where she had the honor of winning the class medal,—a high testimonial to her skill and talent. In 1896, she was obliged to give up her studies on account of ill-health. Alexander R. was born July 19, 1878, and is studying medicine, being a member of the graduating class of 1901. James McArthur was born May 20, 1881, and is a student in the preparatory department of Geneva College. Benjamin Clair was born October 16, 1884, and is attending the public schools.

The subject of this biography is a devout Presbyterian, and is very active in church work, having been a ruling elder since 1883. He is a trustee of the church. Politically, he is a Republican.

———— ◆ • ◆ ————

WALTER C. JONES is one of the most prominent and popular young business men of Beaver county, and is esteemed and much respected by the citizens of Beaver Falls, where he is recognized as a valuable member of that community. He has always been connected with various iron and steel industries, and has gradually worked his way up to his present high position,—that of general superintendent of the American

Steel & Wire Company, in which capacity he has efficiently served since April, 1898.

Mr. Jones was born in Zanesville, Ohio, and obtained his elementary education at Newark, Ohio, which was supplemented by a course of study in the schools of Pittsburg, Pennsylvania. In 1888, he accepted a position as general shipping clerk and assistant to the superintendent of the old Braddock Wire Company, of Rankin, Pa.,—living in Pittsburg, Pennsylvania. He remained in the service of that company until the year 1895, when he was transferred to the position of secretary of the Consolidated Steel & Wire Company at Beaver Falls, Pa., which company was the owner of both plants. Mr. Jones occupied that position until April, 1898, when he was promoted to general superintendent of both the office and the mills, and now has charge of all the business transacted at the great plant in Beaver Falls. This immense plant covers twenty-three acres of ground, upon which are five main buildings, with the following departments,—rod, wire, barbed-wire, galvanizing, and nail,—and when in full operation, gives employment to about nine hundred men. Mr. Jones commands the respect and good-will of the many employees under his supervision, as well as the confidence and esteem of his superior officers; he is a very energetic young man, full of business, thoroughly understands all lines of the iron industry, and is fully competent to fulfill all the duties of his present high position.

Mr. Jones formed a matrimonial alliance with Miss Ruth Mattern, of Pittsburg, Pa.,

and their home has been blessed by the birth of one son, Robert. He is a faithful member of the Royal Arcanum and of the Heptasophs.

————◆•◆————

DR. JOHN J. ALLEN, a gentleman of high educational attainments, and a well-known educator for many years, has achieved particular success in the field of medicine, having a large and lucrative practice in Monaca and vicinity. He is a son of Robert and Elizabeth (Wiley) Allen, and was born in County Meath, Ireland, February 22, 1859.

Robert Allen, the father of John J., was born in County Antrim, Ireland, and was the youngest son of a family of thirteen children. He was fortunate in his boyhood, as he was given a good education to fit him for the station of a country gentleman. After his marriage and the birth of the subject of this sketch, the family met with reverses, and he came to the United States, settling in Beaver county, Pennsylvania. He was joined in marriage with Elizabeth Wiley, who was born and educated in County Meath, Ireland, and they became the parents of three children: John J., the gentleman whose name appears at the head of this narrative; Robert II., a farmer by vocation; and Emily K. W. (Moore). The two last named were born after Mr. Allen moved to this country.

Dr. John J. Allen, who was three months old when he was brought to this country by his parents, has risen to a high station in life entirely through his individual efforts. A series of adverse events prevented his family from giving him an education, and at the immature age of eight and one-half years, he left home to seek a livelihood, obtaining a position on the farm of D. W. Scott. He was very ambitious and remained with him until he was nineteen years of age, working upon the farm during his summer months and attending school during the winter. Dissatisfied with the life he was leading, and feeling confident that better things were in store for him if he would but strive for them, he became impressed with the necessity of a good education. He gave up farming and entered Piersol's Academy, taking a normal course in order to fit himself for a teacher's work. He was subsequently a teacher in the New Sewickley township schools, for one year, principal of the schools of Industry, for two years, and then principal of the North Ward School of New Brighton, for two years; at the same time he was instructor in the night school,—working hard and conscientiously. Giving up teaching for the time being, he entered Geneva College, at Beaver Falls, taking an eclectic course, during which time he competed for a permanent state certificate, and was successful. He was elected principal of the Glenfield schools of Allegheny county, Pa., and at the same time finished a business curriculum in Curry University of Pittsburg,—also serving as bookkeeper in the music store of Mellor & Hohne. This is but one evidence of the industrious life he has led, but with eyes fixed upon the distant goal,

which he was slowly but surely approaching, he would allow no obstacle to stop him. He was re-elected principal of the Glenfield schools and also of the Bellevue schools, and chose the latter connection as being the more desirable of the two. For three years he was the incumbent of that position, also teaching night school in New Brighton. During the latter part of this period, he desired to satisfy his ambition to become a physician, and read medicine under the tutelage of Dr. James McCann. He then entered the medical department of the Western University of Pennsylvania, and after his graduation in 1890, began practice at Phillipsburg, now Monaca. His choice of fields was a wise one as there is no borough in the state in a more flourishing condition or one which gives more promise of future growth. He has since been located there and his practice has grown apace with the town, his patients including many of the best citizens of the community. As he was eminently successful as an educator, so has he been as a doctor. He at once won the confidence of the citizens in a professional way, and they have since become his friends.

Dr. Allen was joined in hymeneal bonds with Jeannette N. Armstrong, a native of Beaver county, and a daughter of John Armstrong, of Brighton township. She is an accomplished musician and art student, having pursued a course at the Pittsburg School of Design. They have two children: Harold A., born December 24, 1895; and Jeannette Juay, born December 26, 1898. The residence in which the Doctor lives is the finest on the south side, and is a feature of the town. It is a handsome three-story building of fourteen rooms, being constructed of buff brick. Its interior is beautiful,—finished in hardwood and equipped with all modern arrangements for comfort and fine appearance. The Doctor's office is on the Eighth street side of the building. He is a public-spirited man and is anxious to see the town progress,—taking an active interest in all its affairs. He was one of the hardest workers in obtaining the bridge across the Ohio, and he is now a stockholder in the bridge company. In politics, he is an ardent Republican, and has been a member of the school board for seven years. He is borough physician, holds a position on the poor board, and is a member of the staff of the Beaver Valley Hospital. Religiously, he is a Presbyterian and has been an elder ever since he has been in the borough. Fraternally, he belongs to the following orders: Royal Arcanum; Woodmen of the World; Knights of Pythias; and Rochester Lodge, F. & A. M. His portrait, in connection with this sketch, is shown on a foregoing page.

GEORGE WILSON. Conspicuous among the successful attorneys who devote their whole attention to the active practice of their profession, stands George Wilson, the subject of this brief biography. Mr. Wilson attended the Beaver High School, and after completing its course, he began the study of law with his father. After diligently pursuing his studies for some time, he was admitted to the bar, March 4, 1889, soon after the death of his father. He began the practice of his chosen profession by entering into partnership with R. S. Holt, under the firm name of Wilson & Holt, of which he is still a partner. Mr. Wilson's undivided attention is given to his chosen profession, and like his father, he has built up a splendid reputation.

Sarah Cummings, an attractive daughter of David and Sarah Cummings, of Freedom, Pa., became the wife of Mr. Wilson. Their home is brightened by the presence of four children namely: Marion, Caroline, Samuel B., and Richard. In his political attachments, Mr. Wilson is a stanch Democrat, and, although he labors zealously for the success of his party, he has never sought office nor cared for political distinction, being very much like his honored father in that respect. He is a member of the Masonic fraternity of Beaver.

Our subject is a direct descendant of Samuel Wilson, who was of Scotch origin, and his wife was a descendant of the early Knickerbockers. Early in the eighteenth century, he married Mary Van Wier, who was born in Holland. This worthy couple owned and occupied a farm along Marsh Creek, near Gettysburg, Pennsylvania. There he engaged in tilling the soil, and spent a peaceful and happy domestic life, and there they both died, leaving two sons: Samuel, and Marmaduke, who was the great-grandfather of our subject.

Marmaduke Wilson was born upon his father's homestead, and in 1744 was united in marriage with Susan Beatty. The young folks started out in life at the homestead, caring for the old parents very lovingly until the death of the latter. They then removed to Westmoreland county, Pa., and continued to follow agricultural pursuits for many years. The names of their children were: Patrick; Samuel; Rachel (McFarlan); Jane (Dunlap); Susan (Marshall); Easter (Rambo); Martha (Gibson); Sarah (Mitchell); and Elizabeth (Byers).

About 1801, Patrick Wilson located in Beaver county, the part now called Lawrence county. There he followed mercantile pursuits, and in 1804 his marriage with Rebecca Morehead, a daughter of William Morehead, occurred. They had the following children: William; Marmaduke; John; Susan (Phillips); Nancy (Chriss); Sarah (Harper); and Samuel.

In 1811, Mr. Wilson purchased a farm near New Castle, where he spent many happy years, and finally died in 1866. This farm is still owned by his descendants. Samuel B. Wilson, father of George, was born February 20, 1824, and from early childhood his aspirations were beyond those of his playmates. He was a faithful student in the district schools, from which he entered Jefferson College at Cannonsburg, Pa., graduating therefrom in June, 1848, with about the highest honors of his class. He enjoyed the distinction of being a noted linguist, and his mastery of the English, Latin, and Greek languages was never questioned by either his fellow students, or the professors. Moreover, he not only kept up with his studies when the college course was ended, but greatly increased his knowledge of the ancient classics by daily reading and timely reviews. Soon after leaving college, he was chosen principal of Darlington Academy, a position which he held until the fall of 1849, when he went to Somerset county, and became a law student in the office of the Hon. Jeremiah S. Black, who was then president judge of the Sixteenth Judicial District of Pennsylvania. Mr. Wilson was admitted to the bar, November 12, 1850, and immediately thereafter went to Beaver, where he practiced in the several courts of the county, and in due time acquired a lucrative practice, which occupied his time for more than a quarter of a century. He was engaged in the interests of the most important legal business that has been transacted in Beaver county. His receipts for professional services have perhaps been greater in amount than that of any other resident lawyer who has at any time practiced at the Beaver county bar.

Samuel B. Wilson, although an active politician in the interest of the Democratic party, never sought office. The height of his ambition was to become a thorough scholar, and an honest and successful lawyer; he loved justice, law, and peace. In the practice of his profession, he outlived the ambition of display before courts and juries, he learned to bear criticism without irritation, censure without anger, and calumny without retaliation. He

SAMUEL HENRY MOULDS.

learned how surely all schemes of evil bring disaster to them that support them, and that the granite shaft of a noble reputation can not be destroyed by the poisoned breath of slander.

In 1856, he purchased of Judge Agnew, the Susan Cochran estate, one of Beaver's oldest homes, and a substantial building for its day, located on the north side of the Park, on Turnpike alley. Here Samuel Beatty Wilson had his office and reared his family around the old-time fireplace. This handsome old estate is today owned by the subject of this sketch, as his father left it later in life, and purchased a handsome brick residence on the adjoining lot, which was built by Senator Quay. There Mr. Wilson spent the remainder of his days, passing to the life beyond the grave in January, 1889. His widow is still living, and occupies the same home in which he left her. Mr. Wilson was a member of the Masonic fraternity, and passed all the degrees from the F. & A. M., to the Knights Templar. April 11, 1854, he led to the hymeneal altar, Elizabeth Robinson, a daughter of George Robinson, who was then sheriff of Beaver county. As a scholar, a student, and an assistant, Mrs. Wilson had been of great assistance to her husband, besides being a kind and loving mother, who reared a family, and is loved and esteemed by all. Their children were: Sarah, now deceased; Anna, wife of A. R. Whitehill, a professor of physics in the University of West Virginia; Mary, wife of George Davidson; and George, the subject of this sketch.

George Wilson is held in high repute in his community, and is a man whom all respect and honor. He has a pleasing address and is liberal in his sentiments. His genial disposition and reputation for honesty have made him a favorite not only with his brother practitioners, but among all classes.

SAMUEL HENRY MOULDS, under whose personal supervision and direction as foreman and assistant manager, the Rochester Tumbler Company has been operated since its organization, is a man who understands the business of manufacturing glass from beginning to end. Since he was ten years old he has been connected with such work, and the high state of efficiency in his office has rendered it possible for the company to lead all others in the world at that particular industry. He is also a stockholder and director of many of the most successful enterprises in the borough,—being a man of great shrewdness and foresight. He was born near Milltown, County Antrim, Ireland, December 9, 1845, and is a son of John and Nancy (Henry) Moulds.

John Moulds, the father of Samuel Henry, was born in County Antrim, Ireland, and after his marriage removed to America with his family,—landing in the city of New York. He located at Steubenville, Ohio, where his wife had a brother and a number of friends, and there became a glass worker, which continued to be his employment until within a short time of his death. He then was engaged in packing, working until the last. He was a man of remarkable dexterity for his age, and shaved himself, as was his custom, up to within three days of his death, which occurred in 1890, at the age of seventy-five years. He married Nancy Henry, whose father was William Henry, and the following offspring resulted: Jane, who married Joseph S. Mellor, employed in the Rochester Tumbler Works, and a stockholder in the company; William, whose biography appears elsewhere in this work; Samuel Henry, the subject of this record; Annie, the widow of Albert Albin, of Columbus, Ohio; Sarah, the wife of Eli Capers, of Steubenville, Ohio; Robert, who lives at Rochester; John, also a resident of Rochester; and Elizabeth, who makes her home at Steubenville, Ohio.

At the age of ten years, Samuel Henry Moulds entered the glass manufacturing establishment at Steubenville, being employed in the press department until 1868, when he went to Pittsburg and continued in the same line of business until 1872, when he became an organizer, and one of the original stockholders, of the Rochester Tumbler Company. He has also been one of the directors from the first. Owing to his well-known skill and thorough knowledge of every detail of the work, he was chosen as foreman and assistant manager, and has since remained in that position. They manufactured both blown and pressed tumblers, and the demand for their product increased with amazing rapidity, compelling them to increase their facilities and enlarge the business, until now it is the largest of its kind in existence, and the most important industry in the borough of Rochester. They ship to all parts of the globe, sending out from three to ten carloads per day. Their capacity is 150,000 dozen blown tumblers, and 150,000 dozen pressed, per month, twelve hundred skilled workmen being employed the year around. They make their own boxes, barrels and crates for shipping, grind the clay and make pots, and also make their own molds. They have a large water tank containing 3,100 gallons, and have private water works and a private electric light plant. They also have an ice house for drinking purposes. The place is kept in the best of order, and reflects great credit upon the work of the gentlemen in charge. Our subject exacts the best work from each man under him, yet treats him with the greatest consideration and kindness, thereby retaining his good will to the highest extent. Mr. Moulds is a stockholder and director of the Rochester & Monaca Suspension Bridge Company, of the Rochester Electric Plant, and of the Rochester Daily Star. In 1885, he built a fine residence at No. 103 West Washington street, on the corner of New York street, which was burned down and rebuilt in 1886.

The subject of this writing was united in marriage with Belle Krewson, a daughter of Horace Krewson, and they have two children: Horace Fuller, who is engaged in the insurance business at Rochester; and Agnes K. Mr. Moulds has served as school director and held various other borough offices. His portrait accompanies this sketch, being presented on a foregoing page.

---◆·◆---

REV. R. MORRIS SMITH, a gentleman of high educational attainments, is pastor of the Baden Lutheran church, the Rehoboth church, the House of Mercy, and the Trinity church, of Freedom, Pa., and resides in the borough of Baden, where he is held in the highest esteem by his parishioners and fellow citizens. The extensive duties of his charges are very confining, but being a man of unusual energy and ability, and deeply absorbed in the work of Christ, he has performed them faithfully, as the increased membership will indicate.

Mr. Smith was born in Easton, Northampton county, Pa., January 25, 1862, and is descended from a long line of distinguished ancestors. The first of the family of whom there is any record extant is his great-great-grandfather, who was a professor of dogmatic theology at Copenhagen University. His son, the great-grandfather of our subject, was a minister of the Gospel in the Lutheran church, of Denmark and was the first member of the family to come to America, prior to which he was united in marriage with a woman of German birth. He was the first Lutheran minister to preach in the old town of Easton, Pa. His son, P. F. B. Smith, grandfather of the subject of this record, was born seventeen days after the arrival of his parents in this country; he also studied for the ministry. He preached in Easton until his health failed him, when he resigned. His popularity is shown by the fact that he was immediately elected to the office of register and recorder of the county,—a position he held for a period of nine years,—when he retired and was then elected justice of the peace. Being a very fine penman, he had plenty to do in the way of writing wills and deeds. He and his wife had seventeen children, three of whom are still living.

George Q. F. Smith, the father of the subject hereof, was the oldest son, and was born January 1, 1825, at Easton, Pa., and was intellectually trained in the Easton public schools. He became a merchant tailor and very successfully followed that vocation all of his active life, becoming quite prominent, but is now living a retired life in Stockertown, Pennsylvania. He is a Republican in politics, and, although he has been a hard worker for the party's success, he has never accepted office other than that of school director. Religiously, he is an active member of the Lutheran church, and has held all of the church offices. He is a member of the Masonic order, Knights Templar, and the Jr. O. U. A. M. Mr. Smith was united in marriage with Mary A. Millar, who was born at Mt. Bethel, Northampton county, Pa., and they have five children: Emma C. (Uhler); Millard Fillmore; Mary E. (Sandt); Amanda A. (Kiefer); and R. Morris, the subject of this biographical record.

R. Morris Smith received his primary education in the public schools of Easton, after which he took a classical course at Trach's Academy and entered Muhlenberg College. He graduated from that institution in 1883, with the degree of A. B., and three years later with the degree of A. M., taking third honors in his class. He then went to Texas, where he was given charge of the Mission Valley Academy, but in 1884 he entered the Lutheran Theological Seminary, from which he was graduated in 1887, being ordained in June of that year. He was then called to Baden to accept his present charges, as successor of the Rev. Dr. Passarant, who, assisted by his son, had been established there for twenty-one years. It is the oldest church in Baden and he is its second pastor. Faithfully and well is he discharging the multifarious duties of these charges, and that his efforts have not been without their reward, we need but mention that the congregation of the Baden church has increased to double its size when he went there. He also erected a handsome new church edifice at Freedom, and is deeply interested in its future. Besides his pastoral duties, Rev. Mr. Smith has completed a post graduate course in the Chicago Theological Seminary, in the study of liturgics. He is at present engaged in literary work, and has several pamphlets on this subject, in the press. He is a member of the college fraternity, Alpha Tau Omega.

On October 13, 1887, Mr. Smith was united in marriage with Minnie Balliet Trumbower, a daughter of Harrison and Josephine (Balliet) Trumbower, who was born in Hokendauqua, Pa., and obtained her education in the public schools of Allentown, graduating from the high school in 1886. Two children were born to bless their home, namely: Phillip M., deceased; and Mary J. Mr. Smith is a Republican in politics, and, although he does not desire office, believing they should be filled by the laity, he consented to accept the place of school director.

———◆◆◆———

GEORGE GOULD, superintendent of the Butts Cannel Coal Company, and a resident of East Palestine, Ohio, was born near Bath, England. He accompanied his parents to this country, when but seven years old. He received his educational training at East Palestine. After leaving school he determined to learn the business of coal operating, and started in at the bottom of the ladder as a digger in the coal fields of Pennsylvania. He gradually worked his way up, and his first appointment to a position of responsibility was as superintendent under Captain Hicks in his mine at Bagdad, Westmoreland county. About fifty men found employment in this mine, and most of the mine's product was sold to the railroads.

After retaining that position for three years, Mr. Gould resigned. In 1888, he bought an interest in the Sterling Mining Co., producers of coal and clay, at Cannelton, Beaver county, Pennsylvania. He was superintendent of the company's mines for five years, having under him one hundred men.

1900

DR. CONSTANTINE T. GALE.

Later he sold his interest to Mr. Heilman. Mr. Gould had also been manager for the Butts Cannel Coal Co., but finding the duties of both positions too arduous, he decided to give his entire attention to the Butts Company, and consequently resigned the superintendency of the Sterling Company. He opened and developed the Butts Company's mines. They are producers of very fine cannel coal.

They employ fifty-two men and have a nine-foot vein of cannel coal. This coal is very fine for making gas and is found in few places in this country. Two other places where it is found in paying quantities are at Falling Rock, West Virginia, and Bear Creek, Kentucky. The products of the Butts Co.'s mines are shipped to all parts of the United States and Canada.

Mr. Gould married Belle Atchison, of East Palestine, Ohio, and resides in a handsome residence a short distance from the mines, to which he drives daily. Mrs. Gould is a native of East Palestine, where she also received her scholastic training. Four children bless the home of Mr. and Mrs. Gould, namely: William, aged eleven; Charles, aged seven; Ellen, three years old; and George, Jr., a baby of eight months.

Mr. Gould is a stockholder of the Elk Run Mining Co., miners of soft coal, and is president of the same. Other members of the company are Messrs. Lanor, Flynn and Bycroft,—the first named being also secretary and treasurer. The offices of the company are at Lisbon, Ohio. The subject of these lines is a Republican. He is a member of the town council, a school director, and is serving on the board of education. He belongs to the M. E. church, of which he is a trustee. He is a member of the Palestine Lodge, F. & A. M., also of the I. O. O. F.

———————

DR. CONSTANTINE T. GALE. The well known physician and surgeon whose name heads this sketch, and whose portrait we present on the opposite page, has one of the largest practices in Beaver county, and his ability as a physician is undoubtedly of the highest. His patronage extends over New Brighton, his present home, and through Beaver county, and the counties adjoining, and he is held in high esteem by all who know him. Dr. Gale is a son of the late well known physician, Dr. George W. Gale, and was born at Newport, Washington county, Ohio, January 18, 1850.

The paternal grandfather, George Gale, was born in Ireland and came to America prior to the year 1800. On the way over, he met on the ship a Miss McKernan, whom he afterward married. They located in Hampshire county, in what is now West Virginia, and followed farming, until they were well along in life, when they sold their property, and went to what is now Pleasant county, West Virginia, and, a few years later, moved to Cape Girardeau, Missouri, where they both died at the advanced age of eighty years. Their children were, as follows: Thomas;

James; McKernan; George; W., M. D.; Robert; John; Constantine; William; Bridget; Catherine; Ellen; Maria; and Theresa; all of whom grew to be men and women, and attained an old age. Three of the oldest sons served in the War of 1812.

George W. Gale, the father of Constantine T., was born in Hampshire county, West Virginia, and was educated in Cumberland, Maryland. He chose medicine as a profession, and was one of the most successful practitioners of the time. He was a self-made man in every respect, and won for himself a name which time cannot efface. He began his professional life in Tyler county, West Virginia, in 1831, and then located at Newport, Washington county, Ohio, and obtained a large practice on both sides of the Ohio River. His career as a physician started in the saddle-bag days, when there were but few roads to reach the pioneers' homes with wagons. Dr. Gale rode many miles on horseback, and in those days a physician had to take grain, provisions, and even timber, for services, as money was very scarce. Good physicians were not to be found within many miles of each other, therefore the Doctor was kept very busy. Being a lover of nature, he purchased a large farm, and spent many happy hours in having it improved, for he was a man of fine tastes and a progressive disposition, and in a short time, he had in his possession a very fine farming property.

He died in September, 1871, aged eighty-one, but although he had given up his long rides several years previous to his death, he was called on at his home and office, to the very last days of his sickness. His name is known in every household in the vicinity of his former home, and his memory will ever be warmly cherished. He assisted four of his sons to become doctors. Dr. Gale married Catherine Wells, a daughter of Nicholas Wells, of Tyler county, West Va., and she died at the age of seventy. They were both faithful members of the Catholic church. Their children were: John W., M. D.; Mary; Alcinda B.; Rachel; Ellen; Nicholas W., a farmer; Veronica; Constantine T., the subject hereof; George T., M. D.; Samuel Hammett, D. D. S.; Adah L.; and C. Bernard, M. D.

Dr. Constantine T. Gale, whose name heads this personal biography, attended the public schools of his native town, and also the St. Thomas Seminary, and began reading medicine with his father at the age of twenty. He then entered the Jefferson Medical School at Philadelphia in 1876, and graduated in 1878. He began practice at Parkersburg, West Va., and in 1880 went to New Brighton, where he has since lived. He was an entire stranger there, but it was not long until he had a most promising beginning, and his services were soon sought by many residents of New Brighton. He rapidly rose in the profession, and has proven himself to be a complete master of the science of medicine. His practice is a large and lucrative one, and he is greatly loved by all in the vicinity. The Doctor has a fine home at Eleventh street and Fifth avenue, where is, also, his office. This place was formerly the residence of Dr. Simpson. Dr. Gale was united in wedlock with Lucy L. Stephenson, a daughter of Hon. James Stephenson, of Parkersburg, West Virginia. He has served several years on the staff of the Beaver County Hospital, is a member of the Beaver County Medical Society, State Medical Association, and American Medical Association. He is a stanch Democrat, but has never sought political distinction. He is also a member of the order of Elks, of Rochester, Pennsylvania.

———— ◆ ◆ ————

D R. WILLIAM S. GRIM, a leading practitioner of Beaver Falls, Pa., is a pleasant, companionable gentleman, with a liking for company, and a genial manner that wins him large numbers of friends. Dr. Grim has been actively engaged in the practice of medicine ever since his graduation from the medical department of the Western University of Pennsylvania, at Pittsburg, in 1888, when he located immediately in Beaver Falls. He makes a specialty of diseases of the nose, throat, ear, and chest. He was first assistant surgeon of the 10th Reg. of Pennsylvania Militia for a period of six years. He is a member of the Beaver County Medical Society and also of the Pennsylvania State Medical Society. He acted as delegate from the latter to the State Medical Society of New Jersey in 1889. He is also a member of the Pittsburg Obstetrical Society. Politically, the Doctor is an ardent Democrat, but has never sought nor held office, being too busily occupied with his professional duties.

The subject of this article is a son of Dr. William and Lucinda (Spangler) Grim, and was born August 26, 1864, in Rockville, Dauphin county, Pennsylvania. He received an excellent scholastic training in the common schools of Beaver Falls, which was supplemented by a course at Piersoll's Academy at Bridgewater, and a finishing course at Geneva College in Beaver Falls. He received the degree of B. S. in 1885, and the degree of M. S. in 1889. For his future life work he elected to become a physician, like his honored father. With him, he began the study of medicine in 1885; after studying diligently for some time he attended the Western University of Pennsylvania, at Pittsburg, graduating in 1888, as previously mentioned. His energy, determination, and skill have won for him a high reputation as a physician, and have secured for him an extensive field of practice, besides having fairly given him a place among the leading practitioners of his profession. Dr. Grim is a past master of Beaver Falls Lodge, No. 478, F. & A. M., and is also a member of Harmony Chapter; a member of Valley Echo Lodge, I. O. O. F.; Lone Rock Lodge, K. of P.; and Schuyler Grove, No. 8, United Ancient Order of Druids.

Louis Philip Grim, the great-grandfather of the subject hereof, was a native of Germany, and, on coming to the United States, settled in York county, Pa., at an early date. His son, Michael Grim, was the grandfather of William S. and was born in York county,

Pa.,—settling in Beaver county, about the beginning of the present century. He located near Unionville, where he followed agricultural pursuits, and spent the remainder of his life. He rendered valuable services to our country during the War of 1812, being under the command of Captain Henry, in the battle of Lake Erie, under Commodore Perry.

William H. Grim, father of William S., was born in Beaver county, Pa., about 1833. He was a pupil in the common schools, and at Beaver Academy. He then read medicine with Dr. W. W. Simpson, of Rochester, Pa., after which he entered the Cincinnati Medical College, from which he graduated.

After practicing a few years in Lawrence county, and at Rockwell, Dauphin county, he took a special course at Jefferson Medical College in Philadelphia, graduating therefrom in 1869. He then went to Beaver Falls, where he practiced until his death, April 29, 1897. He was a member of the Beaver County Medical Society, and the Pennsylvania State Medical Society. He made a specialty of surgery, and when in active practice, was considered by many to be the leading surgeon in Beaver county. He was a Democrat in his party affiliations, took an active part in politics, and was vice-president of the State Democratic league. He took a deep interest in the educational institutions of his county, and served as a school director for (perhaps) twenty years. He was appointed postmaster under the administration of Benjamin Harrison, and served faithfully in that official capacity. In the Episcopalian church, he

was recognized as one of the prominent members, and had a record for piety of the most earnest character. He was twice married. His first wife was Lucinda Spangler, mother of the subject of this biography. She was a native of Lebanon county, and was a daughter of Levi Spangler. Some time after the death of his first wife, Dr. William H. Grim re-married, his union in this instance being with Amelia Ann Robinson, a daughter of Hon. Archie Robinson, who was state senator of the Beaver-Lawrence district in the early days. Dr. William H. Grim was a very prominent man in the Masonic fraternity. He was past master of the Beaver Valley Lodge, No. 478; a member of Harmony Chapter; Pittsburg Commandery; and of Syria Temple, A. A. O. N. M. S.

Levi Spangler, maternal grandfather of the subject hereof, was an extensive coal operator at Tremont, Pennsylvania. His grandfather settled in Philadelphia in 1737, in what is now known as the First Ward, but later in life went to what is now Myerstown, in Lebanon county. There he built a stone house which was called "Stone Fort." In this the people of that vicinity took refuge at times to protect themselves against the Indians. Levi Spangler and his brother Christian, were engaged many years in coal operating at Tremont, Pennsylvania. Christian Spangler was a prominent man of his day. He was one of the thirteen original directors of the Pennsylvania R. R. Company, and continued to be an officer of that road up to the time of his death, being the last of the thirteen to die.

LIVER B. ELLIOTT. Among the most important public institutions of Beaver county is the Home for the Poor and Infirm, a fact which is largely due to its successful management by the gentleman named above. It is situated on a tract of one hundred and thirty acres in Moon township, on the banks of the Ohio River, and commands a beautiful view. The place was formerly known as the Stone farm, and a part of the old farm house is now used as the superintendent's residence. A large brick building was erected for the use of the inmates which is a model of convenience in its arrangement, being heated and lighted with gas, equipped with numerous fire escapes and extinguishers, and a 250-barrel tank to insure safety from fire; its sanitary equipments are of the finest. There are thirty-two large, airy sleeping rooms for the accommodation of from eighty to one hundred and ten inmates, and the lower floor is given to separate parlors for the males and females; these are fitted up in comfortable style, and good literature is supplied. The pest house is placed in an isolated position on the farm, but, fortunately, owing to the absolute cleanliness of every portion of the place, this is but little used. The cellars and every out-of-the-way corner are scrupulously clean,—and all of these conditions received due praise from the state superintendent. The building is surrounded by beautiful grounds, and a greater part of the farm is under cultivation, the product being used upon the table, leaving nothing but flour and meat to be bought for daily·use. The inmates are well cared for and are provided with an abundance of good, wholesome food, and treated on holidays to special dinners. In addition to this, entertainments are frequently given for their benefit, and they are allowed plenty of freedom. The inmates are very useful in the kitchen, laundry and bakery, and elsewhere; one man is placed in charge of the chicken coops,—500 fowls being kept. About 1,400 dozen eggs per annum are gathered, of which 1,000 eggs are kept for setting and the remainder are used for home consumption. The young inmates are instructed in useful ways, and are taught to lead a life of independence and self-reliance. As soon as possible they are placed in good homes, and in many instances have become useful and honored citizens. Mr. Elliott is eminently fitted for the position he holds, and it is to be hoped that for the advantage of the inmates and the benefit of the county, he will be retained for many years to come. He has made a study of human nature, and seems to comprehend every desire and want of his charges; these he endeavors to satisfy, if reasonable, and within his power. Kind and considerate, he has their respect, without exception.

Oliver B. Elliott was born in Moon township, Beaver county, June 20, 1857, and attended the district schools until he reached the age of sixteen years, after which he assisted his father on the farm until he was married. He later purchased a portion of his grandfather's old estate,—in all eighty-four acres. It was partially improved land, but Mr. Elliott improved both land and buildings still further,—setting out excellent orchards and vineyards. He raised six tons of grapes annually, besides large quantities of berries, cherries, apples, plums, etc. He also engaged in general farming. His place was well stocked with good horses, registered Jerseys and Holsteins, and sheep. He continued at this until he was appointed superintendent of the County Home, in 1897, since which time the place has been rented.

Mr. Elliott was united in marriage with Ellen Dunn, a daughter of Walter and Ellen Dunn, of Scotch birth, and they have three children: Bertha A., born in January, 1883, a student of Beaver High School of the graduating class of 1901; Frank W., born in August, 1885; and one who died in infancy. Politically, Mr. Elliott is a Republican, and served as assessor and collector for a long time. He was also constable until 1897, and has filled all the township offices except that of justice of the peace. Religiously, he is a member and elder of the Presbyterian church. Socially, he is a member of the K. of P.; Jr. O. U. A. M.; Woodmen of the World; and Rochester Lodge, B. P. O. E. Mr. Elliott's portrait accompanies this sketch.

————◆•◆————

WILLIAM·DELOSS HAMILTON, county, Pa., is one of that town's postmaster of Freedom, Beaver most active and popular business men, was born in Freedom, March 24, 1863, and is a son of Oliver James Hamilton. His great-

grandfather, James Hamilton, was born in Ireland, and on coming to America, settled among the early pioneers of the western townships of Beaver county. While assisting the sheriff to make an arrest, he was shot by some one who supposed him to be the sheriff. He was the first white man shot in Beaver county. His children were: James; Oliver; and Martha.

James Hamilton, the grandfather of the subject of this record, went to Beaver, where he learned the trade of a tailor, and afterward settled in Moon township, where he followed farming the rest of his life. He was born March 22, 1789, and died October 12, 1870. He married Elizabeth Weigle, a daughter of John Weigle. She was born December 6, 1799, and died May 7, 1866, at the age of sixty-six. Their children were, as follows: John, born January 16, 1824; Oliver James, born April 4, 1825; Caroline J., born August 3, 1826, and married to Daniel Irwin; Oscar, born April 20, 1828; Eleanor, born June 28, 1830, and married to Milo Jones; Susannah, born June 24, 1832; Sibeam, born November 1, 1834; Juliana, born October 14, 1837, and married to Milfred Webb; Samuel, born November 3, 1839; and Martha, born October 16, 1843. Oliver James Hamilton, the father of William Deloss Hamilton, followed farming early in life, and then learned ship carpentering, and became one of the members of the Freedom Barge Building Co., which built boats for many years. Then Mr. Hamilton followed house carpentering, and built himself a home on Fourth street, which he sold later. At present, he is retired from active life. He married Lovina Minor, a daughter of James Minor, of Hookstown, Beaver county. Mrs. Hamilton died August 15, 1853, at the age of thirty-four years, and eleven months. Their children were as follows: B. Deloss, deceased; James Oscar, born August 31, 1851, married to Cynthia Davis, and having six children, as follows: Elmer; Fay; Eva; James; and Adam and Nancy J., both deceased. Mr. Hamilton was married again, this time to Mary Jane Calvert, a daughter of James Calvert, of Allegheny, who was born in County Down, Ireland. Miss was born in County Down, Ireland. Miss Calvert was born July 13, 1827. The second union resulted in seven children, as follows: Lizzie L., born March 14, 1859, now deceased; John C., born October 19, 1860, and married to Lydia Cuppo, whose children were,—Lizzie, Rubie, John O., and Gertrude; William Deloss, the subject of this biography; Milo J., born November 25, 1864, and married to Joanna Lopp; Frank S., born April 8, 1867, and married to Clara Harshman; Alexander O., born May 19, 1869, married to M. Cronk, and having one child.—J. Earl; and Thomas, born April 23, 1871. Mr. Hamilton is a Republican in politics, and a member of the M. E. church.

William Deloss Hamilton, whose name heads this sketch, was educated in the schools of Freedom, and as early as twelve years of age, began work in the Rochester Tumbler Works,—spending several years also as a glass blower, in Pittsburg. When the Key-

stone Tumbler Works were established in Rochester, he was one of the organizers and stockholders, and is at present a stockholder. He worked there until January, 1898, when he was appointed postmaster of Freedom. The postoffice of Freedom was established about May 28, 1832, with Stephen Phillips as postmaster. The officials who preceded him in that capacity were as follows: William Smith, May 9, 1836; T. F. Robinson, March 6, 1840; Henry Bryan, April 30, 1844; Frederick Schumacker, September 25, 1845; William P. Phillips, February 18, 1850; John Graham, June 16, 1853; William Kerr, March 13, 1861; William D. Fisher, May 26, 1871; T. C. Kerr, September 6, 1880; Francis M. Grim, February 15, 1886; J. L. Conner; and G. W. Jack. The assistant is Miss Annie C. Lewis. Miss Elizabeth Wright served as assistant from 1880 until 1898.

Mr. Hamilton built, on Fourth avenue, a beautiful residence, which he occupies. He was united in marriage with Margaret Fehr, a daughter of Conrad and Mary Fehr. She was born in Pittsburg, but was reared in Freedom. The children which have blessed this union are: Clyde D.; Milo S.; Mary G.; Harry C., and an infant son, unnamed. Mr. Hamilton is a member of the I. O. O. F., of the Woodmen of the World and is a member, and ex-steward, of the Methodist Episcopal church. His present position he has filled to the entire satisfaction of all the citizens, and he has fully demonstrated that he is worthy of all the trust and confidence reposed in him.

FREDERICK DAVIDSON, vice-president of the Union Drawn Steel Co., of Beaver Falls, Pa., is among the most prominent citizens of his town. His career gives evidence of careful training in early youth. When young, he moved to Beaver, where he received his primary education, and later took an academic course at Chester Military School. His business tact and abilities attracted the attention of an official of the National Bank of New Brighton, and he obtained a situation as clerk in the bank, which he held for three years. He then accepted the responsible position of cashier of the Beaver National Bank. At the death of his brother, James J., he became president of the Union Drawn Steel Co., of Beaver Falls. His life has been a steady, onward and upward advance in every field of usefulness to which he has been called, in which respect his career is suggestively similar to that of his father. Socially, Frederick Davidson is affiliated with St. James Lodge, No. 457, F. & A. M., of the borough of Beaver, where he now lives. His political preference is with the Republican party. The subject of this writing is the youngest son of Daniel R. and Margaret C. (Johnston) Davidson, and a grandson of William and Sarah (Rogers) Davidson.

Hon. William Davidson was of Scotch-Irish origin, and was born in Carlisle, Cumberland county, Pa., February 14, 1783. He was a very prominent man of his day, both in religious and political circles. He was a clergyman of the Christian church and a very active worker in that denomination; he was equally influential in the political arena, having served as a member of the State Legislature, as state senator, and as speaker of the House. He died at the age of eighty-five years.

Daniel R. Davidson, father of Frederick, was an active business man of Beaver, Pa., and was born in Fayette county, Pa., January 12, 1820, where he was a pupil in the select schools. He was a man of notable commercial tact and ability; his business relations were varied and extensive. He dealt largely in coke and coal, and owned valuable mines. For many years, he was a successful and influential railroad official, having built the B. & O. R. R. from Pittsburg to Connellsville, Pa., in connection with which he held various offices, and for a time was president of that branch. After severing his connection with that road, he was the main promoter of the Fayette county branch of the Pennsylvania Railroad. At the time of his death, he was president of the Commercial National Bank, of Pittsburg, having been one of the organizers of that institution. He was also one of the board of directors of the National Bank of Commerce, of Pittsburg, from the time of its organization. He was the owner of two plants in the coke regions, and was president of the Love Manufacturing Co., of Rochester, Pa., during its existence. In politics, he was a Republican, and gave the weight of his influence to the advancement of the principles of that party, believing his own, as well as the public interests, were best advanced by Republican policies.

WILLIAM HENRY WAGONER.

Daniel R. Davidson was married in Fayette county, Pa., in 1846, to Margaret C. Johnston, daughter of Alexander Johnston, who was of Scotch-Irish descent. Seven children blessed this union, and were named as follows: Charles, who lives in Connellsville, Pa.; Sarah, William J., and Elizabeth, deceased; George, who is cashier of the National Bank of New Brighton; James J., deceased; Louis R.; and Frederick, the subject of this sketch. Daniel R. Davidson died March 18, 1884, and with his death ended a very useful and exemplary life.

———— ♦ • ♦ ————

WILLIAM HENRY WAGONER, a noted machinist, whose portrait is presented on the opposite page, has been a resident of Beaver Falls since 1883, when he accepted a position with the Hartman Steel Company, but subsequently engaged with the American Steel & Wire Company. He learned the trade of a rod roller, —becoming quite an expert at that business. On December 22, 1892, he was promoted to the position of a boss roller or that mill. The plant is an important one, and, when running full time, night and day, furnishes employment to 151 men, many of whom are under the direct supervision of Mr. Wagoner. August 24, 1899, Mr. Wagoner accepted a more responsible position with the same company, at Rankin, Pa., and has charge of the company's works there, as boss roller.

Besides the important position he occupies

with the above-mentioned firm, Mr. Wagoner is also interested in various other enterprises of minor note. In the many years he has exercised his right of suffrage, Mr. Wagoner has always voted with the Republican party, and takes an unusually active part in politics. He is a thorough advocate of good systems of public instruction and was elected to the office of school director from the sixth ward; he has taken a deep interest in affairs under consideration by the directors, and has served on some of the most important committees. Our subject is a member of the Masonic fraternity, in good standing,—being a past master of that order. He is also a member of Lodge No. 225, Knights of Pythias; of Lodge No. 311, Royal Arcanum, and is a member of Sr. O. U. A. M., Council No. 385.

William Henry Wagoner was born January 7, 1867, in Sewickley, Allegheny county, Pa., and is a son of Andrew and Sarah Jane (Marlatt) Wagoner, and grandson of Joseph Wagoner. Joseph Wagoner was a Pennsylvanian by birth, and was one of the pioneer settlers of Sewickley, Allegheny county, Pa., where he lived many years, and finally died. He was a carpenter by trade, and a steamboat builder. He assisted in building many boats on the Ohio River, and was an excellent workman. Andrew Wagoner, father of William Henry, was born in Sewickley township, December 16, 1832. He was reared in the same locality, and attended the district schools, remaining there even after attaining his majority. Like his father, he also engaged in carpenter work and steamboat building, and is now located in Van Wert, Ohio.

He was joined in matrimony with Sarah Jane Marlatt, a daughter of Joseph Marlatt. She was also a native of Allegheny county, and bore her husband eight children, four of whom are now deceased. The names of the children are: Elias, who resides in Little Chippewa township, where he follows the occupation of a farmer; Cecelia, deceased; William Henry, the subject of this sketch; Frank L., who died at the age of twenty-two years; James and Joseph, twins, who died young; Mary Luella, wife of W. J. Harris, of Beaver Falls; and Alfred. William Henry Wagoner was the recipient of a practical education acquired in the public schools of Sewickley. After leaving school his first position was with the Bentley & Goehring Works, of New Brighton, where he remained until 1883, when he went to Beaver Falls, as before mentioned.

The subject of this record was joined in marriage with Elizabeth A. Tucker, an attractive young lady. Their home was brightened by the presence of four children, one of whom is now deceased. Their names are: Winifred M.; Samuel Anderson; Warren Henry, deceased; and Merle Edwin. Besides his cares and duties, Mr. Wagoner has time to devote to other affairs, and takes much interest in the progress and welfare of his community. He is abundantly qualified to fill his present, or any similar, position, for his life has been spent in factories and in following mechanical arts. He is found ready and willing to undertake new projects, but is still conservative enough to withhold his support from visionary and wild cat schemes. He is broad and liberal in his ideas, and is esteemed and respected by his many acquaintances; he performs the varied duties which fall to his lot with a ready tact and ease that come only from thorough experience.

———— • • ————

HENRY SECHRIST, a progressive dairyman, and stock and feed farmer, of Big Beaver township, ranks among the most up-to-date agriculturists of Beaver county, Pa. Mr. Sechrist commenced the dairy business about 1872, when he purchased the homestead farm from his father. Previous to that, he had followed farming ever since leaving school, and the complete management of the farm had been left to him for several years. He removed to Beaver county, when nineteen years of age. Having good business ability he was quick to realize that money was to be made in the dairy trade. He started with only twelve cows, but has since had as many as thirty-five. At first, he kept only the short-horn variety, but later changed to the Holstein breed, and now keeps only Jerseys. The dairy products of his farm were formerly shipped to Allegheny and Pittsburg. Later, he purchased a retail route in Beaver Falls. Disposing of that, Mr. Sechrist now ships to Beaver Falls. He also raises hogs and horses, and large quantities of grain and hay. Most of the latter is, however, feed for his stock. Soon after purchasing it, our subject built a new house on his farm; this house was destroyed by fire in 1894. In March, of the same year, was begun the erection of his present handsome residence, which was constructed from plans drawn by himself. He also built fine, large barns, equipped with all modern conveniences. Only the latest and most improved farming implements are to be found on his farm, and when not in use, these are carefully sheltered under neat sheds prepared for the purpose. Everything about his place goes to show the superior ability and management of its owner, the entire premises being a model of neatness and convenience. Besides keeping up the old orchards on the farm, Mr. Sechrist has recently planted a fine, large peach orchard containing the choicest varieties to be found.

Henry Sechrist was born in Johnstown, Pa., July 18, 1840. He is a son of Henry, Sr., and Nancy (Flinchbaugh) Sechrist, and comes of good German stock. Henry Sechrist, Sr., was born in York county, Pa., in 1806. He was instructed in the public schools, and afterward learned milling. He subsequently built a mill, which he conducted himself, carrying on a successful business for twenty years. He then moved to Cambria county, Pa., and rented a farm for a brief period. Removing to Indiana county, he rented another farm, but did not like the country, and moved again. This time he located in Allegheny county, where he followed agricultural pursuits for eleven years.

In 1860, he purchased a farm in Beaver county, and immediately occupied it. This is the identical farm now occupied by the subject of our sketch. It was then an improved farm of 140 acres, with a frame house and barns. It was much deteriorated, however, —with buildings out of repair. Henry Sechrist's father rebuilt the house and barns and set about enriching the land. He set out fine fruit orchards and put many modern improvements on the place. His marriage was celebrated in New York City, where he espoused Nancy Flinchbaugh. Mrs. Sechrist was a native of York county, Pa., where she received a good scholastic training. She proved a worthy helpmeet to her husband in every way. Eight children were born to them, namely: Sarah (Scott); William; Jacob; Henry, the subject of this sketch; Susan (Miller); Annie, who died in infancy; Mary, who never married; and Sylvester, who also died young. Henry Sechrist, Sr., was a prominent Democrat. He served as supervisor and as school director. Early in life he embraced the faith of the Methodists, but subsequently became a member of the United Presbyterian church, of which he served many years as trustee and steward.

The subject of this record was the recipient of a practical education while yet in Allegheny county. In 1887, he wedded Lizzie M. Dillon, a charming daughter of James and Barbara Dillon. Mrs. Sechrist was born, reared, and educated in Beaver county. One son, William L., born July 11, 1895, blesses their home and renders life more happy. In politics, Mr. Sechrist is an ardent Democrat. He has served as school director and supervisor, has held many of the township offices,— among them, that of treasurer. He favors the Methodist religion, and is trustee and steward of the church of that denomination. In fraternal associations, he is an active member of Meridian Lodge, No. 411, F. & A. M., and of Harmony Chapter, of Beaver Falls. Such men as Mr. Sechrist are valuable acquisitions to any community.

———— ◆ ◆ ————

APT. FRANK MARATTA is one of the oldest and most respected men in Beaver county, and makes his home at Rochester. He has owned many steamers during his life time, and has undoubtedly served as captain on more boats on the Ohio River than any other man in that section of Pennsylvania. He is a son of James and Elizabeth (Walker) Maratta, and was born in Beaver county, October 25, 1819. His father was also born in that county, but his grandparents were natives of France.

James Maratta, the father of Frank, took up the trade of a carpenter and later became a contractor, settling at Bridgewater, where his father before him had lived. He lived there the remainder of his life and died at the age of sixty-two years. His union with Elizabeth Walker resulted in the birth of the following children: Caleb; Margaret; Mahala; Peter; Frank, the gentleman whose name appears at the head of this sketch; Cynthia; James; Ann; Mary; Hines; Daniel; and three others who died in infancy. Those who grew to maturity are all respected citizens of the various communities in which they reside.

Capt. Frank Maratta started life as a pilot on the river, and became very skillful in that capacity on keel boats. He subsequently engaged as cook on a steam packet, run between Pittsburg and New Castle, Pa., but a man of his ability and ambitious nature does not remain down long. He bettered his position as the opportunity presented itself, and became a captain of steamboats. He became owner of many boats and was interested in others. He built the Forest Rose at California, Pa., and the Paris and Princess at Freedom, all of which he ran a few years, and then disposed of to the government. He built the Champion, at Freedom, the Sunny Side, at Brownville, and the Mansfield. His next two boats, the Henry A. Jones and the Belle of Texas, after crossing the Gulf of Mexico, he sold at Galveston, Texas. He then built the Forest Rose No. 2, and the Leonidas, which he ran before selling them. He was also part owner and captain of Scotia Packet; Ironsides; and was captain of the Alaska; Golden Eagle; Robert Burns; Bostonian No. 1; Bostonian No. 2; and the Alice Dean. After many years of the greatest activity, in 1890, he retired from the river, but is still financially interested in a number of enterprises. He was an organizer and a stockholder of the Conway Bank, and is president of the Big Beaver River Bridge Company, and a director of the Brighton Bridge Company. He also served as councilman of the borough.

Captain Maratta was united in marriage with Lydia Ransom, who was born in Jeffersonville, Ind., and was a daughter of James Ransom. She died in 1893, at the age of seventy-three years. The subject of our sketch formed a second marital union with Millie P. Seidell, a daughter of J. G. Seidell, of Scioto county, Ohio. In 1890, he built his present handsome residence in Rochester, having previously built what is known as the Dr. A. L. Shallenberger residence. He then erected another residence which he sold to William Moulds. At the advanced age of eighty years, Captain Maratta is enjoying excellent health, having never been sick in his life until the spring of 1899, when he suffered from an attack of "la grippe." He is a man of good habits, never using tobacco or liquor in any form, and to this may be attributed more than anything else his wonderfully strong constitution. He is a man of pleasing personality, a clever conversationalist, and stands high in the estimation of his fellow men.

WILLIAM MOULDS, who has attained prominence throughout Western Pennsylvania as the general manager of the Rochester Tumbler Company, a firm employing the largest number of hands in the service of any concern in the borough, has been engaged in the manufacture of glass in various departments of the work for almost a half century. He is a man of tried business ability, which, coupled with his years of experience, has been an important factor in the thriving condition of the establishment with which he has been connected since its inception. It is, unquestionably, the largest enterprise of its kind in the world. Mr. Moulds is also president of the Olive Stove Works of Rochester, which occupies an important place among the manufacturing industries of that community. He was born near Milltown, County Antrim, Ireland, December 9, 1842, and is a son of John and Nancy (Henry) Moulds.

John Moulds was also born in County Antrim, Ireland; upon coming to the United States he landed in New York City, but subsequently located at Steubenville, Ohio, where his wife had a brother and friends. On arriving here he was without a trade, but soon learned the art of glass blowing, which he followed nearly all of his life. During his last days he was engaged in packing, and was a man of remarkable activity up to the end,—dying in 1890, at the age of seventy-five years. He was a man of sturdy constitution and enjoyed fine health, having shaved himself just three days prior to his demise. He married Nancy Henry, a daughter of William Henry, and their children were as follows: William, the subject of this personal history; Samuel H., a record of whose life also appears in this work; Annie, the relict of Albert Albin, of Columbus, Ohio; Sarah, the wife of Eli Capers, of Steubenville, Ohio; Robert, who lives at Rochester; John, also a resident of

Rochester; and Elizabeth, who makes her home at Steubenville, Ohio.

William Moulds left school at an early age, being eight years old when he was instructed in the art of mold-making for the use of blowing glass. He became a very skilled mechanic, and followed that line of work at his Ohio home until 1866, when he removed to Pittsburg and there engaged at his trade. In 1872, he assisted in organizing the Rochester Tumbler Company, which comprised the following prominent business men: H. C. Fry; G. W. Fry; S. M. Kane; William Moulds; S. H. Moulds; Thomas Carr; William Carr; Thomas Matthews; John Hayes; J. H. Lippencott; and Richard Welsh. Mr. Moulds and H. C. Fry went to Rochester and there purchased the ten-acre estate of A. Lacock, which was at one time a fine maple grove, and, later, partly used as a brick yard. They immediately broke ground and soon a factory was built and in full operation, their success being manifest from the start. Misfortune (through fire) overtook them when they had been running for two years, but they rebuilt without delay and made many valuable improvements which greatly facilitated manufacture, and greatly increased the output. At that time three new members were added to the firm, namely: George Searles, and Robert and John Carr. The plant has grown to be the largest enterprise of its kind in the world, their shipments being directed to all parts of the United States, Canada, England (and other parts of Europe), South America, Africa, Australia, Mexico, China and Japan.

They ship from three to ten carloads per day, and have a monthly output of 150,000 dozen of blown goods and 150,000 dozen of pressed, giving employment to twelve hundred persons. They have their own dynamos, and the factory is equipped with 1,000 incandescent lights. They also have their own ice house and water works, containing a tank with a capacity of 3,100 gallons. The firm at the present time is organized as follows: H. C. Fry, president; William Moulds, general manager; S. H. Moulds, assistant manager; J. H. Fry, secretary; and Clayton Vance, treasurer. Mr. Moulds has also been closely identified with other business interests about Rochester,—prominent among them being the Olive Stove Works, of which he is president. He has taken an active interest in the progress of the borough, and has made many friends throughout this section by the honorable manner in which he conducts his affairs.

He was united in matrimony with May Jane, a daughter of Captain John Wallace, of Steubenville, Ohio, and they have three children: Mary W., widow of H. B. Shallenberger, of Rochester; John W., deceased; and Jessie Agnes. Mr. Moulds resides in a fine home on West Adams street, and has served in the council for two years. Fraternally, he is a member of the Odd Fellows and Masonic orders. He served in the Civil War, enlisting in 1864, as a corporal in Company C, 157th Reg., Ohio Vol. Inf. Religiously, he is a member of the Baptist church. We present a portrait of Mr. Moulds on another page, in proximity to this.

CHARLES M. HUGHES is the present popular and efficient cashier of the Beaver National Bank; he has had a broad and useful experience in this line of business, as he has been connected with various banking institutions almost continuously since his early manhood. Our subject is a man of fine business ability, is a favorite in both business and social circles, and he always lends his influence in favor of such enterprises and measures as he deems best for the advancement and prosperity of the borough, county, state and country at large. He was born in Lima, Ohio, May 24, 1856, and is a son of Richard T. Hughes. Richard T. Hughes was a farmer in early life, but later conducted a mercantile store at Lima. He was county treasurer of Allen county, Ohio, for a period of four years. He died March 7, 1879, at the age of fifty-one years.

Charles M. Hughes was intellectually trained in the public and high schools of Lima; at the age of eighteen years, he accepted his first bank position, that of clerk in the First National Bank, of Lima, Ohio; two years later he became assistant cashier of the Allen County Bank, of Lima,—remaining in that capacity until 1881. In that year he returned to the First National Bank, of Lima, and became cashier of that institution. Having spent a life of indoor occupation up to this time, Mr. Hughes decided to seek some open air exercise, and accordingly, in 1894, he resigned his position in the bank and entered the employ of the Mutual Life Insurance Company as traveling agent out of

Cleveland, Ohio. In 1896, Mr. Hughes returned to his former occupation,—accepting a position as cashier of the Beaver National Bank, succeeding cashier Fred Davidson. This bank is practically a new institution, having thrown open its doors to the public July 1, 1896; it has a capital stock of $100,000.00 and is one of the most solid banks in the county. The officers of the Beaver National Bank are J. R. Leonard, president; E. K. Hum, vice-president; C. M. Hughes, cashier; and William P. Judd, assistant cashier. In 1895, a handsome brick and stone building was erected for the bank; in the center of the building is the large safe and vault, and also the deposit drawers; in the rear is the directors' room, while in the front is a private office; the interior is finished with quartered oak, presenting a very neat appearance, and the building throughout is heated with hot water and lighted by both electric lights and gas.

Mr. Hughes was married June 18, 1878, to Miss Katherine M. Colbath, a daughter of J. A. Colbath, of Lima, Ohio, and they are the proud parents of three children, namely: Clarence L., corresponding clerk in the Columbia National Bank, of Pittsburg, Pa.; Margaret, who is a student at Beaver College; and Dorothy. Fraternally, our subject is a member of the F. & A. M., of Lima, Ohio, No. 205; Chapter No. 49; Shawnee Commandery, No. 14, and is past commander of the same; he is also a member of the K. of P. lodge, of Lima, Ohio. Religiously, he and his family are Presbyterians. During the short period Mr. Hughes has been a member of the community, he has, by his courteous manners and superior business ability, won hosts of friends, who greatly esteem and respect him for his sterling worth; he is well read and intelligent, and fulfills all the obligations of a dutiful citizen.

———•••———

ALEXANDER T. FORSYTH, a prominent citizen of the borough of Baden, Beaver county, Pa., is a contractor of wide reputation, and has built many of the principal buildings in that section of the county. He was born in Allegheny county, Pa., in 1829, and received the ordinary instruction of the public schools.

Although his educational advantages were limited, he made the best of his opportunities, and has acquired a good degree of practical knowledge by close observation and reading. He was taken from school at an early age to learn a trade, but continued to learn what he could in private. There were six children in the family, and they all studied out of the same old arithmetic. He adopted farming and followed that line of work until he reached his twentieth year, when he learned the trade of a carpenter, which he followed until 1852. He then removed to Beaver county, and subsequently to Wheeling, West Virginia, where he worked in a sash and door factory until 1861. Owing to the central situation of Wheeling, there was a division of sentiment on the war question,

which resulted in a depressing effect on all kinds of business. He then began contracting for himself at Baden, Beaver county, Pa., and has since been one of the most prominent men of that place. His first contract was to build the Lutheran church, in which he has always been a most earnest worker, and he has since had the contracting of all the principal buildings in that locality. He recently completed a church in Braddock, Pa., and now has a school building in course of construction at Remington, Pa. He is also agent for Dr. Daly, of Pittsburg, and has the management of his real estate interests in this district. He has always been a popular citizen of the borough, and served in the first council after its incorporation. He has since served as school director and councilman, and was burgess for four years. He was then elected justice of the peace, an office he is now filling for his third term. He has always given good satisfaction in this capacity, his aim being rather to keep people from litigation than to increase his own revenues by promoting it. That his policy is appreciated was forcibly demonstrated at the last election. He ran on the Democratic ticket, and out of a voting list of 100, he only received an opposing vote of seven. This is all the more remarkable when the fact is taken into consideration that the county is strongly Republican.

Mr. Forsyth was united in marriage with Sarah J. Romigh, and they became the parents of three children, namely: James F., a foreman in the tin-plate mill; William Taylor, now working in the oil fields; and Walter A.,

REV. WILLIAM G. TAYLOR, D. D.

who is with Jones & Company, of Pittsburg. Mrs. Forsyth died on her thirty-eighth birthday, and the subject of our sketch subsequently formed a second union, with Mary J. Sickles, to whom have been born three children: George, weigh master in the tin-plate mills; Alma; and Margaret. Mr. Forsyth is a very active member of the Lutheran church and for thirty-seven years was superintendent of the Sunday School. He is also a deacon of the church.

REV. WILLIAM G. TAYLOR, D. D., of Beaver, Pennsylvania, whose portrait appears on the opposite page, has done as much to advance the education, elevate the morals, and give prosperity to the people under his charge as any other man in Western Pennsylvania. It is appropriately and truly said of him that "he loves to undertake things others are afraid to touch, and with pluck, tact, labor, patience and perseverance, succeeds." His intellectual faculties are uncommonly clear, forcible, and powerful, rendering him a superb organizer; his reasoning is clear and right to the point. He possesses the happy faculty of making deep thoughts so plain that even the uneducated think them simple truths; he is preeminently adapted to treat of moral and religious subjects, and is a natural theologian, minister, Sabbath school and Bible class teacher. In fact, he is an expounder of moral truths, and is peculiarly fortunate in making appropriate and happy illustrations. These char-

acteristics of Dr. Taylor make him a natural educator of the young. He is not a bargain driver, but is capable of prompt and instant comprehension of the facts involved in active business matters of any kind, and is most likely to succeed. He is a keen judge of human nature, and can lay plans and think for others, attending to a great variety of affairs simultaneously, with rapidity and ease, and apparently without the least confusion. Dr. Taylor is of Scotch-Irish origin, and is a son of James and Margaret Taylor. He was born at Pittsburg, Pa., March 3, 1820, and had nine brothers, six of whom died in infancy. The other three lived to advanced age; one, a half brother, was Rev. J. B. Walker, D. D., an author of note; the other two were successful and prominent manufacturers and merchants of Pittsburg, for over forty years. Dr. Taylor also had three sisters who reached old age.

The father of the subject hereof was one of the Irish patriots who settled in Pittsburg, in 1798. He was a druggist, and was most anxious to have William G. succeed him in that business, and began training his son while yet in childhood for that purpose. James Taylor was ambitious, however, beyond his strength; and his career was cut short by death in August, 1827. Thus the education and training of William G. was left entirely to his mother.

Mrs. Taylor, although a woman who possessed only the common education of those days, had a vigorous and poetical mind, plenty of good common sense, devout piety, and implicit trust in God. She was a strict disciplinarian, and rigidly enforced the rules of obedience, industry and study. She believed that the youth should have plenty of work, study, and play,—leaving no time for idleness, and bad habits. These inculcations developed, in time, into the fixed habits, the untiring industry and studiousness and the unconquerable energy, which characterized Dr. Taylor in his manhood. During the intervals between school-terms he was kept at work in some business house from the time he was nine years old, and at a later period in life he always found employment readily in such concerns, during his college and seminary vacations. He loved to teach and excelled in discipline; his versatility of talent, education, and training, fitted him for the ministry, the educator's task, and for the arena of business.

Dr. Taylor left the manufacturing and mercantile life in Pittsburg, in which he was engaged as a partner and business manager, to finish his education, and to prepare himself for the ministry, with the view of laboring among the churches which were unable to pay a full salary or were broken down, or involved in some kind of difficulty. For this unusual department of church work he felt that he had an especial adaptation, and his invariable success proved that he was not mistaken in his calling.

The subject of this biography graduated at Jefferson College (now Washington and Jefferson) in 1847, and took a full course in the Western Theological Seminary, from which he graduated in 1849. He was licensed to preach the Gospel by the Presbytery of Pitts-

burg, in April, 1848, and was ordained by the same presbytery as an evangelist in April, 1849, with a view of laboring among the broken down, feeble churches, or those unable to support a pastor, or working in new fields.

He was invited to become assistant-editor of the Prairie Herald Publishing Company, of Chicago, Illinois. This company published two religious weeklies, and worked off on their small power press two dailies, and one monthly, and two quarterly, journals. In connection with the company was a bookstore, in which Dr. Taylor found additional employment; he also assisted the pastor of the Third Presbyterian church in his pastoral duties as the latter was in feeble health. The intense labor occasioned by his various duties, together with an attack of chills and fever, finally broke down his health and he sought rest in assuming charge of a small New England congregation; but the chills and fever continued and at last compelled him to go back to Pittsburg, his native city.

On his return, he commenced his work on unbroken ground, at Mt. Washington, on the hill above South Pittsburg, assuming charge of that field, in April, 1851. There a good Sabbath school was organized, and the foundation laid for a flourishing church. About that time, the Presbyterian church of Beaver, having declined from one hundred and ninety-six members to forty-two, gave Dr. Taylor a call, for half time. He accepted the charge, devoting his full time, however, as that was necessary in order to insure success. A neighboring church of three hundred members, all active, zealous workers, was gathering into its folds, as many as possible who formerly belonged to the Presbyterian church. But under the labors of Dr. Taylor and his faithful few, a reaction took place in favor of the old church, its edifice was handsomely repaired, and in the course of four years its congregation and membershp were increased one-half, and a good Sabbath school was organized. The church of Tarentum had been in trouble for several years, and needed special labor; there was some discord, and difficulty in raising the salary, although for only half time, as the Bull Creek church raised the other half,—the same minister serving both flocks. The calls for Dr. Taylor to assume these charges being unanimous, were accepted by him, and he entered upon his work. Soon harmony was restored and a missionary point at Natrona was added to this field. In four and a half years, each of these churches was enabled to command the full services of a pastor, and one of them was able to build a parsonage. This ended the necessity for Dr. Taylor's labors in that sphere.

His next field was at Mount Carmel, Pennsylvania. This church had been without a pastor for twenty years, and lacked unity, and ability to support a pastor half of the time. Commencing in May, 1861, Dr. Taylor gave his full attention to this charge, restoring harmony, and very soon bringing the church into better condition; he remained there for four years. In 1865, the pastor of North Branch church left, and Dr. Taylor took that place for his extra service, in order to unite the two churches in one pastoral charge to support a pastor. Soon these churches were prepared to make a call for full time, and, his work in them being done, were placed in the hands of Rev. R. J. Cummings, D. D., with a salary of $1,000. Soon the church was able to build a fine new church edifice at New Sheffield, near the old church.

His next field of labor was the old disbanded church of Concord, on Southern avenue, now Pittsburg, Pa. With eleven Christian workers and no Sabbath school, he commenced work and succeeded in building and paying for a new church and Sabbath school rooms, and establishing a Sabbath school which enrolled two hundred and fifty pupils in four years, with a good library.

For ten and one-half years, Dr. Taylor was principal and chaplain to the Soldiers' Orphan School, and preached twice every Sunday. This was the great work which has made him famous as an organizer, educator and character builder, and was done in connection with the Phillipsburg Soldiers' Orphan School, an institution practically established by his efforts. The labors performed by him in connection with this school will be briefly described at the close of this sketch.

On April 15, 1849, Dr. Taylor was united in marriage with Charlotte Thompson, a daughter of John and Mary Thompson, of Allegheny, Pennsylvania. This estimable and thoroughly educated lady and devoted wife, has been a valuable companion and assistant to him in filling his various charges. Their home was rendered doubly attractive and happy by the addition of the following children: Mary M.; Charlotte E.; James W.; Ellen S.; John T., and Harvey J. Mary M. is the widow of C. Martin, a lawyer. They had three children, namely: William T., Erwin S., and Charlotte E. Charlotte E., the second daughter, now deceased, was the wife of T. L. Kerr. James W. is a machinist, of Beaver, Pa. Ellen S. is the wife of William J. Stewart. They have three children: William J., Herbert T., and Ethel T. Mr. Stewart is a stockholder and superintendent of the Fallston Fire Clay Company. John T. is a capitalist and real estate dealer, of Monaca. He married Ida M. McDonald and has four children: Jean K., Vera, William G., Jr., and Ida M. Harvey J. married Hester L. Potter, and has two children: James S., and Harold A. Dr. Taylor owns, perhaps, the finest modern house in Beaver. It was built in 1897 and 1898, and is situated on East Third street. His former home was built in 1854, and is near his present residence. He also owns several other houses in Beaver. He values money for its use only; he is regarded as a man of great wealth, all of which has been made in a legitimate business way, and not by speculation, or the neglect of his professional calling. As early as 1847, he commenced making investments in real estate, and his close economy gave him means for any good investment which his keen foresight pronounced good. He has always been a liberal giver, is public-spirited, and has assisted others to prosperity. It was principally in this way that

his handsome competency was secured. His observation and experience are to the effect that moral character, integrity, temperance, courtesy, industry, economy, value of time, and public spirit are the highest way to success in life.

From boyhood, Dr. Taylor took strong grounds on the temperance, the Sabbath, and anti-slavery, as well as religious, questions. He felt from his anti-slavery views, as well as for the unity of the government, a deep interest in the Civil War, and immediately after the firing upon Fort Sumter (in fact, the same evening), he commenced recruiting for the conflict. He was deeply interested in the great work of the Christian commissions at home and in the field. The Beaver county commission, of which ex-Chief-Justice Agnew was chairman, placed Dr. Taylor in charge of the work in Beaver county. Dr. Boardman, the United States secretary of the commission, made the statement that Beaver county was the banner county of the Union in the ratio of its population to the amount raised. Dr. Taylor's labor in this capacity was entirely gratuitous. His enterprising spirit, courage and foresight prepared him to take the risk of progress and improvement.

The subject of this biography was one of the seven who met at the call of Mr. Nelson to organize the Beaver County Agricultural Society. He was also one of the principal organizers of the Beaver Female College and Musical Institute. With Prof. Blees, he was the first to publicly advocate the necessity for a county superintendent of public schools, and conducted the first teachers' institute for Hon. Thomas Nicholson, the first county superintendent of Beaver county. He and Mr. Mair, of Rochester, Pa., were the originators of the Sabbath School Institute, and held the first institute in Rochester, and the second in the East Liberty Presbyterian church, Pittsburg. These annual institutes are now generally held. He was for years a member of the Prison Society of Western Pennsylvania.

Dr. Taylor served as director of the Third National Bank, and also of the Germania Savings Bank, of Pittsburg, and is a trustee of the Western Theological Seminary, of Allegheny, Pennsylvania. He earnestly pressed the necessity for, and the claims of, the Pittsburg & Lake Erie R. R., when that company was securing the right of way and stock subscriptions. He was also a director of the Freedom & Beaver Street Railway.

Dr. Taylor has a very large and well selected library; books on theology, biblical criticism, commentaries, practical religion, controversial, a large reference library, works on metaphysical subjects, on science and philosophy, physiology, biography, history and many miscellaneous works. He has given at various times over 1,000 volumes to other libraries and individuals.

HISTORY OF PHILLIPSBURG SOLDIERS' ORPHAN SCHOOL.

This was a new and most difficult field which opened for the labors of Dr. Taylor. The county superintendents of Beaver, Alle-gheny and Washington counties, together with Colonel Quay, recommended Dr. Taylor's appointment as principal, to open the first regular and exclusively soldiers' orphan school in Western Pennsylvania. Many friends of the Union and of the soldiers' orphans, knowing the Doctor's fitness for work of the kind, urged him to accept the trust. But there were very serious difficulties in the way, namely: The state would provide neither ground, buildings, books nor furniture; the uncertainty of the necessary appropriations was another obstacle; it would require $20,000 for the purchase of farm, buildings, furniture, house supplies, school room, books, and apparatus, etc.; the small amount allowed each orphan for board, clothing, schooling, books, etc., was insufficient. This amount was according to age,—for those under ten years of age, $115 per year, and for those from ten years of age to sixteen, $150 per year. This was all the allowance made to meet all demands, including those of teachers, employees and medical attention. The work of caring for one hundred and fifty orphans would require twenty assistants, to be paid, also, out of this amount.

These obstacles made considerable risk in the undertaking, but Dr. Taylor took the risk and succeeded. It was difficult to obtain a suitable location in the congressional district. At last the former "Water-cure," later used as a summer resort, was purchased. It was repaired and refurnished throughout, and was enlarged by a dwelling 34 by 44 feet; girls' hall, 20 by 41 feet, with high ceiling,—the hall including laundry, bakery and additional cook room; an additional building, a school room, 27 by 44 feet; a boys' hall, 24 by 46 feet; and a chapel, 26 by 46 feet. In addition to this, 210 acres of land was purchased,—the plant costing in all $48,000. This amount was all furnished by Dr. Taylor. This made literally a family home.

The next difficulty was to obtain and train teachers and help for this new and peculiar work, which required some time and changes. All the buildings were handsomely and tastefully furnished, as taste is essential to culture in girls and boys. The music rooms were carpeted with Brussels carpet and furnished with chairs, and a piano and organ, and the chapel was provided with an organ.

EDUCATIONAL.

The state prescribed eight grades as the extent of the educational course. To this Dr. Taylor found he could add four grades of a mathematical and scientific course, and one-fourth of the orphans were able to finish these four grades. The average annual progress of the school, on examination of the state committee, was one and five-eighths grades, while one-third made two grades, and an average standing of from 92 to 95. No one was promoted unless his or her standing was at least 75.

HYGIENE.

The laws of health and life were practically understood and carried out by Dr. Taylor, as the result shows. Food was given for bone-making, muscle, nerve, and brain. All clothing was fitted and adapted, perfect cleanliness of body, house, school rooms and work houses was required, and out-houses were thoroughly ventilated and supplied with an abundance of light. The following regulations were enforced: Nine hours of regular sleep; two hours of moderate, but diligent, work on fixed details; two hours of exercise, play or amusement, and, for boys, one hour of military drill, morning and evening; clean, warm feet; good shoes with common-sense heels, fitted by Dr. Taylor personally. Thus six hundred orphans were cared for, and it may be mentioned that two hundred of them required medical attention, on being received. Only four of the six hundred died in ten years, and three of these were incurables. All the rest, on examination by the state surgeon at the time of their discharge when sixteen years old, received the grading of "100," as to health,—with the exception of one thought to be incurable, who was marked "95,"—and she is now in perfect health.

INDUSTRY.

With the aid of his excellent and well educated wife, his constant and efficient assistant, who was the recipient of a remarkable domestic training in all the branches of housekeeping and household economics, Dr. Taylor was able to originate a system of industrial details of labor, and to have recitations daily in classes under competent teachers, for thirty days in each department. By this method each girl in the institution, without losing a recitation in school, acquired an intelligent system and practical knowledge of the domestic work, such as scrubbing, washing, ironing, house-cleaning, dining-room work, cooking, baking, mending, darning, plain family sewing and fine dressmaking, all of which work was subject to the daily inspection of either Mrs. Taylor or the Doctor. Every room and department was open for the scrutiny of visitors daily, except Sunday, from 8 a. m. to 5 p. m., and all visitors were furnished with a guide to accompany them. All the surroundings and training in the work department were designed to form and confirm habits of system, to instil industry, refine the tastes and manners, and give beauty and ease to the person. These results can not be secured without regular habits of industry. The effects of this culture and training manifested themselves everywhere—in private, in public, at church, and in their success and influences in after-life.

MORAL, RELIGIOUS, AND GENERAL INSTRUCTION.

Dr. Taylor had a Bible class of all the scholars and employees of the institution, and also of his own family. He preached Sabbath morning, he taught the Sabbath school in the afternoon, and lectured in the evening on religious biography, Bible history, and archaeology. During the week, he also gave table talks each day,—talks about ten minutes in length on some subject, historical, moral, or economical,—on government, on passing events, or on incidents that occurred in school.

In addition to this, teachers of the institution were required, in evenings and on the Sabbath, to read, for the benefit of the scholars, an average of seventy-five volumes per year. By this method, their intelligence was increased, and their conscience educated to become the guiding and controlling motor of their lives and conduct. Dr. Wickersham, state superintendent of public instruction in Pennsylvania, in writing to Dr. Taylor about the institution, said: "I read, twice a year, the history of the fifty boys and girls you wrote at my request, and it seems to me you have found out the true secret of elevating our race." Each teacher was required to be a model to the scholars. Dr. Taylor's success in giving education, culture, self-control and good habits to his scholars, is commented on in the report of Prof. Beamer's lecture in the M. E. church; he said, in conclusion: "In my entire experience as a public lecturer, traveling through the United States, Canada, and Europe, I have never seen such perfect development of the physical organization as there is in the entire body of the children of the Phillipsburg Soldiers' Orphan School, under the care of Dr. Taylor, and as is presented tonight by the one hundred and fifty boys and girls here present. I have never seen in my experience on both continents, such perfect discipline and order as is here shown tonight by these attentive children, whose happy countenances testify that this discipline is the result of proper government, and not of fear. As a soldier of the war that made them orphans, I am happy to meet them, and thrice happy in seeing their home, their training, their education, and their preparation and prospects for usefulness in life."

———————

MATTHEW NICKLE. The Book of Biographies of Beaver County would certainly be incomplete if mention were not made of the gentleman named above, a highly respected citizen and one of the wealthiest farmers in the county. His life has been one of industry, and he is now spending its declining years in the happy enjoyment of the fruit of his toil, on the old family homestead in Green township. He was born on July 7, 1822, in Hanover township, Beaver county, and is a son of David and Mary (Morrow) Nickle. David Nickle, the father of Matthew, came from Scotland, in 1820, and located in Hanover township, Beaver county, Pa., upon the farm on which the latter was born. He purchased that property and lived upon it two years, and then for a time rented another farm. He bought a farm in the northern corner of Hanover township, consisting of one hundred acres, which was left to his son, David, and is now owned by a son of the latter. He erected a fine house and barns, and cleared most of the land, devoting the closing period of his life to sheep-raising. He died in March, 1847, aged sixty-six years, and his wife died in 1872, at the age of seventy-two. While a resident of Scotland he married Mary Morrow, and five children were born to them before coming to this country, namely: James; George; William; David; and Elizabeth. Thereafter three children were born: Matthew; Alexander; and Margaret. They are all deceased but the subject hereof.

Matthew Nickle was born on the first land purchased by his father and continued to live with his parents until he reached the age of twenty-three, although previously to that time he rented and cultivated a farm owned by his father. Upon his father's demise he became possessed of a portion of his estate, and has since made his home upon it. During the oil excitement, he leased his property, and realized large returns. He is a self-made man in every particular, as a boy being industrious and ambitious. He improved his condition in life steadily and grew to be one of the most influential agriculturists in the district, owning at the present time some five hundred and fifty acres of rich farm land. In 1867, he erected a handsome residence, which is well-arranged and appropriately furnished, and also put up fine barns and out-buildings. While he has attained more than ordinary success in his life's work, he has at all times been most liberal with his money,—lifting many of his less fortunate fellow men to their feet when in distressing circumstances. He is of a modest and retiring disposition, and would have his charitable acts overlooked, but his numerous friends, who have known him so well for many years, delight in telling of his generosity. Being a man of good character and pleasing habits, and a clever conversationalist, he is very popular.

WILLIAM IRWIN BEBOUT.

In 1847, he married Margaret Patterson, by whom he had nine children, four of whom are now living, namely: Thomas F., who lives on the home farm; Alexander, who lives in Liverpool, where he is employed as a clerk in Robert Hall's lumber yard; Margaret R., who lives with her father; and William, who, when an infant, was adopted by Alexander and Mary Scott, of Ohio. Mrs. Nickle was called to her eternal home in 1868, and Mr. Nickle formed a second union, with Jane Hall, nee Bigger, who is also deceased. Politically, Mr. Nickle was formerly a Democrat, but is now a supporter of the Prohibition party. He is an elder of the U. P. church, and it was through him that the present fine church of that denomination was erected.

———— ♦ • ♦ ————

WILLIAM IRWIN BEBOUT, proprietor of a large general store in Darlington, Pa., whose portrait we present on the preceding page, has been found at the same stand for the past twenty-seven years. He deals in drugs, hardware, groceries, harness, paints, house furnishings, tin, granite, and enamel ware. Mr. Bebout was born in Mercer county, Pa., July 25, 1843. He is a son of Ellis and Olivia (Campfield) Bebout, and grandson of Peter Bebout.

Peter Bebout was a native of Green county, Pa., but at an early date removed to Mercer county, where he bought two hundred acres of wild land. After clearing a portion of it, he built a house and barn, and followed farming all his life.

Ellis Bebout, father of the subject hereof, was born in Mercer county, where he received his scholastic training. He afterward assisted his father on the farm; one hundred acres of the homestead farm were given him as his share of the estate. He married Olivia Campfield. Olivia was born in Mercer, where she was also educated. The following seven children were born to them: John C., who was killed in the army when twenty-one; Wesley S., a merchant in Mercer county; William Irwin, the subject of these lines: Alfred S., a retired merchant; Andrew J., a merchant, of Pittsburg. Pa.; Elizabeth Jane (Hewett); and Mary A. Ellis Bebout was a Whig. He was a member of the M. E. church, of which he was Sunday school superintendent for years. He died in 1852, at the early age of thirty-eight years, and was survived by his widow until 1896 when she, too, crossed the river of death.

William Irwin Bebout was mentally instructed in the public schools, which he attended constantly until he attained the age of seventeen years. He then enlisted in the Union Army, September 2, 1861; he entered Company B, 76th Reg., Pa. Zouaves, and participated in the following battles: Pocotaligo, Fort Wagner and Strawberry Plains. He was engaged in the siege of Petersburg, in Butler's and Grant's campaigns in Virginia, in connection with the Mine Explosion, and other historical events. He was honorably discharged November 30, 1864. He was severely wounded by a gun shot at Fort Wagner, July 11, 1863. He was in the hospital at Hilton Head for about nine months. While there, he was treated not only for his wound, but for lung and heart ailments and for neuralgia. At Botany Bay Isle, he was treated for laryngitis for several weeks. Mr. Bebout's brother, John C., was in the same company, and was killed while on picket duty at James Island, June 15, 1862.

Mr. Bebout was joined in marriage April 2, 1872, with Margaret M. McConnell. Mrs. Bebout was a native of Mercer county, Pa., where she was born, February 8, 1847. She was a daughter of Henry and Julia A. (Bruce) McConnell. Her primary education was received at her native place. Afterward, she entered Edinboro State Normal School, from which she hoped to graduate. Ill-health prevented this, however, compelling her to leave the institution. To Mr. Bebout and his amiable wife, one child, Anna Maude, was born; her birth occurring in Darlington, in September, 1873. After preliminary schooling she took a finishing course at Darlington Academy. From the time of the death of her beloved mother, in 1889, Anna Maude kept house for her father until her marriage with Mr. S. S. Leiper, of Darlington.

After the war, the subject of this sketch engaged in farming for one year and then for several years was a carpenter. He subsequently clerked awhile for his brother, who was a druggist. In 1872, he purchased Dr. Ball's business and started a drug store at his present location in Darlington. At a late date he added the lines previously mentioned, and enjoys a liberal patronage. As a business

man he is exceedingly popular. In politics, Mr. Bebout is a Republican. He has served in the borough council for several terms, and is still a member of that honorable body. He is in accord with the United Presbyterian church. Fraternally, he is enrolled as a member of the I. O. O. F., of Sharpsville, Pennsylvania.

⸺ ◦ •⸺

S. J. FAIR, the genial proprietor of a large general store at Smith's Ferry, Ohio township, has perhaps one of the best arranged and splendidly stocked country stores in Beaver county, Pennsylvania. Some time ago, Mr. Fair purchased the general store of T. L. Minesinger, at Smith's Ferry, and has since carried on a very successful business. This store is orderly in all its arrangements, and contains a large and very complete stock of groceries, hardware, house furnishings, cutlery, patent medicines, feed, dry goods, notions, boots and shoes, hats and caps, clothing, gent's furnishings, crockery, harness, ploughs, harrows, and all kinds of farm implements. Mr. Fair is special agent for Johnston's Harvester Company's machinery, and carries in stock a thousand and one things necessary in a country store.

S. J. Fair was born in Armstrong county, Pa., in September, 1866. He is a son of Philip and Nancy J. (Gregg) Fair, and grandson of John and Susannah (Christman) Fair. John Fair was born in Armstrong county, Pa., in 1804. He was a descendant of a prominent German family, that settled in Armstrong county in early days. They bought a good-sized farm of forest land. After making a clearing, they built a log house and barns; a part of this farm,—240 acres of improved land,—was left to the different members of the family. John Fair was instructed in the schools of his native county, but, as was unavoidable in those early days, his schooling was limited. However, he made the most of his opportunities. He learned the art of tilling the soil on the old homestead, which he eventually owned. His marriage with Susannah Christman resulted in the birth of four children, namely: William; Philip; Chambers, who was killed in the Civil War, while serving as drummer; and Susannah (Yerty). John Fair followed general farming until his death, in 1888.

Philip Fair, father of the subject of this biography, was born February 26, 1832, in Armstrong county, Pa., one-half mile from the birthplace of S. J., his son. He became a very fair scholar and after leaving school, learned the trade of a stone mason. He worked for his father until he attained the age of twenty-four years. He then bought a farm of sixty-five acres which he cultivated, but still continued to live with his parents until his marriage, in 1860. He was joined in matrimony with Nancy J. Gregg. Nancy was born May 2, 1840, and was a daughter of George Gregg. Eight children resulted from this union, viz: Harvey, a blacksmith; George, a merchant; Annie (Hellam); S. J., subject of this sketch; Charles, an engineer; Ross, Barney, and Claude, the last three being engaged in mercantile pursuits. After his sons grew up, Philip Fair left the care of the farm to them, and worked at his trade as stone mason. He followed that business as a contractor for about fifteen years. He was a Republican, but had no ambition for office. He was a member of the Lutheran church, of which he was an elder for fifteen years. His death occurred May 4, 1898.

S. J. Fair attended public school and became quite proficient in all studies required in a business course. He assisted his father on the farm during summers, and acted as clerk in the general store of his uncle, John Fair, during the winter months. This was continued until his twenty-first year. He then followed contracting and building at Leechburg, Pa., in partnership with one of his brothers. For two years they were very successful. Mr. Fair then sold his interest to his brother and retired from this line of work. In company with his brother George, he bought property and started a bakery and confectionery store. One year later, our subject sold his interest to his brother. Mr. Fair then went to Williamsport, Lycoming county, Pa., and started a similar store, which he conducted for three years. In 1892, he sold his store in Williamsport and moved to New Brighton, Pa., where he opened a grocery store. He did a successful business there for over two years, but finally sold out. He then invested in a dwelling house in New Brighton, which he rents. Soon after he purchased his present store and removed to Smith's Ferry.

Mr. Fair married Wildia McCracken. She was born in Armstrong county, in 1867, and is a daughter of James McCracken. One child, Margie Ethel, now brightens their home. She was born October 22, 1893. The subject of this narrative is a prominent stockholder in the Iron City Building & Loan Association. He is a Republican, but is too busy for political ambitions. He favors the Presbyterian church. Socially, he is allied with the Knights of Pythias. He is also a member of Glasgow Lodge, No. 485, F. & A. M., and is now passing through the chairs.

———— ◄ • ► ————

DAVID G. PATTERSON, a progressive farmer of Beaver county, Pa., was born in Darlington township, in this county, on November 26, 1859. He is a son of Rev. Samuel Patterson, who was a native of Ireland, but came to America in company with his brothers, when fourteen years old. He located in Allegheny, Pa., and there received his primary education. He pursued a clerical course in Allegheny Theological Seminary, and was ordained a minister in the United Presbyterian church. He was given a pastorate at New Galilee, in 1849, a charge he held all his life. He took advantage of the opportunities of the locality, and purchased a farm, which he also managed in connection with his professional duties. He had one of the best farms in the county, and raised considerable stock, making a specialty of sheep and dairying. The tract he bought contained two hundred and seventy acres. Soon after purchasing, he made extensive improvements,—tearing down the old house and replacing it with a fine country home,—a large brick residence, which commands one of the finest views of the Little Beaver Valley. The out-houses are in keeping with the nice dwelling, and speak volumes for the industry and progressive nature of the family. The buildings are large and constructed on modern plans, presenting an ornamental as well as comfortable appearance.

Mr. Patterson was always a busy man. In his younger days he taught school at the Darlington Academy; he also conducted a school in the basement of his church at New Galilee, and had a private school on his own farm. His business interests extended beyond that of farming; he was a large stockholder in the Little Beaver Woolen Co., and was for many years president of the company. His political belief was on the side of the Republican party, but he constantly refused to accept any office. He was a public-spirited man and took an active interest in all things pertaining to the welfare of the community. He married Eliza J. Gilliland, a daughter of David Gilliland, a pioneer of Beaver county. They reared seven children: Jennie (McCready); John; David G.; Isabella; Robert; Samuel; and Ada.

David G. Patterson was a pupil of Darlington and Bridgewater academies. After receiving his intellectual training, he returned to the farm and assisted his father in its management. In a few years he and his brothers

GEORGE W. DIXON.

assumed the full care of the place, and he has continued in that connection until now. After his father's death the property was left to the heirs, but as yet the shares have not been allotted. The brothers operate a large dairy,— having at times as many as forty-five cows.

Mr. Patterson is a member of the U. P. church. His political affiliations are with the Republicans, and he has satisfactorily served as assessor, collector, and constable, for his townsmen. He is a stockholder in the creamery of his native place.

————— ◆ ● ◆ —————

GEORGE W. DIXON, road master, master mechanic, and train master of the Pittsburg, Lisbon & Western R. R., whose portrait is shown on the opposite page, resides in a pleasant cottage in New Galilee, Pa., and has spent the whole of his active life in railroad service.

Mr. Dixon was born in Dalton, Luzerne county, Pa., March 26, 1852. He received a limited schooling there, being taken from school when ten years old. At that early age, he began to work on the railroad, carrying water for the section gang. When large enough, he commenced work on the section, and continued in that capacity until April, 1869. After spending one year on the steam shovel, he was employed the year following on the D., L. & W. R. R.; June 11, 1871, he was placed in charge of the track gang on the New Jersey Midland R. R. The track under his care was thirty-seven miles long. A short

time afterward, he was appointed assistant road master on the same line.

In June, 1874, Mr. Dixon commenced work on the New York Central R. R. and had charge of laying the tracks of the third and fourth lines on the Rochester and Syracuse division. The following year, however, he was induced to return to the New Jersey Midland R. R., where he was placed in charge of 87 miles of track. He remained on that road until 1881; at that time he went to Warren, Pa., and accepted a position as superintendent of a construction train on the Western New York & Pennsylvania R. R., between Warren and Salamanca. He held that important post until 1882. His next move was to engage with the road with which he is still connected. He was first superintendent of track-laying and overseeing the building of the road. When the road was completed, he was appointed superintendent, which position he held until 1887. Later, the road changed hands and Mr. Dixon remained as conductor. In 1893, he was appointed to his present important position as roadmaster, and has the entire charge of building tracks, bridges, locomotives, and everything outside of general office work. He is also master mechanic and train master. The subject of this record is a son of B. D. and Ruth A. (Calvin) Dixon, and grandson of John and Christiana (Ireland) Dixon.

John Dixon descended from an old Connecticut family. When a young man he located in Luzerne county, Pa., where he bought 100 acres of land. He followed farming all his life. His union with Christiana Ireland resulted in the birth of a large family of children, of whom Mr. Dixon's father was the second born. B. D. Dixon, this gentleman, was born in Dalton, Luzerne county, Pa., in October, 1826. After attending the public school, he learned how to till the soil, and followed that line of occupation until 1857, when he began railroad work. After working in the carpenter gang for a short time, he was promoted to be section foreman, and then to be supervisor, in charge of the track-laying gang. Ruth A. Colvin became his wife. She was a daughter of George Colvin, and was also born in Luzerne county, in 1824. Seven children resulted from this union. They are: Mary, now deceased; Caroline (Waldron); Emily M. (Latimer); George W., the subject of this biography; Florence A. (McCullom); Frank; and John, who died in infancy. In politics, B. D. Dixon was a Democrat. Religiously, he was an active member of the Baptist church. He died in 1885, but is still survived by his widow.

George W. Dixon was joined in marriage with Margaret A. Poole, a fascinating daughter of William Poole. Mrs. Dixon was born in Morris county, N. J., May 10, 1856, and received her mental training in the public school. Her marriage resulted in the birth of eight children, namely: Caroline A. (Beeson); Georgiana (Harris); Frank D.; Mary (McCowin); Howard G.; Irene, a student; Nellie; and Cornelius. Mr. Dixon is faithful to the interests of the Republican party. He has served as school director and as a member of

the council. He is a faithful member of the M. E. church. Socially, he is a member of Meridian Lodge, No. 411, F. & A. M., at Darlington, Pennsylvania.

––––––•••––––––

JOHN LAUGHLIN, a prosperous grocery merchant in the little town of Glasgow, Beaver county, Pa., is justly regarded as a power in that place. During the whole of his active business career in their midst, the citizens of Glasgow have felt his enterprising spirit in all movements to advance the welfare of the community. Mr. Laughlin is a native of Beaver county, where his birth occurred in 1834. He is a son of Robert Laughlin, a native of the same county, and grandson of Thomas Laughlin, a worthy pioneer. His great-grandfather was Thomas Laughlin, who married Sarah Simpson in 1765, and they had five sons, as follows: Thomas; James; Robert; John; and William. After receiving a limited education in the public schools, the gentleman whose name heads this sketch entered upon his career as cabin boy on the river. Shortly afterward, however, he rose to the position of steward, and was employed in that capacity with Charles Hurst, the well-known steamboat man of Pittsburg, Pennsylvania. In 1856, he resigned his position and went west to seek his fortune in California. After locating in Sacramento City, he established claims of his own and engaged in gold mining. In this venture, his fortune varied, although on the whole he was fairly successful. After working his claims diligently for three years, Mr. Laughlin returned to the Keystone State, and invested considerable money in the Laughlin Steamboat Company. He acted as steward on one of the numerous boats owned by that company, and his brother was captain of the same boat. Our subject subsequently sold his interest in that company, resigning his position at the same time. He then accepted a position with the Brown Company, and remained in their employ until 1873. Mr. Laughlin then retired from river life, having followed that occupation fully twenty-five years.

In 1887, the subject of our sketch built his present store in Glasgow, and started a grocery. Glasgow is located on the C. & P. R. R. near the Ohio River, and is the terminus of the C. & P. branch railroad, recently constructed to New Lisbon, Ohio. Mr. Laughlin went into business there during the oil excitement, and the place at that time boasted of five hundred inhabitants. The oil interests of the place were, however, then on the decline, and the town has gradually gone back to its present state. It is simply another illustration of the rise and decline that has characterized so many oil towns. But during all the fluctuating fortunes of the town, our subject has remained at the same old stand where he has ever enjoyed a fair patronage. In addition to handling a fine line of staple and fancy groceries, he has also a choice stock of notions, patent medicines, hardware, confection-ery, flour and feed; he deals also in tobacco and cigars.

July 19, 1860, Mr. Laughlin was united in marriage with Priscilla Calhoun, a charming daughter of James Calhoun, a well-known boat builder. Priscilla was born in Beaver county, where she also received her scholastic training.

To the subject of this biography and his esteemed wife, have been born five children, all of whom received a practical education in the district schools. Their names are: Charles D., a plumber; James O., a gauger in the employ of the Standard Oil Co.; Bertha M. (Childs); William, a prominent plumber in Rochester, Pa.; and Abner L., who is also an expert plumber. Mr. Laughlin takes an active interest in the affairs of his town and is a prominent member of the Republican party. He has served as councilman and as school director. He resides in a fine residence, beautifully located on the bank of the Ohio River. Mr. Laughlin worships at the M. E. church of which he is steward. He is exceedingly popular.

JAMES R. CAUGHEY, a miller residing in Darlington, Pa., on the ancestral homestead, was born in the same house which he now occupies, March 22, 1831. He is a son of James Caughey and a grandson of Samuel Caughey.

Samuel Caughey was born in the eastern part of Pennsylvania, and went west to Beaver county, settling near Hookstown, about the beginning of the present century. In 1810, he moved to the farm where the subject of this memoir now lives. About that time the Land Population Company began their attempt to dispossess the settlers of their land. This, naturally, caused alarm and indignation among the people. Finally, one member of the Company was shot by an irate settler, and when the Company realized what a hornet's nest they had brought about their ears, they were forced to suspend operations. When Samuel Caughey settled in Darlington, that place contained only one or two buildings. It was then called Greersburg, and is the oldest town in that section of the Keystone State. The old academy, which was built in 1802, was then only eight years old. It is now used as a depot by the P. L. & W. R. R. Company. Few settlers had then located in the district, and roads were far from numerous. The one extending in front of the residence of the subject of these lines was then the old stage line between Pittsburg and Cleveland, long before the advent of railroads in that vicinity.

Mr. Caughey owned forty acres of land and, in 1812, built a grist mill, run by water power. This was one of the first mills in Beaver county, and was in the family for three generations. It was operated until 1870, James R. Caughey's grandfather having spent all his life as a miller. He and his good wife reared five children, namely: Betsy (McGeorge); Polly (Hanna); Hetty (Duff); Samuel; and James.

James Caughey, father of James R., was born in Octoraro, Pa., in 1782, and received the greater portion of his mental instruction in the eastern part of Pennsylvania. After leaving school, he assisted his father until the War of 1812 broke out. He took an active part in that conflict, serving under General Harrison at Fort Meigs. On returning from the war, he assisted his father in the milling business. Upon the death of that beloved parent, the mill became the property of James and his brother Samuel. They operated it in partnership until James purchased the interest of his brother. At first the mill was of the old-fashioned stone process type, and later had the Burr process. All kinds of grain and feed were ground. The capacity of the mill was 20 barrels of flour and 150 bushels of chop daily. James Caughey was largely self-educated, but made the most of his opportunities, and was known to be a well-informed man. He was a discriminating reader and a clear thinker. He enlarged and enriched the library left him by his father. He was an Abolitionist of the most intense type. He was executor and administrator for several estates in the district, and served as school director and supervisor. He and his family were in accord with the Reformed Presbyterian faith. Margaret Johnston became his wife. She was reared and educated in Beaver county, and bore her husband four children, namely: S. G.; James R., the subject of this sketch; Margaret, deceased; and Jane, who still prefers single blessedness.

James R. Caughey received his primary in-

WILLIAM A. GARTSHORE.

struction in the public schools, and later graduated from the academy at Darlington. He then assisted his father in the milling business and became an active partner. His progressive nature made him quick to note and take advantage of any improvement in machinery. He put in steam power in 1856, and doubled the capacity of the mill. August 28, 1861, he enlisted in the "Roundhead," or 100th Reg., Pa. Vol. Infantry. He was second lieutenant of his company, and was assigned to duty in South Carolina, under General Sherman. Exposure and the southern climate, caused him to contract malarial fever, and he was sent home as unfit for further service. As soon as he recovered his health he again assumed his duties at the mill, which he continued to operate for years afterward. In 1876, he sold this mill and purchased a portable saw mill. For ten or twelve years he conducted that successfully, but finally sold it and started a chop mill, which he still runs.

In 1865, Mr. Caughey was joined in marriage with Mary A. Johnston, an attractive daughter of Andrew Johnston. She was born in Fayette county, Pennsylvania. Three children, Paul, James G., and George, blessed this union. Paul learned blacksmithing, and is now working in the silver mines of Idaho. James G. is a competent engineer, and holds a good position in the silver mines of New Mexico, being employed in a stamping mill. George died at the age of twenty-one years. The old house occupied by the subject of this sketch was built in 1820, and is still in a good state of preservation. He built the present barns, and now does a little farming also. In politics, he works hard for the success of the Republican party, and has been supervisor for three terms. He cares nothing, however, for political distinction, and is not an office-seeker. He is an ex-member of the G. A. R., and unites in worship with the Reformed Presbyterians.

———— • • ————

WILLIAM A. GARTSHORE, a progressive and enterprising citizen of Aliquippa, Pa., whose portrait is shown on the preceding page, is superintendent of the J. C. Russell Shovel Company, one of the most flourishing establishments in Beaver county. It was one of the first plants to locate at Aliquippa, which is admirably situated in the famous Beaver Valley and on the Ohio River,—extending to the tracks of the P. & L. E. R. R. It was organized in 1892 by the gentleman named above, with others. The following are the officers: J. L. Cooper, president; William A. Gartshore, vice-president; E. H. King, secretary; and J. J. McKee, treasurer. They manufacture shovels and drain tools of all kinds, which are shipped to all parts of the country.

The process of shovel manufacturing is a very interesting one, and these works are of a modern type, the latest machinery and improved methods being employed under the personal supervision of Mr. Gartshore, who has had many years of experience in that line. In the main building, whose dimensions are

240x80 feet, all of the shovels are made. A solid bar of steel is heated and passed between rollers of great power, and there the first rough shape is made; it is then pickled, placed in proper dies, where it is cut and trimmed to the proper shape, and then taken to the machine which forces the handles on, and rivets them in place. They are then polished, taken to the shipping room, and thence sent to all parts of the world. While this meagre description makes the process appear simple, the opposite impression is conveyed upon a visit to the factory. There the ponderous machinery with its immense fly wheels, rapidly revolving rollers, gigantic presses, and intricate machinery of various kinds, compels a respect for the shovel, which was not felt before seeing this useful implement in the course of manufacture. Adjoining the mill is the machine shop, with its full equipment, and on its other side is the drying room which is used to dry handles. Mr. Gartshore, the gentleman in charge of this important plant, is a man of wide experience in his business. He is held in the highest esteem by the men under his supervision, and by his associates, and he deports himself toward everyone with the greatest kindness and consideration.

The subject of this sketch was at one time a trusted employee of Hubbard & Company, of Pittsburg, Pa., and had charge of their shovel works, for a period of eight years. He faithfully discharged his duties to the best of his ability, and it was with regret that they permitted him to resign, in 1892, when the J. C. Russell Shovel Company was organized. He became vice-president, and a director, of the company, and has put forth his every effort to make the venture a successful one.

In September, 1888, Mr. Gartshore was united in marriage with Miss Laura Dunhorn, of Pittsburg, Pennsylvania. They have two children,—Laura and Park.

———— • • ————

SAMUEL LEVINE, a gentleman who by means of the superior faculties with which he is endowed by nature, has worked his way from a lowly station in life to one of prominence in his community, is proprietor of the leading general store in Aliquippa, Hopewell township, Beaver county, Pennsylvania.

Mr. Levine was born in Poland, Russia, in 1861, and got his education there in the public schools, after which he assisted his father, who was a commission merchant, until he was old enough to go into business for himself. He came to this country in 1886, landing in the city of New York with but twenty cents. Thrifty and ambitious, he immediately set to work, and what he has since acquired has been due exclusively to his own industrious efforts. It is a boast which he may well feel proud to make, that he has never worked for another, but has always been his own "boss." Remaining in New York City but two months, he went to Troy, N. Y., and purchased a horse and wagon,—becoming an itinerant merchant. He carried the thousand and one things for which there is a demand in the country, and worked up a very successful business, at which he continued until he settled in Aliquippa, when that town was first started. He has a splendid business and the most complete line of merchandise carried by any dealer in the county. He purchased the two-story building which he now occupies, and has divided it into three departments. The left wing is a fully stocked shoe store in the front, and the rear is used as a ware room. In the rear of the main store is the grocery department, and in front, the dry goods department. He is a man of great enterprise, and has endeavored to equip his store with every article which his customers may demand, having a comprehensive line of dry goods, clothing, boots and shoes, hats and caps, hardware, house furnishings, notions, carpets, oil cloth, jewelry, tobacco and cigars, feed and seeds, millinery and gentlemen's furnishings, china and glassware, wall paper and tinware. He built his store seven years ago, and added the shoe store annex later. His efforts to please the people are being rewarded, as his patronage is steadily increasing, and he is rapidly earning for himself the title of the most progressive merchant in the borough. Besides this business, in which he employs five hands, he owns valuable building lots in Aliquippa. He has erected another two-story frame building adjoining the old one,—the first floor, 50x 20 feet, being used as a dry goods store, and the second floor, 58x24 feet, being devoted to the purposes of a public hall.

In 1889, Mr. Levine and his wife, Rebecca, were married, and they have five children, two of whom are attending school. Fraternally, he is a member of the order of Odd Fellows. In politics, he is always ready to exercise his privilege as a citizen, but has never sought office.

———— · · ————

JOHN CONWAY, president of the John Conway Banking Co.; president of the Keystone Tumbler Co., and at one time a leading dry goods merchant of Rochester, Beaver county, Pa., is, today, one of the most influential men in that thriving borough, and is notable for sound judgment and sterling integrity. He has been a very successful business man, and his opinion in all matters pertaining to business and financial questions, is of great worth. Mr. Conway was born in Economy township, Beaver county, Pa., March 27, 1830, and is a son of Michael and Mary (O'Brien) Conway.

Michael Conway was born in County Kerry, Ireland, and came to America in 1825. He located in Economy township, and bought 230 acres of partially cleared land on the bank of the river. There he built a log cabin, and later a frame house. The farm is now owned by John Conway and his sisters. He made many improvements on the place, and it became one of the best kept and most prosperous farms in that section. He married Mary O'Brien, who died at the age of seventy-eight, her husband dying when sixty-six years old. Their children were as follow: Abigail, deceased, who was the wife of James McGuire; Thomas, deceased, who was a farmer; James, attorney, who married Jane Sheldon, served as captain in Company H, 139th Reg., Pa. Vol. Inf., was wounded in the battle of the Wilderness, and later died from the effects of the wound: John, the subject of this biography; Joanna, who married Peter Ivory, of Perrysville; and Mary, the widow of William Emery, of Indiana.

John Conway, whose name heads this sketch, was reared on the farm, and attended the common schools and the college of Vincennes, Indiana, and then returned home, and became a clerk in a dry goods store at Pittsburg, where he remained for one year. He was then a clerk for eight years on a steamboat on the Ohio River when he returned to Rochester. In 1856, he opened a dry goods store in New Castle, Pa., and after two years spent in that place again came to Rochester and bought the building at 749 West Madison street, which was built, in 1848, by Bonbright and Irwin. There he started a dry goods store, in 1857, and was very successful, continuing in the business until 1871. His store was the principal one in Rochester at that time. In 1871, he closed out, and established a general banking business, the company being comprised of the leading men in Rochester. Gradually Mr. Conway bought out the interests of his partners, until, at this time, he is the sole owner of it. The bank was built by Bonbright and Irwin, but purchased from J. H. Whisler. The subject of this sketch has built and sold many fine residences in Beaver county, and has dealt quite extensively in real estate. He has always taken an active interest in the progress of Rochester, and was one of the original promoters and stock-holders of the Olive Stove Works and of the Heat & Light Company. He is president of the Keystone Tumbler Co., of which a description is given elsewhere.

Mr. Conway married Thalia Bentel, a daughter of Philip Bentel, of Freedom, Beaver county, and to them have been born two children, namely: Lilian M., married to N. F. Hurst, of Rochester, Pa.; and Charles B., who is his father's assistant,—he married Emma Pfeiffer, a daughter of Benjamin Pfeiffer, of Rochester, Pennsylvania. Mr. Conway is widely known throughout the county, and wherever he goes he makes many friends, and keeps them. In politics, he is an active Democrat, and has served in the borough council and as school director. He is a Mason, and a member of the Presbyterian church. He was one of the promoters of the project to build the Masonic block at Rochester.

VICTOR MANUFACTURING COMPANY. Another of the many manufacturing establishments for which Beaver county is noted is that of the Victor Mfg. Co., where cast-iron, enameled bath-tubs are made.

There are but about a dozen concerns of this character in the country, the principal ones being in Pittsburg and vicinity. The officers of the Victor Mfg. Co. are: J. F. Bruggeman, president; John Rebman, Jr.,

HERMAN F. DILLON.

secretary and treasurer; and F. D. Cook, manager of the works. The works are located in Aliquippa, Beaver county, Pa.

The company has a fine site of 3½ acres of land lying between the P. & L. E. R. R. tracks and the Ohio River. Their plant comprises foundry, pickling and cleaning shop, enameling boiler and engine rooms, and warehouse and office. They have had success in marketing their product, and have always had sufficient orders to keep the works running steadily. Their plant, with exception of warehouse and office, was destroyed by fire in May, 1898, since which time the manufacturing has been carried on in temporary buildings.

The Victor Mfg. Co. was organized in 1896, through the agency of William C. Degelman, of Pittsburg, who for two years was general manager. Mr. Cook, the present manager, is from New York, and, before engaging in the bath-tub manufacturing business, had been interested in the making of enameled advertising signs. Mr. Cook is an independent Republican, in politics, and, fraternally, a member of the Royal Society of Good Fellows.

———— ◆ • ◆ ————

ERMAN F. DILLON. The gentleman whose name heads this sketch, and whose portrait is shown on the preceding page, has for many years been one of the active and influential residents of Beaver Falls, Pa., and it is in terms of highest praise that his fellow-citizens speak of him.

Having long been one of the leading business men of that thriving borough, he has done much to promote high business standards, and in every sense of the word has been an exemplary citizen, one of whom the people are justly proud. Mr. Dillon was born in Beaver, November 2, 1856, and is a son of Henry N. Dillon.

Henry N. Dillon, the father of Herman F., was born in Big Beaver township, Beaver county, Pa., in 1824. He was a pupil in the district schools of Beaver county, and after farming for a time upon his father's estate, moved to Beaver and engaged in the teaming, hauling and general contracting business. In 1884, he removed to Beaver Falls, and went into the wholesale oil business, which he followed during the remainder of his active life. In early years he was a Whig, but on the formation of the Republican party, he cast his vote with that organization, and gained quite a local fame by virtue of his personal association with Abraham Lincoln. Mr. Dillon was an active and aggressive worker in his party, but never sought office. He was a liberal supporter of the Methodist Episcopal church. He was united in marriage with Mary A. Supplee, a daughter of the late William Supplee, who was for many years a resident of Beaver county, having come from Chester, Pa., in 1839.

The father of the subject hereof died in March, 1892, and his death was greatly mourned by all in the community. The Dillon men are all of large size, and are well-known for that physical trait.

Herman F. Dillon received his early mental training in the common schools of Beaver, and in Beaver Academy, and when fourteen years of age removed, with his parents, to Ohio township, his education being completed in that district. When but sixteen years old, he went to Pittsburg, where he was placed in full charge of a milk depot and route, owned by Jesse Smith, of Smith's Ferry, Pennsylvania. After two years he returned to Beaver county and went into the oil business at Island Run, where he became a general contractor. He remained there until January 1, 1882, and then accepted a position with the Beaver Falls Gas Company, for which he worked until 1885, when he was appointed superintendent of the entire plant. He continued with this company until 1897, when other business interests and political duties made it necessary for him to resign.

Mr. Dillon was one of the promoters of the Beaver Falls Improvement Company, a society formed of public-spirited men, whose object was to attract manufacturing interests to that town. He is a promoter and director of the River View Street Railway Company and also a promoter and director of the People's Building & Loan Association,—a most substantial organization which had its inception in 1884,—and is also a member of the Tribune Publishing Company, printing a daily and weekly newspaper at Beaver Falls, and doing also a large business in job printing. Mr. Dillon is one of the stockholders in the Beaver Falls Water Com-

pany, which was started by several public-spirited men for the purpose of supplying the town with pure water at a much lower rate than had previously prevailed. Too much credit can not be accorded to this company, as the relief from the oppression of the old water company has been a great blessing to the people of Beaver Falls. Mr. Dillon is a Republican of the strongest type, and was elected to the council, the first term, in 1893, and served until 1897, when he resigned his seat to accept the office of register and recorder. The subject of this sketch cast his first vote for President Garfield, and has been active in politics ever since. For many years he was a member of the county committee, serving as its secretary and treasurer, and was also chairman of its executive committee. He is a member of the Methodist Episcopal church, of which he has always been a most faithful supporter. He is a member of several fraternal organizations, namely: Glasgow Lodge, No. 485, F. & A. M., of which he has been a member twenty-one years; Harmony Chapter, of Beaver Falls; Pittsburg Commandery, No. 1, of Pittsburg; Beaver Falls Lodge, No. 293, K. of P.; Rochester Lodge, No. 283, B. P. O. E.; Walnut Camp, of Beaver Falls, Woodmen of the World; Beaver Falls Tent, No. 53, K. O. T. M.

Mr. Dillon married Jennie M. Kerr, a daughter of John Kerr, of Darlington. She was born at Darlington, in 1853, and pursued a course of study in Darlington Academy, afterwards teaching school until her marriage. The children which resulted from this union are: Herman Ross, born in Beaver Falls, who is now a student; Blanche V., born in Ohioville; and Walter E., a student, born in Beaver Falls.

———— ◆•◆ ————

ROBERT G. YOUNG, a well known lumber merchant of Beaver county, is located at New Galilee and deals in all kinds of building materials, sashes, doors, blinds, mantels, inside finishings, shingles, agricultural implements, barbed and galvanized wire fencing, and also does considerable business as a slate-roofer. He is one of the substantial business men of that section and is everywhere respected as a citizen of worth and influence. He is a son of Robert and Jane (McAnlis) Young, and was born April 4, 1845, in Big Beaver township, Beaver county, Pennsylvania.

Peter Young, his grandfather, was born in Ireland, where he was educated and spent the early part of his life. He came to America, located east of Pittsburg, Pa., and entered the employ of Captain Crawford, a hero of the Revolutionary War. He subsequently went to Saw Mill Run, and in the year 1800 removed to Beaver county, where he purchased from Mr. Wylie, the original patentee, a farm of 100 acres of wild land. He built log sheds and a log house, and at that time there were but three white families in the district. Indians were very numerous, and many interesting stories are related in connection with adventures and encounters with them. Mr. Young remained on the farm the remainder of his life and successfully confronted the many difficulties and hardships to which the early pioneers were subjected. He reared the following children: John, a farmer; William; Algeo; Nancy (Wright); Elizabeth; Rebecca; James, a practicing physician of Westmoreland county; and Robert, father of the subject hereof.

Robert Young was born in Beaver county, Pa., in 1803, and was reared on the old homestead farm, receiving such an education as circumstances would permit. He learned farming and assisted his father until the latter's death, when he succeeded to the home property. This he greatly improved by erecting new buildings, clearing the land and raising an orchard. He was an Abolitionist, and then a Republican, in politics. He was a consistent member of the Presbyterian church, and for twenty years served as elder. He died in 1862, at the age of fifty-nine years. His union with Jane McAnlis resulted in the following issue: James M., who died at the age of fifteen years; Margaret; Susan (Patterson); W. J., a farmer; Robert G., the subject of this biographical record; Hamilton A., a farmer; and Lizzie.

Robert G. Young obtained his elementary education in the schools of Beaver county and received an excellent business training in the Iron City Business College, of Pittsburg, in 1867. He learned the trade of a carpenter after spending some time as a bookkeeper in New Castle, Pa. He plied his trade in the states of Iowa and Missouri, until 1870, when he returned to Beaver county and became a contractor. In 1882, he started in business as a lumber dealer, being the first in the locality to take up that line of trade. His yard is located near the Ft. Wayne tracks at New Galilee, and there he carries all kinds of sawed lumber, in addition to the articles enumerated above. He is also an exporter in walnut logs, selling to various foreign markets. He owns a fine home, and a small farm in Lawrence county, Pennsylvania.

In 1876, Robert G. Young formed a matrimonial alliance with Lucy Wallace, who was born in Lawrence county, and is a daughter of John and Margaret Wallace. Seven children were born to them, as follows: Clarence, who is in partnership with his father, and is a graduate of the Beaver Falls high school; Maggie; Rutherford J.; William Harvey; Mary E.; James G.; and Kenneth W. Personally, Mr. Young is a genial man, of public spirit, and is very popular locally. He is an earnest church worker, having built the Presbyterian church, and has been an elder since 1894. He is very liberal in his contributions toward its support. He is, politically, a Republican.

———◆•◆———

LORENZO C. KIRKER, a veteran of our Civil War, is a much respected citizen of Beaver Falls, where he has been engaged in the carpentering business for many years. He is a son of John S. and Elizabeth (Rutter) Kirker, and was born in that part of Beaver county which now forms a part of Lawrence county, August 21, 1843.

His grandfather was Robert Kirker, a native of this county, but his entire life was spent in Butler county, Pennsylvania. The father of Lorenzo C. was born in Butler county, Pa., but came to Beaver county early in life, where he resided during his remaining days. His occupation was that of a shoemaker, at which he was quite successful. He belonged to the old state militia, in which he was a major.

The subject of this writing was reared in Lawrence county, Pa., and obtained his elementary education in the public schools of his native district, and then took up the carpentering trade, which he made his principal occupation. Prior to 1880, he resided in New Castle, Pa., where he was employed in a planing mill, but in that year he became a resident of Beaver Falls, where he has since lived. He engaged in the grocery business soon after coming there, but gave it up and resumed his former occupation. Mr. Kirker is quite prominently known throughout this vicinity, and enjoys the reputation of an honest, upright and conscientious citizen. When the Civil War broke out, our subject laid aside all plans for the future, and went to the aid of the Union, enlisting July 14, 1861, in Company H, 9th Reg. Pa. Reserves for a term of three years. He was wounded at the battle of Antietam, in September, 1862, and was taken to the German Reformed Church Hospital at Frederick, Md., where he remained six months; upon recovering, he again joined his regiment, with which he remained until he was honorably discharged at Pittsburg, Pa.,

ABRAHAM WEST.

May 12, 1864. While with his regiment, he took part in the battles of Dranesville; Mechanicsville; Miner's Hill; Savage Station; Malvern Hill; Second Bull Run; South Mountain; Antietam; Gettysburg; and in many small skirmishes.

Politically, Mr. Kirker is a prominent Republican of the community, and is now serving as judge of elections. February 5, 1863, he was joined in marriage with Miss Jeannette Cunningham, and they reared six children: Evelyn L., the wife of C. B. Jolley, of Beaver Falls; Cecilia, the wife of Charles D. Garrett, also of Beaver Falls; Flora A., the wife of John Richards, of Beaver Falls; Harry V. (wedded to Jeannette Craig, of Afton, N. Y.), who is engaged in carpentering with the subject of our sketch; Rosa, who is the wife of A. C. Bellis, of Beaver Falls; and Edward L., who also works with his father at the carpenter's trade.

———

ABRAHAM WEST, deceased, who was for many years one of the foremost farmers of Marion township, was a descendant of an old and highly respected family of Beaver county. He was a son of Peter and Agnes (Boyd) West, and was born in New Sewickley township, Beaver county, Pa., in 1825.

Peter West, the father of Abraham, was born in West Virginia and, in 1805, removed to Beaver county, Pa., with his parents. He rented a farm in Franklin township, but later bought one known as "The Knob," in New Sewickley township, where he lived and farmed for a period of twelve years. He then purchased a tract of four hundred acres in Marion township,—a portion of which is now owned by Mrs. West,—and upon this he erected a fine brick residence. He died there in 1865, and his wife, whose maiden name was Agnes Boyd, died in the year of 1879.

Abraham West, the subject of this sketch, always lived upon the home farm, the original property being divided upon the death of his father, and Abraham receiving two hundred and fifty acres. He carried on farming and was extensively engaged in sheep-raising and dairying,—in late years shipping the milk to Allegheny. He died on July 30, 1897, and his death was universally mourned, as he was everywhere respected as a man of true worth and influence in the community. Since his demise, Mrs. West, aided by two of her sons, has carried on the farm with good results. They still continue to ship the milk to Allegheny, and have a herd of twenty-two cows. Their farm is mostly flat land, and is very productive, being unexcelled in that vicinity.

Abraham West, on March 6, 1860, was joined in wedlock with Mary Jane Sowash, who was born in Brighton township, Beaver county, and is a daughter of Frederick Sowash. The latter came from Mercer county to Beaver county when a young man, and was a stone mason by trade. This union resulted in the birth of seven children, as follows: Virginia (Wilson); William B., a fireman on the Fort Wayne R. R., who lives at Allegheny; Clinton P., a farmer in Butler county; Joseph

F., deceased; Abraham G., who is living at home; Charles, who lives in Zelienople, Butler county; and John F., who is at home. Politically, our subject was an active supporter of the Democratic party. We take pleasure in presenting his portrait, which appears on a preceding page.

JOHN HENRY LOWRY. As one of the representatives of the agricultural class of citizens of Beaver county, we take great pleasure in presenting the life record of the gentleman named above, one of the most progressive and influential farmers in North Sewickley township. He was born on Main street in Allegheny City, Pa., and is a son of John and Sarah (Wagoner) Lowry.

John Lowry, the father of our subject, was born in the vicinity of Harrisburg, and was a young man when he removed to the city of Pittsburg. He was a bridge blacksmith by trade, and many old landmarks are standing, today, as monuments of his skill. The old covered bridge at Beaver Falls, and, in fact, nearly all of the covered bridges built in that region during his time, are the result of his workmanship. In the spring of 1857, he moved to North Sewickley township, where he bought a farm of one hundred acres. Prior to this, however, he had given up his trade, and for some years had been a stationary engineer in the city of Allegheny. After his removal he devoted all his time to farming, and when he purchased his property it was an unbroken piece of timber, but before his death most of it was cleared. He was a very industrious man and at the time of his death was in comfortable circumstances, financially. He was united in marriage with Sarah Wagoner, and their happy home was blessed by the birth of eight children, as follows: David E.; Martha Jane, the widow of A. J. Steele; Elizabeth Ann, deceased; John Henry, the subject hereof; Lucinda V., the wife of William Chaney, who resides at Conway, Pa.; William J., who resides at the home of John Henry Lowry; and two who died in early childhood. Politically, Mr. Lowry was a stanch supporter of the Democratic party, and was elected to a number of the township offices.

The subject of this writing was but nine years of age when he removed with his father from Allegheny, where he had attended the common schools, to North Sewickley township. He continued to attend the public schools, acquiring a good intellectual training, and has lived on the farm, coming into full possession of it upon his father's demise. He has very successfully managed his affairs, and since buying an additional hundred acres of land, has as fine a property for agricultural purposes as Beaver county contains. He employs only the most approved methods of farming and has more than one thousand dollars' worth of improved machinery. His land is exceedingly rich with coal, having a five-foot vein, but is mined by outside parties, this being a source of considerable income to Mr. Lowry. He is a man of exceptionally strong character, a true friend and a devoted husband and father. He has many friends and acquaintances throughout this section of the state, who respect him as a man of influence and true worth to the community.

On September 2, 1882, Mr. Lowry was united in marriage with Elzena Fombell, of North Sewickley township, and three children are the issue of their union, as follows: Myrtle; Lulu; and John Roy. Politically, Mr. Lowry is a Democrat of the sturdiest type, and has been the incumbent of all the township offices. In a religious connection, he and his wife are conscientious members of the Presbyterian church.

———•♦•———

ENERAL J. S. LITTELL, ex-sheriff of Beaver county, now a representative farmer of Big Beaver township, Beaver county, Pa., is a descendant of 'Squire William Littell, an old Revolutionary hero, and one of the early settlers of Beaver county. 'Squire William Littell was born in Belfast, Ireland, in 1740. He attended the public schools of Belfast and came to America while still a young man. He wedded Elizabeth Walker, who was also a native of Ireland. They reared nine children, namely: Elizabeth (Reed); Jane, now deceased; Mary (Todd); Alice (Sharp); Agnes; James; William, father of the subject hereof; David; and Thomas.

At the outbreak of the Revolutionary War, General Littell's grandfather held a clerkship in the army (being private secretary to Gen-eral George Washington), and served in that capacity throughout the war. His brother, James, was a soldier, and served under the illustrious Washington until the war was ended. A letter written in Fort McIntosh in 1779, by James to William, is still in the possession of the subject hereof, and is in a good state of preservation. It proves James to have been a good scholar. After the war, William went to Beaver county, Pa., where he took up a large tract of land in Hanover township. This tract was all wild land. Settlers were few, and wild game was abundant. William Littell made a clearing and built a large hewed-log cabin upon it,—also building a barn. He was appointed "Squire" by the governor of the state,—a position which he filled until the time of his death, in 1819. He died aged seventy-nine years.

William Littell, Jr., father of General Littell, was born upon the old homestead in Hanover township, in 1794. He attended the district schools, after which he taught for several years. He was joined in marriage with Cynthia Smith, a daughter of John and Nancy (McClure) Smith. Mrs. Littell was born in Adams county. Twelve children were the result of this happy union. Their names are: J. S., the subject of this sketch; Eliza (Robertson); Rebecca (Calhoun); Maria (Ewing); Nancy (Ewing); Cynthia, wife of J. McHenry; William M., who died in infancy; a second William M.; David; Washington; James M.; and Henry. The wife of William Little, Jr., died in 1853. Our subject's father was a farmer by occupation, and lived many years on the old homestead farm. He sold this, however, and bought 155 acres near Beaver. His farm products were disposed of in Beaver and vicinity. He served in the War of 1812, and was ordered to duty on Lake Erie. While crossing the Ohio Swamps, he contracted the measles which nearly proved fatal. In politics, he was first a Whig and later a Republican, but had no aspirations to office. He belonged to the Seceders' church.

General Littell was the recipient of a good scholastic training, which he obtained by attending district school. He subsequently learned surveying, although he never followed that profession. He taught school for three terms in Beaver county. In 1845, his marriage with Mary Calhoon was solemnized. Mary was born in Raccoon township in 1821, and was a daughter of Richard and Sarah (Moffet) Calhoon. She was called away from her earthly home, August 1, 1897. Seven children were born of this union, viz.: Richard W.; William P.; Robert C.; Isidore S. (White); Harriet (Rhodes); Joseph; and Isabell. Richard W. served three and one-half years in the 76th Reg., Pa. Vol. Inf., as drummer boy (this being his father's regiment). William enlisted in the 6th Reg., Ohio Cavalry, and had some narrow escapes. On one occasion he was sent to the hospital. Joseph, the youngest son, resides on the farm with his father.

After his marriage, General Littell engaged in blacksmithing for ten years. He then bought the first portable saw mill ever used in Beaver county, which he operated for one year. In 1853, he joined a militia company, of which he was elected captain. He was afterward appointed brigade inspector of the 19th division. In the fall of 1861, he recruited a company for the 76th Reg., Pa. Vol. Inf., and was chosen captain, and was ordered to the South. From a volume entitled "Martial Deeds of Pennsylvania," the following extract is taken: "Brig. Gen'l. J. S. Littell fought with his company of the 76th Pa. Vol. Inf., at James Island, and a few days later at Morris Island. He also took part in the first and second assaults on Fort Wagner, where he led his company with great bravery." On Morris Island, General Littell had charge of the entire regiment for thirty days. On the first of July, 1862, he was severely wounded, but continued to fight and would not give up, although suffering great pain. The next morning, he received a serious wound in the right arm and side.

The attack on Fort Wagner was very disastrous, as it resulted in the loss of almost one-half of the regiment. On May 31, the subject of our sketch was promoted to be lieutenant colonel. The very next day he was again wounded, a ball passing through both thighs. After remaining in the hospital for some time, he was removed to his own home. His recovery was slow. On August 17, he was promoted to a colonelcy, and, the following January, sailed with the expeditions under Generals Butler and Weitzel, and later served under General Terry in the attacks on Fort Fisher, which commanded the approach to Wilmington. In the midst of an engagement, while gallantly leading the assault, General Littell was again wounded by a ball. This ball struck him in the left thigh, passed through a pocket-book, and lodged in his body. While a disastrous day for him, it was a glorious one for the Union Army. Although suffering severely, General Littell was able to exult in the splendid victory. He was removed to Fortress Monroe, the ball having been extracted while on the field. Later, he was sent to his home. Upon the recommendation of General Terry, as a merited recognition of his distinguished valor, he was created a brevet-brigadier general. While recovering from the wounds received at Cold Harbor, a party of inferior officers tried to secure the General's discharge from the army. This was done to better their own chance of promotion. Rumors of the situation reached the General before their plans had finally matured, however, and, with his wound still running, he returned to his command. It is a fact worthy of note that of all the commissioned officers who went out with the regiment, the subject of our sketch and one other alone returned.

After such a notable war record, General Littell was urged to be a candidate for sheriff, and was elected by a large majority, in 1866. Immediately after the expiration of his first term, he settled upon the farm where he still lives. This farm contains 233 acres of fine, improved land and was purchased from Harrison Power. The General erected another house and built better barns, and his farm is conceded to be one of the best in his section. For many years he operated a dairy. He was one of the organizers of the creamery in Darlington, of which he is still a stockholder. He was president of the same until he declined to serve longer, but is still retained on the board of directors. He now makes a specialty of raising early lambs for the market. He is a Republican, and has served as school director and as supervisor. He is also an elder of the United Presbyterian church.

———— ◆•◆ ————

CLYDE W. INMAN, a manufacturer and merchant of Cannelton, Pa., was born in Chippewa township, Beaver county, in 1867. He received his scholastic training in the schools of his native town, and in Darlington Academy. After leaving school, he began to work in a coal mine, doing the work of a bailer. This he followed for a short time, and then commenced work on the N. Y., P. & C. R. R., which was during the construction of the road. After a few months, he again returned to the mines as a coal digger for Mr. Mansfield, a well-known operator. In 1884, he made another change, this time entering the carpenter department of the Allegheny car shops. One year later, he returned to work for Mr. Mansfield as a carpenter, to do the wood work in the manufacture of the Grimm drill. In 1886, he opened a general store in Cannelton in partnership with his father and brother. Fifteen months later, he bought out the interests of his partners, and has since conducted the store alone. He also bought the plant of, and the right to manufacture, the Grimm drill. In 1893, he built a new work shop and put in new machinery. He has an upright engine and boiler, two screw-cutting lathes, a large drill press, forges, and numerous jigs, and labor-saving devices.

In connection with his factory, Mr. Inman operates a general blacksmith shop, where he manufactures picks, sledges, wedges, bars, etc. The market for his goods extends through the states of Virginia, West Virginia, Ohio, Pennsylvania, Alabama, Illinois, and Michigan. The Grimm drill is a tool subjected to years of actual test, and has been demonstrated to be the most durable, effective, and economical drill in the market. It finds a sale in every land, and has everywhere been crowned with the highest competitive honors. These drills bore one and one-half to three inch holes, and eight feet deep at any angle, in coal, fire clay, rock, and slate.

Mr. Inman keeps a stock of general goods in his store, varying from groceries to hardware. He has a large warehouse and is well equipped to satisfy the demands of miners and farmers. He is also a member of the firm of Inman Brothers, miners and shippers, his partner being his brother, G. W. Inman. Their coal trade is local, but they ship a clay, which is like Cannel coal, peculiar, and as fine a quality as can be found in any part of the world.

The subject of this sketch married Laura E. Hays, daughter of Charles Hays, the well known blacksmith, of South Beaver township. They have three children: Lena W.; Zoe M.; and Hannah E. Mr. Inman is a strong Republican, and a member of the county committee. His fraternal associations are with the I. O. O. F. and Meridian Lodge, No. 411, F. & A. M. He also belongs to the Junior Order of United American Mechanics. His sympathies are with the church of the Seceders.

———— ◆ • ◆ ————

DR. JAMES S. LOUTHAN, a prominent physician and surgeon of Beaver Falls, Pa., has, by his perseverance and strict attention to professional duties, placed himself in the foremost rank of physicians in Beaver county, and has built up a large practice in the home of his adoption, where he has been located since 1890. Dr. Louthan was born in South Beaver township, Beaver county, Pa., April 28, 1856. He received his early scholastic training at Darlington Academy. after which he followed the profession of teaching for four years, subsequently attending Westminster College. He began the study of medicine under Dr. Moon, and later studied with Dr. Strouss. He took the required course of lectures at Cleveland Medical College, graduating in the class of 1882. Dr. Louthan began the practice of his profession immediately after his graduation, locating at Fairview, Beaver county, Pa., where he remained until 1890, when he located in Beaver Falls, and is still to be found there.

Dr. Louthan is a quiet, unassuming gentleman of a very pronounced, studious nature.

To him it is a pleasure to keep in step with the wonderful advances made of late in his profession. No new thing escapes his attention, and he is quick to grasp and utilize any modern discovery, which may be used to the advantage of his patients. Careful and conservative, he is a strict adherent to the ethics of his craft, and possesses the traits of a true professional worker. Dr. Louthan descended from one of the first families of Virginia. He is a son of James Louthan, Jr., grandson of James Louthan, Sr., and great-grandson of Moses Louthan.

Moses Louthan was a native of Scotland, and his parents were the first representatives of the family in America. They settled in Virginia, where their son Moses, in early manhood, engaged in farming. Later in life, however, he removed to South Beaver township, Beaver county, Pa., being one of the earliest settlers of that county. He was a member of the Salem church congregation, and was one of its first elders. Moses Louthan lived to be over eighty years of age. His wife, Betsy, bore him seven children, as follows: James; George; William; Samuel; Henry; and Betsy. James Louthan, the next in line, was born in Beaver township and received his mental training in the vicinity of his home. Like his father, he followed the occupation of a farmer, settling on a farm adjoining the old homestead, where he remained a few years, and then sold it and moved to the state of Ohio, settling near Worcester. There his death took place, in his forty-third year.

He was joined in wedlock with Anna Brad-shaw, a daughter of Robert Bradshaw, of South Beaver township. Mrs. Louthan died at the advanced age of eighty-three years. As her husband died early in life, the rearing of the family fell mostly upon her shoulders. Two sons and three daughters were the offspring of this worthy couple, named as follows: Moses; Sarah (Sebring); Eliza; Susan (McConnell); and James, Jr., father of the subject hereof. They are now deceased, except James, the youngest.

James Louthan, Jr., was born near Worcester, Ohio, but obtained his schooling in South Beaver township, Pa., whither his mother had removed soon after the death of her husband. At the time of his father's death, James was but six years old. Upon reaching manhood, James became apprenticed, and learned the carpenter's trade in New Brighton. In that capacity he worked upon the first brick building in that flourishing borough, and followed his trade almost uninterruptedly for over forty years, making his home in South Beaver. He was an industrious, enterprising citizen, with a love for work and a capacity for achieving success in whatever he undertook to accomplish. He also followed agricultural pursuits, and was respected by all men of character and position. Purchasing twenty acres of woodland, he cleared some, and built a home, very soon adding sixty acres more. In 1838, he wedded Nancy Strain, a daughter of James Strain, of Chippewa township. Mrs. Louthan passed away from her earthly home in June, 1879, after assisting in rearing a family of ten children. Mr. Louthan sold the homestead, and removed to Darlington, remaining there until 1896, when he went to Beaver Falls, and is now spending the sunset of life in retirement. One remarkable fact concerning this family is their general good health; neither the father nor any of the children ever had any serious illness. Mr. Louthan was first a Whig, then a Free-soiler, and later a Republican, in his political attachments. He is strong in his belief, and is intensely interested in the governing policy of the nation. In his religious views, he is a Covenanter. His children's names are: Mary A. (Craig); Asa (Martin); Rebecca (Rayle); Susan M. (Hartzell); Elizabeth W. (Cox); Bradford; Allie (Bradshaw); James S. (subject); Nancy (Patterson); and John.

Dr. J. S. Louthan was united in marriage with May Johnson, an entertaining daughter of Joseph Johnson, who now resides in Beaver Falls. Their nuptials were consummated in 1884, and their home is brightened by the presence of two daughters: Ethel Zoe; and Elizabeth Gemiska.

Dr. Louthan is a Republican, and takes a fitting interest in party affairs. He is a member of the Beaver County Medical Association. Aside from his professional duties, he is a very energetic gentleman in the town and county. He was one of the organizers of the Dime Savings & Loan Association, of Beaver Falls, and is one of its directors. He is also a director of the Farmers National Bank.

J O. BROWN is the junior member of the firm of Steffler & Brown, manufacturers of paving brick, in Darlington, Pennsylvania. Mr. Brown was born in Armstrong county, in October, 1867. After receiving a practical education in the public schools of his native county, he learned the trade of a carpenter, working as a journeyman in Armstrong county, and later in Pittsburg, Pennsylvania. He went to the latter place in 1885, and entered the employ of Mr. Steffler, a prominent contractor and builder of that city. He remained in the employ of Mr. Steffler for a period of ten years, and became an expert workman.

In 1896, in company with Mr. Steffler, Mr. Brown purchased the plant of the Darlington Fire Brick Company, then owned by Messrs. Cook, Sturgeon & Cook, and since then business has been carried on under the firm name of Steffler & Brown. Their plant is strictly up-to-date, and covers about three acres of ground. Adjacent to it is a bed of fine clay and coal. The clay from this district is as fine as may be obtained in any part of the world. Large quantities of the raw and ground clay are shipped to all parts of the United States. At the works are five large draught kilns and three large dry tunnels. Each kiln holds 60,000 brick. The kilns are kept going all the time.

The engine house adjoins the machine room, and is equipped with two 100 horse power boilers and an 80 horse power engine. This large engine runs the crusher and dry pan for grinding clay, also the wire cutting

WILLIAM H. FOX

machine, the soft mud machine and the re-pressing machine. One brick-making machine has a capacity of 20,000 bricks per day. A smaller engine operates the fan for the dry tunnel.

The company owns its own railroad siding, and a network of train and trestle roads for the transportation of clay and coal from the banks to the works. The main offices of the company are in Pittsburg. About twenty men are constantly employed, and the products of the plant are shipped to Pittsburg and throughout the West.

Mr. Brown was united in marriage with Lily Steffler, the accomplished daughter of his business partner. Their marriage took place in Pittsburg. Mrs. Brown was born in Lawrence county, in 1872. One son, Harry, born June 8, 1896, is the result of this most happy union. Mr. Brown is a stanch Republican, but has given his attention strictly to his business interests, having no time for political campaigning. Both Mr. and Mrs. Brown are faithful attendants of the United Presbyterian church, and contribute generously towards its support. They also assist worthy charitable institutions. Both are well and favorably known in social and religious circles throughout Beaver county.

* * *

ILLIAM H. FOX, whose portrait is shown on the opposite page, is the leading blacksmith of Beaver Falls, and he is recognized as having no superior in Beaver county, Pa., in the line of shoeing horses. He owns a large, brick shop and gives employment to several skilful hands who are constantly kept busy in order to meet the demands of his large patronage; he is also a prominent and industrious citizen, commanding the respect and good-will of a host of acquaintances. He was born in Lawrence county, Pa., in 1862, and his parents are David and Rachael (Van Horn) Fox.

His grandfather, Peter Fox, was born in Westmoreland county, Pa., where he followed his trade as a millwright during his active life. His wife was Miss Saddler by whom he reared five sons and three daughters: Joseph; Michael; John; Peter; David; Mrs. Morrison; Mrs. Kennedy; and Mrs. Ryhel.

David Fox was born in Lawrence county, Pa., in 1818, and was reared to agricultural pursuits, which occupation he successfully followed throughout his active career. He was joined in marriage with Miss Rachael Van Horn, who was born in Lawrence county, Pa., in 1825, and they became the parents of seven children, as follows: William H., the subject of this narrative; Abram V.; Rebecca J. (McCurdy); Mary M. (Dick); Katie (Golden); Emma (Williams), and Agnes (Cameron).

William H. Fox received a common school education in Venango county, Pa., and at the age of sixteen years, he began life on his own account. Leaving his father's farm, he sought to learn the trade of a blacksmith; after mastering the trade, in 1884 he located in Beaver Falls, where he has since established the reputation of being the most expert and competent blacksmith in the county. His patronage increased to such a large extent that it was necessary for him not only to enlarge his shop but also to employ more hands to cope with the growing demands. Accordingly, he erected a fine two-story shop facing Third avenue on the corner of Eighth street, and he is now able to accommodate his patrons. Mr. Fox is well deserving of the success that has met his efforts; he is enterprising and progressive, and supports all measures that tend to promote the welfare of the community.

Mr. Fox was joined in the bonds of matrimony with Miss Mary A. Hitchin, a native of England. Socially, he is a member of the Order of Maccabees, Woodmen of the World, and Independent Order of Good Templars. In politics, he is a Republican, while in religious views he favors the Methodist church.

———— • • ————

JAMES S. WILSON, who is a prominent and independent farmer of North Sewickley township, Beaver county, Pa., is a veteran of the Civil War and bears an excellent record for honorable and valiant service. He is a son of James and Barbara (Showalter) Wilson, and was born November 27, 1833.

James Wilson, the father of James S., was born on Hickory Creek in Allegheny county, Pennsylvania. His father died when he was a young man and his mother was again married to a Mr. Ralston, and he soon after went to Butler county, where he remained for some time. He moved to Beaver county at an early day, and worked as a farm hand until 1832, when he bought the farm now owned by the subject of this sketch. It consisted of one hundred and seven acres of wooded land, and he worked early and late until he cleared all but twenty acres, upon which the timber still stands. He was one of the prosperous and substantial men of the township, and was everywhere held in the highest esteem. He died in 1891, aged eighty-six years. He married Barbara Showalter, and they became the parents of twelve children: Salina, the widow of H. M. Biddell, who lives in Beaver Falls; Nancy, who died at the age of thirty years; William F., who moved West; James S., the subject of this personal history; Joseph F., who lives in New Brighton; Harrison, who died at the age of nineteen years; Mary Jane, deceased; Jefferson; Aaron, a dry goods merchant and Baptist minister, who lives at Rochester; John, who died in the army during the Civil War; Thomas, who is engaged in the grocery business at Rochester, Beaver county; and one who died in infancy. In political belief, Mr. Wilson was a Republican. Religiously, he was a devout Christian and attended the Methodist Episcopal church. Mrs. Wilson died in 1893.

James S. Wilson was born on the farm on which he now lives, and received a first-class scholastic training in the common schools and in North Sewickley Academy, and pursued a course in Duff's Business College at Pittsburg. He spent his time working on the farm until the Civil War was in progress, and then, in answer to the call for volunteers, he enlisted, August 23, 1861, in Company C, 63d Reg., Pa. Vol. Inf., as a private. He saw much hard and continued fighting, but was ever willing and even eager to perform his full share of the work, and more. He is of a cool and even temperament, and in times of danger was undisturbed, and always to be seen in the very thickest of the fight. In 1863, he was promoted to a first lieutenancy. He took part in the following important engagements: The siege of Yorktown; Williamsburg; Fair Oaks; Seven Days Battle; second battle of Bull Run; and Chantilly. He then went home on recruiting service, remaining six months, and upon returning to the regiment, participated in the battles of Chancellorsville and Gettysburg, following Lee to Manassas Gap, where an engagement took place. He fought in the battles of Mine Run, Kelly's Ford, and in the battle of the Wilderness, where, on May 5, he was severely wounded in the thigh and hip. He was compelled to go to the hospital for three months, and upon going home, used a pair of crutches for two years. He then resumed agricultural pursuits, his farm being under a high state of cultivation, and one of the best in that section. It is supplied with good substantial and convenient outbuildings, which are so essential to success in farming, and the house in which he resides is a large brick dwelling. He is a man of pleasing personality, a clever conversationalist, and has a host of friends.

On July 24, 1866, Mr. Wilson was joined in wedlock with Miss Jemima A. McCreary, a daughter of William and Mary McCreary, of North Sewickley township, and six children were born to them: Mary E., the wife of E. U. McDaniel; Sarah Jane, the wife of Henry Bonzo; Cecelia N., who married Jefferson Kinney; and Anna, Aaron, and George, who live with the parents. Religiously, the family are Presbyterians.

HENRY M. CAMP is one of the most active and prominent business men in the borough of Rochester, Beaver county, Pa., where the Camp family has resided and contributed to its growth and prosperity since its early days. Our subject is interested in many of the local enterprises, and since 1887 he has acted in the capacity of superintendent of the Rochester Heat & Light Company. He was born in Rochester in 1850, and is a son of Michael Camp and grandson of Michael Camp, Sr.

Michael Camp was born in Hanover, Germany, and, with his brother John, came to the United States in 1832, first locating in Philadelphia, then in Butler county, and finally in Beaver county, where he spent his remaining days. They crossed over the mountains in a wagon, and at Rochester made a stop, and there John erected the old National Hotel on Water street; he later owned the one now adjoining, known as the Farmer's Hotel. Michael Camp was engaged in the making of shoes, the work being all by hand; the leather was purchased from near-by tanners and much of the work was let out to men who would complete it at their homes. His home and shop were located in Beaver, near where Mr. Frank Laird now resides. During his latter days he retired to Rochester, where he passed from this life, aged seventy-five years. His wife was Annie Barbara Schlesman, and they became the parents of the following children: Elizabeth, who died in Germany; Catherine, who married John Frick; Michael; Mary, who was born while her parents were crossing the ocean, and who is the wife of John Miller; Christian and Martin, who are twins; Margaret, who was married to Benjamin Dawson; Henry; John; and Barbara, who is the wife of James Robinson.

Michael Camp was born in Hanover, Germany, in 1827, and upon coming to this country, learned the trade of a brickmaker, but soon discontinued that occupation and accepted a position as clerk in the National Hotel. John Buchler was proprietor, and died the second day after taking possession of the hotel. Mr. Camp continued as clerk in the hotel, and later married Mrs. John Buchler, whose maiden name was Magdaline Weise. She died in 1877, aged sixty-four years, and had been married three times. Her first husband was Mr. Zerker, by whom she reared three children: Magdaline, Mary, and John. Her second husband was John Buchler, and four children were born to them: Frederick, William, Caroline and Emma. Her third union was with Michael Camp, and their only child was Henry M., the subject of this sketch. Mr. Camp formed a second union, with Mrs. Catherine (Mauser) Smith, widow of John Smith. Mr. Camp owned and conducted the Pavilion Hotel, now known as the St. James, from 1861 to 1886; in the latter year he sold out to C. H. Clarke, and moved on the farm formerly owned by William Johnson, which is located on the east side of Adams street. Mr. Camp still resides there, and is spending his latter days in comfort and happiness. He has always been a stanch Democrat, and has served in the council, as assessor and in many minor offices. Mr. Camp was one of the promoters, and is a large stockholder, of the Rochester Insurance Company; he is a stockholder in the Rochester Flint Vial & Bottle Works,—now known as the Point Bottle Works,—a stockholder in the Olive Stove Works, a member of the Rochester Heat & Light Company, a director in the Big Beaver Bridge Company, and a stockholder in the Keystone Tumbler Company. He built his present residence and has also erected many houses for tenement use.

The subject of this sketch attended the schools of Rochester until he attained the age of seventeen years, when he went to Pittsburg to learn the machinists' trade, and followed it for five years. Returning to Rochester, he went into the hotel business with his father, but upon the organization of the Rochester Heat & Light Company, he became superintendent and a stockholder. This company is composed of two hundred stockholders and has a capital stock of $18,-000. The gas used is furnished from Beaver

JOHN BEUTLER.

and Allegheny counties, and the company has not only been a success, but a means of great saving to the residents of Rochester. Our subject is a stockholder in the Rochester Insurance Company, the Flint Vial & Bottle Works, the Big Beaver Bridge Company, the People's Electric Railroad, and the High River Bridge Company. In 1883, he erected a handsome brick residence on the corner of Jefferson and Connecticut streets, and has resided there ever since.

Mr. Camp was joined in marriage with Miss Tillie E. Scheinder, a daughter of Louis E. Scheinder, of Rochester, and this happy union has been blessed by the birth of three children: Charles A.; Marl Etta, and Emma Maria, deceased. Our subject is a solid Democrat, and has served as a councilman. Religiously, he is a member of the Lutheran church; socially, he is a member and past master of the Masonic fraternity; and member and past regent of the Royal Arcanum. Mr. Camp is a man of high business principles, is respected by all who know him, and is always active in advancing the prosperity of his adopted town and county.

———◆•◆———

JOHN BEUTER, a prosperous and successful pharmacist of Beaver Falls, Pa., whose portrait is shown on the opposite page, wants it distinctly understood that he is a Republican of the deepest dye, and always has affiliated with that party ever since he was old enough to vote. He has been one of its most active members in Beaver county, and was one of the three Republican delegates to the state convention, held in Harrisburg, in 1898, and the only one of the three from Beaver county, who supported William A. Stone for governor, and had the satisfaction of seeing his man not only nominated, but elected.

John Beuter was born January 29, 1860, and is a son of John and Pauline (Tyfel) Beuter. His father was a native of Germany, and came to America with his parents when but twelve years of age. He located in Wheeling, West Virginia, where he followed the retail liquor business for a period of forty years. He laid down the burden of life, in 1894, and entered into rest.

John Beuter received his scholastic training in the public schools and afterward attended St. Vincent's College in Wheeling,— from which he graduated. After leaving college, young Beuter entered the employ of Logan List & Co., wholesale and retail druggists of Wheeling, and remained with that firm for a period of eight years. He then took a course in the Philadelphia College of Pharmacy in the autumns of 1879, 1880 and 1881. As these courses included only the fall months, he improved his unoccupied time by taking a special course in chemistry in the University of Pennsylvania.

After he became a full-fledged pharmacist, he took charge of the laboratory of the wholesale drug business of Bailey & Porter, of Zanesville, Ohio. Leaving Zanesville, he went to Pittsburg, where he entered the employ of George A. Kelley & Co., having complete charge of their second floor shipping department, where he remained for a short period. He then went to Beaver Falls, and was for some time a clerk for W. H. Hamilton. On seeing an opportunity to better his condition, he went to Pittsburg and took charge of the Twenty-fourth street drug store of Emil G. Stookey,—the same business now being conducted by N. B. Stookey. Mr. Beuter remained there until 1894, and then went into the drug business for himself at 619 Seventh avenue, Beaver Falls, where he conducts a first-class drug store.

In connection with his regular line of drugs, he is the patentee and manufacturer of the celebrated medicine known as "No-Dys-Pep" compound, having a large sale throughout the country.

The subject of this biography won for his bride, Hattie W. Hays, daughter of Charles Hays, of New Brighton, Pennsylvania. Mrs. Beuter has a kind and sweet disposition and is a great favorite in all classes of society. She is well and favorably known throughout Beaver county. Mr. Beuter is a member of the Benevolent and Protective Order of Elks, of Rochester, Pa.; of Beaver Falls Lodge, No. 293, Knights of Pythias, and of Walnut Camp, No. 2, Woodmen of the World, of Beaver Falls.

John Beuter has worked hard and earnestly, and with a determination that is bound to be rewarded by success. He believes in doing thoroughly everything that is required of him; he keeps a fine line of pure drugs for his customers, and also makes a specialty of filling prescriptions with promptness and care.

EDWARD KNOX HUM. The Beaver National Bank, of Beaver, Pa., was fortunate in having as an originator and promoter the gentleman whose name heads these lines, who now serves efficiently as vice-president of that institution. He is a man of thorough business ability and a sturdy supporter of all enterprises tending to improve the interests of the community,—his name being one familiar to the residents of Beaver county. He was born in Beaver, August 11, 1858, and is a son of James W. and Margaret (Briggs) Hum.

His great-grandfather, who established the Hum family in this country, was Jacob Hum, a native of Germany, who settled in Ohio and there followed the trade of a hatter. His business was first located at Columbiana, Columbiana county, Ohio, but he thereafter engaged in a similar line of business at Salem, Ohio. He married a lady of Scotch birth, who bore him the following children: David; John; Jacob; Adam; Margaret; and George. He died at the age of eighty-three years.

David Hum, the grandfather of Edward Knox Hum, was born in Columbiana county, Ohio, and early in life undertook the trade of a hatter, but, later, became a merchant of Lisbon, Ohio, where he died at the age of eighty years. He was four times married, and by his first wife, Mary Ann Hickox, who died at the age of thirty-six years, he had the following offspring: Angelina (Hatcher); James Winnard, who married Margaret Briggs; Richard Winchester, an early settler of Lowellville, Ohio; Columbus C., who lives near Toledo, Ohio; Martha (Throne), of East Palestine, Ohio; and Elizabeth, deceased. His second union, with Rebecca Thorn, was blessed by the birth of a son, John. His third wife's given name was Esther, and his fourth union was with Mary Silverthorn.

James W. Hum, a record of whose life appears elsewhere, and the father of the subject of this sketch, was born in Deerfield township, Columbiana county, Ohio, February 16, 1827. He left home at the age of ten years to live with his uncle, John Hum, with whom he remained four years. He then began to shift for himself and received employment on a steamer on the Ohio River as a cabin boy, and later learned the trade of boat carpenter. He manifested considerable natural ability in this line, and, after leaving the river, manufactured an ingenious machine known as a fanning mill. Threshing was at this time all done by hand, and this machine was used to clean the grain. It met with marked success on the market and his business increased rapidly, resulting in the employment of a goodly number of men. He subsequently became interested in the lightning rod business, and in 1849 was one of the founders of the American Lightning Rod plant at Philadelphia. The western section of the country was assigned to him, and he established a large wholesale and retail store at No. 19 Market street, Pittsburg. In 1882, he was joined in the business by his son, E. K. Hum, and together they continued until the father retired from active business duties in 1892. He built the home residence, in which Mrs. Hum now lives, in 1868,

and he was also possessed of considerable real estate in Bridgewater and Beaver at the time of his demise, March 17, 1895. James W. Hum's faithful companion in the pathways of life was Margaret Briggs, a daughter of Henry and Mary (Westcoat) Briggs. Henry Briggs was born in Dighton, Mass., and was a son of Matthew and Cecelia (Reed) Briggs, and grandson of Matthew Briggs, a blacksmith by trade, who came to this country from England. Matthew, Jr., was born in Dighton, Mass., and was also a blacksmith, following that occupation all of his active days. By his first wife he had three children, as follows: Matthew, Elizabeth, and Deliverance. He formed a second union with Cecelia Reed and they had five children: Henry, Nancy, Mary, Joseph, and Cecelia. Henry Briggs, the father of Mrs. Hum, learned the trade of a blacksmith, and, in 1836, removed to South Beaver township, Beaver county, Pa., where he purchased a farm. In addition to general farming, he was engaged at his trade all of his active life, but spent his last days in retirement, dying at the home of his daughter, Mrs. Hum, in the eighty-fourth year of his age. His wife survived him several years, and died at the remarkable age of eighty-nine years. She had made several trips to her native state, Massachusetts, and had returned from one of these trips but two months prior to her death. Their children were: Henry, who died young; Mary; Julia; William; Elizabeth; Margaret; and Spencer.

Mr. and Mrs. James W. Hum were the parents of the following: Henry Thornton, now of Pike county, Ill., who first married Josephine Blake, by whom he has one child, Harry C., and secondly married Elizabeth Hughes, by whom he has one child, Carl D.; Edward Knox, the subject of this personal history; Mary Elizabeth, deceased, the wife of Frank Robinson, by whom she had one child, Lois; James Weston, a farmer of Columbiana county, Ohio, who married Matilda Hineman, and had the following children,—Edward K., Guy H., Mary A., Martha T., James W., and Wayne A.; Fred Cook, deceased, who married Florence King, by whom he had a son, Forrest, deceased; Arthur Westcoat, an electrical engineer, of Bridgewater, who married Mary Doing, deceased; and Margaret Mott, the wife of Samuel P. Provost, a flour manufacturer and merchant, of Pittsburg. Fraternally, he was a member of the Masonic lodge at Beaver, being one of its charter members.

Edward K. Hum attended Beaver College, and while a young man became associated in business with his father, under the firm name of J. W. Hum & Son, wholesale and retail dealers in lightning rods and fixtures, at Pittsburg. Some twelve years later, after the death of his father, he formed a partnership with W. M. Leatherman, the firm name being Hum & Leatherman, at No. 8 Market street, Pittsburg. The subject of this sketch was the leading spirit in the organization and building of the Beaver National Bank, of Beaver, Pennsylvania. It has a capital of $100,000, and its officers, who are among the most substantial and public-spirited citizens of Beaver

county, are as follows: Jesse R. Leonard, president; Edward K. Hum, vice-president; Charles M. Hughes, cashier; and W. P. Judd, assistant cashier. The directors are: Jesse R. Leonard; Edward K. Hum; U. S. Strouss, M. D.; Thomas F. Galey; Joseph H. Evans; Winfield S. Moore, and Agnew Hice.

The Beaver National Bank is one of the prettiest specimens of business architecture in Western Pennsylvania, being constructed of Cleveland sandstone and having large plate-glass windows. It is richly finished, furnished in elegant style, and its arrangement is most convenient for the transaction of business. The bank has shown its patrons the greatest courtesy, and by their enterprise its officials have made it one of the leading financial institutions in the county.

Mr. Hum, although his business was for many years located at Pittsburg, has always been a loyal citizen of Beaver, and when not attending to business affairs he is always to be found enjoying the companionship of his family at his elegant home. In 1885 he built a residence on Third street, in which he resided until 1896, when he disposed of it to James Galey and built his present dwelling, a fine brick structure supplied with all modern conveniences for the highest enjoyment of life. He also owns considerable real estate in Beaver. On September 26, 1882, Edward K. Hum was joined in the holy bonds of wedlock with Emma L. Young, a daughter of Jacob and Lucinda M. Young, of Columbiana county, Ohio, and they have two children, namely: James Winnard and Anna. Fra-

ternally, Mr. Hum is a member of St. James Lodge, F. & A. M., of Beaver; Eureka Chapter, R. A. M., of Rochester; Pittsburg Commandery, No. 1, Knights Templar, of Pittsburg; and Syria Temple of the Mystic Shrine, Pittsburg. A man who has ever faithfully endeavored to be of benefit to his fellow-citizens of Beaver county, the subject of our sketch is held in the highest esteem, and numbers his friends by the score.

THOMAS M. FITZGERALD, a recent portrait of whom is shown on the opposite page, is descended from a line of ancestral gardeners, and is very fond of the culture of flowers, which he has made his like-work. He conducts one of the most beautiful gardens in Beaver county, situated in the borough of Beaver, and he has established a reputation as one of the best artists in his profession. He was born in Hulton township, Allegheny county, Pa., February 27, 1868, and is a son of Thomas and Mary (Healey) Fitzgerald.

The father of Thomas M. was born in Listowel, County Kerry, Ireland, and when a boy, learned the trade of a gardener and became an expert in the culture of flowers; for nine years he managed the grounds and hot-house of Lord Colliss, of Tarbert township, County Kerry, Ireland; he then engaged with Dr. Barrington, of Glin, County Limerick, Ireland, for fifteen years. He subsequently went to Hamilton, Canada, where he spent two years, and, as he had many friends and acquaintances in Pittsburg, Pa., he located there in 1866, and worked for many prominent men of that city, who owned large and handsome properties; he was employed by Mr. Murdick, Mrs. Deeny, and Mr. Charles McGee; he now has charge of Mr. M. C. Miller's grounds at Turtle Creek. While working in the employ of Lord Colliss, he made the acquaintance of his present wife. Both being poor and not able to buy a home in their native country, Thomas decided to come to America in the effort to seek home and fortune; his plans being crowned with success, three years later he wrote for his intended wife, and, upon her arrival here, they were happily united in marriage. A few years later the health of Mr. Fitzgerald's mother began to fail, and he sent his wife and five children to his old home in Ireland, where they remained four years,—returning in much better health and spirits. Mr. and Mrs. Fitzgerald are the parents of eight children: Joseph, deceased; John; Thomas M.; James; Annie; Mary; Edward, who served at Manila in Company B, 10th Reg., Pa. Vol. Inf.; and William, deceased.

The subject of this memoir attended school, four years, at Tarbert, Ireland, and in this country, at New Castle, Pennsylvania. While a mere boy, he assisted his father in the cultivation of flowers and improved every opportunity to gain a thorough knowledge of the art; in 1889 he came to Beaver to take charge of the beautiful grounds and hothouse of Hon. J. F. Dravo, but a year later he leased the hothouse, and a part of the grounds, of his employer, and now keeps one of the finest displays of flowers ever seen. The beds and plants are artistically arranged, and the choice, blooming flowers present an exquisite appearance; he is prepared to furnish flowers, on short notice, for funerals, weddings, and other occasions, and he also ships largely to other points. Mr. Fitzgerald is well deserving, and worthy of his large patronage, and he has shown the people of the vicinity that they always have at their command the most select assortment of floral beauties. He is genial and accommodating to all, and his pleasant manners and honest business methods, have won for him the esteem and good will of all who know him. He has not only adopted Beaver as his place of business, but likewise as his home, and he owns two fine lots on Commerce street, upon which he erected a handsome residence in 1893. In July, 1899, he purchased the Campbell estate, consisting of six and one-half acres on Fifth street, on which he will erect a large range of greenhouses to better accommodate his growing business.

Mr. Fitzgerald wedded Nora, a daughter of Jeremiah Minihan, of County Cork, Ireland, and three children have resulted from their union: Mary Catherine, born July 16, 1896; John Leo, born February 23, 1898; and Joseph Thomas, the last two being twins. Religiously, our subject is a member of the Catholic church; politically, he is independent in his views.

JOHN R. EAKIN, who owns a controlling interest in the Olive Stove Works, at Rochester, Pa., of which he is secretary and treasurer, is one of the most esteemed citizens of Beaver, Pa., and, although in the seventieth year of his age, he is today as active a man as can be found in Beaver county. He has seen Beaver grow from the little settlement called Beaver Town, to its present stage of development, as one of the finest and most prosperous boroughs in Western Pennsylvania. John R. Eakin was born July 20, 1829, in Beaver, Pennsylvania. He is a son of James and Mary (Quaill) Eakin, and grandson of John Eakin, who was of Scotch-Irish descent.

James Eakin, father of John R., was born in County Derry, Ireland, within fourteen miles of Londonderry. He was reared under the old Presbyterian methods, and took a great dislike to the controlling element of Ireland. In 1808, at the age of sixteen years, he packed his few belongings and started for "free America." Having a fine education for that day, and being active and energetic, he had no fear of meeting with failure in the new world, but looked eagerly forward to the time when he could make a home for himself, and rear a family in accordance with his own ideas. Upon his arrival in the United States, he drifted to Philadelphia, Pa., where he began working at the trade of a chandler, which consists of candle making. He remained at that place for about fourteen years, removing, in 1822, west to Pittsburg, and followed the same occupation with B. C. Sawyer, of that city.

Later, he began teaching school; being a fine scholar and a splendid writer, he experienced no difficulty in obtaining a desirable situation. He went to Beaver, Pa., where he taught in the old academy which stood there many years ago. Mr. Eakin also opened a store on the same site where the Quay business block was later erected. Still later, he built a residence and store on the corner of Third street and College avenue. There his death occurred, in 1847, at the age of sixty-four years. In politics, he was a Whig, and served many years as justice of the peace, and as burgess of Beaver. He also owned a fine farm, which was subsequently the property of Mr. Hardy.

James Eakin was united in marriage with Mary Quaill. She was born in Washington county, Pa., in 1804, and passed away from her earthly home in 1892. Their union was prolific of the following children: Mary Jane; John R.; Eliza Ann; Sarah; James Q.; Margaret; Victoria; Emma; and Matilda. Mary Jane is the wife of Daniel Risinger, a prominent blacksmith of Beaver. John R. is the subject of these lines. Eliza Ann is the widow of John D. Davidson; she resides in Middlesex, Pennsylvania. Sarah is the wife of Abraham Wolf, of Beaver. James Q. is deceased; he married Elizabeth Strock, who still survives him, and resides in Bridgewater. Margaret is the wife of J. M. Dunlap. Victoria is the wife of H. H. Newkirk, of Rochester, Pennsylvania. Emma, who is deceased, was the wife of Jacob M. Johnson. Matilda is the wife of J. B. Wilson, of Beaver.

John R. Eakin pursued a course of study at Beaver Academy, and, like his honored father, he adopted the profession of instructing youthful minds. But upon the death of his father, who left a widow with a family of small children, it devolved upon John, the eldest son, to assist his mother in rearing the smaller ones. He realized this to be his first duty, nor was that duty shirked; rather may it be said that it was performed in a faithful manner, quite worthy of emulation by those similarly situated. He accompanied his bereaved mother and the family to the farm which the father's thrift and prosperity had provided. This farm he conducted and managed to the best of his ability, and assisted his mother in every possible way to rear and educate the children. After eight years upon the farm, he felt free to seek other pursuits, and became a steamboat clerk on the Ohio River; he followed river life for a period of twelve years, during all of which time he held the position of either clerk or captain. Desiring to settle down in order to be more with his family, he then accepted a place as clerk in the county commissioner's office, and also became deputy treasurer, serving two years. Later, he was interested in the manufacture of glass at Beaver Falls, for five years. In 1875, he was elected county treasurer of Beaver county, serving one term. Subsequently, in company with others, he purchased the Olive Stove Works in 1879. This plant was established in 1872, and was sold at sheriff's sale, in 1879. Mr. Eakin was at once appointed secretary, treasurer, and general manager of the works, and under his careful, judicious management, the business took another turn, and has since been a very progressive and prosperous plant. The original works have been enlarged, in addition to which new buildings have been added; with increased facilities and capacities, the plant now turns out as fine a line of stoves and ranges as any plant of its size in America. It is located on Railroad street, and the controlling interest is now owned by Mr. Eakin. In addition to his business interests, Mr. Eakin also owns the premises on Third street, formerly belonging to his beloved father, and his present residence on College avenue, which is a beautiful, modern brick dwelling.

John R. Eakin was joined in the holy bonds of matrimony with Margaret Mitchell. This most happy union resulted in the birth of two daughters and one son, whose names are: Annie M., Emma E. and Joseph Mitchell. Annie M., the eldest daughter, is the wife of J. Rankin Martin, a leading attorney of Beaver Falls, whose sketch also appears in this volume. Emma E., the second daughter, is the widow of James J. Davidson, whose life history appears elsewhere in this volume of biographies. Joseph Mitchell, the third child, and only son, is in business with his father, being a partner and bookkeeper in the Olive Stove Works. He pursued a course of study in the Beaver high schools, and at Beaver Falls, and, when seventeen years of age, became interested in the plant to which his whole life has been devoted. He is fast assuming the heavier duties of the works. He

wedded Minnie White, and they have a son, whom they call John Mitchell. Joseph M. Eakin is a Knight Templar Mason, a Shriner, an Odd Fellow, and a Knight of Pythias.

Our subject and his family are of the Presbyterian faith. Mr. Eakin is a member of the borough council, and has always been a public-spirited man, having done much to further the progress of Beaver. He is spending the sunset of life, surrounded by loving friends and many comforts, and is reaping the just reward of earnest and well-directed efforts.

Joseph Mitchell, father-in-law of John R. Eakin, was born in Ireland and came to the United States in 1822, at the age of thirty-four years. He located at New Brighton, Pa., and engaged in agricultural pursuits, removing in 1826 to Beaver, where he went into mercantile pursuits. He was very successful in this line, and purchased ground adjoining Beaver on the north and west, until he was the owner of much valuable acreage. He built a handsome brick residence at Vanport, now known as the Purdy farm. He continued to prosper until he had accumulated a nice property. He served as a justice of the peace and as a school director. He did business at the Pittsburg Bank, and at the advanced age of eighty-seven years, just as he was about to start to Pittsburg on business, he slipped and fell, breaking his leg, which caused his death shortly afterward, in 1876. He was joined in marriage with Anne McCreary, a daughter of James McCreary, of Beaver county, Pennsylvania. She died in 1846 at the age of thirty-six years. Their children were: Eliza, deceased; Sarah, wife of Jesse Cruthers, of Beaver county; Margaret, wife of the subject of this sketch; Esther, wife of H. M. Cunningham, of Ohio; Maria L., wife of the late T. B. Cunningham, of Ohio; James, who married Lucinda Greenlee, of Vanport, Beaver county; and Shannon R., who married Annie E. Stokes.

——— ◄ • ►— ———

DR. JOHN D. COFFIN, deceased, was for many years a most distinguished physician of Beaver Valley. Having an established reputation before locating there in 1865, he soon acquired an extensive practice. His profound knowledge of therapeutics and his most thorough manner of diagnosing, first gained for him the confidence of the people in a professional way, and as closer relationships sprang up he became the honored friend of his patients. In the latter years of his life he lived in partial retirement in Beaver Falls, just retaining sufficient practice to employ his time. The Coffins are an old English family with genealogical records dating back to the twelfth century. The family is one of the most prominent in New England, and includes many bankers and men of mark in all professions. At the family reunion held at Nantucket in 1884, there were about eight hundred names registered as descendants of a common ancestry, who were then living. The first of the line in America was Tristam Coffin, who came from Devonshire, England, early in the seventeenth century and settled at Nantucket Island, Massachusetts. In the course of time one branch of the Coffin family went over to Newburyport, Mass., and settled there. It is from this latter branch that Dr. Coffin is descended. He was born in Newburyport, Mass., in 1809, and was a son of Nathan E. and Eunice (Emory) Coffin.

Nathan E. Coffin was a well-known ship builder of Newburyport, Mass., but about the year 1820, he relinquished that occupation and moved to New Lisbon, Ohio, where he became a contractor. Upon moving to Allegheny, subsequently, he retired to enjoy the benefits of his industrious past. His wife died there, of cholera, and he survived her some years, dying in 1854. Their children were: Charles, at one time a celebrated judge of the Cincinnati courts; Emory, deceased, who was a practitioner of medicine; Gardiner, who became a wealthy manufacturer; Harrison, at one time president of the Des Moines Loan & Trust Company, who was succeeded by his son; Carey, a merchant; Emeline McMillan, whose husband is a printer of Pittsburg; Harriet (Nesbit); and John D., the gentleman whose name heads these lines.

John D. Coffin received his intellectual training in the common schools of Newburyport, Mass., and after his parents removed to New Lisbon, Ohio, he began the study of medicine under Dr. McCook. After thoroughly mastering the science, he began to practice at New Lisbon in 1830, remaining there for five years, and moving to Petersburg, Ohio, in 1835.

After practicing there for a period of fifteen years' duration, he located in Westmoreland county, Pa., where he continued with much success until 1865. He then secured a good practice in Rochester, Beaver county, Pa., where he remained for ten years. Possessing some property at Homewood, he then betook himself there to follow his profession. These years of hard and continuous labor resulted in placing him in good financial circumstances, and in September, 1882, he decided to retire, as he was getting old, and moved to Beaver Falls. But inactivity was not suited to one of his energetic nature, and we soon find him again caring for a limited practice, a few old patients, just enough to keep him moderately busy. The Doctor was called to his final rest in August, 1893, aged eighty-four years.

Doctor Coffin was united in marriage, in 1851, with Margaret Harrah, who came of one of the pioneer families of Western Pennsylvania, and was a daughter of William and Eliza (Stewart) Harrah. Her grandfather was also William Harrah, who was born in Massachusetts, in 1767, and followed the occupation of a farmer. He later moved to Petersburg, Ohio, in the latter part of the eighteenth century, and became one of the very early pioneers. He bought a farm of four hundred acres of wild land, on which, after making a clearing, he built a log house. He then built a fine frame house, in which he lived the remainder of his days. He was a devout Presbyterian and served as elder a great many years. He left the following children: William; Hugh; Samuel; John; Nancy (Nesbit); Margaret (Adams); and Mary (Watson). William Harrah, the father of Mrs. Coffin, was born in Massachusetts and removed to Petersburg, Ohio, with his parents, making the trip by wagon. They did their own cooking and lived in the wagon, and at the end of six weeks they arrived at the end of their journey. He received his educational training in the schools of Beaver county, and took up the occupation of a miller, building what was probably the first mill in the county, on Beaver Creek, near Enon Valley. He followed that until he reached his declining years, and then opened a small grocery store, from which he realized a sufficient amount to spend his last days in easy circumstances. He married Elizabeth Stewart in 1826, and they had seven children, namely: Harvey; Jane; Margaret; Mary (Magee); James Ritner of Beaver, Pa.; Stewart; and Laura (Fowler), of Vanport, Pennsylvania. Harvey died young. Jane (Saltsman) is deceased; her husband was a very successful merchant of Saltsman Station, Jefferson county, Pa., and also a wealthy land owner. Stewart is a physician residing in Allegheny county, Pennsylvania. Margaret was born near Enon Valley, in Lawrence county, Pa., and was a pupil in the public schools. At the early age of 18 years, she was married to Dr. Coffin, and they had the following children: Lizzie; Jennie E.; Ella (Strock), whose husband is a real estate and insurance agent; Matilda; Anna M.; John W.; and Laura M.

Lizzie Coffin was born in 1853, in Petersburg, Pa., is a graduate of Beaver College and Edinboro State Normal School. Prior to her marriage she taught school in New Brighton and is now teaching in the public schools of Chicago. She married W. Fitch, who, after graduating from Oberlin College, was principal of a Chicago high school. He died in Honduras while representing the Honduras Land & Fruit Company. They had one child, Alice.

Jennie E. (Sunderlin), whose husband read law and then took up teaching, lives at Tekamah, Nebraska, where Mr. Sunderlin is principal of the Tekamah public schools. He is a native of Michigan. She was graduated from the Edinboro State Normal School and taught at New Brighton for some years.

Matilda (Ford), who enjoys a national reputation as an educator and a lecturer on institute work, was born in Westmoreland county, Pa., in 1861, and attended Beaver College and the Edinboro State Normal School. She taught two years at New Brighton and one year in the Beaver Falls High School, after which she took a course of study in the Cook County Normal School under Col. F. W. Parker. She held a position as instructor in that institution for three years, when she accepted a similar position in Millersville (Pa.) State Normal School; still later she was employed as principal of the Model School, for three years. Becoming interested in institute work, she lectured in every state in the Union, and established a high reputation throughout the country, which brought her many handsome offers at a high salary. She

became assistant principal of the public schools of Detroit, and continued thus for five years, having three hundred teachers under her direction. In 1897, she was united in marriage with Franklin Ford, a member of a well-known commercial agency firm in the city of New York. She was offered the position of assistant principal of the schools of that city at a salary of $4,000, but this she declined. She is a successful lecturer on geography and reading, and, with one exception, she has been offered the highest salary ever offered to a woman. She contemplates a public career and her future certainly has a brilliant outlook.

Anna M., who was educated in the Edinboro (Pa.) State Normal and the Cook County (Ill.) State Normal schools, is now attaining considerable success as a teacher in the public schools of Chicago.

John W. Coffin was born in Greensburg, Pa., and obtained his primary education in the schools of Beaver Falls and in the high school of that place. He then studied medicine at Cleveland, and was graduated from the Western Reserve University in 1889, receiving the degree of M. D. He built up an excellent practice in Beaver Falls, being located at No. 1402 Seventh avenue. He was appointed surgeon with the rank of lieutenant, in the National Guards, by Gov. Pattison, and, on May 1, 1898, he enlisted in the same grade in the 10th Reg., Pa. Vol. Inf., and accompanied the regiment to Manila, helping to establish its brilliant record, there made. Dr. Coffin is also interested in considerable realty. He is a member of the Masonic order and of the Elks.

Laura M. Coffin, who was born in Rochester, Pa., October 23, 1870, attended the public schools of Beaver Falls, and graduated from the high school there. She took a course of study under Col. Parker in the Cook County (Ill.) State Normal School, after which she taught for one year in the Beaver Falls public schools. She is a young woman of many admirable traits of character, and her friends and acquaintances in the vicinity of Beaver Falls are numberless.

Dr. John D. Coffin, deceased, was an independent Democrat in politics, but respectfully declined all offices. Religiously, he was a conscientious member of the First Christian church. Socially, he was a prominent member of the Masonic order.

———— ♦ • ♦ ————

SAMUEL THOMAS, deceased, was for many years an extensive farmer and sheep-raiser of Beaver county, in which he lived all his life. A man of exceedingly strong character and excellent habits, he was greatly respected by all with whom he was acquainted, and his friends were without number. He was born in Chippewa township, Beaver county, March 6, 1818, and was a son of Elam and Barbara (Baker) Thomas.

Elam Thomas, the father of Samuel, was a native of Wales, and after coming to this country spent most of his life in Beaver county, in that section which is now Lawrence county. As a result of his union with Barbara Baker, eight children, all of whom are now deceased, were born,—the youngest of them being our subject.

Samuel Thomas spent ten years of his early life with an uncle, during which time he acquired the money with which he bought a farm of one-hundred acres in Beaver county, the one on which Mrs. Thomas now lives. The farm was partially cleared and he leased it until after his marriage, when, on April 3, 1848, they moved upon it. He had taught school prior to his marriage, and continued so to do for two terms thereafter. They lived in a rude old log house until about twenty years ago, when he erected the one which now stands. In addition to the home farm, he owned a property of one hundred and twenty-three acres, which he cultivated, but since his death, it has been sold. He was a great sheep-raiser, having some 300 head of the finest in the county. Mr. Thomas was called to his final rest in 1883, and his widow has since very successfully managed the farm, which is worked by her brother, William T.

On December 7, 1847, he formed a matrimonial alliance with Eliza Jane Crans, a daughter of James and Elizabeth (Thomas) Crans, and a granddaughter of John Crans, who was a native of New York State, but moved to Ohio in early life. Mrs. Thomas was born December 8, 1824, and was one of a family of ten children, eight of whom now live, as follows: Eliza Jane, the wife of Samuel Thomas; Mary Ann; John J.; Ellen J.; Laura; William T.; Elizabeth; and James.

ALBERT M. JOLLY.

Those deceased are David R. and Julius L., both of whom were taken ill and died while serving in the army during the Civil War. After the death of her husband, Mrs. Thomas, who has no children of her own, adopted Maggie E. Ruby, whose family lives in Franklin township. She is a woman of sympathetic and charitable disposition, and has many friends who love her for her excellent traits of character. She is a remarkably well preserved lady, for one of her years.

Mr. Thomas was what may be termed a home man, a good husband, and very fond of the society of his wife. He had excellent habits, using neither tobacco nor intoxicating liquors. In politics, he supported the Republican party, but favored the cause of Prohibition. He was not an aspirant to office, yet served as supervisor. Religiously, he was a faithful member of the Baptist church, as is his widow, and for forty years was a deacon in the church.

ALBERT M. JOLLY, whose portrait is presented on the preceding page, has for many years been recognized as one of Beaver county's most substantial and enterprising business men, and is an esteemed resident of Beaver Falls. He is connected with one of the largest contracting concerns in Western Pennsylvania,—that of A. J. Jolly & Sons, his association with this prominent firm dating back to 1877. He was born in December, 1855, at what is now known as Monaca, Beaver county, and is a son of An-

drew J. Jolly, and grandson of Kenzie Jolly.

Mr. Jolly traces his family line back to Colonel Henry Jolly, of Revolutionary War fame, who after that eventful struggle moved to Marietta, Ohio, where he became a prominent citizen. He presided as judge over the first court ever held in that state. His wife was a Miss Ghriest, who was scalped and tomahawked by the Indians, and, though the wound never healed, she survived this barbarity for forty-three years, dying at an advanced age. Colonel and Mrs. Jolly were the parents of the following children: William, Kenzie, Albert, and Siddy, the wife of Vashel Dickerson.

Kenzie Jolly was born in Washington county, Ohio, in 1778, and there resided all his life engaged in agricultural pursuits. He married Elizabeth Dickerson, a daughter of Thomas Dickerson; she was born in 1795 and died aged one hundred years and five months. She was the mother of the following children: Rachel, the wife of John Ankron, of New Orleans, La.; Rebecca, wife of Abner Martin, of Washington county, Ohio; Henry, also of Washington county, Ohio; Dickerson and Andrew Jackson residing in Phillipsburg, Pa.; Alpheus B., a resident of Keokuk, Iowa; William M., who died in his infancy; Electa M., the wife of James Hutchinson, of Washington county, Ohio; and Owen F., a resident of Dayton, Kentucky.

Andrew Jackson Jolly, father of the subject hereof, was born in Washington county, Ohio, May 28, 1828, and continued to reside there until 1844. He accepted the opportu-

326 BOOK OF BIOGRAPHIES

nities afforded by the primitive schools for an education, and at the age of sixteen years, he came to Pittsburg; there he embarked as a boatman on the Ohio and Mississippi rivers, beginning as a deck-hand and advancing through various grades until he became captain. This river life was continued until 1866, when he engaged in prospecting and drilling for oil in Beaver county, but soon resumed the life of a boatman, which business he followed until 1872. In that year he entered upon his present business of furnishing stone for building and street-paving. Like many other great enterprises the business of A. J. Jolly & Sons has developed from small beginnings, and is the outgrowth of hard labor, perseverance, and indomitable energy. It required a great amount of work to secure the cobble stone from the river banks, but the greatest task was to meet the opposition of the older firms in the same business; this was happily done, and the present firm now ranks among the foremost and most successful contractors of the state. Their first contract was with the Pittsburg & Lake Erie Railroad Company, for whom they still continue to furnish stone and to do masonry work; they also supply other railroads with stone, and the stone for the court house and custom house at Pittsburg was supplied by them. They erected a bridge across the Ohio River at Point Pleasant, West Va., one and one-half miles long and 103 feet high; they erected the bridge at Parkersburg in the same state and furnished the stone for lock Number 4, on the Monongahela River, and for the bridge at

Cold Centre, Pa., on the B. & O. R. R. Politically, Mr. Jolly is a stanch supporter of the Democratic party. He was wedded September 26, 1850, to Miss Sarah Srodes, a daughter of John M. Srodes, of Beaver county, and they are the parents of the following children: William A., deceased; John K.; Albert M.; Marilla E., the wife of David Anderson; Eddie, deceased; and Frank L.

Albert M. Jolly acquired his primary education in the district schools of his native town and, in 1874, was graduated from Duff's Mercantile College of Pittsburg. Returning to Phillipsburg in 1877, he became interested in contracting, and was made secretary and treasurer of the firm of A. J. Jolly & Sons; at that time the business was chiefly confined to quarrying, but at the present day they do all kinds of contracting. The subject of this biography gives much attention to the details of the business, and is frequently to be found in the various localities where the work is progressing,—West Virginia having recently been his base of operations. Of the many important contracts completed by this firm were the Government lock on the Muskegon River, the construction of which occupied nearly one year; the large bridge that spans the river at Wheeling, West Va.; several bridges across the Beaver River; the firm built the railroad from Point Pleasant to Huntington, Pa., and also the Twelfth street inclined plane at Pittsburg, one of the first of its kind to carry street cars. They have accepted large contracts from the P. R. R., the B. & O. R. R., and the P. McK. & Y. R. R. The other members of the firm are J. K. and F. L. Jolly. Aside from his interests with the above firm, our Mr. Jolly is interested in many other enterprises, among which are the Beaver Valley Street Railway Company, of which he was vice-president seven years and is now a stockholder and a director. He was, five years, manager of the Wheeling Street Railway Company; is president of the Sharon Street Railway Company; with other members of his family, he built the Bellaire, Bridgeport and Martin's Ferry Railroad, which was consolidated with the Wheeling lines in the fall of 1898; he is a director of the Ohio River Bridge Company, which owns the bridge which connects Rochester and Monaca, of which company his father is president; he is president of the People's Water Company, a corporation formed to supply the residents of Beaver Falls with pure water at a low rate, and to relieve them from the oppression of the old company (one of the greatest blessings the borough now enjoys); he is a director in the National Bank, a director in the Home Protective Bank & Loan Association, and a director of the Columbia Building & Loan Association. Mr. Jolly has built many dwellings in the village of Beaver Falls, including the handsome residence he has occupied for the past few years.

Mr. Jolly was united in marriage March 23, 1882, with Miss Jennie E. Small, a daughter of Elmira Small, and to this union two children have been born: Clarence D., a student in the Chester, Pa., Military Academy; and Leila V., a student in the district school.

Socially, Mr. Jolly is a member of the F. & A. M., Valley Echo Lodge, No. 622; Pittsburg Commandery, No. 1, of Pittsburg, Pa., —which is next to the largest commandery in the United States; the I. O. O. F., of Beaver Falls; Lone Rock Lodge, No. 222, K. of P.; Royal Arcanum; and the Beaver Falls Mechanics' Lodge, No. 28, A. O. U. W. Religiously, he belongs to the Methodist denomination.

The father of Mr. Jolly's wife is one of the oldest residents of the county, the date of his birth occurring in March, 1822, and his birthplace being Bridgewater, Pennsylvania. He was a son of Boston Small, who was born in 1781. Boston was one of six brothers who came to Beaver county about the year 1800, at which time the place was a vast forest filled with roaming Indians and wild animals. Those of his family who accompanied Boston to this vicinity were Jacob, a gunsmith; Frederick, a blacksmith; and John, Henry and Peter, farmers. They were the sons of Jacob, who was born in Germany, and who came to America many years prior to the War of Independence. Boston Small was educated in Pittsburg, Pa., and at an early age came down the Beaver valley to the sugar camps, and being favorably impressed with the appearance of the place, he decided to locate there; later he was followed by his five brothers. They bought large tracts of land, which was covered with great quantities of black, red and white oak, and hickory. Boston moved to Bridgewater in 1833, and there he spent his remaining days, being suddenly cut off by an attack of apoplexy, in 1858. He was married, in 1809, to Margaret Graham, who was born September 6, 1788, and was a daughter of Hughey Graham, a soldier of the Revolutionary War. Mrs. Small was born at Fairview, and received her mental training in the old log school in that district. Five children were born to them: Catherine (Calhoon), born in December, 1809; Jane (May), born in 1811; Maria (Swager), born in 1817; Martin, born in 1819; and Socrates J. Boston Small was a devout Christian, a member of the Presbyterian church, and assisted in the building of the churches at Bridgewater and Beaver. He never allowed a morning or evening to pass without having family prayers. He was a Whig, and served as supervisor and school director.

Socrates J. Small was mentally instructed in Brighton township, in the old log school house, and was obliged to walk three and one-half miles daily during the terms; when seventeen years of age, he learned the trade of a cabinet-maker. He built the first hearse in the county; at that time the coffins were made of cherry wood, and the undertakers were compelled to take the rough wood, cut it into necessary shapes and boil it in whisky in order to get the requisite color; then the coffin was covered with beeswax melted with a hot iron and polished with a cork. There was no rough box, no handles on the coffin, no ceremony, and it was difficult to secure anything but a wagon to convey the corpse to its final resting place. The coffins were sold for one dollar a foot. Mr. Small had many strange orders to fill while in the undertaking business; one was to furnish a steel casket of polished metal, that weighed three hundred and fifty pounds. Mr. Small first engaged in the business in 1842, with his brother Martin, in the town of Bridgewater, but three years later he sold out and worked for Robert Gilmore and Milton Swager, with whom he had learned the trade. In 1846, he returned to the furniture and undertaking business,—buying out the stock of Mr. Johnson.—and successfully conducted the establishment throughout his active life,—retiring in 1887. A few years prior to 1875, he was in business at Beaver but in that year he moved to Beaver Falls. Mr. Small wedded Elmira Swager, a native of Mercer county, Pa., who came to Beaver county when she was but eight years of age. Eleven children were born to them: Ursula (Johnson), an artist now in the treasury department at Washington, D. C.; Hiram; Margaret (Coleman), of Rochester; George, a farmer; J. Emma (Jolly), wife of the subject hereof; Ann M. (Jolly); Maria (Allen); Kate (Sterling); Eliza (Owery); Frank; and Charles, who died in infancy.

———— ◆ • ◆ ————

DR. HENRY C. ISEMAN is a skilful physician residing in the town of Beaver Falls, Pa., and his exceedingly large practice and wide experience have placed him in the foremost ranks of the profession in Beaver county. The Doctor makes a specialty of hemorrhoids and has been called to various cities to treat some of the most

P. M. WALLOVER.

prominent men in Western Pennsylvania and Eastern Ohio. He was born in Westmoreland County, Pa., August 16, 1839, and is a son of Christopher and Maggie (Sober) Iseman. His parents were both natives of Westmoreland county, Pa., and his father was a veterinary surgeon and resided in Burrell township.

The Doctor obtained a common school education in his native district, and having decided upon the medical profession, he entered the office of Dr. George Wallace of Westmoreland county, and subsequently completed the required study with Dr. Charles Jarvis. In 1869, he opened an office in Allegheny City, Pa., but after a year had elapsed he located in Beaver for six months; he then made Petersburg, Ohio, his headquarters, in the vicinity of which he successfully practiced his profession for a period of twelve years. At the expiration of that time, he returned to Beaver,—remaining there ten years. Since then he has been practicing in Beaver Falls and vicinity. Dr. Iseman realizing the great prevalence of hemorrhoids, early began to give special attention to the study and treatment of this disease; in addition to his own investigation along that line, he spent one year under the instruction and tutelage of that well-known specialist, Dr. Wendman. Certainly the Doctor has shown a wonderful skill in the treatment of hemorrhoids, and counts among the patients that he has successfully treated, many of the prominent business and professional men throughout this part of the state, and Eastern Ohio. Dr. Iseman is popular as a business man and citizen, and is held by his many acquaintances in profound respect and esteem. When the crisis of the Civil War was upon us, true to the patriotic instincts of his nature, Dr. Iseman volunteered his services in defense of the Union. In 1861, Dr. Iseman was joined in marriage to Annie E. Edger, daughter of "Squire" I. A. W. Edger, of Darlington, Beaver county, Pa., and unto them have been born four children, as follows: Maggie, who married J. C. Naugle, of Wampum, Pa.; William, who married and settled in Miduga,—the maiden name of his wife not being known; Alice E., unmarried; and Frank. In religious belief the family are Presbyterians. In political action, he casts his vote for the man best qualified, regardless of party or creed.

P. M. WALLOVER, an extensive oil producer and refiner of Smith's Ferry, Beaver county, Pa., whose portrait appears on the opposite page, was born near Philadelphia, Pa., in 1824. Several generations of the Wallover family were born in that vicinity. The birth of his father, William H., and of his grandfather, after whom he was named, also occurred in that part of the state. His grandfather, M. P. Wallover, was the son of a well-known sea captain. He was reared and educated in the city of Philadelphia, and at an early age became interested in the manufacture of paper. In those pioneer days all the work was done by hand, and to do an extensive business required considerable capital. He was successful in his operations and established two mills, one on Mill Creek, the other on Wissahickon Creek. He became very wealthy. At that early day, only wealthy people could afford to buy a piano, and he bought one of the finest instruments shipped to this country. The whole family became expert players on this instrument.

He reared a family of six children, namely: Peter; William H.; Harry, who went to Mexico, and there formed a partnership with a Mr. Bellfield (both of whom showed their patriotism by offering their place to the government for a garrison); Harriet, who became the wife of a Mr. Duckett, a wealthy paper manufacturer; Margaret (Shee); and Mary Ann.

William H. Wallover, father of the subject of this sketch, obtained his intellectual training in Philadelphia, and, although the advantages were meagre, he received a fair education. His first business relations were those with his father, whom he assisted in the paper mills. He was interested in that business during all of his active career. He married Harriet Mervine, and they reared three children: P. M., the subject of this sketch; Anna, the wife of General Daniel Dare; and Henry, who died at the age of six years.

William H. Wallover died in 1829, and his widow married a Mr. Stott, a mechanic of no mean ability. He it was who put the machinery in the United States steamship Princeton. He was superintendent of the Phoenixville Iron Works for many years, and retained this position up to the time of his death, which occurred very suddenly.

P. M. Wallover received his education under private tutorship. He learned the trade of a machinist, but, although he never followed it, he has found his knowledge of mechanics very useful during his business life. His first work was in a paper mill of his uncle, near Philadelphia, where he labored for eight months; he was then given the management of the establishment. Afterwards he became interested in two mills, working them on shares,—and continued thus until 1854, when he came to Beaver county to manage a mill opened by a relative on Little Beaver Creek. This mill was operated for three years. Mr. Wallover purchased property near Smith's Ferry, and on February 9, 1860, he began to drill for oil. March 1, of that year, he struck a five-barrel well. This gave him encouragement, and he leased more property and struck a well which produced $60,000 worth of oil. He has drilled and operated twenty-eight wells, and all of them were good producers.

In 1863, he started an oil refinery,—it being the first one in this district. He at once began to experiment in the oils, and his efforts were crowned with success. He made the first signal oil used on the Ohio River; he also made the first brand of wool oil used in the woolen mills, and got several brands of fine machinery oil. In those days the war tax was twelve cents per gallon, and one dollar per barrel. The firm name of the refinery was the Wallover Oil Co., but there were three parties interested in it. Two of them were railroad men, and when the railroad was put through that section, the railroad partners had to withdraw from the Wallover Oil Co., as it was against the rules of the railroad company for any of its stockholders to hold outside interests. Consequently Mr. Wallover purchased their shares and continued the business alone.

Our subject was joined in the bonds of wedlock with Margaret Arthur. She was also born in Philadelphia. They have a family of eight children: Charles A., now engaged in paper manufacturing; William H., who is in the oil business, in Indiana; Robert A., who is with his father; Joseph D., a contractor for drilling oil wells; Bert S., deceased; Edwin S., a salesman and teacher of music; Katie, deceased; and Laura (Boyd). Mr. Wallover is a Republican, and has served in minor offices of his town. The family is in accord with the M. E. church, of which he is a liberal supporter.

———◆◆———

JAMES W. HUM, deceased, an early resident of Beaver, Beaver county, Pa., was for many long years a very prominent business man of Western Pennsylvania, conducting a large wholesale and retail lightning-rod house at No. 19 Market street, Pittsburg, Pa. He was born in Deerfield township, Columbiana county, Ohio, February 16, 1827, and was a son of David and Mary Ann (Hickox) Hum, and grandson of Jacob Hum.

Jacob Hum, with a brother, early in life emigrated from their native country, Germany, and settled in Ohio, where he worked at his trade, that of a hatter. He established a business at Columbiana, Columbiana county, Ohio, but subsequently engaged in the same line of work at Salem, Ohio. He formed a matrimonial alliance with a lady of Scottish birth, and those of their children who grew to maturity were named as follows: David; John; Jacob; Adam; Margaret; and George. Mr. Hum lived to reach the advanced age of eighty-three years.

David Hum, the father of James W., was born in Columbiana county, Ohio, and at Columbiana followed his father's business for some years. Later in life, however, he became a merchant of Lisbon, Ohio, where he died when eighty years old. His first wife's maiden name was Mary Ann Hickox, who died at thirty-six years of age, leaving the following offspring: Angelina (Hatcher); James Winnard, who married Margaret Briggs; Richard Winchester, an early settler of Lowellville, Ohio; Columbus C., who resides near Toledo, Ohio; Martha (Throne), of East Palestine, Ohio; and Elizabeth, deceased. By his second wife, Rebecca Thorn, Mr. Hum had one son, John. His third wife's given name was Esther, and his fourth union was with Mary Silverthorn.

James W. Hum left home at the age of ten years to live with his uncle, John Hum. He remained with him until he reached the age of fourteen years, when he obtained employment on a steamboat on the Ohio River, as a cabin boy. Later he learned the trade of boat carpenter, a vocation for which he was naturally well qualified. Subsequently he established himself at Bridgewater, and displayed considerable genius by manufacturing fanning mills, by the means of which grain, then threshed by hand, could be cleaned. His business became very prosperous, and he employed a large number of hands, as his product was extensively used in Western Pennsylvania. The lightning rod business next claimed his attention, and he was one of the founders of the American Lightning Rod Company, of Philadelphia, in 1849. The western section of the United States was his exclusive territory, and he established a wholesale and retail store at No. 19 Market street, Pittsburg, Pennsylvania. Under successful management the business expanded, and, in 1882, he took his son, Edward Knox Hum, into partnership with him, and they continued together until 1892, when the subject of this sketch retired from active labors. It was in 1868 that he built the handsome residence in which his widow now lives, and he also owned considerable valuable realty in Bridgewater and Beaver at the time of his death, which occurred March 17, 1895. He was a man of high principles, a loving husband and a fond father, and his friends throughout the state were very numerous.

James W. Hum formed a marital union with Margaret Briggs, a daughter of Henry and Mary (Westcoat) Briggs. Henry Briggs was born in Dighton, Mass., and was a son of Matthew and Cecelia (Reed) Briggs, and a grandson of Matthew Briggs, a blacksmith

by trade, who came to this country from England. Matthew, Jr., was born in Dighton, Mass., and was also a blacksmith, following that vocation all of his active days. By his first wife he had three children, as follows: Matthew; Elizabeth; and Deliverance. By a second marriage, with Cecelia Reed, he had five children, namely: Henry; Nancy; Mary; Joseph; and Cecelia. Henry Briggs, the father of our subject's wife, learned the trade of a blacksmith, and, in 1836, removed to Western Pennsylvania, locating in South Beaver township, Beaver county. He purchased a farm, and, in addition to general farming, was engaged at his trade all of his active life, but lived his last days in retirement, dying at the home of his daughter, Mrs. Hum, in the eighty-fourth year of his age. His wife survived him several years, and died at the remarkable age of eighty-nine years. She had made several trips to her native state, Massachusetts, and had returned from one of these trips but two months before her death. Their children were: Henry, who died young; Mary; Julia; William; Elizabeth; Margaret; and Spencer.

Mr. and Mrs. James W. Hum were the parents of the following: Henry Thornton, now of Pike county, Ill., who first married Josephine Blake, by whom he had one child, Harry C., and second, married Elizabeth Hughes, by whom he had one child, Carl D.; Edward Knox, whose life is also recorded in this Book of Biographies; Mary Elizabeth, deceased, the wife of Frank Robinson, by whom she had one child, Lois; James Weston,

PETER J. HUTH.

a farmer of Columbiana county, Ohio, who married Matilda Hineman, and had the following children,—Edward K., Guy H., Mary A., Martha T., James W., and Wayne A.; Fred Cook, deceased, who married Florence King, by whom he had a son, Forrest, deceased; Arthur Westcoat, an electrical engineer, of Bridgewater, who married Mary Doing, deceased; and Margaret Mott, the wife of Samuel P. Provost, a flour manufacturer and merchant, of Pittsburg. Politically, our subject was a Democrat, and was a public-spirited man. He was also a Mason, and was a charter member of St. James Lodge, F. & A. M., at Beaver.

PETER J. HUTH, an enterprising and energetic business man of Rochester, Pa., whom we are pleased to represent with a portrait on the opposite page, is secretary and treasurer of the Point Bottle Works, Limited, one of the most flourishing establishments in Western Pennsylvania. He was born in Baltimore, Md., in 1859, and is a son of Charles and Veronica (Becker) Huth.

Charles Huth, the father of our subject, was born in Lomborn, near Hanan, Germany, and was a single man when he came to America, locating in the city of Baltimore. After his marriage he removed to Pittsburg, and later to Freedom, Beaver county, Pa., in 1864, and, being a cooper by trade, was employed in that line of work. Upon moving to Rochester, in 1865, he operated a cooper shop, and, in connection with this, he opened a store for raftsmen and boatmen, located on Water street. He also purchased what had formerly been a river warehouse, rebuilt it into a residence, and lived there the remainder of his days, dying at the age of fifty-eight years. His union with Veronica Becker resulted in the following issue: Adam, a grocer on Water street, in Rochester; Peter J., the subject of this biographical record; Lizzie, the wife of John Schies, of Anderson, Ind.; Josephine, the wife of Henry Heuring, a record of whose life appears elsewhere in this volume; Andrew, a printer, of Cleveland, Ohio; Kate, the wife of Michael Kinney, of Anderson, Ind.; John, a glass blower, of Rochester, Pa.; Caroline; George, a glass blower of Rochester; and Annie, a bookkeeper in the office of the Point Bottle Works. Veronica Becker, mother of Peter J., was born January 22, 1832. She is a daughter of Henry and Barbara Becker, natives of Bruckenau, Bayern, Germany. She came to this country in 1852, and settled in Baltimore, Maryland. She married Charles Huth in 1853, she having previously met him in the Old Country. Since the death of her husband, she has resided on Water street, in a comfortable home, surrounded by many friends and acquaintances.

Peter J. Huth attended the public schools of Rochester until he reached the age of fourteen years, when he began work in the pressed glass department of the Rochester Tumbler Works, continuing there until he entered the cutting department of the Phoenix Glass Company, of Monaca. He served in that capacity for four years, and then in the main office, for a like period, as custodian, clerk, and paymaster. In 1887, the Point Bottle Works, Limited, was re-organized, and he became one of the stockholders, as well as secretary and treasurer, in which capacity he is still officiating. This plant was established in 1879, as the Rochester Flint Vial & Bottle Works, and was located at the present site on the lower end of Water street, by David McDonald, its president, and C. I. McDonald, vice-president and manager. The estate was subsequently sold at sheriff's sale, and was bought by the following business men: J. M. Buchanan, S. B. Wilson, J. C. Cunningham, J. C. Irwin, and P. McLaughlin, who served as president. In 1887, it was purchased and re-organized with the name of Point Bottle Works, Limited, and Henry Heuring was made president. The subject hereof was selected as secretary and treasurer, and performed his duties with such satisfaction that he was again chosen in 1897, when C. A. Dambacher was made president. The directors are C. A. Dambacher, P. J. Huth, William O'Leary, R. Rodke, John Flint, J. R. Dougherty, and L. Hollander. The main building of the plant is 60x120 feet; on the lower floor are located the mold room, the mixing room, and the engine and boiler rooms. On the second floor are the packing and warehouse rooms. The second building is 64x64 feet, fitted with a twelve-pot furnace, eighteen ovens, and four glory holes. They give daily employment to 125 men, and manufacture all kinds of bottles, the yearly output amounting to $90,000.

Peter J. Huth was united in marriage with Grace O'Leary, a daughter of John and Annie (Ingles) O'Leary, and she died at about the age of thirty years. They had two children: Charles and Lawrence,—both of whom died in infancy. Mr. Huth formed a second marital union, with Mary Emery, a daughter of William F. and Mary A. (Conway) Emery, and they had three children: the first born being a son, who died in infancy; the next, Alexander, who died at the age of one year; and Peter Emery. Mr. Huth built a handsome home on Hull street, but resides on Dees Lane. Religiously, the family are devout members of the Catholic church. Mr. Huth is a man of strong personality, and has gained many friends throughout this section of the state.

———•◦•———

FRANK SMITH READER, journalist, New Brighton, Pa., was born in Coal Center, Washington county, Pa., November 17, 1842. His father, Francis Reader, was a native of Warwickshire, England,—his parents removing from there to Washington county, Pa., in 1802. His mother, Ellen Smith Reader, of the same county, was of Scotch-Irish descent. Her paternal grandfather, Rev. John Smith, was a prominent minister of his day, and her maternal grandfather, Lieut. William Wallace, was a soldier in the Revolutionary War.

The subject of this sketch worked at farming and carpentering, and acquired at the schools of his town, and at Mount Union College, Ohio, an academic education. He lived among the scenes of the Monongahela Valley, Pa., until 1861, when he enlisted as a soldier, on April 27, 1861, serving in Company I, 2nd Reg., Va. Inf., in the commands and departments of Generals Rosecrans, Reynolds and Milroy, until April, 1862, in Western Virginia; he took part in the campaign of Gen. John C. Fremont in the Shenandoah Valley, and in that of Gen. Pope in Eastern Virginia, in 1862. His regiment returned to Western Virginia in October, 1862. June 1, 1863, the regiment was changed to the Fifth West. Va. Cavalry. He was offered a promotion in his company but declined it, and was assigned to duty at Gen. W. W. Averill's headquarters, July 1, 1863, and afterwards to the headquarters of Gen. Franz Sigel and Gen. David Hunter in the Shenandoah Valley, taking part in their campaigns. After the victory under Gen. Hunter, at Piedmont, Va., June 5, 1864, he was one of the first Federal soldiers to enter Staunton, Va., and there had charge of paroling five hundred wounded Confederates. He was captured on this expedition, June 20, 1864, and after being thirty days a prisoner, made his escape from a train, with three comrades, twenty miles south of Bunkersville Junction, Va., while on the way to Andersonville prison. Having undergone eleven days and nights of great suffering, hardships and hunger, hiding in the woods by day and traveling by night, he reached Gen. Grant's headquarters at Petersburg, Va., June 30, 1864,

having passed through the right wing of Gen. Robert E. Lee's Confederate Army. His term of service having expired July 10, 1864, and being so broken in health that further duty was impossible, he was discharged in August of that year. He taught school the following winter, and in July, 1865, accepted a position in the U. S. Civil Service, in which he served at different periods for over ten years; he was chief deputy collector of internal revenue nearly eight years, and acting collector for some months.

On December 24, 1867, Mr. Reader was united in marriage with Miss Merran F. Darling, of New Brighton. Her father, Joseph Darling, was a native of Vermont, his paternal grandfather serving in the Revolutionary War, and her mother, Rebecca Cobb Darling, was a native of Chautauqua county, New York. Two sons were born to the couple, Frank Eugene Reader, attorney-at-law, and Willard Stanton Reader, journalist. Mr. Reader became a member of the Methodist Episcopal church December 15, 1865, and entered the North Missouri Conference of the church, in 1868, as preacher in charge of a circuit of nine appointments, but owing to the failure of his voice, he was compelled to retire after one year's service. He has held an official relation in the church ever since, and has been Sunday school superintendent for over twenty-two years. Mrs. Reader is a member of the Presbyterian church. Mr. Reader is the author of a life of Moody and Sankey, the noted evangelists,—and also of the history of the Fifth West Va. Cavalry, besides historical sketches of the Harmony Society, Economy, Beaver county, Pa., of New Brighton, Pa., and the Beaver Valley, in which his paper is published. On May 22, 1874, he and Major David Critchlow established the "Beaver Valley News," at New Brighton; on January 1, 1877, he bought the major's interest in the paper, and on February 4, 1883, he began the publication of the first daily paper in the county,—"The Daily News." He was secretary of the Republican county committee for several years; while in that office he prepared and presented in the state legislature the first law enacted in Pennsylvania for the government of primary elections; he was alternate to the Chicago convention which nominated James G. Blaine for president in 1884; he was suggested as a candidate for congress and for the state senate, but declined to be a candidate; he served in the council and school board of his borough, and held other positions of trust, but never solicited any public position.

Frank Eugene Reader, attorney-at-law, New Brighton, Pa., son of Frank S. and Merian D. Reader, was born at Greencastle, Mo., December 15, 1868. He attended school at New Brighton, Geneva College, Beaver Falls, Pa., and entered Johns Hopkins University, Baltimore, Md., in the fall of 1885, from which he was graduated in 1888, second in a large class, with the degree of B. A. He studied law with Brown & Lambie, a prominent law firm, of Pittsburg, Pa., and was admitted, on examination, to the bar of Allegheny county, Pa., in 1891, and

later was examined and admitted to the bar of Beaver county, Pennsylvania. He became a partner of the law firm of Moore Bros., Beaver, Pa., in 1892, the new firm being Moore, Moore & Reader. In April, 1892, he was elected solicitor of the Beaver County Building & Loan Association, New Brighton. In 1896, he retired from the law firm and opened an office of his own in New Brighton. He was elected secretary of the council of New Brighton in March, 1899. On June 3, 1896, he was united in marriage with Miss Jennie B. Nesbit, a daughter of Rev. Samuel H. Nesbit, D. D., one of the most prominent, able and influential members of the Pittsburg Conference of the M. E. church; he was, for twelve years, editor of the Pittsburg "Christian Advocate"; presiding elder, and pastor of some of the best charges in the conference. A daughter,—Dorothy Nesbit,—was born to Mr. and Mrs. Reader, the date of her birth being May 8, 1897. They are members of the Methodist Episcopal church.

Willard Stanton Reader, journalist, was born at New Brighton, Pa., September 28, 1871; he attended the public schools of his native town, and was a pupil in Geneva College, Beaver Falls, Pennsylvania. He entered the office of the Beaver Valley News as an apprentice, and in 1889 was appointed the New Brighton reporter of the paper. September 28, 1892, on his twenty-first birthday, he was admitted to partnership in the business, and has since held the position of city editor. In addition to the duties of this position, he has written for leading papers in Pittsburg and other cities; has served on the Republican county committee, and is now secretary of the board of health of his native town. He united with the Methodist church, in January, 1885.

Mr. Reader was united in marriage with Miss Lily Robinson, a daughter of Thomas and Mary Robinson, March 1, 1897. Mr. Robinson was a soldier in the Civil War, serving his country with fidelity and courage. Both Mr. and Mrs. Reader are members of the Methodist Protestant church. They have one child, a son, Willard Donald Reader, born December 20, 1897.

———◆ ● ◆———

ILLIAM A. PARK is treasurer of the well known firm, the Park Fire Clay Company, and is a respected citizen of Rochester, Pa., where the main office of the company is located. He is a man of extraordinary business capacity, and energetic and honest in the methods which he pursues. He is a native of New Sewickley township, Beaver county, Pa., where he attended the public schools and assisted his father in the lumber business. He continued to do so until he entered the general merchandizing business with his brother, John H., at Park Quarries. He afterward became identified with the Park Fire Clay Company as treasurer, and has since served in that connection. The other officers are: J. I. Park, president; J. H. Park, superintendent. The capacity of the works is 250,000 bricks per

day, and three hundred and fifty men are employed. They have filled paving contracts in Pennsylvania and adjoining states, and have an established reputation, shipping their product to all points in the United States and Canada. In 1884, he, with his brother, John H. Park, built a line connecting their establishment with the main line of the Pennsylvania Railroad Company, at Conway, but this they have since disposed of to the Ohio River Junction Railroad Company of which Mr. Park is treasurer. Mr. Park has been located in Rochester for many years, and has conscientiously endeavored to further the interests of the town. He is widely known throughout the district, and has many friends.

William A. Park is of Irish ancestry, being the great-grandson of William Park, who was born in Cookstown, County Tyrone, Ireland, where he received an education. He was a man of good character and of high standing in that country, as is shown by papers which are now in the possession of the subject of this sketch. These papers are evidence of the fact that he became a member of Lodge No. 479, F. & A. M., at Tullaghoge, County Tyrone, Ireland, December 3, 1783. In 1791, on April 26, he was given a demit from that lodge, together with one from the Knights Templar, of which he was also a member,— accompanied by testimonials as to his character. He landed in Philadelphia, Pa., in May, 1791, where he remained for about four years, in the meantime learning the trade of stone mason, and then located in Wilkinsburg, Allegheny county, Pa., where he instituted what was, for many years, the only Masonic lodge in that section of the state. He followed his former vocation there and many houses now remain standing in that village as the result of his work. He lived to reach the advanced age of eighty-eight years, and was buried in the Beulah burial grounds. He married Mary McGahey, who died at the age of ninety-four years, and they had the following issue: John, who married Margaret Duff; David, whose wife was Ann Hamilton; Jane; William, who married Nancy Johnson; Robert, who married Elizabeth Loney; and Thomas from whom our subject's wife is descended.

David Park, the grandfather of William A. Park, was born at Wilkinsburg, Pa., and there learned the trade of wagon-maker and wheelwright, which he followed until he moved upon a farm, purchased by him in New Sewickley township, Beaver county, Pa., in 1845. There, in addition to cultivating the soil, he plied his trade for many years, dying when eighty-six years old. The property is now owned by his son Theodore. The maiden name of David's wife was Ann Hamilton, and she was born in Warren county, Ohio, in 1806, and died at the age of seventy-nine. Their children were: James F., the father of the gentleman first named above; William; George, who married Mary Beal; Elizabeth, the wife of Hiram Phillip; Mary, the wife of Rev. John Brown; and Theodore, who married Kate Campbell.

James I. Park was born at Wilkinsburg, Allegheny county, Pa., and adopted the trade of a carpenter, but early in life removed from his native place to Freedom, Beaver county, where he became a contractor and lumber dealer. He was very successful, and now owns a farm near Freedom, upon which he is living a retired life. He married Emiline McDonald, a daughter of William and Rebecca (Magee) McDonald, who was of Scotch ancestry, and she died leaving four children, as follows: William A.; John H., a record of whose life appears elsewhere herein; Annie V., the widow of Milton McCullough; and George I., who is also identified with the Park Fire Clay Company. He formed a second union,— in this instance with Mary Dean, a daughter of Samuel Dean, and they have two children: Mabel D. and Nellie D.

William A. Park was joined in the bonds of wedlock with Mary J. Park, a daughter of Thomas and Helen (Duff) Park. Thomas Park, a son of William Park, the first of the family to locate in this country, was born in Wilkinsburg, Allegheny county, Pa., and settled in Penn township, where he became a farmer of considerable prominence. He died at the age of sixty-three years. His wife, Helen, who now resides with William A. Park, is a daughter of David Duff, and they had two children: James Graham, of Cripple Creek, Colo.; and Mary J.

Socially, the subject of this sketch is a member of the Masonic orders, F. & A. M., and R. A. M., of Rochester, Pa., and of the Commandery, of Pittsburg. He is also a member of the Mystic Shrine, of Pittsburg.

DAVID PHILIPS ESTEP, deceased, a gentleman whose life was marked by years of activity in the industrial world, was a prominent dairyman in Chippewa township, Beaver county, Pennsylvania. He was a son of Ephraim and Susanna (Philips) Estep, and was born in Washington county, Pa., March 9, 1822.

His grandfather was Robert Estep, who was born in Baltimore, Md., in 1750, and was of Welsh parentage,—his father having come from Wales to America, in 1720, and settled in Baltimore, Maryland. Robert Estep, after reaching maturity removed to Bedford county, Pa., making the trip on horseback,—and there engaged in agricultural pursuits. He subsequently bought a farm in Washington county, Pa., and lived there during the remainder of his life. He was a Democrat in politics, and served as a "squire" under the old laws, being appointed by the governor. He was also burgess of Lawrenceville, when that was a busy little town, entirely apart from Pittsburg. He was united in marriage with Dorcas Wells, and they became the parents of thirteen children, namely: Eliza; Nathan; Jemima (Dailey); Ruth (Potter), of Darlington, Pa.; John; James, a physician, and later, a minister of the Gospel; Ephraim, whose business was that of a merchant; Mary (Gaston); Elizabeth (Holmes); Thomas; William, who died in infancy; Joseph; and William.

Ephraim Estep, the father of the subject of this sketch, was born in Washington county, Pa., and was mentally trained in the public schools, after which he took up the occupation of a farmer, but subsequently learned the trade of a blacksmith,—buying a place which was furnished with water power. He then removed to Pittsburg and became a prominent manufacturer of shovels and axes,—buying the old plant of Orrin Waters. He supplied all the jobbers of Pittsburg, and employed about forty-five men. Some time later, he moved to New Brighton, Beaver county, Pa., and built a factory in which he manufactured all kinds of edge tools, employing seventy-five men, and in 1849, he retired, and turned the management over to two of his sons. He married Susanna Philips, a daughter of John Philips, who was a very successful merchant in Philadelphia. He was appointed an ensign in Washington's army during the Revolutionary War, and the commission is highly prized by the subject hereof, in whose possession it has remained. He was a man of extensive business interests, and besides conducting his store he was an extensive weaver; for many years he was a "squire" of his district. Religiously, he was a Baptist; politically he was a member of the Whig party. Susanna Philips was born and educated in Philadelphia, and as a result of her union with Ephraim Estep, she became the mother of nine children: Mary Hall, deceased; Joseph Philips, manufacturer of wagons; William C.; David Philips, the subject of this sketch; Dorcas (Marquis); Elvira; Harriet; Ephraim; and Robert.

David Philips Estep was mentally trained and educated in Washington county, Pa., in

the public schools, and in the schools of Pittsburg, and thereafter became prominently
identified with his father's business interests.
In 1849, he went to California, and became an
active speculator,—being one of the first miners in that field. While in California he turned
his attention to seine fishing in the Sacramento River and supplied the camps and
towns with fish,—in this way doing a good
business. In 1851, he returned to Pittsburg
and was employed at the Lippencott axe factory, for a time, but subsequently became
foreman for Hubbard & Bakewell. He
served in that capacity for thirty-two years,
and as a workman was unexcelled. He
seemed to possess the happy faculty of pro-
curing the best efforts from the men under
his direction, and yet, by showing them kindness and consideration, he gained their esteem and affection. In fact, it was with great
regret that they saw him take his departure
from their midst in 1879, and he was presented with what is, probably, the hand-
somest set of engrossed resolutions ever
drawn up in Pittsburg. It was an extraordinary exhibition of their regard for him,
and was signed by a committee of seven, and
by over two hundred of the employees. It
is a gift of which any man would feel proud.
He then removed to Beaver county, and purchased a tract of two hundred and seventy-
one acres of land in Chippewa township, one-
half of which was in a state of cultivation. The
handsome brick house was then standing, and
was known as the McKinley homestead, but
was subsequently owned by William David-

son and then by Mr. Hamilton, from whom
the subject of our sketch purchased it. He
made many important improvements on the
place,—clearing a considerable portion of
it,—and engaged in dairying and farming.
He possessed fifty head of cattle,—making a
specialty of Jersey stock,—and retailed milk,
keeping two wagons busy in selling directly
to the consumer. Up to the time of his death,
he was ably assisted in the management of the
farm by his son Edgar, who attended to all
of the active duties incident to so extensive
a business. He also had eleven head of fine
horses, one of them being twenty-six years
old, and still a very good horse,—a fact which
speaks well for the treatment and care it has
received. Mr. Estep made a host of friends
after locating in Beaver county, and was
everywhere received as a man of worth to the
community.

His wife was Hannah Squires, who was
born in 1823, and received an excellent mental
training in the schools of Pittsburg,—being
an exceptionally bright woman. He was deprived of her companionship by death in
1892, when she was sixty-nine years old.
They had the following children: Frances M.,
who died in infancy; Thomas S.; Albert D.,
who died in infancy; Susanna Catherine, who
also died in infancy; Edgar S., who assisted
his father; and Harry Clay, a prominent real
estate dealer, of Pittsburg. Politically, the subject of this memoir was a Republican. In religious attachments he was a member of the
Baptist church, of New Brighton. He was a
member and past master of Pittsburg Lodge,

REV. JAMES L. DEENS.

F. & A. M.; past commander of Pittsburg Commandery, No. 1; past commander-in-chief of Pittsburg consistory; and a member of Arsenal Lodge, No. 480, I. O. O. F., of which he was, for some time, deputy grand master of the Pittsburg district. His death occurred September 22, 1899, and he was buried with Masonic honors in Allegheny Cemetery, Pittsburg, Pennsylvania.

————◆ ◆ ◆————

REV. JAMES L. DEENS, who for many years served in the ministry of the Methodist Episcopal church, became thoroughly identified with the interests of Beaver county, after his retirement from active ministerial service, when his preference of the freedom of country life asserted itself in the choice of a home here. Prior to a permanent residence on his farm, however, he had served as pastor of several local charges, and thus strengthened his interests in the Beaver Valley.

His thorough enjoyment of farm life, exempt from the strain of routine service, was marked by evidences of vitality and adaptability to surroundings seldom experienced by one of his years.

James L. Deens was born in County Armagh, Ireland, January 3, 1820, being the only child of James and Margaret (Graham) Deens. His father, of direct Scotch descent, died when a young man, and the widowed mother, during a period of general emigration from Ireland, brought her infant son to America,

locating in Pittsburg, which became to them a permanent home around which their interests ever centered: for there Mrs. Deens subsequently married John Lompre, a French Canadian, whose paternal interest in the boy was marked by a voluntary embodiment of the step-father's name in the boy's full name of James Lompre Deens, and by a close companionship in business, interrupted only by the sudden death of the father just as James was entering manhood.

To the mother, thus left a second time with a family of which only Lydia Sergeant and Eliza Lompre Irwin attained maturity and established families of their own, the best tribute that can be paid is the acknowledgment of the respect accorded her for half a century by all who came under the influence of her unselfish spirit, which remained young and sympathetic until the close of a long life of loving interest in family and friends. In 1887, at the age of eighty-seven, she peacefully passed away.

James Lompre Deens during his early years was sent to both private and public schools, and when opportunity afforded, or necessity required, was reared by his father's side as a tobacconist, of which trade he became master. His general education was completed in the Western University of Pennsylvania, after which careful and thorough preparation for the ministry was made under the leading teachers of Methodism, to whose influence was largely due his connection with the Pittsburg Conference in 1846.

After traveling several circuits, he became

pastor in charge of various stations in Ohio and Pennsylvania, serving as Presiding Elder of the Barnesville District, Ohio, during that period of unrest in our Nation's History—the Civil War—in which he was commissioned Captain of the Barnesville Company, Monongahela Regiment of Unattached Departmental Troops Volunteers.

Subsequently, as pastor, he was stationed successively at Brownsville, Pa., New Brighton, Pa., Main street and Bingham street charges, Pittsburg, and at Mansfield Valley. His last appointments were all in Beaver county, at Georgetown, Homewood, Noblestown, and Shoustown; after which a supernumerary relation, later changed to superannuated, was taken.

Two years after his admission to the conference he was united in marriage with Mary E., daughter of Samuel McKinley, who stood high in the Masonic fraternity, and was also a prominent Methodist.

The wife shared faithfully her husband's itinerant life, and still survives him in her home in Beaver, surrounded by her children,—Margaret A., who resides with her mother; James C., representing the pottery industry of East Liverpool; Anna M., engaged in scientific work in the Pittsburg High School.

The three other children have established their own homes in Beaver: Minnie G., whose union with James Dowdell, a paper manufacturer of Wellsburg, W. Va., resulted in the following issue,—Grace P., Marie E., James Deens, John Irwin, Anna M., and Olive S.;

Charles H. A. conducts his farm on the south side of Beaver county, but occupies a Beaver residence for the educational advantages offered there,—his marriage with Anna M. daughter of John Adams, the pioneer glass manufacturer of Pittsburg, has been blessed by the following children,—Harry Adams (recently deceased), Walter Lompre, Mary Natalie, John Adams, Charles Wilfred, Jean Annette, Alta Carol, and Helen Elizabeth; John L., a pharmacist, became united in marriage with Lydia Ferguson, to whom have been born two children. Louise and Lillian.

The paternal spirit showed itself strikingly in the watchful interest exercised by this father over children and grandchildren alike, and undoubtedly bore fruit in the community of family interests now centered in the Beaver Valley.

It would be a depreciating familiarity toward a man like James L. Deens to attempt to sum up in a few paragraphs his life of service, the responsibilities faithfully met, the hardships cheerfully undergone, or to describe his life as a husband, father, friend, and citizen. Brief mention, however, of a few striking traits may be permitted. He knew men as few are able to know them; he believed his brethren, and with a loyal devotion he stood by his friends. As a preacher he knew what he wished to say and had unusual ability in making himself understood. Thoroughly fitted for his work, scriptural, evangelical, simple, fearless, though tender of heart, he taught his people righteousness. A despiser of shams, he could strip the borrowed garments from assumed humility or pretentious ignorance. Master alike of pathos and invective, able to see at a glance the strong and the weak points of an issue, capable of clear statement, his arguments had oftentimes a startling suddenness, always a clearness, and kindly wit, which made him in an age of great conference debaters easily the foremost; already some of his speeches belong to the traditions of the conference.

A lifelong student, when years of failing health came to him, he never lost interest in things which are and are to be. Questions of church polity, the civic discussions of the time, the welfare of the church and the work of his brethren were matters of living interest and constant conversation. Only the outward man grew old; mind and heart remained young. When retirement from active ministry became necessary, his nobleness of spirit was strikingly exhibited. Unwilling to be idle, fearful of an aimless existence, he located on his farm near Beaver, Beaver county, Pa. His children and their children always found this place of rest beautiful, as did also his old companions in the ministry, and other acquaintances who shared his hospitality. There he passed from this earth at Eastertide in 1892, and from the altar of home and church, he was borne to the Beaver Cemetery, and tenderly laid to rest in the beautiful Ohio Valley.

The publishers of this work take pleasure in announcing that a portrait of Rev. James L. Deens is presented in connection with the foregoing account of his life and deeds.

JOHN H. PARK, one of the reliable business men of Rochester, Beaver county, Pa., is superintendent of the Park Fire Clay Company, a prominent firm whose products are shipped to all parts of this country and Canada. He is a son of James I. and Emiline (McDonald) Park, and was born in New Sewickley township, Beaver county, Pa., in 1856.

William Park, the great-grandfather of John H., was born in Cookstown, County Tyrone, Ireland, whence, after attending school, he moved to Philadelphia, Pa., where he learned the trade of a stone mason. Papers in their original state, now in the possession of W. A. Park, show that he was admitted as a member of lodge No. 479, F. & A. M., at Tullaghoge, County Tyrone, December 3, 1873. When he came to America, April 26, 1791, he was given a demit from that order, and also one by the Knights Templar, together with high recommendations as to his character. He landed in Philadelphia, in May, 1791, but located in Wilkinsburg, Allegheny county, Pa., in 1796, where he instituted the first, and for many years the only, Masonic lodge in that region. He followed his trade the rest of his life, and there are many houses standing in that county today which are the result of his work. He died at the age of eighty-eight years and was laid to rest in the Beulah burying grounds. His wife was Mary McGahey, who died at the age of ninety-four years, and they had the following offspring: John, who married Margaret Duff; James, who married Betsey Duff; David, whose wife was Ann Hamilton; Jane; William, who married Nancy Johnson; Robert, who married Elizabeth Loney; and Thomas, who married Helen Duff.

David Park, the grandfather of the gentleman whose name heads these lines, was born at Wilkinsburg, Pa., and early in life learned the trade of a wheelwright and wagon-maker. In 1845, he removed to Beaver county, purchasing a farm in New Sewickley township, where he followed his trade, and engaged in agricultural pursuits until his death. This property is now owned by his son, Theodore. He died at the age of eighty-six years, and was buried in Oak Grove cemetery, near Freedom. His wife, Ann Hamilton, was born in Warren county, Ohio, in 1806, and died at the age of seventy-nine. Their children were: James I., the father of the subject hereof; William; George, who married Mary Beal; Elizabeth, the wife of Hiram Phillip; Mary, the wife of Rev. John Brown; David; and Theodore, who married Kate Campbell.

James I. Park was born at Wilkinsburg, Allegheny county, Pa., and learned the carpenter's trade, but early in life removed to Freedom, Beaver county, where he became a contractor and lumber dealer. He was very successful, and is now living in retirement near Freedom, where he owns a fine farm. He was first married to Emiline McDonald, a daughter of William and Rebecca (Magee) McDonald, who was of Scotch ancestry, and she died leaving four children, as follows: William A., a record of whose life appears elsewhere in this Book of Biographies; John H.,

the subject proper of this sketch; Annie V., the widow of Milton McCullough; and George I., who is also identified with the Park Fire Clay Company. Mr. Park formed a second union, in this instance with Mary Dean, a daughter of Samuel Dean, and they had two children: Mabel D. and Nellie D.

John H. Park was reared on the farm and studied in the public schools. He assisted his father in the lumber trade and later entered the field of business on his own account, opening a general store at Park Quarries, which he conducted under the firm name of J. H. Park & Co. He also opened a stone quarry there, and in 1882 established another at New Galilee, from which he furnished fine sand stone for building,—shipping it to Pittsburg and Philadelphia. In 1885, the Park Fire Clay Company was organized at Park Quarries, with J. I. Park, president; W. A. Park, treasurer, and John H. Park, superintendent. They have a capacity of 250,000 brick per day, and three hundred and fifty men are employed. The product is nearly all from Beaver county. The general office is at Rochester, Pennsylvania. They have filled large paving contracts in Pennsylvania and adjoining states, and ship brick to all parts of the United States and Canada. John H., and W. A. Park built a railroad three miles in length, connecting their establishment at Park Quarries with the main line of the Pennsylvania Company at Conway, in 1884, and this they later sold to the Ohio River Junction Railroad Company. Of this the subject of this sketch is now president.

DR. JAMES SCROGGS, JR.

He is a man of great energy, is sagacious and possessed of keen foresight. He has always exerted his greatest efforts in whatsoever he has undertaken, and the fruit of his work is evidenced by the prosperous condition of the plants under his supervision.

Mr. Park was joined in hymeneal bonds with Jennie M. Sproat, a daughter of James Sproat, of Economy township, Beaver county, and they are the parents of three children, namely: Emma, aged nineteen years; William, who is seventeen; and Lizzie, who died at an early age.

R. JAMES SCROGGS, Jr., an eminent physician and surgeon of Beaver, Pa., a recent portrait of whom is shown on the opposite page, has seen twenty-four years of practice in Beaver alone, and stands at the head of his profession in Western Pennsylvania. Especially is this assertion true of his position in the field of surgery, to which he devotes especial attention, having probably done more work in that line than any other physician in the county. Dr. Scroggs, Jr., was born in Allegheny county, Pa., July 19, 1850, and is of Scotch ancestry. He obtained a good education in the Pittsburg schools, after which he began the study of medicine with his father, who was one of the ablest physicians of his day. The subject of this review then entered the University of Michigan, Ann Arbor, Mich., and, after taking a course of lectures there, he graduated from the Cincinnati College of Medicine and Surgery in 1873. Engaging in the practice of his profession at Fairview, Pa., for two years, he met with a good degree of success. From Fairview, he went to Beaver, Pa., and became a partner with his father. In 1890, he took a trip to Europe, where, after visiting the place where his ancestors came from in Scotland, he attended the Charing Cross Medical College in London, taking a special course in surgery, and visiting the leading hospitals on the Continent. He served eleven years as surgeon of the Beaver County Infirmary, and contributed some valuable articles to the press. He was also one of the first promoters of the Beaver County Hospital at Rochester, Pa., and is one of its charter members.

The Doctor was united in marriage with Annie M. Aber, an accomplished daughter of John Aber, of Industry, Beaver county. This happy union resulted in the birth of four children, namely: A. Emily; James Joseph, at present a student of Pennsylvania University; Hal E., at present a student at Geneva College; and Fred J. Dr. Scroggs, Jr., has ever taken a deep interest in the educational affairs of his home, having served on the board of education for a period of eleven years. He has always taken a great interest in the progress and development of Beaver, and is one of the directors of the Beaver National Bank.

Dr. Scroggs, Jr., is a son of Dr. James and Emily (Seaton) Scroggs, grandson of James and Elizabeth (Gilbraith) Scroggs, great-grandson of James Scroggs, and great-great-grandson of James Scroggs, of Scotland, who was found when a small child by the side of his dead parents, victims during the "Rebellion of the Covenanters." This child was named Scroggs, which in Scotch means bush. He was thereafter called James Scroggs, grew to manhood and became one of the representatives to the Lord Chief Justice of Scotland. According to history, James Scroggs, the great-grandfather of our subject, immigrated to America about 1760, from near Edinburgh, Scotland, locating near Cumberland, Cumberland county, Pa., where he settled in company with some Scotch Covenanters. He acquired a large tract of land in that vicinity later in life, and was either a minister of the Gospel, or a physician,—it is not definitely known which. He brought eight children with him to America, having two children born to him later in this country. His first wife, who was a Miss Jack before marriage, bore her husband the following children: James, Ebenezer, John, Ellen, Polly, Reynold, Rachel, and Joseph. His second matrimonial alliance was contracted with a Miss Cowden, but the names of their children have not been preserved. The old homestead in Cumberland is still known as the Scroggs estate, although it is now owned by a Mr. Armstrong.

James Scroggs, grandfather of our subject, was born in the Cumberland Valley, Pennsylvania, and in early life moved to Washington county, Pa., where he came in possession of a large tract of land, near Midway, and, being an ardent lover of the beauties of nature, he devoted his life to agricultural pursuits. He was married to Annie Paxton, who bore him two children: Margaret; and James Paxton,

commonly known as J. Paxton Scroggs, M. D. After the death of his first wife, Mr. Scroggs re-married, choosing for his second bride, Elizabeth Gilbraith. Being determined to have a son who should be called James, the favorite name in the family for many generations, he called the first son of his second marriage by that name alone. The following children were the result of the second union: James, George, Samuel, Elizabeth, Nancy, Joseph, Robert and Ann, and one more who died at birth. James Scroggs, our subject's grandfather, studied medicine but never practiced it.

James Scroggs, father of our subject, was born upon his father's farm in Washington county, Pa., studied medicine under his half-brother, J. Paxton Scroggs, M. D., and engaged in the practice of his chosen profession, at Allegheny City, and at Pittsburg, establishing at the latter place a large and successful practice. In 1875, he decided to locate in Beaver, one of the finest boroughs on the Ohio River. There he built a home in the midst of beautiful scenery, in the hope of enjoying a more quiet life. But his valuable services were soon sought there also, and were in demand among the leading families, who soon discovered his knowledge in medical matters to be far above that of the ordinary physician. Although it was his earnest desire to spend his closing years in retirement he never found time to do so. In his seventy-third year he was stricken with apoplexy, and when able to be consulted he was even then called upon for his valuable judgment. As a citizen he was highly esteemed and as a physician not excelled. He died in 1894, aged seventy-four years. He was joined in marriage with Emily Seaton, a daughter of Catherine Seaton, whose death occurred at Louisville, Ky., at the very advanced age of ninety-seven years. Mrs. Scroggs bore her husband five children, and lived to attain the age of sixty-two years. Her children were: James, subject of this sketch; Katie, wife of Clark Hunter, of Beaver county, Pa.; Joseph, a prominent physician of Lincoln, Neb.; Mary, wife of John Scott of Beaver; and Elizabeth, who also resides in Beaver.

Like his fore-fathers in this as well as in many other respects, our subject is a lover of nature, in all its beautiful and varied forms. Some years ago, he purchased the M. Graves farm, which is located on an elevation of splendid height, overlooking the beautiful Ohio Valley, with its picturesque villages and boroughs, with ten minutes drive of this farm. Upon this splendid and desirable location, Dr. Scroggs built a handsome brick cottage, tenement houses, barns, etc., and set out thousands of fruit trees of all kinds both small and large. The broad, spacious lawns, surrounding the cottage, contain many beautiful shade trees and fine ornamental shrubbery. Here the Doctor has one of the finest summer resorts in Beaver county, where he spends many happy hours and entertains his friends, although his profession does not allow him half the time he desires to enjoy the beauty and pleasures of such a home, where he hopes to spend his closing years in retirement.

JAMES A. IRONS, who for many years was a prominent contractor, stands foremost among the progressive citizens of Monaca, Beaver county, Pennsylvania. He is a man of public spirit, and when he deems an improvement necessary for the future welfare of the borough, he puts forth a strenuous effort for its accomplishment. His aggressiveness in public affairs has been in evidence for years, and it may safely be said without fear of contradiction, that no one man has done as much for the community; for this he is held in the highest esteem.

Mr. Irons comes of Irish ancestry, and is descended from one of three brothers, Solomon, Samuel and George, who came to this country from County Derry, Ireland. They were sons of a very wealthy man who held ninety-nine year leases on considerable property. Solomon Irons, the grandfather of the subject hereof settled in Washington county, Pa., in 1771, and moved to Beaver county about the year 1800, taking up several hundred acres of wild land, which was almost virgin forest, and traversed by few roads. He made a clearing and built a log house and barn,—becoming a very successful farmer. Religiously, he was a member of the United Presbyterian church. He died at the age of seventy-six years. His marriage with Rachel Dickson, a lady of Scottish birth, was blessed with eleven children: James; George; John; William; Andrew; Samuel; Joseph; Rachel (Maloney); Mary (Douds); Rosanna (Nevin), and Elizabeth.

John Irons, the father of James A., was

born in Hopewell township, Beaver county, in 1811, on the old homestead, and received his intellectual training in what schools the community afforded. He learned the trade of a tanner under Mr. Scott, one of the first "squires" appointed in the county, and subsequently went into the tanning business for himself. He was very successful, but preferred farming, and as a result, purchased two hundred acres of partially improved farm land in 1840. He moved upon the place in 1845, dealt considerably in horses, raised wheat, and carried on general farming,—being fairly successful. He was a shrewd business man. He was united in marriage with Ann Moore, a native of Pittsburg, Pa., and a daughter of Joseph Moore. They became the parents of seven children, as follows: Joseph, who is now a real estate agent, and justice of the peace, in Greenfield, O.; James A., the gentleman whose name heads these lines; Elizabeth A. (Laird); Rachel J. (Peoples); Rosanna (Minor); John D., a farmer in Pittsburg, Kas.; and Amanda (Wallace). Religiously, he was a member, and for many years an elder, of the United Presbyterian church. He was a Whig, in political affiliations. He died of typhoid fever at the age of forty-two years, and, eight days afterwards, his wife died of the same disease.

James A. Irons was born in Hopewell township, and attended the public schools until he was thirteen years of age, when he became apprenticed to the blacksmith's trade, under George Denny and Mr. Couch. He then followed the trade at intervals for a period of eight or ten years, and in 1856 he entered Beaver College, which he attended for two years. From 1857 to 1862, he worked on the river, and in the latter year, on the 28th of April, he enlisted as a blacksmith and assistant engineer in the navy, on the steam ram Lioness. He participated in the fight which resulted in the destruction of the rebel fleet at Vicksburg, and has the distinction of being the first Union man to set his foot in Memphis at the time of its capture. He has many interesting relics of the war,—one of them being an old boarding pike in excellent condition, which he intends presenting to the Carnegie museum. After his discharge, he took up contracting, in 1867, and during the oil excitement, went to Oil City and engaged in that business. Subsequently he became interested in gas lands, and leased three hundred acres in Moon and Hopewell townships. Upon drilling for gas he made one of the two best strikes in the county, and its roaring could be heard seven miles away. The company disposed of this property to the Bridgewater Gas Company, of which he was secretary and treasurer, and it yielded him handsome returns.

Mr. Irons, since his residence at Monaca, has ever exerted a wholesome influence in public affairs, and has fought with his utmost vigor for many public improvements. When a system of water works for the town was proposed, its supporters succumbed to determined opposition, one by one, until the subject hereof alone stood as its champion. Realizing the great benefit it would be to the

HON. HENRY HICE.

citizens, he would not yield, but fought to the bitter end, and had the satisfaction of seeing it established. Although for a time he was harshly denounced by the opposition, he is now accorded the respect of his gratified fellow citizens. Similar were the conditions in his fight for grading and paving, and for the telephone line. He purchased the line, and having it in good condition, disposed of it to the telephone company. His energy in furthering these enterprises entitles him to recognition as one of the progressive men of Beaver county. He is a Republican and has served as burgess for three terms, and on last May received his fifth commission as justice of the peace. He is a member of the G. A. R.

James A. Irons was united in marriage with Margaret Quinn Srodes, a daughter of John M. Srodes, one of the early river pioneers, and for many years a pilot and captain on the Ohio River. They became the parents of four children, as follows: John E., deceased, who was a very successful business man; James C., a glass manufacturer; Anna, deceased; and B. C., chief of police of Monaca.

HON. HENRY HICE, who enjoys a wide reputation as a member of the legal profession, has been engaged in practice for almost a half century, and for a period of eleven years was judge of the Thirty-sixth Judicial District of Pennsylvania. He was born in Independence township, Beaver county, Pa., January 24, 1834, and is a son of William and Hannah (Eachel)

Hice, and grandson of Henry and Catherine Hice. Mr. Hice was the second child born to his parents, and received his scholastic training in the public schools of his native county,—taking a finishing course at Beaver Academy. Choosing as his life-work the profession of law, he became a law student under the preceptorship of Richard·P. Roberts, of Beaver, Pa. Mr. Roberts was a man of prominence in that section, and during the Civil War became colonel of the 140th Reg., Pa. Vol. Inf., meeting a brave but unfortunate death at the terrible battle of Gettysburg, where so many gallant defenders of the Union fell. Under his preceptorship, young Hice made rapid progress, and was admitted to the Beaver county bar in 1859. He was immediately taken in as a partner with Mr. Roberts, in the practice of his profession, and remained as such until the death of the latter. In 1867, Frank Wilson became associated with Mr. Hice, and continued to be his law partner until, 1874, when the subject of this sketch was appointed judge of the Thirty-sixth Judicial District of Pennsylvania, which office was filled by him in a most acceptable manner, until 1885. His opinions were delivered firmly and courageously, and with full intent to treat each case fairly and impartially. He was courteous alike to the youngest attorney and to the oldest member of the bar. At the expiration of his term, Judge Hice resumed his long neglected practice, and was joined, in 1894, by his son, Agnew Hice,—the firm name becoming Hice & Hice.

Judge Hice first married Ruth Ann Ralston, a daughter of Joseph and Mary Ralston, of Hanover township, Beaver county, where Mr. Ralston was a prominent agriculturist. Their happy union resulted in the birth of two sons and two daughters, viz.: Mary, who is unmarried; Richard, who is superintendent of the Fallston Fire Clay Company, and who married May Kells; Agnew; and Laura. Agnew studied law with his father, with whom he is now associated as partner, having been admitted to the bar in 1894. He is fast assuming the heavier duties of the firm, thus enabling his father to enjoy more leisure and the rest so richly deserved. Judge Hice was deprived of his much beloved companion in 1872, when she was called to the life beyond, having attained the age of thirty-six years only. Judge Hice contracted a second matrimonial alliance,—in this instance with Mrs. Sarah H. Minis, a daughter of ex-Chief Justice Daniel Agnew.

Henry Hice, the grandfather of the subject hereof, is believed to have removed from New Jersey to Indiana county, Pa., whence after purchasing a tract of land in the forests of the Ligonier valley, he returned to New Jersey after his family, who accompanied him to his new home, where they lived the simple, unpretending lives of sturdy pioneers,—enduring with others the many hardships and privations incident to such a life. Mr. Hice engaged himself in felling the forest trees and improving the land as best he could with the few facilities of a newly settled country. Here on this farm Mr. Hice's grandparents spent their last years and reared their family, consisting of three sons and one daughter, whose names are as follows: John; George; Catherine; and William.

William Hice, father of the subject hereof, was born on the old homestead in Indiana county, Pa., in 1793. As he grew to manhood, he assisted his father in clearing the land, and in 1819 or 1820, he removed to the vicinity of Clinton, Allegheny county, Pa. After purchasing a farm but little improved, he extended the improvements by clearing more land, and building a set of buildings, which have since been replaced by new ones. The farm, then occupied by the elder Mr. Hice, is now owned by John Miller, and was sold by William Hice, in 1840. He then bought a better farm at Frankfort Springs, which became his permanent home during life. Upon this farm, known as the J. Stephenson farm, he built a very substantial dwelling, which is still standing; but the barn, then built, has long since been destroyed by fire. Starting out with nothing except a determined will power and a strong constitution, by persistent and untiring efforts, together with successful management, he amassed considerable property. Although he was a shrewd business man, he was kind of heart, and a liberal neighbor, never turning a deaf ear to an appeal for charity. Thus he endeared himself to many, and his loss was deeply mourned. His death occurred in 1868, at the age of seventy-three years. His life companion was Hannah Eachel, a daughter of Andrew Eachel, and she died when about fifty years old. Their children numbered seven, five daughters and two sons, as follows: Mary Ann, deceased; Catherine, also deceased; Eliza, still residing at Beaver, and unmarried; Sarah, wife of Joseph Brown, of Iowa; Hannah, of Beaver, also single; William, a retired farmer residing in Kansas City, Mo.; and Henry, the subject of this brief sketch.

Judge Hice purchased for his home the R. P. Roberts homestead, on the corner of Market and North Park streets. Removing the old house, in 1876, he built upon the same attractive and well selected spot a handsome, modern brick house and office. Both are appropriately and handsomely furnished. He has taken an active part in the progress of his home borough and county. Aside from attending to his practice, he has been associated with manufacturing, banking, and other enterprises. Judge Hice worships with the Presbyterians, and liberally supports that denomination. His portrait is shown on preceding page.

———◆•◆———

D R. GEORGE A. CRISTLER, who through years of careful training in the intricacies of medical science, has attained a degree of skill which but few physicians of the county possess, commands an extensive practice in the vicinity of Hookstown. He is a native of Beaver county, and is a scion of one of its oldest and most highly respected families, having been born at Shippingport, Green township, Beaver county, Pa., October 9, 1852.

The early history of the Cristler family is one of deep interest, but our limited space will not permit us to give the many details. Michael Cristler, the great-grandfather of the subject of these lines, was born in Germany, and at an early day settled in America, in the western section of Pennsylvania, which was at the time a howling wilderness, inhabited only by Indians and infested by wild beasts. What courage must have coursed in the veins of these pioneers, who came from a prosperous but too thickly settled country, and endured the many hardships and trials that fell to their lot while endeavoring to convert the forest land into tillable farms! Courage, perseverance, an indomitable will, were characteristic of every man of that day, else they would have succumbed to hunger or the hostile natives. At the time this sturdy old ancestor settled in that section, the Indians were very troublesome, and he was employed as a government spy. Every two weeks he would make the trip from Brownsville, Pa., to Wheeling, West Virginia, on foot, a journey attended by the greatest danger, not only from the Indians, but also from wild animals. Many interesting stories have been handed down to the present generation of the family, concerning his adventures and his many miraculous escapes. He was a very prominent man, and bought a tract of land on which the village of Shippingport is now located. Here he toiled, and, before his death, the most of his four hundred acres was cleared, and under a high state of cultivation. He was married, and among his children was one, Samuel, the grandfather of the subject hereof.

Samuel Cristler spent his youthful days upon his father's farm, but soon after reaching maturity, he purchased a farm of three hundred and forty acres, which is now owned by John and Jacob Green, and John Calhoun. His occupation was that of a farmer, and he followed it with unqualified success throughout his life. When the War of 1812 broke out he was among the first to volunteer his services, but they were only required for a term of three months, when he received an honorable discharge. He was united in marriage with Catherine Baker, and they had a family of ten children, as follows: Michael; Susan; Mary; Henry; Martha; Jemima; Anthony W.; Elizabeth; Philip; and another who died in infancy. They are all now deceased. Samuel Cristler was a Democrat in his political affiliations.

Anthony W. Cristler, the father of Dr. George A., was born on his father's farm in 1817, and early in life learned the trade of a mason, at which he became one of the finest workmen in that section. He remained on the farm until 1867, when he moved to Shippingport, and there followed his trade during his active life,—dying January 12, 1884. He married Elizabeth Hayward, a daughter of Robert Hayward, of the state of New York, and today the family is one of influence and prominence. Her parents moved to Beaver county, Pa., in 1846, settling at Safe Harbor, opposite Rochester. Mr. Hayward died in the winter of 1895, and his wife is still liv-

ing, enjoying life at the age of eighty-three years, at the home of a son, at Shippingport. Her maiden name was Hill. Mr. and Mrs. Cristler reared nine children, as follows: George A., the subject of this personal history; Sarah A., who died at the age of eight years; Lucinda Jane, the wife of W. B. Appleton, who lives at Industry, Beaver county, Pa.; Amanda, who resides at the home of the subject of these lines; William B., who died in infancy; Melissa; Elmer E., who lives at Shippingport; Ella, who died in infancy; and Willard, who also lives at Shippingport. Mrs. Cristler died on July 26, 1898. They were both faithful members of the Presbyterian church. Mr. Cristler was an active worker in the ranks of the Republican party, but never held office.

Dr. George A. Cristler was reared on the old homestead and attended the public schools, after which he learned the trade of a mason under his father. He was a journeyman before he was twenty-one years old, and followed the trade for fourteen years. During this time he taught school for five winters, and followed his trade in the summer. He then decided to study for the medical profession, and began reading with Dr. Davis, of Shippingport. In the fall of 1887, he entered the Pittsburg Medical College, now called the Western University of Pennsylvania, and was graduated in the spring of 1889,—immediately thereafter locating at Murdocksville. After remaining there for a period of three months, he began practice at Shippingport, where he successfully continued until 1895.

He removed to Darlington, Beaver county, where he spent eighteen months, and then located at Hookstown, where, in a remarkably brief space of time, he has worked up a large and paying patronage. He has always made his home in Beaver county, and is widely known throughout its bounds,—being held in the highest esteem everywhere. He is also a member of the Beaver County Medical Society.

In January, 1891, Dr. Cristler formed a marital union with Lizzie Laughlin, a daughter of William Laughlin, and they had one child, Martha, born January 12, 1894. Mrs. Cristler was called to her final rest on August 16, 1896, and thus, when but little over two years of age, her child was deprived of a mother's love and careful training. Martha is an interesting little girl, and is receiving a Christian training under the guidance of loving eyes. The Doctor is a Presbyterian in religious belief, and has been an elder in the church for twelve years. He is a member of Smith's Ferry lodge, No. 485, F. & A. M.

—— ◆•◆ ——

BEN COOK, stock raiser and general farmer, of Darlington township, Beaver county, Pa., has traveled a good deal throughout the country. On account of ill health he was obliged to give up school, but received a fair degree of instruction in the public schools of Beaver county. He subsequently learned farming. He wanted to see something of the world, and while still a young man went west. He traveled through all the western states and was interested in various occupations. He remained in the West until 1889, and then returned to Beaver county, where he purchased his present farm. This farm contains one hundred and fourteen acres, and is almost entirely cleared. A fine brick house is standing upon it and it is considered one of the best country homes in the district. A large, three-story bank barn, built by the subject hereof, also ornaments the place and adds to the comfort of the stock, which is Mr. Cook's "hobby." The gentleman of whom this narrative treats led to the altar Julia Morton, a favorite daughter of Dr. Woodson Morton. She was born, reared and educated in Illinois. Mr. and Mrs. Cook have four children, namely: May, Howard, Carrie and George. All are regular attendants at the Presbyterian church.

Mr. Cook is a hard worker in the cause of the Republican party, but never accepted office. He was born in Darlington, Pa., March 21, 1855, is a son of A. J. and Margaret (Robinson) Cook, and grandson of Benjamin R. and Susannah (Johnston) Cook. Benjamin R. Cook was a native of Chambersburg, Pa., and went to Western Pennsylvania in the latter part of the eighteenth century. He was a carpenter by trade and followed that occupation for many years. Later he engaged in mercantile pursuits in Darlington. He was one of the first three merchants of that place. The others were Andrew Leach and David Gilliland. After some years he sold his store and bought a farm east of the town. A few years further on he moved one mile west of the present home of the subject hereof. There he purchased eighty acres of partly cleared land. An old cabin then on the land still exists. Here upon this farm Benjamin R. Cook remained until 1845. He then went south in quest of better health, but never found it, and died there April 6, 1845. He wedded Susannah Johnston, a native of Beaver county. She was a daughter of Andrew Johnston, a pioneer of prominence in this section of Pennsylvania. Six children were born to Mr. and Mrs. Cook, viz: Mary; A. J., father of N. Ben; John; James; Martha A. (McClure); and Emeline. Mary, the eldest of these, was a college graduate and followed the profession of teaching for a number of years. She became one of the best educators in this country, and gained for herself a national reputation. Her sister Martha was also a successful teacher before her marriage.

A. J. Cook was born at Darlington, Pa., October 1, 1821. After attending district school he finished his education at Darlington Academy. He then learned farming. Subsequently he purchased a half interest in a threshing machine. The other half was owned by John Davis. At a later period A. J. Cook sold his interest, and for a brief period resumed farming. He afterward bought a hotel in Darlington and followed the hotel business for seventeen years. On relinquishing this, he became the first permanent station agent of the Fort Wayne R. R. at New Galilee. He resigned that position, however, and opened another hotel, which he sold after awhile, and purchased an eighty-five acre farm, where his son, L. J., now lives. Mr. Cook continued to reside upon this farm for nine years, when he was deprived of his beloved wife by death. Since then he has rented his farm, and makes his home with the subject hereof. His wife was Margaret Robinson, a daughter of Andrew Robinson, of New Castle, Pa., where Margaret was born. This happy union was blessed with eight children: Andrew J.; Lucinda; William; L. J.; N. Ben, to whom these lines pertain; Amelia; Carolina; and Lizzie. The first two died in infancy. William Cook received his education at Darlington Academy, and taught school for some time afterward. He then studied medicine under Dr. Sherlock, and later under Dr. Clendenning, of Cincinnati. He practiced medicine at Freeport, Pa., but was cut off by death at the early age of thirty-five years. L. J. Cook is a farmer of prominence, and is also an agent for farm machinery. Caroline died aged thirteen, and Lizzie at the tender age of two years.

EFFERSON WILSON, an extensive fruit grower and prominent farmer of Chippewa township, Beaver county, Pa., is a son of James and Barbara (Showalter) Wilson, and was born in North Sewickley township, Beaver county, in the year 1839.

James Wilson, the father of Jefferson, removed to Beaver county when a very young man and was one of the earliest settlers. He located in North Sewickley township and engaged in farming,—soon after, buying a tract of one hundred acres of wild land. He made a clearing, erected a log house and barn, and resided there with his family for a number of years. He subsequently built a handsome brick house, in which he spent the rest of his active days. He followed general farming and was successful beyond the average. He was a Republican in politics, and held the office of school director, for a time. Religiously, he was a member of the Methodist Episcopal church. His marriage was blessed by the birth of eleven children.

Jefferson Wilson received a limited education in the district school, but made the utmost of his opportunities and is now considered an intelligent and well read man. Upon leaving school he learned the trade of a plasterer, and then moved to Nebraska where he engaged in that line of work. He returned to Beaver county, and still later went to Allegheny county, following his trade until 1868. Many of the oldest houses in Beaver Falls were plastered by him, as he was the leading plasterer there at that period. In 1868 he bought the Thomas farm of one hundred and six acres of partly cleared land, and as there were no buildings standing, except a barn, he erected a house and the necessary out buildings. There was also a very small orchard upon the place, and this he enlarged, until he now has what is undoubtedly the equal of any fruit farm in the county. He has always been interested in that line of work, and has made a study of it, being a well informed man in matters pertaining to fruit growing. He has thirty acres of fruit trees, mainly apples,

pears, peaches, plums, and cherries, and in addition to these he has a large tract set out in berries of various kinds,—a branch of the business which he has found very profitable. Besides retailing, he ships a portion of his produce to Pittsburg markets. He also raises a little stock, grain and potatoes. During his spare time he has invented and patented a number of useful and valuable articles. Mr. Wilson is a man of pleasing characteristics, and has a large circle of friends throughout this section of the country.

Jefferson Wilson was united in marriage with Elizabeth Couch, daughter of John and Mary A. (Hickman) Couch. Mrs. Wilson was born and educated in Lawrence county, Pa., and they have eight children, a record of whom follows: Nanna J., a graduate of Bucknell University, was a missionary to Upper Burmah and Japan, for several years. She returned to America and was married to Dr. Leroy Stephens, secretary of the Pennsylvania Baptist Educational Society. Charles A. attended Butler University, read law, and is a graduate of the University of Michigan. He practiced law a short time, and then entered Crozier Theological Seminary, where he was prepared for the ministry, and has been pastor of churches in the Pittsburg and French Creek associations. Thomas J. attended Geneva College, read law, and is a graduate of the University of Michigan. He is now a prominent lawyer in Pittsburg. Mamie, who attended Geneva College, in pursuance of the study of music, is now at home with her parents. Frank G. attended school at Mount Hermon, Mass., and is now a farmer in Beaver county. Della A. attended Hall Institute, and was married to Rev. T. J. Edwards, a prominent Baptist minister. Harry studied art and is now engaged in that work. Nora, after attending Mount Pleasant College, graduated in Byron King's School of Oratory, and then taught dramatic art. She was subsequently married to G. A. Johnson, a prominent attorney of Pittsburg, Pennsylvania.

In addition to his farm land, our subject owns property in Beaver Falls, in the form of building lots and houses. Politically, he is an independent Republican. In religious belief, he is a faithful member of the Baptist church.

----◆◆----

SAMUEL M. HERVEY, burgess and justice of the peace in Rochester, Beaver county, Pa., is one of the leading business men of that borough, and is highly esteemed by all of his fellow-townsmen. He is very well known throughout the county, and comes from an excellent family. He was born January 4, 1856, in Brownsville, Fayette county, Pa., and is a son of the late Rev. D. W. C. Hervey, and a grandson of James Hervey, who was of Scotch-Irish descent. James Hervey was a farmer in Fayette county, but was a weaver by trade, and also conducted a cotton and woolen mill; after the factory burned he retired.

Rev. D. W. C. Hervey, the father of Samuel M., became in early life a Baptist minister, and occupied the pulpit in Freeport, Kittanning and New Castle; he also served six years in the Providence church in Beaver county, and in Jefferson county, Pa. He then went to Illinois and Kansas, but in a few years retired to Mount Gilead, Ohio, where he lived until his death, which occurred at the home of his son at New Castle, at the age of sixty-seven. He married Kate McCune, who died in Illinois at the age of sixty. Their children were as follows: John P., principal of the fifth ward school of New Castle; Hazen J., a printer in Illinois; Herbert B., deceased; Ella B., who married S. B. Skinner, of Indiana; Kate, who married Mr. McCann, of Illinois; and Samuel M., the subject of this sketch.

Samuel M. Hervey attended the North Sewickley Academy, and then began teaching school. For several years he taught at Hillsville, Lawrence county, Pa., where he met and married Annie E. Davis, a daughter of William Davis; they are the parents of three children, namely: Walter D.; Nellie; and Kate. Subsequently Mr. Hervey taught school in New Castle, and then engaged in painting. In 1886 he moved to Rochester, continued teaching, and carried on painting by contract. He also taught night school in Rochester until 1893. In 1894 he formed a partnership with J. T. Conlin in the insurance business. They are today the most extensive insurance agents in the county, and represent the Royal, Lancaster, American, Fire of Philadelphia, Providence, Caledonia, Northwestern, Milwaukee, Milwaukee Mechanics, Netherlands, Springfield, Fire &

WILLIAM HENRY ANDERSON.

Marine, and other insurance companies. In February, 1893, Mr. Hervey was elected justice of the peace, and has been re-elected; he was appointed burgess by the court in March, 1898. In politics he is a stanch Republican. He has served as trustee and auditor of the Baptist church for the past three years, and is secretary of the Sunday School. He is a member of the I. O. O. F., Royal Arcanum, and B. P. O. E. In 1891 he built a fine residence on New York street, which reflects much credit on the taste of its owner. His office is also on New York street.

━━━━━━━━━━

WILLIAM HENRY ANDERTON, secretary, treasurer and general business manager of the Anderton Brewing Company of Beaver Falls, Pa., whose portrait we present on the preceding page, received his primary education in the Beaver Falls schools,—taking a collegiate course at the Iron City Business College of Pittsburg, Pennsylvania. In 1883, he entered the employ of the Hartman Steel Co., of Beaver Falls, in the capacity of clerk, remaining in their employ until 1889. He was a prime mover in the organization of the Union Drawn Steel Co., and was secretary and treasurer of that company, until December, 1890. At that date, Mr. Anderton became secretary, treasurer and general business manager of the Anderton Brewing Co., which position he still holds. He assisted in organizing the People's Water Company in 1897, and is its vice president. He is a believer in the principles

of Democracy, and an active worker for that party. Socially, he is a member of the Masonic fraternity, being included among the members of Beaver Valley Lodge, No. 478; he is also treasurer of the B. P. O. E. lodge, No. 348.

William Henry Anderton is one of a family of five children. He was born October 23, 1866, is a son of James and Betty (Greenwood) Anderton, and grandson of James and Sarah (Morris) Anderton. His grandparents came to America from England in 1856, accompanied by their son James, and settled at Fallston, Beaver county, Pa., where their two sons, John and Joseph, had located a few months previously. There father and sons worked in the mines for some years. John died at Fallston, in February, 1899. but Joseph now resides in Rochester, Pa. The beloved father departed this life in May, 1879, at the age of seventy-nine years, and was preceded to the grave by his faithful wife and companion, who died in March, 1878, in her eighty-fifth year.

James Anderton, the father of William Henry, was born in Streetbridge, Royston, Lancastershire, England, June 26, 1830. He worked for eighteen years in the mines in his native place, beginning at the early age of eight years. In his youth he had no educational advantages whatever,—his only mental training being a night school organized by himself and his fellow miners, known as the "Youth's Seminary." There the boys taught each other, being too poor to afford an experienced teacher. The school organized by these lads has grown into a famous institution of learning, and is now known as the Literary Institute of Oldham, England.

James Anderton accompanied his parents to America when twenty-six years of age, worked in the mines at Fallston, until 1866, and then removed to New Brighton, Pennsylvania. He continued to follow this occupation at the latter place until March, 1868, when he removed to Beaver Falls, purchased his present residence, and engaged in the hotel business. The following year (1869), he went into the brewing business in a small frame building, situated quite near the elegant structure in which he at present officiates. The first brewing was made November 30, of the same year, and consisted of only nine barrels. In 1875, Mr. Anderton built the old part of the present structure, and with a much increased capacity, he continued to brew ale and porter until 1895, when he built a large brick addition, with all the modern improvements, and began brewing beer. The Anderton Brewery is now one of the most complete up-to-date breweries in Pennsylvania, and has a capacity of 30,000 barrels per year. There are many larger breweries in the Keystone State, but none more complete.

While still in his native land, James Anderton was united in marriage with Betty Greenwood, a daughter of Joseph and Mary Greenwood. This event took place in 1852, and their union is blessed with five children, viz.: Jonathan ; Mary G.; William H.; William H., second ; and Sarah A. Jonathan was born June 22, 1853; he is vice president of the Anderton Brewing Company. He wedded Margaret Hart, a daughter of Hilton and Ann Hart, and their home is made happy by the presence of four sons: James, Hilton, Jonathan, Jr., and William H. Mary G. was born February 1, 1858. She became the wife of C. W. Rohrkaste, who is now superintendent of the Anderton Brewery. They have three children: James A.; Mary A.; and Florence E. William H., the third child, died at the tender age of five years, and the same name was given to the next child. William H., the fourth child, is the subject of this brief sketch. Sarah A., the fifth child, was born October 14, 1869, and died in early childhood, aged three years.

James Anderton is a fine illustration of a self-made man, which in a great measure is due to his progressiveness, reliability and integrity. He ranks among the most esteemed citizens of Beaver Falls, and takes an active interest in fraternal organizations, being a member of Lone Rock Lodge, K. of P.; Valley Echo Lodge, I. O. O. F.; Mechanics Lodge, A. O. U. W.; and Beaver Valley Lodge, F. & A. M., of which he has been treasurer for the past nineteen years. He was one of the organizers and original stockholders of the Union Drawn Steel Co., and is one of the stockholders of the People's Water Co., of Beaver Falls. In his religious convictions, the elder Mr. Anderton is an Episcopalian, of which denomination he and his family are members. Politically, he is a stanch Democrat, but could never be persuaded to seek or accept public office.

William Henry Anderton chose for his wife Emma J. Bailey, a daughter of James and Emma Bailey. In his business ventures he has met with success and, like his father, he is known to be an upright, honorable man. His home bears evidence of comfort in all its surroundings, and he always lends his aid and influence to the support of measures which he believes will be conducive to the general good.

— ⟶ • ⟵ —

ETHAN HAZEN THOMAS, chief burgess of New Brighton, Pa., is also an insurance agent of that place, and deals largely in real estate. New Brighton is one of the best business towns in Beaver county, Pa., situated as it is in a fine location, and containing many beautiful homes, streets, walks, and shade trees. The mammoth manufacturing industries operated within its limit, are among the best in this section of Pennsylvania. New Brighton is located upon lands known as tracts No. 91 and 95, and was laid out in lots in 1814. About the same time, a bridge was built connecting it with Beaver Falls, and was rebuilt in 1833 or 1834. In 1832, a canal was built around the falls in order to market the products of the first manufacturing concern located there, —that was the Townsend Flouring Mills, which were built in 1837, destroyed by fire about 1846 and replaced by woolen mills. New Brighton is situated on the banks of the Beaver River, which gives abundant water supply for various manufacturing concerns,

and is only a few miles from the Ohio River. It contains two railroads,—direct lines east and west; they are the P., F. W. & C. R. R., and the E. & P. R. R. In addition to this, the place is supplied with a trolley line through the main streets, and broad walks, finely shaded; it has many beautiful residences, surrounded by spacious and well-kept lawns.

In 1838, New Brighton was made a borough, and now has a population of 9,000. It contains fine stores, public halls, local banks, eight churches, splendid schools, a young men's library, building and loan associations, a daily paper, and is well supplied with electric lights and natural gas for illuminating and manufacturing purposes; the water supply is inexhaustible. It is no small honor to the subject of this sketch to be at the head of such a prosperous and flourishing borough. Mr. Thomas was elected chief burgess of this enterprising town on the Republican ticket in 1897, and fills the seat of honor in a very creditable manner. He was born in North Sewickley township, Beaver county, Pa., February 29, 1856. He is a son of John Thomas, and grandson of Ethan Thomas. Our subject was educated in the public schools and in Burns' Seminary, after which he embarked in the drug business, purchasing the store of Kennedy & Patton. He continued in that line for five years, selling out his business to H. L. Schwieppe; he then embarked in the feed and grain business, and conducted that for several years, after which he entered his present real estate and insurance business. In 1888 he added an insurance department to his business, representing the following companies: Home, of New York; New York Underwriters; National, of Hartford; Agricultural, of Watertown, N. Y.; Northwestern, of Milwaukee; and Lloyd's Plate Glass Ins. Co., of New York. Mr. Thomas handles as much, if not more, real estate than any other man in New Brighton, and has established a large patronage by his upright dealings. He resides at the corner of Sixth avenue and Eleventh street, and has an office adjoining, at No. 602 Eleventh street.

Ella Kilpatrick, an attractive daughter of Daniel and Margaret Kilpatrick, of New Brighton, became the wife of Mr. Thomas, and has borne him five children, namely: Edith, a student; Edna, who died in infancy; Clara Emma, who also died young; Frank; Carl, who is ten years old; and an infant daughter.

Mr. Thomas is a consistent member of the Immanuel Baptist church, and has served as clerk, trustee and treasurer, while his worthy wife worships with the Methodist Protestant church. Mr. Thomas served several years as a member of the borough council, and also as notary public, and is known as one of the most enterprising citizens of New Brighton.

Ethan Thomas, grandfather of the subject of this sketch, was born in the state of Maryland. He was united in marriage with Elizabeth Eads, a native of Virginia. They went to Beaver county, Pa., among the earliest settlers,—following agricultural pursuits. They settled first in Patterson township, but later removed to Chippewa township, where

their son William now resides. Ethan Thomas cleared this farm, which was, at the time of its purchase, only a wilderness. He also placed many improvements upon the place, such as dwellings, barns, etc., and was a very successful farmer for his day. Mr. and Mrs. Thomas reared a family of eight children, six sons and two daughters. Their names are: Isaiah; John; James; David; William; Daniel; Mary, wife of Daniel Daniels; and Elizabeth, wife of Mr. Brittain. The beloved father and mother now rest in the churchyard at Darlington, and William is now the only living member of their family.

William Thomas, uncle of our subject, now resides upon the homestead farm, and is known as a successful man, respected by all. In his early life, he was a merchant at Beaver, for three years. He was in business later at New Brighton, for three years, and then retired to the homestead farm, which he has since cultivated. He has served as county auditor one term, and as justice of the peace for several years. He was joined in matrimony with Mary A. Young, a daughter of Jacob and Susan Young, of Columbus, Ohio.

John Thomas, father of our subject, was born at the homestead in Chippewa township, Beaver county, Pennsylvania. He was a farmer by occupation and settled in Franklin township for a while, but removed later to North Sewickley township, where his death took place in 1864, in his fifty-sixth year. His life partner and cheerful helpmeet was, before marriage, Miss Margaret Hazen, a daughter of Samuel Hazen. She survived her husband

ROBERT DOYNE BURNSIDE DAWSON, M. D.

until 1889, when she, too, crossed the dark river, at the age of seventy-one years. Nine children blessed their union, viz.: James, who served in the Civil War as a member of Company H, 101st Ohio Vol., from 1861 to 1863, when he was discharged for disability, and who died January 28, 1869; Pamelia, who is the widow of Dr. James E. Jackson, and still resides in New Brighton; Clara, who died, single, in 1871; Elzena, who married J. M. Hazen, and also died in 1871; Elizabeth, Jane, and Samuel, who all died young; Ethan H., the subject of this sketch; and Maggie E., wife of John W. Withrow.

John Thomas was a Whig, and later, a Republican. He served as school director and in minor offices in the township. He was a deacon of the Baptist church, of which denomination both he and Mrs. Thomas were devout members.

———— ✦ ● ✦ ————

ROBERT DOYNE BURNSIDE DAWSON, M. D., a well-known and popular physician of Beaver county, Pa., a portrait of whom accompanies this sketch, is a descendant of one of Beaver county's oldest families. His great-great-grandfather, Benoni Dawson, was a native of Montgomery county, Maryland, but the date of his birth is not known. He was a descendant of an old English family, who were given a large grant of land in Maryland, by King George; in recognition of this favor, the Dawsons were loyal to the mother country. They firmly believed it to be to the best interest of the com-

munity to maintain allegiance to the British empire. During the Revolutionary War they were Tories, and owing to their influence and the respect they commanded in their neighborhood, they proved themselves valuable allies of the English.

After his marriage with Rebecca Mackall, the daughter of a prominent family of Maryland, Benoni with his wife moved from Montgomery county, Md., to Beaver county, Pa., and took up a farm where the village of Georgetown is now located. His son, R. D. Dawson, laid out the village of Georgetown in town lots, which he disposed of. Benoni lived upon his farm until his death in 1806, having located upon it about the year 1784. He and his wife were the parents of the following children: Thomas; Nicholas; Benoni; Mackall; John Lowe; Robert D., who died in 1801, at the age of twenty-one years; George; James; Elizabeth, the wife of Charles Blackamore; Nancy, the wife of John Beaver; Mary, wife of James Blackamore; and Rebecca, wife of William White. When Dr. Dawson's great-great-grandfather first came to Beaver county, there were few white settlers in that vicinity and no roads had yet been built. Indians and big game were alike plentiful. Mr. Dawson became an extensive landowner, and established a comfortable home there. His third son also bore the name Benoni, a favorite name in the family for many generations. He was the next in line of ancestry and was the great-grandfather of the subject of this sketch.

Benoni Dawson, Jr., assisted his father on

the new place for some time, and then began to look around for a location for himself. He made a trip across the river, and is supposed to have been the first white man who ever made the journey with the idea of settling there. He selected a place, but a Mr Mc-Laughlin, also, had the same locality in view, and the latter hurriedly built a log cabin, and secured "squatters' rights" to it. Benoni, Jr., was then obliged to withdraw and seek a new location. He selected four hundred acres near by, where Ohioville now stands. His marriage with Catherine McKennon resulted in the birth of the following eight children: Robert Doyne; Benjamin; James, a physician of prominence; Daniel; Elizabeth, who remained single as did Sarah, the next one; Ruth (Evans); and Mary Ann (Johnston). All the boys, except James, became farmers. Their father was particularly active in road building. The land he took up was of course wild and he used every effort to make the spot habitable and to provide a comfortable home for his family. He followed farming up to the time of his last illness. In politics, he was a Whig, and religiously, was reared in the faith of the Protestant Episcopal church in which he served many years as vestryman.

Robert Doyne Dawson, grandfather of the subject hereof, was born July 30, 1801. He received his scholastic training under Master Steele, a private pedagogue. Robert worked upon his father's farm for some time, but subsequently followed river life between Pittsburg and New Orleans. He worked in that capacity until his marriage with Elizabeth Reed. Elizabeth was a favorite daughter of Ruel Reed. She was born in Beaver county, Pa., in 1803. She bore her husband ten children, namely: Mary Ann, Catherine and Rebecca, who all remained single; Benoni, Dr. Dawson's father; Ruel; James; Benjamin; Robert D.; Daniel D.; and William McKennon.

After his marriage, Robert Dawson relinquished river life and returned to farming. For a short time he was located on his father's homestead farm. Then, for a brief period, he rented a place. Later, he purchased one hundred acres of land from his father-in-law. After farming that for some time, he sold out and purchased the farm where Daniel D. now lives. Here he prospered, and was soon enabled to add three other farms to his original purchase. Thus he became the owner of three hundred and forty acres, which he improved in a superior manner. He built a good brick residence, and his farm was considered one of the finest and best improved in the county. In addition to producing large quantities of fruit, he devoted much attention to stock raising. He was the first to introduce Durham cattle and Leicester sheep in Ohio township, and was among the first to introduce these breeds into the county. He disposed of his stock at Pittsburg and in local markets. Like his honored father, he was vestryman in the Protestant Episcopal church. In his political affiliations he followed the leadership of the Republican party. At the time of his demise, he was a comparatively wealthy man.

Benoni Dawson, father of the subject hereof, was born in Ohio township, in 1830, and obtained the rudiments of an education in the district schools. He learned farming and bought a farm for himself in 1854. This farm contained one hundred and twenty acres, and was partly improved, having a fine log cabin on the premises. This was torn down and replaced by a convenient frame and log residence, which is standing to this day. Dr. Dawson's parents were married in 1858. His mother was, before marriage, Rolena Brisbane. She was a native of Pittsburg, Pa., and was educated in Allegheny City. She was the mother of seven children, viz.: Elizabeth (Nicholson); Rebecca C. (Murdock); Robert D. B., the subject of this sketch; Charles H., deceased; Anna F., wife of Dr. C. C. Taylor, of New Waterford, Ohio; Benoni R., a farmer; and Rolena I., now deceased. Mr. Murdock. who married Rebecca C., is a professor of music in Allegheny, and a composer of some note. He is the inventor of the Murdock system of guitar instruction.

Dr. Dawson's father is still actively engaged in cultivating his fine farm. He grows fruit in large quantities. He also devotes much time to stockraising,—selling mostly to East Liverpool markets. He is a stanch Republican, and has served as a school director, and in various other township offices. In early life he was a member of the Episcopal church, and assisted materially in building the church at Georgetown. Later in life, he joined the Presbyterian denomination in which he has been a trustee for twenty-five years.

Dr. Dawson was born in Beaver county, Pa., January 13, 1864. He obtained his primary education in the district schools, which he attended during the winter months, until he attained the age of twenty years. In the summers, he assisted his father on the homestead farm, and followed that line of work until his twenty-third year. He then decided on a professional career, and began the study of medicine. He studied one year under Dr. R. J. Marshall, of Fairview, merely as a preparatory course. In 1890, he entered Western Reserve University, of Cleveland, Ohio, as a medical student. He graduated with high honors in the class of 1893. Dr. Dawson then took a post-graduate course at Lakeside Hospital, Cleveland, and was appointed house surgeon, filling that position very creditably, for sixteen months. During that time, he gained valuable experience in surgery, and gained an enviable reputation for himself. Dr. Dawson is very skilful in his profession, and is an enthusiastic operator in surgical cases. He first began practice in East Liverpool, Ohio. After an eight months' stay, an opportunity occurred whereby he could practice in his native town. He purchased the property of Dr. George J. Boyd and opened his present office in Fairview. He is a general practitioner, but devotes especial attention to surgery. He supplies his own medicine to his patients, and is decidedly popular. By his cleverness and skill he has won the confidence of his clients in a very notable manner.

Dr. Dawson was joined in matrimony

October 4, 1893, with Eleanor Loretta Coll, a gifted daughter of Hugh Coll. Mrs. Dawson is a native of Pittsburg, where her birth occurred in 1862. She was educated in the St. Mary's Academy at Pittsburg. Dr. and Mrs. Dawson have one son, Robert Doyne. He was born July 9, 1894, and in him all their domestic hopes are centered. Politically, the Doctor is a Republican, but is too busy to accept office. He worships with the Presbyterian denomination.

───◆─◆───

OHN A. CAMPBELL, junior member of the firm of D. Campbell & Son, contractors in heavy masonry, is one of the most successful and prosperous men of Beaver Falls. He was born near New Galilee, Beaver county, Pa., in 1863, and is a son of David Campbell, whose father was John Campbell, a native and life-long resident of Scotland.

David Campbell, the father of John A., was born in Ayrshire, Scotland, and received a thorough mental training in the common schools there. He was then bound out as an apprentice to the trade of a mason, and after serving his time, worked as a journeyman until he came to this country. He located at Beaver Falls, Beaver county, Pa., in 1864, at the age of twenty-two years, and at once resumed work at his trade, being employed on the Ft. Wayne R. R. construction. He subsequently started in business for himself, as a general contractor, and being one of the first business men in the district, Bea-

ver Falls, at that time, not having a population of more than two hundred, he laid the foundations for nearly all the buildings built in that section of the county. He worked on the construction of an arch at Wallace Run. This was a long and difficult task, the wall under ground being thirty feet thick; and it required three years for its completion. He did all the masonry work for the cutlery shops, built the Economy Bank and Geneva College, did the masonry on the File Works and Axe Factory, and also considerable work on the P. & L. E. R. R. He has for many years been one of the foremost business men and most reliable citizens of Beaver Falls. In 1861, he was joined in wedlock with Margery McKim, of Scotland, and nine children resulted from this union, as follows: James, deceased; Jeanette (Gaston); John A., the subject of this personal history; Robert, a stone mason by trade; Samuel, who follows the occupation of a master plumber; Elizabeth, deceased; Jane, deceased; Margery; and Myrtle, a graduate of the Beaver Falls High School, and of Beaver College, who is now a successful teacher at College Hill school. Mr. Campbell is a strong supporter of the Republican party, but has never accepted office. He is a member of the F. & A. M., and of the mother lodge in Scotland; the Ancient Order of United Workmen; and the Odd Fellows.

John A. Campbell received his education in the public schools at Beaver Falls, and upon completing his schooling, became associated in business with his father. In 1887, he purchased the interest of Mr. Moffit in the

MAJOR GILBERT L. ELERHART

firm, and has since devoted his entire time to its success. Although it has always been the leading firm of the kind in that district; since our subject has been identified with it, its business has increased steadily until it encounters some difficulty in keeping apace with its contracts. At the present time it has a contract to build the shops of the Atlantic Tube Company, which will cover three acres of ground, at Moravia. Pennsylvania. The subject of this sketch is an enterprising and energetic young man, popular with his fellow citizens and he has a host of friends wherever he is known.

Mr. Campbell was joined in hymeneal bonds with Mary C. Robel, a daughter of Lewis and Sophia (Cleis) Robel, of Germany, a native of Morgantown, West Virginia, where she received her education. Our subject is a Republican in politics, and like his father, is a member of the Presbyterian church, of which he is an elder.

———————

MAJOR GILBERT L. EBERHART, of New Brighton,—editor, author, lawyer and soldier, Interesting references to his life and public service.

Some of the Eberharts came from Germany to Pennsylvania as early as 1727, landing at Philadelphia on the 16th of October, in that year, on a vessel named "Friendship."

All descended in a direct line from the celebrated "Eberhart mit ihm bart," first duke of Wurtemberg.

John Adam Eberhart, duke of Elsass, Germany, had four sons (Andrew, George, Martin and Adolphus), all of whom came to America in the ship "Banister," under command of Capt. John Doyle, landing at New York in the fall of 1758.

Andrew settled first in Sherman's Valley, Cumberland County, Pennsylvania, and afterwards removed to Washington County, where he died in August, 1799. on his farm on which he and his wife were buried within three miles of the present location of the court house of that County.

His wife was Catherine Elizabeth Mercer. a sister of Brig. Gen. Hugh Mercer, M. D., who fell fatally wounded at the battle of Princeton, N. J., on the second day of January, 1777.

Adolphus, youngest brother of Andrew Eberhart, served in the Revolutionary War, although quite young. He was the first man to make glass in America, and went into the business with Albert Gallatin in Fayette County, about 1786.

His descendants have continued in the business in the Monongahela Valley to the present day.

Andrew Eberhart was the father of two sons and four daughters. His eldest son, John, was born in Cumberland County, Pa., May 9, 1766. He removed from Washington to Beaver County in the year 1804, and settled on a farm within sight of the court house where he lived till his death, November 9, 1831. He was the father of two sons and seven daughters. He called his eldest John, who became a man of fine attainments, although he had no collegiate training. He spent a part of his early life in teaching, and was many years an active business man. He learned the trade of cabinet maker, and specimens of his handiwork, made of native maple, cherry and walnut, are still in use in some of the homes of the children of the older inhabitants of the County.

He was an active politician although never a candidate for office; and some of his articles written in behalf of his favorites can yet be found in the files of the county journals of "ante bellum" days.

Although but a boy at the time, he enlisted and served in Capt. Thos. Henry's Company in the War of 1812. His wife was Sarah Power, second daughter of Gen. Samuel Power, and sister of James M. Power, who was one of the Canal Commissioners of Pennsylvania, and Minister to Naples and the Kingdom of the two Sicilys. She was a sister, also, of the late Gen. Thos. J. Power, of Rochester, Beaver County, who was a prominent politician and several years Adjutant General of the State. And as a civil engineer, he had much to do, in conjunction with his brother James, in promoting the public works, state and national, in Pennsylvania, notably in the first improvements made in the navigation of the Ohio River from the mouth of the Beaver to Pittsburg.

Her father, Gen. Power, was sheriff of Beaver County from 1809 to 1812, and served as a major in the War of 1812, and took a battalion to Lake Erie to protect our frontier from a threatened invasion of the British. He was of Scotch parentage, born in Virginia, and came to Beaver County, Pa., in 1804.

Gen. Power afterwards became Adjutant General of the State, which office he held for six years. He was also a member of the House and Senate from 1819 to 1836, and while in the Legislature he took a very active interest in all enterprises that tended to develop the wealth of the state, and advance the welfare of the people. And it was mainly through his vigorous efforts, while a member of that body, that the necessary appropriations were secured to connect Pittsburg and the Ohio River with Lake Erie, at the City of Erie, by canal through the Beaver and Shenango Valleys; and, by means of the Pennsylvania and Ohio canal, through the Mahoning valley, to bring Pittsburg and intermediate towns in closer commercial relations with Cleveland, Ohio, some twenty-five years before the advent of railways into Western Pennsylvania and Eastern Ohio.

John Eberhart, Jr., grandson of Andrew Eberhart and Catherine Mercer, was the father of five children by Sarah Power; three boys and two girls. All, except the youngest, now are dead, the eldest, the Rev. Wilford Avery Power Eberhart, having died at Cedar Rapids, Iowa, February 14, 1899.

Gilbert Leander Eberhart, the only survivor of the family, and the subject of this sketch, was born in North Sewickley township, Beaver County, Pennsylvania, January 16th, A. D. 1830. His mother died when he was nineteen months old, and he was then taken into the care of his maternal grandfather's family.

His first instructions in letters were received in a select school in the Beaver Academy, and the first public school-house built, in Beaver. His first Sunday school lessons were given him in the old Presbyterian Church that stood on the public square in Beaver, while he was a member of an infant class taught by the late Captain John D. Stokes. Later he received some very wholesome drills in Kirkham's Grammar, the Western Calculator, the English Reader and the New Testament, in a log school-house which stood on the banks of Big Brush run in South Beaver township, where one of his teachers was George McElroy, who made quill pens for his pupils with a razor; and, when needed, stirred them up to a sense of their duty with a hickory "ox-gad" seven feet long, without leaving the chair he occupied in the centre of the schoolroom. The other was James Bliss. Both were thorough and efficient teachers.. In his later school-boy days, Mr. Eberhart was sent to the Academy at Mercer by his uncle, the Hon. Jas. M. Power, who was then a merchant and iron manufacturer at Greenville, in Mercer County. Finally he entered Washington (Pa.) College, where he spent two years. Soon after he left that institution, he engaged in civil engineering on the Erie and Pittsburg railway of which his uncle, Gen. Thos. J. Power, was then President. He pursued that profession some five years, when he engaged in teaching in Greenville, Mercer County, and soon became Superintendent of Public Schools of that county.

A short time prior to the outbreak of the Slaveholders' Rebellion, he took charge of the Conneautville (Pa.) Academy, but resigned that position, and on April 17, 1861, he enlisted for a term of three months as a Sergeant in "D" Company in Col. John W. McLane's Erie Regiment.

At the expiration of that term, he enlisted in the 8th Regt., Pa. Res. Vol. Corps, and was mustered in for three years at Washington City, July 28, 1861, as a member of the non-commissioned regimental staff. He served in that capacity until August 21, 1862, when Gen. Geo. G. Meade, then commanding the Second Brigade of the Pa. Reserves, assigned him to duty on his staff as his Commissary of Subsistence, and he remained in the Subsistence Department of the Army of the Potomac as long as that army was in the field, and afterward served at Beaufort, S. C., and Jacksonville, Fla., until October, 1865.

During the Second Bull Run campaign, he served on the staff of Gen. John F. Reynolds, then commanding the third division (Pa. Reserves) of the Fifth army corps; and was honored and highly complimented by both Reynolds and Meade for the coolness and courage by which, on August 28, 1862, he saved the division trains from capture and destruction during a severe shelling by Rebel artillery.

In that action Maj. Eberhart's horse was so badly injured by a shell in the left shoulder that he was obliged to abandon the poor, animal to his fate.

September 3, 1862, he received a commission as Quarter Master of the 8th Pa. Reserves, and was mustered to rank as such from July 1st, 1862.

November 19, 1862, he became quite ill, and in a few weeks was reduced in weight from one hundred and forty to one hundred and fifteen pounds, as a result of the hard march through rain and snow from the battlefield of Antietam to Brooks Station, near Fredericksburg.

Major Eberhart, however, in spite of his severe illness, was present on duty in the field at the battle of Fredericksburg, December 13, 1862, where, by the discharge of a heavy cannon, near the muzzle of which he was standing, he lost his hearing for a time. When it gradually, but only partially returned, it was discovered that the drum of his right ear was perforated and the hearing totally destroyed.

The disease contracted in November, 1862, resulted in chronic disease of the digestive organs, and muscular rheumatism, from which he has been a constant sufferer to the present time; and not until the year 1890, did he regain the twenty-five pounds of flesh lost in the winter of 1862-3.

Under date of September 15, 1865, while on duty at Jacksonville, Fla., he received a letter from Maj.-Gen. Rufus Saxton, then Asst. Commissioner of the Bureau of Freedmen and Abandoned Lands for the states of South Carolina and Georgia, in which was this sentence: "I am pleased to offer you the position of Superintendent of Freedmen's Schools for the state of Georgia." Maj. Eberhart ac-

cepted the offer, and under date at Charleston, S. C., October 2, 1865, he received Special Order No. 18 directing him to "report in person, without delay, to Brig.-Gen. Davis Tillson at Augusta, Ga." October 6, 1865, he was "assigned to duty as Superintendent of Freedmen's Schools for the State of Georgia." He remained on Gen. Tillson's staff until October, 1867, in the meantime having established, in the face of difficulties and menaces which only the military power of the Government could curb and resist, over two hundred and fifty schools for freedmen. In the City of Atlanta and, also, in Savannah, he secured the erection of a fine school-house— the first buildings of the kind ever erected in Georgia for negroes.

On his return to civil life, he resumed teaching, and, in the fall of 1867, became Superintendent of the public schools of Rochester. The next year, without his seeking, he was elected Superintendent of the Kittanning Schools, where he organized the first graded schools that City ever had. He held that position four years, when he resigned to enter on the practice of law, having in the meantime read with the late Judge Brown B. Chamberlin. He was admitted to the Beaver bar June 14, 1870, and soon after to Lawrence, Mercer and Butler, and the Supreme Court of Pennsylvania.

In November, 1876, he was elected to represent Beaver County in the lower house of the General Assembly, and served during the sessions of 1877 and 1878.

In 1883, he was elected without any solicitation on his part, to the office of Chief Burgess of New Brighton, and re-elected to succeed himself; and, so well pleased were his fellow-citizens with his administration of the office, that they tendered him a third term, but his private business so engrossed his time he was obliged to decline the honor.

In 1884, he was a prominent candidate for Congress, for which in all the counties of the district there were aspirants, producing a divisive and somewhat bitter rivalry; and, subordinating his own desires to the good of his party, he withdrew, rather than jeopardize the success of his party.

In 1891, he was elected a delegate to represent the senatorial district composed of Beaver and Washington Counties in a proposed convention to amend the State constitution.

His popularity in the district, as well as in his own County, was well attested by the fact that he received nine thousand, three hundred and fifty votes out of a total poll of thirteen thousand, one hundred and thirty-three.

In 1879, at the earnest solicitation of a number of the young men of New Brighton, he organized a military company of which he was commissioned Captain and which was admitted to the National Guard of Pennsylvania as "B" Company, of the 15th Regiment of Infantry, in 1880, and the next year to the 10th Regiment,—the Hawkins regiment,—which became famous, as well for being the only volunteer regiment east of the Mississippi in the War with Spain in the Philippines, as for its heroism and gallant partici-

pation in the battles about Manila after their capture by Admiral Dewey in 1898.

Major Eberhart, ever since boyhood, has been a member of the Episcopal Church, and is one of the judges of the Ecclesiastical Court, and a trustee of the diocese of Pittsburg. Among the fraternal orders, he is a Mason, Odd Fellow, and Knight of Pythias as well as a member of the Grand Army of the Republic and the Union Veteran Legion, in all of which he has passed through the highest chairs. He has been twice President of the Law Association of Beaver County, and of the Soldiers and Sailors' Association of Beaver County. His wife is the youngest daughter of the late Dr. Peter Smith, formerly of San Francisco, but latterly of Wimpole street, London, England, where he practiced his profession the last ten years of his life. Their only surviving child is the wife of Dr. H. S. McConnel, of New Brighton, one of the most prominent and successful physicians and surgeons in Pennsylvania.

For some eight years Major Eberhart was owner and editor of the Daily and Weekly Tribune of Beaver Falls, and in that capacity distinguished himself as a brilliant writer on all current topics, and gave his paper a wide reputation. His most notable political articles were those on Protection by invitation of the N. Y. World during the Blaine campaign. He has devoted much time to literature, and is the author of a large number of disquisitions on Philology and other scientific subjects. He has established a good practice in his profession; and, as a public official, made a marked impression upon his constituents for his fidelity to their interests, and the unswerving tenacity with which he adheres to the principles of his party.

As a public speaker and lecturer, he is fearless, as well as entertaining and instructive; and he has attained considerable notoriety as a poet, his poems entitled "The Fife," and "Ruth and I," having given him a very wide reputation. A fine collection of his poems appears in Herringshaw's "Poets of America," and many in other anthological publications.

— ◆ • ◆ —

HENRY HEURING, a stockholder and director of the Point Bottle Works, of Rochester, Pa., is the general manager of the establishment, and it is almost entirely due to his efficient service in that capacity that the plant is one of the most flourishing in Beaver county. He was born in Pittsburg, Pa., November 11, 1857, and is a son of Theodore and Mary (Renner) Heuring, —being of German parentage.

Theodore Heuring, the father of our subject, was born in Munster, Germany, and was a young man when he came to America, obtaining employment as a common laborer. After his marriage, he became a raftsman on the Ohio River and settled at Pittsburg, but later became a sawyer, and then foreman of the saw mill of McClintoc & Co., of Pittsburg. In 1873, he removed to Rochester, Beaver county, Pa., where he was employed as foreman of the L. Oatman Mills, and later as foreman of the box makers of the Rochester Tumbler Company. He was an ambitious man and a hard worker, and rose from the ranks of the day laborer to a prosperous condition in life. He died in 1898, when sixty-seven years old, and his wife now enjoys life at the age of sixty-five years. She resides in the house built by her husband on New York street. Her maiden name was Mary Renner, and she is a native of Elk county, Pennsylvania. Their union was blessed by the birth of the following offspring: William, of Chicago; Henry, the subject of this biographical record; Annie, the wife of J. T. Conlin, whose personal history also appears in this book; Kate, the wife of John Beck, of Carnegie, Pa.; John, deceased; Frank, a boxmaker; Theodore and Charles, twins, both of whom work in the Rochester Tumbler Works; and Andrew Packer, who is also employed at the Rochester Tumbler Works; and Joseph, a glass blower at the Point Bottle Works.

Henry Heuring was reared and educated in the borough of Rochester, and at an early age entered the box manufacturing department of the Rochester Tumbler Company. He continued to work at that until 1887, when he became an organizer, stockholder and president of the Point Bottle Works, Limited. This plant was established, in 1879, as the Rochester Flint Vial & Bottle Works, by David McDonald, president, and C. I. McDonald, vice-president. The business did not flourish as was expected, and it was later sold at sheriff's sale,—being purchased by the following: J. M. Buchanan; S. B. Wilson; J. C. Cunningham; J. C. Irwin; and P. McLaughlin. The name was changed to that of the Point Bottle Works, the concern was re-organized, and P. McLaughlin was made president. Under this head business was continued until 1887, when the enterprise again changed hands and was completely re-organized under the name of the Point Bottle Works. Henry Heuring, the subject of these lines, was chosen president, and P. J. Huth, secretary and treasurer, and under this management the plant for the first time was made a paying venture. Mr. Heuring continued as president until 1897, when he assumed the duties of general manager, his former position being filled by C. A. Darmbacher. The plant is one of the principal manufacturing establishments in Beaver county, and its products are shipped to all parts of the country. The yearly output amounts to $90,000, and the company gives constant employment to one hundred and twenty-five men. The factory consists of two large buildings, both of which are well equipped with the latest of machinery used in the business. A switch is also run up into the yard to the shipping house, making the best of facilities for shipping. Mr. Heuring has given his entire time and attention to the business, and under his skilful guidance it has prospered and is increasing with great rapidity. The subject of this memoir was, for two years, president of the Central Building & Loan Association, of which he was one of the organizers.

Mr. Heuring was joined in matrimonial bonds with Josephine Huth, a sister of P. J. Huth, whose sketch appears elsewhere in this Book of Biographies, and their children were: Agnes, deceased; Harry; Gracie; Marilla; Irene; and Richard, deceased. Fraternally, he is a member of the Elks.

————◦•◦————

SAMUEL CLARENCE GORSUCH, a machinist by trade, has been connected for many years with iron and steel works and has been a resident of Beaver Falls, Pa., since 1883, being, until recently, a heater in a plant there, which he assisted in building. He was born February 21, 1860, in Springfield, Blair county, Pa., and is a son of Henderson and Elizabeth (Gates) Gorsuch, and grandson of Benjamin Gorsuch. The first of the family who came to America, was the great-grandfather of Samuel Clarence, and was a native of Wales. After reaching America, he settled in Baltimore, where he spent his last years. He, with his brother, was engaged in the cotton business. His son Benjamin, the grandfather of the subject hereof, was reared near Baltimore, where he became apprenticed to learn the trade of a blacksmith. After completing his apprenticeship, he engaged in that line of business on his own behalf, and was known as a very successful business man and a skilled mechanic; he followed that line of business all his life. He removed to Huntingdon county, Pa., for some years, but later settled in Blair county, near Klopperstown. He followed blacksmithing until middle age, when he went into the iron business.

Henderson Gorsuch, father of the subject of this record, was born in June, 1833, in Huntingdon county, Pa., where he was reared, receiving a limited education in "book learning" in that county, and also in Blair county. In early manhood, he lived at Springfield, Blair county, where he, too, learned the trade of a blacksmith, thereby following the same inclinations as his father. Henderson also learned the art of making axes entirely by hand. He held an important position at the Springfield furnace for a period of three years, as master mechanic, and subsequently accepted a similar position at the Martha furnace. At a later period, he discontinued working about machinery, and engaged in the transfer business,—taking contracts for general hauling. Being frugal and industrious, he soon saved considerable money with which he purchased a fine farm. He then moved to Roaring Spring, and built himself a fine residence, blacksmith and carriage shop, and conducted this business the balance of his life.

In his political views, Henderson Gorsuch was, in early life, an ardent Republican, but later became a strong Prohibitionist and a great temperance worker. He was a member of the Methodist Episcopal church for the twenty-five years preceding his death, and was a class leader and trustee of that denomination. His demise occurred February 11, 1896, and his life was considered well and nobly spent. His wife was Elizabeth Gates. She proved to be a most helpful companion, and assisted in rearing a family of nineteen children, one of whom was Samuel Clarence, the subject of these lines.

Samuel C. Gorsuch attended the public schools, after which he partly learned the blacksmith's trade, and then acquired the trade of puddling, in the Cambria Iron Works, at Johnstown, Cambria county. He then learned heating at Tyrone, and subsequently went to Beaver Falls, where, after working for about a year and a half, he became a heater, and assisted in building the plant of the American Steel & Wire Co. there, from which he was transferred to that company's plant in Rankin, where he has charge of the heating department.

In his political action he has always followed the leadership of the Republican party, but has had no political aspirations, whatever. Socially, he is a member of the Masonic fraternity, of Beaver Falls, and also of the I. O. O. F. lodge. He was joined in marriage with Harriet McClellan, a lady with many graces. Their marriage occurred October 15, 1883. Mrs. Gorsuch is a daughter of James McClellan, and is a native of Blair county, Pennsylvania. Seven bright, attractive children came to bless their home; their names and ages are as follows: Alpha, born March 26, 1885; Nellie, born January 22, 1887; Clarence, born September 19, 1889; Clifford, born June 27, 1891; Hazel Belle, born January 9, 1893, and deceased September 13, 1893; Olive, born November 3, 1895; and Forest, born June 17, 1899.

The subject of this sketch and his family are

regular attendants of the Methodist church and contribute liberally to its support. By careful and judicious management he has been able to acquire a snug competence,—due entirely to his own efforts,—while at the same time, he has gained for himself a reputation for honesty and uprightness in all his dealings.

JOHN McFARREN BUCHANAN, son of Thomas C. Buchanan, and Eliza A. Mayhew, his wife, was born near Florence, Washington County, Pennsylvania, April 25, 1851. His father dying of cholera, June 18, 1852, on the overland route to California, his mother removed to Fairview, Virginia (now West Virginia), in 1856, near where her father, John Mayhew, was living. Our subject remained here with his mother and sister, Georgiana, until June 1, 1858, when he was taken by a paternal uncle, Joseph K. Buchanan, to his home in Hanover township, Beaver County, Pennsylvania, where he attended the district school and worked in vacation upon the farm of his uncle.

In the fall and winter of 1864-65, he attended The Collegiate Institute, East Liberty, Pennsylvania, taught by Rev. J. P. Moore, a brother-in-law of his uncle above-named. In the winter of 1866 he recited in the evenings to Thomas Nicholson, Esq., a famous teacher and well known citizen of Frankfort Springs. In April, 1867, he entered Washington and Jefferson College, then under the presidency of Rev. Jonathan Edwards, D. D. Mr. Bu-

chanan was aided in his efforts by his uncle, Joseph K. Buchanan, and by his mother, and by tutoring and teaching and the like through college, graduating in the class of 1869. On December 1, 1869, Mr. Buchanan was entered as a law student in the law office of Sam B. Wilson, Esq., one of the most eminent lawyers that ever graced the Beaver Bar, and was admitted to the Bar September 2, 1872, the committee being Edward B. Daugherty, Frank Wilson and E. P. Kuhn, all now deceased.

In November, 1874, Mr. Buchanan received the Democratic nomination for District Attorney in the strong Republican county of Beaver and was elected by 94 votes, and in 1877, was re-elected by 303 majority. During the six years of office, Mr. Buchanan never had an indictment quashed nor amended in a single word; nor did he have a grand jury sit over two days at a time,—the Quarter Sessions Court and Grand Jury then sat at the same time. Since that time Mr. Buchanan has enjoyed a large and lucrative practice. He is president of the First National Bank, Beaver, Pennsylvania, and of the Beaver Valley Traction Company, the Beaver & Vanport Electric Street Railway, a director in the First National Bank, Rochester, Pennsylvania, in the Bridgewater Bridge, Sharon Bridge, New Brighton Water Company, The Valley Electric Light Company and in various other companies. He is also attorney for the Pennsylvania Company. Mr. Buchanan has taken an active part in keeping Beaver County to the front in every good work. He is a member of the First Presbyterian Church of Beaver and active in its councils.

In 1896, Mr. Buchanan was the nominee of the Democratic party for Judge of the Thirty-sixth Judicial District of Pennsylvania, and received the largest vote ever received by a Democrat in that District, but failed in the election in this strong Republican district.

The ancestor of this branch of the Buchanans first in the country was Walter Buchanan, who was of Scotch-Irish origin, and emigrated to America from the northern part of Ireland, settling in Little Britain township, Lancaster County, Pennsylvania, in 1745. He was a farmer up to the time of his death, which occurred in Lancaster County, in 1790; his remains lie buried in the Churchyard of Little Britain Presbyterian Church in Lancaster County, Pennsylvania. He was active in church and state, and was one of the signers to the petition found on page 310, Vol. 3—2 Ser., Pennsylvania Archives. The home of Walter Buchanan was blessed with three sons and three daughters, namely: Gilbert; John; James; Jeannette; Mary; and Sarah. Gilbert, the eldest, settled near Poland, Ohio, and became a tiller of the soil. John, the second son, settled near Paris in Washington County, Pennsylvania, and also followed the occupation of a farmer. He was a member of the Associate Presbyterian Church, and served as elder of that denomination. His remains lie buried in the Associate Burial Ground at Paris, Washington County, Pennsylvania.

James, the third son, was the great-grandfather of our subject. In 1791, he located in Hanover township, Washington County, Pennsylvania, about two miles from Florence. James was born May 23, 1761, in Little Britain township, above-named. He served for some months as a member of Captain James Morrison's Company, Porter's Battalion, in the Revolutionary War, and died on the twenty-fifth day of November, 1823. He married Margaret Ross, a relative of George Ross, a signer of the Declaration of Independence. Mrs. Buchanan was of Scotch-Irish ancestry, and was born March 23, 1769, a native of Chester County, Pennsylvania, a member of the Associate Presbyterian Church. She survived her husband for thirty-five years, passing away July 20, 1854, and her remains now lie buried in the Presbyterian Churchyard at Slippery Rock, Lawrence County, Pennsylvania. This highly esteemed and worthy couple reared the following children: Elizabeth, born April 5, 1789, and died September 24, 1855,—she became the wife of John Mitchell, and now lies buried in the United Presbyterian Churchyard at Sharon, Ohio; Walter, born July 14, 1791, and died July 19, 1869, is buried at New Brighton, Pennsylvania; Hannah, born October 21, 1793, and died March 6, 1866,—she married John Smith, and is buried at Sheakleyville, Pennsylvania; Nancy, born January 1, 1796, died October 26, 1873,—she became the wife of Hugh Smith, and is buried at Duncanville United Presbyterian Church, Crawford County, Illinois; John, grandfather of our subject, will be mentioned later; James, born May 29, 1800, and died February 19, 1840; Moses Ross, born October 6, 1803, and died at De Witt, Iowa, July 22, 1878; Joseph Smith, born October 31, 1806, a graduate of Jefferson College and a minister in the United Presbyterian Church for nearly fifty years, died March 31, 1887, at De Witt, Iowa; Margaret, born January 29, 1808, and died June 17, 1876; Mary, wife of Mr. Caldwell, was born May 9, 1813, and died June 18, 1893; and George Black, born September 14, 1815.

John Buchanan, grandfather of our subject, was born on the twenty-eighth day of May, 1798, in Hanover township, Washington County, Pennsylvania, was a farmer, purchasing a farm just across the line in Virginia, where he spent the remainder of his life, and where his death took place, May 6, 1830; his remains lie buried in the Presbyterian grounds in Fairview, West Virginia. He married Margaret Chambers, a daughter of Thomas Chambers, a native of Scotland, who came to America as a Scottish soldier in Cornwall's Army. Mr. Chambers settled in Hanover township, in 1789, on a farm which is now owned by our subject. Mrs. Buchanan survived her husband four years, dying July 25, 1834, at the age of thirty-one years. This worthy couple left four sons, orphans, to mourn the loss of their parents; James, born in 1824 and wedded Mary A. Craig; Thomas Chambers, father of our subject, heretofore mentioned; John F., born in 1828, and twice married,—his first wife being Jane Greenfield, his second, May Elligood; and Joseph Kerr, born in 1830 and married Martha T. Bigger.

HARRY CALHOON, district attorney of Beaver county, Pa., ranks high among the members of the legal profession of the county, and is a much respected citizen of the borough. He was born at New Brighton, September 15, 1862, and is a son of John and Nancy (White) Calhoon, grandson of Robert and Elizabeth (Scott) Calhoon, and great-grandson of Andrew Calhoon.

Harry Calhoon attended the public schools of New Brighton, taking a finishing course at Geneva College. After this he began the study of law, reading in the office of J. R. Harrah in the evenings, and working through the day in the manufacturing department of the foundry of Logan & Strobridge. He finished reading law in the office of Thompson & Martin and was admitted to the bar, in 1892. He immediately began the practice of his profession in New Brighton. It was not long before his worth became known and brought him lucrative returns; being active and energetic, cases in which he is interested are pushed to a speedy termination, as his efforts are very rarely lacking in the elements of success. About the year 1893, he was elected solicitor of New Brighton; he was elected district attorney of Beaver county, Pa., in 1898,—in which capacity he now serves.

In 1896, Mr. Calhoon married Florence Deitrick, a daughter of Frederick A. Deitrick, a worthy citizen of New Brighton. He and his wife live in a handsome residence recently purchased by him; it is modern in design, very convenient and attractive, and was built by R. E. Hoop.

Andrew Calhoon, great-grandfather of the subject hereof, was a native of County Derry, Ireland. He came to America about the year 1785, while still a single man. For the first few years, he lived in New York City in a log house, which contained one of those historic old fire-places. The usual custom was to draw a huge back-log to the door of the cabin; after the laborious task of getting it through the door, it was rolled into the capacious fireplace, which it completely filled for a time,—smaller logs being gradually burned in front of it. Some of the back-logs were so large that it was not necessary to replace them for several days. During the latter part of his life, Mr. Calhoon used frequently to speak of the change in New York City, and to compare it with its early condition. He died in 1864, at the remarkable age of one hundred and three years. After leaving New York City, Mr. Calhoon settled in Chester county, Pa., and later in Washington county, where he followed agricultural pursuits, and accumulated some money. In the year 1800, he purchased one hundred acres of land where Kennedy Calhoon now resides. There in the forest, he built a log house so substantially that it is still standing, being used as a storehouse. He set out orchards, cleared the forests into fine fields, and spent his closing years upon that farm. While in the East, Mr. Calhoon was joined in marriage with Mary Kennedy, who bore him the following children: Robert; James K.; and John S.

The young wife and mother was called from her earthly home before her children attained manhood. Mr. Calhoon contracted another matrimonial alliance,—his second wife being Mrs. Rogers of South Beaver township. No issue was the result of this marriage. John S., the youngest son, inherited the homestead, and it still remains in the possession of his descendants.

Robert Calhoon, grandfather of Harry, in early life learned the carpenter's trade, and located in Brighton, now Beaver Falls. He built many houses, barns, etc., in that vicinity, and in adjoining counties, and also assisted in building the boat called the "Aaron Burr." He won an enviable reputation as a mechanic and builder, in his day. In 1848, he settled in New Brighton, where he served as justice of the peace, member of the borough council, and as burgess. He was a member of the Old School Presbyterians. His death was caused by consumption, and occurred April 1st, 1859, when aged fifty-four years. His marriage with Elizabeth Scott, of Darlington, Pa., was celebrated in 1828. She survived her husband until she attained the age of seventy-four years.

Their union resulted in the following offspring: Mary Jane, who died at the age of twenty-one years; Thomas, whose death occurred as recently as 1898, at the age of sixty-five years; John C., father of the subject hereof; and Margaret, who died young.

John C. Calhoon attended public school until his fifteenth year. Just previous to his sixteenth birthday, he became apprenticed to learn the harness maker's trade. He served his time with James W. Baker, of New Brighton, completely mastering the trade, and in 1894, went into business for himself, at New Brighton. In 1861, he became employed in the Arsenal in Allegheny, and continued for three and one-half years, working on saddles and harness for the U. S. government. He built his present residence and shop at New Brighton, where he is now located, in 1859, and has engaged in the manufacture of harness, and in custom work ever since, keeping a separate salesroom of harness supplies, blankets, etc. On July 17, 1883, Mr. Calhoon received a patent for the "Calhoon Improved Truss" which he had previously invented, and which has been a great success. The use of this truss has effected many permanent cures. Mr. Calhoon put only the best of materials in these articles, and has built up quite a reputation for that line of goods, although he has not advertised them very extensively. The tidings of a cure effected by one of them are soon transmitted to another sufferer, and thereby his trade is increased. He makes various kinds of trusses to suit the requirements of each separate case. Mr. Calhoon is a man of sterling worth and is esteemed by all who know him. His life has been unusually successful, from a financial standpoint. He was a county commissioner when the present court house was built, has also been a member of the borough council, and is now serving his third term as justice of the peace. He chose for his life companion Nancy White, a daughter of Harvey White. Mrs. Calhoon

was born in 1841, and died in 1867, at the early age of twenty-six years,—leaving the following children: Thomas, a prominent confectionery dealer in New Brighton, who married Emma Sheehan, and has one child, Eleanor; Harry, whose name heads this sketch; Edwin, a lumber dealer, in New Castle, Pa.; Robert, a molder by trade, who married Elva Guntner; and Harvey, who is associated with his brother. Mr. Calhoon married a second time. Miss Ellen McDaniel became his wife; they are both members of the Methodist church, of which he is a trustee and class leader. In politics, he is a Republican.

Harry Calhoon, the subject of this narrative, by good management and careful methods has won success in his profession, and also has a large circle of friends in private life. He is a member in good standing of the Masonic fraternity, the American Mechanics, and the Royal Arcanum. Like his father, he worships with the Methodists.

GEORGE E. SMITH, ex-county commissioner of Beaver county, has seen many years of public service. He was formerly engaged in mercantile pursuits and his record as a public servant is clean and altogether in harmony with the integrity of his successful business life. Mr. Smith is esteemed and respected by thousands of acquaintances, as one of nature's noblemen, and is a man of whom Beaver county may well be proud. He was born in Westmoreland township, Cheshire county, New Hampshire,

February 24, 1841. In his youth, he attended the local schools, where he obtained a good practical education. He went west, to Beaver county, Pa., in 1865, and worked for a period of three years on the Pennsylvania Railroad. The following year was spent by the subject of this sketch in a store at Sharon, Pa., after which he was engaged in a similar way, for two years, at Beaver Falls. Mr. Smith then decided to discontinue business pursuits, and try a new venture; accordingly, in 1871, he began to run a general delivery, which he conducted very successfully for twenty years; he then turned it over to his son, Thomas A. Smith, in order to give his attention to the duties of the office of county commissioner. This change occurred in 1891, when Mr. Smith was appointed to fill the vacancy caused by the death of John Wilson. After filling this unexpired term of one and one-half years, Mr. Smith was elected to a full term of three years, which expired January 1, 1897.

Mr. Smith is known as a stanch, uncompromising, and aggressive Republican, to all who are familiar with his political views. He has been a hard worker in the Republican cause, and occupies an influential position in his party organization.

Our subject is a member of the Beaver Valley Lodge, No. 478, F. & A. M.; of Harmony Chapter, No. 206, R. A. M.; and of Lone Rock Lodge, No. 222, Knights of Pythias. In 1868, Mr. Smith led to the altar Margaret White, an accomplished daughter of Thomas White, of White town-

ship, Beaver county, Pennsylvania. One son, Thomas A., blessed this union, and is now succeeding his father in the general delivery business. The subject of this sketch, who is one of a family of fourteen children, is a son of Hiram and Olive (Arnold) Smith, and a grandson of Benjamin Smith.

Benjamin Smith was a native of the North of Ireland, where he was also reared and educated. In early manhood, he came to America and settled in Westmoreland township, Cheshire county, N. H., where he spent the remainder of his life.

Hiram Smith, father of the subject hereof, was born in New Hampshire in 1800. He was reared and trained to agricultural pursuits, and while not in school did such work as usually falls to the lot of a farmer's boy. This discipline was just the kind needed to make him understand all the details of farm work, which he followed all his active days, spending his last three years in retirement at Walpole, N. H., where his death occurred, in 1875.

His wife was Olive Arnold, a daughter of Thomas Arnold, of Cheshire county, New Hampshire. Mrs. Smith crossed the dark river into the light beyond, at the age of sixty-three years, after rearing a family of fourteen children, viz.: Ralph; Caroline (Scott); Miranda (Roberts); David; Charles; Sarah (Hale); Phineas; Adeline (Angier) and Augusta, twins; Laura; George E., the subject of this sketch; King; Elizabeth, and a child that died in infancy. Hiram Smith was a firm friend of education, and in his political affiliations was a Democrat. Both he and his wife entertained broad, liberal views as to religion, but preferred the Universalist church.

Our subject is a man who, wherever, he is known, is respected for his sterling qualities. He has, like all men, had opportunities, but unlike many men, he has made the most of them. He takes a broad, comprehensive view of life, in this respect being very similar to his honored father. He has knowledge of many other interests than those with which he is intimately connected, and in all matters, his judgment is known to be sound. He is heir to a good name and that good name he proposes to hand down to posterity without tarnish.

———◆◆———

WILLIAM W. HAYS, a prominent blacksmith of Fairview, Pa., was born in Beaver Falls, Pa., November 10, 1849. He learned blacksmithing with his father, with whom he worked sixteen years. He has labored all his life at his chosen trade,—a trade which has been followed until the present day by each succeeding father and son, through many generations of the family. Mr. Hays is a son of Adams and Barbara (Langnecker) Hays, and grandson of Adams and Sissin (Stephens) Hays.

The grandfather of William W. was born in Carlisle, Eastern Pennsylvania. He learned blacksmithing under his father. In those early days all kinds of machinery were made

by blacksmiths, and were merely fitted by machinists. He also learned to make sickles. He wedded Sissin Stephens, and they reared a large family of children, as follows: Martha; John A.; Eliza; Thomas Calvert; Sissin; Belinda; Adams; Caroline; Sallie Adams; Margaret; and William.

William W. Hays' father was one of the younger members of the family. After he had learned blacksmithing from his father, he, in company with two of his brothers, moved to Beaver county. He then started into business in old Brighton, which is now Beaver Falls. He did all kinds of smithing (including tool dressing), on the Ft. Wayne R. R., and later on C. & P. R. R. His first work on the railroad was done when the line was single-tracked. Forty years later, in 1898, he did similar work on the same road when it was double-tracked. His marriage with Barbara Langnecker resulted in the birth of twelve children. Barbara was a native of Germany, and was brought to America when only three years of age. The names of their children are: William W., the subject hereof; Charles L.; George W.; Fanny (Lomax); Frank, deceased; Sissin; Mary (deceased; Samuel B.; Harry P.; James J.; John R.; and Annie, who died at the tender age of nine years. George W. is manager for Butler & Jackson, in Rochester, Pennsylvania.

The father of William W. located in Fairview in April, 1859, and built a shop where the latter is now doing business. He carried on blacksmithing there until 1893, when he retired from active life. In 1892, the old shop was torn down and was at once replaced by a new one, 24 by 40 feet. The elder Mr. Hays is a consistent member of the Episcopal church, which he joined in 1874. He served as vestryman. In politics, his sympathies are with the Republican party. He has always voted for that party's candidates, and has worked hard for its success, but would never accept office. The mother of the subject hereof died in December, 1892. The father still survives.

William W. Hays learned his trade when nails, horse shoes, and almost everything in that line were made by blacksmiths. He acquired all the peculiar features of the art from his father. Mr. Hays has been twice married, and is now a widower. His first union was contracted with Nancy A. Cochran. Nancy was a daughter of John and Jane Cochran, and was born at Egypt (now Midway), Washington county, Pa., where she also received her primary education. This was supplemented by a thorough course at Oakdale and at Cannonsburg, with a finishing curriculum at Mansfield, where she graduated. She then followed the profession of teaching, which occupied her attention for several years. She taught just back of Sewickley, in Allegheny county, and was successful to a marked degree. She bore her husband four children, viz.: Hallie J. (Stoner), who now resides in Youngstown, Ohio; Ross, who died in infancy; Oliver A.; and Edward Otto.

Oliver A., attended Todd's school in Industry, took a preparatory course at Fairview, and finished his education with a three

years' course at Beaver Falls. He is now learning the blacksmith trade with his father. Edward Otto received the same educational equipment as his brother, and is also learning the trade which has been followed by most of the male members of the Hays family.

Years ago William W. Hays went to Washington county, as a blacksmith. He purchased a farm in Industry and did some farming in connection with his trade. This farm contained one hundred and four acres, and was devoted to general farming, for some time. Subsequently, Mr. Hays engaged in the berry business, which he carried on successfully, for six years. He then sold a part of the farm and removed to Beaver Falls, but afterward returned to the property, where the death of his first wife took place. He then sold the remainder of it and purchased a house in Fairview, whither he removed, and went into business with his father. As before mentioned, this partnership lasted for sixteen years, when Mr. Hays conducted the business alone. He is now assisted by his two sons. He does horse shoeing, wagon and carriage work, oil-well repairing, etc. Mr. Hays is also somewhat interested in oil production. He owns a half interest in the Esther Oil Co., in addition to which he has a well on his own place. His neat, attractive residence is situated quite near his shops, and he owns several desirable building-lots in the same vicinity.

Mr. Hays married a second time. In this instance, Mary A. Fowler became his wife. She was born on the old farm in Chippewa township, Beaver county, and died as recently

as June, 1899. Mr. Hays is a member of the Episcopal church, of which he is warden. He is a Republican, but is too busy for the cares of office. He is special representative and secretary for the Iron City Building & Loan Association.

SIMON HARROLD, a prominent contractor of Beaver Falls, and a member of the State Legislature from Beaver county, Pa., has been a resident of that borough since 1866, and it may be said that no man has worked more conscientiously to advance its interests than he.

Mr. Harrold was born in Columbiana (now Mahoning) county, Ohio, November 3, 1840, and is a son of Samuel Harrold.

His grandfather was David Harrold, a native of Bucks county, Pa., whose father fought under General Washington at Valley Forge, and a descendant of the sturdy Saxon race. Samuel Harrold, the father of our subject, was born in Columbiana county, Ohio, August 16, 1816.

Simon Harrold received his education in the schools of Mahoning county, Ohio. Upon leaving school he went to Springfield, Ill., and started in business in partnership with a Mr. Eberhardt as a general contractor, continuing for three years. He then returned to his home and after his marriage moved to Beaver Falls, in 1866, becoming one of the first business men of that town. The population did not exceed 100, the borough being incorporated in 1868. Mr. Harrold built a planing mill in partnership with a Mr. Crane,

and they procured lumber from the North and West. He purchased the first car load of lumber that was ever shipped to Beaver county from the West, the transportation charges from Cleveland amounting to $48. He also engaged in contracting alone and soon established a wide reputation. The planing mill was named the Beaver Falls Planing Mill, and after Mr. Crane's retirement, in 1869, our subject became the principal member of the firm and so continued until very recently, when he retired from the active management of the business. They manufacture doors, window sashes, and all kinds of building material. Mr. Harrold has always been engaged in contracting and has built more houses than any other contractor in the district, and has built every hotel in the borough. He has been awarded many large contracts throughout the surrounding country, including nearly every factory in Beaver Falls, in all or in part; the courthouses at New Lisbon and Coshocton; several locks and dams on the Monongahela and other rivers; street paving,—an example of which is the elegantly paved streets of Beaver Falls; the street railway from Pittsburg to Coraopolis, the People's line, and the Riverview; the waterworks at Beaver, Pa., and Leetonia, Ohio; and the pump station for the Monongahela Company at Becks Run and Esplin.

Mr. Harrold was joined in wedlock with Louisa Schauweker, who was born in Columbiana county, Ohio, and is a daughter of Jacob Schauweker, who was born in Germany, but came to America where he followed the trade of a tanner and leather dealer, a business followed by the family for many generations. This union resulted in seven children: Julia E.; Irvin C.; Alberta A.; Mary; Isadore; Katie; Alfred. They were all educated in Beaver county and are graduates of Beaver Falls High School. Politically, our subject is a Republican and cast his first presidential vote for Lincoln. He has always been an active party worker and although he has never sought office it has at times been thrust upon him. He helped to organize and was one of the first councilmen in the borough, and has served in all fifteen years. In 1898, he was elected a member of the State Legislature from Beaver county, in which body he has always been an active worker, doing his utmost to further the interests of his constituents and those of the state. He voted regularly with the Republican party for the election of Quay in the senatorial contest, and the resulting deadlock has convinced him that the proper way to elect a senator is by the direct vote of the people. Religiously, he is a member of the M. P. church. Fraternally, he is a Mason, belonging to Valley Echo Lodge, F. & A. M., of Beaver Falls, Pa. Mr. Harold's portrait accompanies this sketch.

ELLIS N. BIGGER, county solicitor for Beaver county, Pa., is also a prominent attorney of Beaver. After attending public school, young Bigger took a finishing course at Frankfort Academy, after which he followed the profession of teaching public schools and in Frankfort Academy, for a period of four years. He then registered as a law student with the late Samuel B. Wilson, then one of Beaver county's most prominent and able attorneys. Mr. Bigger was admitted to the bar June 2, 1879, and soon after began the practice of his profession, alone, in Beaver. He continued thus until 1882, when he entered into partnership with Frank Wilson. Mr. Wilson died in 1883, after which the firm became Bigger & Henry (T. M. Henry) until 1891, since which Mr. Bigger has practiced alone. He has been very successful as a lawyer, and is an able writer and speaker. Athough he never aspired to office, he has served in the borough council for six years, and has recently been elected county solicitor for three years, which will make an incumbency of eight consecutive years in the latter office. The subject of this sketch is an ardent advocate of thorough educational systems, being a member of the borough school board. He owns a fine residence on Raccoon street, built by J. F. Dravo, and containing all the modern conveniences. Mr. Bigger's residence is handsomely furnished, and he boasts of having one of the most elegant, select libraries in the borough. He is a man of rare literary taste and is a lover of the best works.

Mr. Bigger chose for his life partner Jean Blanche Love, a favorite daughter of the late Robert and Jane (McClure) Love, of Mercer county. Robert Love was a progressive merchant tailor of that place, and died when seventy-two years old, while Mrs. Love died at the age of sixty-two years. The following children were born to Mr. and Mrs. Love: John, who died young; Emma, wife of A. F. McNair; Alfretta, single; Christopher I., who also died young; Catherine, deceased; and Jean Blanche, wife of the subject hereof.

Both Mr. and Mrs. Bigger are devout Christians, being willing workers in the Presbyterian church, besides giving liberally of their means to many charitable institutions. Mr. Bigger is a thirty-second degree Mason, and a member of the Knights of Pythias. He is in every respect a man of force and influence. He has a fund of experience to draw from, that is of a superior order. As a prominent man in his profession, his judgment and foresight have been brought to a keen edge from contact with the shrewdest of business men. The success which has come to him is but the natural result of his incessant and well-directed efforts.

Ellis N. Bigger was born September 17, 1856, in Hanover township, Washington county, Pa. He is a son of Thomas and Mary (Nicholson) Bigger, grandson of James and Mary (Biggart) Bigger, great-grandson of Thomas and Elizabeth (Moore) Bigger, and great-great-grandson of Matthew Bigger. Matthew Bigger was born at a place called Bigger, in Scotland, and on account of religious persecutions fled to Ireland, settled in County Antrim, near Belfast, where his death occurred. He left a widow and six children. The names of the latter were: John, James, Samuel, Thomas, Jane, and Elizabeth. The three eldest sons remained in Ireland, but

Thomas and his two sisters, Jane and Elizabeth, accompanied by their mother, came to America.

Thomas, the fourth son, was born in 1738, and upon attaining manhood, he fell in love with Elizabeth Moore, the daughter of a wealthy man, who objected to their marriage on account of Thomas being a poor man, and a weaver by trade. But notwithstanding the father's objections, the young folks were married, and shortly afterward Thomas induced his mother and two sisters to accompany them to America. They landed at Baltimore, Md., October 16, 1773. Thomas, upon learning that land was cheap in the "wild west," journeyed overland to what is now Raccoon township, Washington county, Pa., and near Raccoon creek he took up a large tract of land. He was of a proud nature, but was a sturdy worker, and the height of his ambition was to become an extensive land owner. In his native country, only the wealthy had large landed possessions, but, by struggling hard against almost overwhelming difficulties, with the aid of his ever-faithful wife, he gratified his heart's desire. He built a log cabin and felled the forest trees, and he lived as only the brave pioneers did; but he prospered, and at the time of his death he was a well-to-do and progressive farmer. His life shows that "what man has done, man can do." He and his devoted consort reared a family of ten children.

James Bigger, grandfather of Ellis N., served in the War of 1812, as a private, being stationed at Fort Maldon. He was united in marriage with Mary Biggart, in 1816, and the same year purchased a farm in Hanover township, Beaver county, Pa. This farm was formerly owned by Magnus Tate, and contained four hundred acres, mostly new land. He built a two-story house of logs, which was later replaced by a fine, large, brick residence, which is still standing. The farm is now owned by H. R. Wilson. James was one of the earliest men of the county to promote agricultural progress. It is said that he owned the first threshing machine ever used in the township, or in that vicinity. Men came many miles to see it. He also owned the first mower, and obtained many other agricultural implements before his neighbors did. He was very naturally regarded as a leading man in the community. His wife bore him the following children: Samuel, who married Jane Fulton; Jane, who was twice married, her first husband being a Mr. Hall, and her second, Matthew Nickle; Mary, wife of Rev. J. P. Moore; Thomas, the father of Ellis N.; Eliza A., wife of David Nickle; Martha, wife of Joseph K. Buchanan; Ellen, wife of David Nicholson; James M., who married Margaret Morrow; John, who married a Miss Childs; and Robert, who married Ann Kieffer.

Thomas Bigger, father of our subject, Ellis N., was born on his father's farm January 9, 1826. During his youth he assisted his father in clearing the farm and when he attained manhood he still lingered there until his marriage with Mary Nicholson, which occurred on the second day of November, 1854. After his marriage he settled in Hanover township,

Washington county, Pa., but later purchased a part of the old homestead farm, near the famous Frankfort Springs, where he has lived ever since, owning one of the finest farms in Beaver county. This farm is now in a state of fine cultivation, and contains a handsome residence, splendid barns, etc. Early in life Mr. Bigger devoted much time and attention to sheep raising, but subsequently he discontinued that branch and turned his attention to general farming; he has now practically retired. He has always been a public-spirited man, and has served as school director for many years; he was one of the founders and original stockholders of the Frankfort Academy. In politics he was a Democrat previous to the formation of the Republican party, since which he has supported the latter. Both he and his aged wife are Christians, being active members of the United Presbyterian church. This worthy and highly esteemed couple, although on the shady side of life, are hale and hearty, and hope to welcome many friends at their hospitable home for years to come. Mrs. Bigger was born May 6, 1834, and is a daughter of Hon. Thomas Nicholson. She bore her husband two sons, and one daughter, namely; Ellis N., the subject of this sketch; Inez J., wife of David S. Strouss; and James Carl, attorney-at-law in Steubenville, Ohio.

Hon. Thomas Nicholson, the maternal grandfather of the subject hereof, enjoyed the distinction of being the first superintendent of schools of Beaver county, Pa. He was for many years a teacher of Frankfort Academy.

He was also elected to the legislature and served as justice of the peace. His life was considered among the most worthy in the annals of Beaver county.

DR. JOHN H. DAVIS. We may safely say that there is no physician and surgeon in Beaver county better or more favorably known to the public, than the gentleman whose name heads these lines, who commands an excellent practice in the vicinity of Hookstown, where he is located. He has made a specialty of surgery, having had a most thorough training in that direction, and he is very frequently called to attend cases in Pittsburg, Beaver, and Liverpool. The profession of medicine is not the only sphere in which he shines, however, for as an impersonator he has almost a national reputation. Unlike most of the followers of the latter profession he recites from his own works, and is thus enabled to give to his renditions that peculiar earnestness and desired expression, which none but an author can give to his compositions.

Dr. Davis comes of an old and highly respected family of Beaver county, and his great-grandfather, a mechanic by trade, came from his native country, Wales, and located in Western Pennsylvania. His grandfather was John Davis, who was born in West Elizabeth, Pennsylvania, and moved to Beaver county about sixty years ago. His occupation was that of a boat builder, but after locating in this county, he turned his attention to

tilling the soil. He purchased 200 acres of land in Moon township, this becoming the old homestead, and in addition, owned one-hundred and forty acres in Independence township. He died in 1884, having lived a long and useful life. In politics, he was a Republican, and a prominent one, but was not an office seeker.

James Davis, the father of John H., was born on the farm in Moon township in 1847, and received a good scholastic training in the public schools, after which he attended, and was graduated from, Edinboro State Normal School. He then taught school for two terms, after which he bought the 140 acres of land owned by his father in Independence township, where he has since been actively engaged in agricultural pursuits. He has greatly improved his property, and has one of the finest farms in the county, making a specialty of truck gardening. He is a Republican in politics, and is an enthusiastic supporter of that party. He was united in hymeneal bonds with Susan C. Engle, who is a native of Vanport but whose family now resides in Raccoon township, Beaver county. The following children blessed their home: Dr. John H., the subject of this record; Frank F., a graduate of Cleveland University, who is now actively engaged in practice in East Liverpool, Ohio; Henry, who lives at home; Maggie; Annie; and Blanche. Mr. Davis is now serving as justice of the peace.

Dr. John H: Davis was born on the old homestead, and after receiving a common school training, he took a course in Sheffield

Academy and Slippery Rock Normal School. He then took an advanced course in literature under a private tutor and a classical course at Cleveland. He developed exceptional talent as an elocutionist and ventriloquist, and traveled two years as a public reciter and impersonator. His interpretations of emotional lines are of a high order, and are rendered with much dramatic ability. With the cleverness of a true artist, he adapts himself to the character of his piece, and at times shows such realistic feeling that a sympathetic wave sweeps over his hearers, carrying them beyond the affairs of their every day life to the scene portrayed by the rendition. His humorous selections are equally well received, as he injects his own bright, vivacious and humorous spirit into the character he produces. In such entertainments the troubles of the audience are cast into the background, and merriment reigns supreme. He was everywhere well received, and has more than one thousand testimonials from some of the most learned men in the different sections of our country, speaking in the highest praise of his ability, and commenting favorably on his dramatic powers and keen sense of humor. There are but eight authors in the United States who recite from their own works, and we take great pleasure in reproducing one of Dr. Davis' poems. It was written when our country was at fever heat over the destruction of the battleship Maine, and when first given to the public at New Cumberland, West Virginia, was enthusiastically received. It is as follows:

WHEN A NATION MOURNED THE MAINE.

Do you remember the night
   When a nation lost the Maine?
When our jolly tars were murdered
   By the crimsoned hand of Spain?
Their graves are decked with laurels,
   Their names are on tablets of fame
But it counts for naught when we think of the time
   When a nation mourned the Maine.

The Cubans sang their funeral dirge
   When they heard of that terrible blow.
Let us sing it again as a nation,
   Oh! Sing it sweet and low.
Let us sing it over and over again,
   Until nations catch the refrain,
And our hearts will throb as they did at the time
   When a nation mourned the Maine.

You remember in 1775
   When our nation was distressed;
When we were bound down in bondage
   And by cruels tyrants pressed.
We gave the blood of Warren
   And thousands we need not name.
We forgive it all, but never forget
   When a nation mourned the Maine.

Our minds go back to '61,
   When the Freedmen's hands were bound;
We can see the blood of old John Brown
   As it "crieth from the ground."
The heart of the nation divided,
   And our swords together came,
But even that is not half so sad
   As when a nation mourned the Maine.

Do you remember Admiral Dewey?
   How he to Manila went?
How he stole right into the harbor,
   On death and destruction bent?
And his cannons' mouths were opened
   And poured forth their deadly rain.
Don't you think the Admiral thought of the time
   When a nation mourned the Maine?

Our glorious armies will conquer
All the armies that Spain may send.
Her cities may smoulder in ashes.
Her Kingdom in fragments rend;
Her men may fall in the cannon's glare;
Aye! Fall like sickled grain;
But that cannot atone the time
When a nation mourned the Maine.

Our hearts entwine the Maine
As there in the mud she lies.
Let us rear to her a monument —
One that will kiss the skies.
Yes, we will raise the brazened shaft,
And in glorious words proclaim,
These are they who died for a nation
That mourns the Maine.

The silent daisies shall nod their heads
O'er the graves of the heroes we love,
And the God of mercy shall hide his face
In the starry throne above,
And the blackbird shall pipe his lay
O'er the land where freedom came.
Ah! little knows of the wounded hearts
When a nation mourned the Maine.

There is a day that will surely come,
When justice will be shown;
When the Son of Man shall open His court
In front of the great white throne.
'Tis there that a nation shall be avenged—
Avenged of that terrible stain,
When a nation was plunged in sorrow,
When a nation mourned the Maine.

Dr. Davis' success was not only a great pleasure, but it enabled him to secure the necessary funds to attend college, and satisfy his ambition to become a physician. In the fall of 1890, he entered the Cleveland Medical College, in which he devoted one year to hard and careful study. The next four years were spent in the Cleveland University of Medical Surgery, where his training was of the best, and in 1895 he was graduated under H. F. Bigger. During the summer of the same year, he located at Georgetown, Beaver county, Pa., and engaged in practice in partnership with Dr. M. S. Davis. One year later they dissolved partnership, and in 1896, the subject hereof located at Hookstown, where he has since remained and has built up an enviable practice. He is very popular with his fellow-citizens, who repose in him the greatest confidence, and his success is due solely to his own efforts. He has kept thoroughly abreast of the times in the advance made in the science of medicine and surgery, but nevertheless still devotes a portion of his time to literature.

In October, 1897, Dr. Davis was joined in matrimony with Maggie Blackmore, a daughter of John Blackmore, of Hookstown, and they have one child, James, who was born February 12, 1899.

Dr. Davis is a member of the Beaver County Medical Society; the State Medical Society of Pennsylvania; the American Medical Society; fraternally, he belongs to the blue lodge, F. & A. M., of Smith's Ferry; I. O. O. F., of Smith's Ferry; and the Jr., O. U. A. M. He was a state delegate of the latter order at the age of eighteen, and enjoyed a fine trip to Washington, Atlantic City and Philadelphia. Politically, he is a stanch Republican, whilst in religious faith and fellowship, he is a Presbyterian.

ILLIAM APPLETON McCON-
NEL, of the law firm of Buchanan
& McConnel, is one of the members
of the Beaver county bar, of some prominence
although still a young man.

He was born in the borough of Bridgewater, Beaver county, Pennsylvania, October
23, 1866, and is a son of William Phillips and
Lydia Ann (Stewart) McConnel, grandson of
James and Elvira (Phillips) McConnel, and
great-grandson of James and Rebecca (Wisbie) McConnel. This latter James McConnel was of Scotch-Irish descent, and was born
in the northern part of Ireland, from which he
emigrated to America, locating near Green
Garden, Raccoon township, Beaver county,
Pa. He was described as being an exceedingly tall man, very active and exceedingly
witty, and was familiarly known as "Uncle
Jimmy." He was joined in wedlock with Rebecca Wisbie, who died while still a young
woman, and was survived by her husband
until he attained the age of about eighty
years. They were the parents of the following children: Henry; James; John; Jane
(Orr); and Polly (Ensley).

James McConnel, Jr., the grandfather of
our subject, was born in Washington county
(now Allegheny county), Pa., and was a
steamboat carpenter and builder. He settled
in Freedom, Pa., where his death occurred in
1862, at the age of sixty years. He was
united in marriage on Sunday, February 28,
1830, by the Rev. George Holmes, to Elvira
Phillips, who was a daughter of Stephen and
Rhoda (Parsons) Phillips. Stephen Phillips,

was one of the prominent men of Beaver
county in the early days, very largely interested in the development of the country, especially in the line of steamboat building. He
and Jonathan Betz bought a large tract of
land, on the northern side of the Ohio River,
from William Vicary, in 1832, and laid out the
town of Freedom as it is at present; afterwards, associated with John Graham, he
bought a tract of land on the south side of
the river from Frederick Rapp, which afterwards became the borough of Phillipsburg
(named after him), and is now the borough
of Monaca. In both places, boat-yards were
established and the one in Freedom has been
in operation until within very recent years.
The panic of 1837, however, almost bank-
rupted him, and on the 17th of November,
1855, he was drowned off the steamboat
Jacob Poe, at the port of Wheeling, West
Virginia, on his passage home from Ports-
mouth, Ohio, and his body was never recovered. His age was seventy-five years, eleven
months and twenty-one days. His wife,
Rhoda (Parsons) Phillips, survived him until
March 1, 1861, when she died at the age of
seventy-eight years.

Elvira (Phillips) McConnel was a native of
Vermont, having been born March 28, 1811,
on the eastern shore of Lake Champlain,
whence she came West with her father about
1820. She died January 6, 1897, in the
eighty-sixth year of her age, leaving to sur-
vive her the following children: William
Phillips; James, of Bridgewater, Pa.; Alonzo
Henry, located in Pittsburg; Alcinus Clark,

of Allegheny, Pa., Hiram Smith, a leading physician of New Brighton, Pa.; Emma Annette, widow of Ben. J. Stephenson, of Seattle, Washington; and Omar Montague, of Atchison, Kansas.

William Phillips McConnel, above-named, was born at Phillipsburg (now Monaca), and with his father became a steamboat carpenter and builder, engaging in this occupation for about ten years, during which time he assisted in building boats on the Ohio, Mississippi and Tennessee rivers.

After that he engaged in the business of keeping a general store, for several years at Olean, Ohio, and later at Freedom, Pa. But river life suited him better, so he accepted a position as clerk on a steamer, and was soon promoted to secretary and treasurer of Gray's Iron Line of the city of Pittsburg, which position he held for twenty-five years. Having resigned his position with Gray's Iron Line, he became, in 1895, secretary of the Beaver Valley Traction Company, which position he still occupies.

Mr. McConnel was twice married, his first wife being Elizabeth Stewart, a daughter of David and Catharine (Baker) Stewart of Bridgewater, Pa. She passed to the life beyond at the early age of thirty-one years, leaving three children: Ada Annette, who died April 1, 1896; Laura Stewart; and David Stewart. Mr. McConnel was married afterwards to Lydia Anne Stewart, a daughter of Charles M. Stewart of New Brighton, Pa., and a cousin of his first wife. She bore her husband the following children: William A.,

subject of our sketch; Lillian Augusta, who, after graduating from Mount Holyoke Seminary, South Hadley, Mass., in 1891, and teaching in the high school at New Brighton, Pa., died on October 28, 1898; Jessie, who is a teacher in the Allegheny Kindergarten Association; Richard Gray, who served during the War with Spain, in 1898, as an ensign in the U. S. Navy, and is now a lieutenant in the U. S. Marine Corps; Paul George, who graduated in medicine at the Western University of Pennsylvania, in 1899, and is now on the staff of the West Penn Hospital, Pittsburg; and Charles Hiram, a student at Pennsylvania State College.

William A. McConnel attended the public school at Bridgewater until 1882, when he entered the high school at Beaver, Pa. From there, in 1884, he went to Phillips Exeter Academy, at Exeter, New Hampshire. In June, 1886, he took his examinations at Shadyside Academy, near Pittsburg, for admission to Yale University, which he entered that fall. He graduated, with a High Oration standing, from Yale, in 1890.

He then studied law under the preceptorship of John M. Buchanan, Esq., of Beaver, and was admitted to the bar January 23, 1895. He was immediately taken into partnership by his preceptor, under the firm name of Buchanan, Reed & McConnel, which afterwards became Buchanan & McConnel, Lewis W. Reed retiring from the firm. Since then he has risen rapidly in his chosen profession, and today the firm of which he is a member is considered one of the best in Beaver county.

Our subject was united in marriage with Sarah Stokes Bruce on July 10, 1895, in the First Presbyterian church, Beaver, Pa., by the Rev. P. J. Cummings. Sarah (Bruce) McConnel is a daughter of William H. Bruce, a highly respected citizen of Beaver, Pa. This union has been blessed with two children: William Bruce, born May 5, 1896; and Stewart Phillips, born March 10, 1898. Mr. McConnel is a member and trustee of the Methodist Episcopal church of Beaver, Pa., a member of the Epworth League, and teacher in the Sabbath School of that church, taking great interest in all church work.

———————

WILLIAM CALDWELL FRENCH. Conspicuous among the young men of sterling worth in Beaver county, Pa., whom business or professional work has given a wide acquaintance throughout the county, and whose public service is ever highly esteemed, is William Caldwell French, a rising young attorney of Beaver. Mr. French was born in Beaver, Pa., and, after graduating at the high school at that place, he registered as a law student in the office of J. H. Cunningham, one of Beaver county's most noted attorneys. After pursuing his studies very diligently, young French was admitted to the bar, and spent the following three years associated with his preceptor in the practice of his profession. Since that time he has been practicing alone.

Our worthy subject is an influential member of the Presbyterian church, and although an active man in the interests of Beaver county, he has never sought office.

William Caldwell French is a son of Capt. Samuel B. and Emily (Robinson) French, and grandson of Joseph and Martha (Newton) French. Joseph French was born November 3, 1781, at Brown Mills, Burlington county, New Jersey, and while still a young man, learned the art of making shoes by hand in his native state. In Morristown, New Jersey, he met Martha Newton, a young Quakeress who became his wife. The young folks went west to Beaver county, Pa., shortly after the year 1800, locating in Brighton, which is now Beaver Falls. At that place, Mr. French began the manufacture of boots and shoes, giving employment to several hands. After following that occupation very successfully at Brighton for a period of eight years, he removed to Beaver, where he carried on a similar but more extensive business during the remainder of his life. He made fine, and also coarse, footwear of all kinds not only for the laboring classes, but for the most aristocratic families in Beaver, and townships adjoining. Shortly after moving to Beaver, he purchased a home on the southeast corner of Elk and Second streets, where he and his wife lived until their death.

He was a very progressive man and made considerable money, nor was he content to deal in footwear alone; in addition to his very heavy trade in that line, Mr. French also rented several farms, and carried on agricultural pursuits to a considerable extent. Besides rearing a large family, he was exceedingly charitable and assisted many in need,— very often, it is said, to his own disadvantage. Thus he became extremely popular and was much beloved. Several years prior to his death, he was considered a well-to-do man, of his day. His death took place April 2, 1847, and the event caused universal sorrow. His amiable companion was born April 10, 1786, and for nearly eleven years awaited the summons to rejoin her husband,—passing peacefully away June 17, 1858.

Their union was blessed with ten children, namely: Newton, born July 17, 1805, and died February 10, 1827; James, born March 27, 1807, and died April 3, 1836; Charles M., born January 4, 1811, and died March 27, 1877; Joseph, born May 21, 1813, and died November 11, 1871; Thomas, born October 4, 1815, and died November 2, 1886; Samuel B., father of the subject hereof; Maria C., born November 22, 1821, and died May 10, 1891; Billings O. P., born August 8, 1823, and died September 22, 1846; Leander, born September 30, 1825; Caroline, born January 12, 1828,—the only one of this numerous family known to be living. The honored father of these children was a devout member of the Methodist Episcopal church, while his wife belonged to the good, old Quaker sect.

Samuel B. French, William Caldwell's father, was born December 1, 1818, and when a young man, began river life as assistant on a steamboat plying on the Ohio River, between Pittsburg and New Orleans. This life just suited his fancy, and he rapidly rose in the line to be captain, and still later became part owner of several steamboats, among them the "Joseph Pierce," the "Tropic," and the "Shenango." Retiring from river life he engaged in the manufacture of brick under the firm name of French & Quay. He established brick yards and kilns, and was conducting that business at the time of his death. This plant was conveniently located on the south side of the Ohio River, directly opposite Beaver. Shortly after his marriage Mr. French built a large, substantial and handsome brick residence on the northwest corner of Elk and Second streets, where he lived during the rest of his life. This residence is, at the present time, the home of Hon. M. S. Quay.

Samuel B. French was a public-spirited man and a Democrat of much influence and great prominence. His active river life prevented his accepting political offices.

He was a member of the Masonic fraternity, and was a charter member of St. Joseph Lodge, No. 457, F. & A. M., of Beaver, and on February 15, 1854, became a member of Commandery, No. 1, of the Knights Templar of Pittsburg, Pennsylvania. He passed to his final rest January 28, 1874, and was survived by his widow for twenty years. Mrs. French was, before marriage, Emily Robinson; she was a daughter of Hugh Robinson, a native of Beaver county, and was reared in New Brighton, Pennsylvania. She was a member of the First Presbyterian church of Beaver. Her death occurred on September 7, 1894, at the age of seventy years. She was the mother of thirteen children, ten of whom are still living, and all of whom grew to manhood and womanhood, with the exception of one. Their names are: Martha, Nancy, Thomas, Samuel, Franklin, Eliza, Mary, Emily, Sarah, Katherine. Jeannette, Alice, and William C., the subject of this biographical record.

———◆•◆———

HARRY T. BARKER has made surveying and civil engineering his profession, and has occupied the position of city engineer of New Brighton and Beaver Falls since 1879. He is a director of the Riverview Land Company, which had its origin in 1892. The subject of this sketch is a worthy representative of one of the old and prominent families of Delaware, his ancestors having settled in that state many years prior to the War of Independence. Mr. Barker was born in New Brighton, Pa., August 28, 1849, and is a son of Thomas A. and Eliza (Oakley) Barker.

On the paternal side, Samuel Barker was the original immigrant of the family in this country,—he having located in Delaware as early as 1685; he received a grant of two hundred acres from the Penns. The next in line was Joseph Barker, who was the great-great-grandfather of the subject hereof, and his birth occurred on his father's farm in Delaware; he was a strong Episcopalian, as were his parents. Samuel was the great-grandfather of Harry T. Barker, and he married Rachael Ball, by whom he reared a family of children. Mr. Barker's grandfather was Abner, a native of Delaware, who early in life located in Pitts-

burg, Pa.; prior to 1790, he served in the fire department of that city. Being a man of means he retired at an early age, and spent his closing years in that city, in comfort and happiness.

On the maternal side, the family is of English extraction, and the Oakleys, from whom Mr. Barker's mother sprang, have been residents of America since a very early period. The grandfather was Milton Oakley, a native of Baltimore, Md., but later a resident of Butler county, Pa., where he was actively engaged in business. He died in the village of Harmony, in middle age.

Thomas A. Barker was born in Pittsburg, Pa., in 1823, but was reared to manhood in Beaver county,—he having left home to live with his older brother, Dr. Butler Barker, a practicing physician of Beaver; after receiving a common school education in Beaver, he located in New Brighton, where he embarked in mercantile pursuits,—continuing thus until his death, in February, 1859. He married Eliza Oakley, who was born in 1821 and died in 1863; they were the parents of the following children: George O., who died aged five years; Frank A., who died in 1879, from an accidental gunshot wound; Harry T.; and Ellen O., the wife of Harry Brown, of Cincinnati, Ohio.

Harry T. Barker obtained his primary education in the public schools of New Brighton, which was supplemented by a course in the military academy at West Chester, Pa., and upon his graduation therefrom, by a course in the Cooper Institute in New York City;

he then took an engineering course under the professorship of George L. Fox, then a celebrated teacher in mechanics and mathematics. On graduating, he accepted a position in the ship building establishment of the Roaches, of New York City. Returning to New Brighton, in 1873, he and his brother, Frank A., began a banking business under the name of Barker Brothers, establishing a private bank in Beaver Falls; this business was continued until 1878, when the subject of this record took up his profession as a surveyor and civil engineer; in the following year he was elected city engineer of both Beaver Falls and New Brighton, and has served in that capacity until the present time. Mr. Barker was one of the organizers of the Riverview Land Company, in 1892, and he is one of its directors; he has surveyed that section into town lots, and also surveyed the route of the Riverview Railroad, which is about two miles long, and of which company he is one of the directors. Mr. Barker is esteemed by his many friends, and possesses all the characteristics of a loyal citizen and a good neighbor.

The subject of this narrative is a Republican, and has served three years as county surveyor, having been elected to that office in 1882. Socially, he is a member of the A. O. U. W.; and of the K. of P.,—both of New Brighton. Religiously, he and his family are prominent members of the Episcopal church, of which the subject hereof is a vestryman. On May 29, 1873, Mr. Barker and Miss Annie V. McClean were united in the bonds of wedlock, and to them have been born two children, George M., and Adele, both of whom are deceased.

DR. WILLIAM M. MILLER, who has an established reputation as a physician and surgeon, is a successful practitioner at Hookstown, Green township, Beaver county, Pa. His family is one of the old and highly respected families of Hancock county, West Virginia, where he was born October 5, 1863, and he is a son of John and Margaret A. (Campbell) Miller.

David Miller, the grandfather of William M., was born in County Tyrone, Ireland, and in 1775 came to this country, first locating near Pittsburg, Pennsylvania. He afterwards removed to Hancock county, West Virginia, buying a tract of land east of the village of Fairview, where he lived until the Indian outbreak in that locality. He was then driven away and moved to Chartiers, Pa., remaining until peace was finally restored. Upon returning to his former home, he followed farming until his death, in 1848, having almost reached the remarkable age of one hundred years. He married Abigail Martin, and among their offspring was one John P., the father of the subject hereof.

John P. Miller was born on the old homestead, in Hancock county, West Virginia, in 1832, and there he has always resided. He has a fine farm under a high state of cultivation, and has conducted it in a very successful manner. There are gas wells upon it, and at one time he supplied the city of East Liverpool, Ohio, with gas. He is also quite an extensive fruit raiser. In politics he is a Republican. Religiously, he is a member of the Presbyterian church. He formed a matrimonial alliance with Margaret A. Campbell, and they had the following issue: Joseph, deceased; Elmer A., who now does the farming on the old homestead; Dr. William M., whose name heads this sketch; Robert S. and Benjamin S., twins, the former a farmer in Iowa, and the latter in Hancock county, West Virginia; Margaret Ellen, the wife of Lawrence Stewart, who lives near the home farm; Mary Jane, the wife of Frank Mayhew, a farmer, of Hancock county; and Henry O., who is living at home.

Dr. William M. Miller received a common school education, and worked upon the home farm until he reached the age of fifteen years, when he learned the trade of a painter and paper hanger. After continuing thus for a period of four years, he was clerk in a store at Fairview for three years; he then taught school four years, in the meantime taking up the study of medicine. In 1887 he entered the medical department of Wooster University, now known as the College of Physicians and Surgeons of Cleveland, Ohio. Being graduated in the spring of 1890, he entered upon a successful practice at Shiloh, Ohio, where he remained until 1894. Wishing a wider field in which to follow his profession, he wisely, and with good foresight, saw the many advantages offered in Beaver county, and as a result located at Hookstown, Green township. He rapidly acquired a good paying practice, and now has the patronage of the leading class of citizens of the district. Thus he has worked his way up in life from the lowly position of a day laborer to a prominent professional status, in which he ranks as one of the most skilled practitioners in this region. He was ever ambitious and energetic, and his advancement is the result solely of individual effort.

In 1885 Dr. Miller was joined in wedlock with Ama Moore, of Fairview, West Virginia, and three children have been born to them: Cecil E.; John M.; and Edna. In political affiliations, he is a strong Republican. Religiously, he is a faithful member of the U. P. church.

PROF. RUFUS DARR. The public schools are the pride of every community, and from them may be determined the character and enterprise of its citizens. Citizens of an intellectual class and those ambitious for the future of their offspring, always employ the best instructors obtainable, and elevate their schools to the highest degree of efficiency. Thus the residents of Rochester, by securing the services of Prof. Darr, in 1892, took an important step in advancement, the good results of which are evident in the schools as they exist today. He is a man of intellectual attainments, and has passed through the ordeal of practical experience,—facts which place his record as principal above criticism.

Prof. Rufus Darr was born in Rostraver township, Westmoreland county, Pa., and is a son of John Darr, a progressive farmer of that locality. He was reared upon a farm and attended the public schools and Elder's Ridge academy. He then entered Lafayette College and after graduation in 1877, began his career as a teacher, which he has since followed continuously, with the exception of a brief period spent in farming upon the old homestead. Besides teaching for a time, in the public schools, he taught successively at Elder's Ridge Academy, Greersburg Academy, at Darlington, Pa., and for several years at Laird Institute at Murrysville, Pennsylvania. In 1892, he accepted the principalship of the Rochester schools, in which he has since continued to the satisfaction of the board and the general public. He is a man of enterprise, and has introduced new and approved methods of teaching.

It is an interesting matter to trace the development of the schools of Rochester from their beginning to their high standard under the present public school system.

The public school system of Pennsylvania dates back to the year 1834. Prior to that time schools were maintained only by private subscriptions, and very frequently were held in private houses. Singularly enough, the town of Rochester got its first actual start in that year. Early records show that two plats were made and recorded in 1834,—one by Joseph Hemphill and the other by Joseph Hinds. In this year the canal between Rochester and New Castle was completed,

and its effect was to build up the new town, which was then called "Fairport." Three years later an early directory gives a population of two hundred inhabitants. The only school house was a log structure, located on what is now the corner of Jefferson and Connecticut streets. There is no record as to when it was built or by whom. It was occupied as a school building for several years and was replaced by a frame school building now occupied by the Evangelical Association church as a parsonage. Rochester borough was organized March 20, 1849, and its first school board was named at a meeting held in this building, May 22, 1849. The board was composed of William Martin, president; Dr. Thomas J. Chandler, secretary; John Berryhill, treasurer; Robert Smith, George C. Speyerer and John McClung. The first teachers were elected May 31, 1849. They were Philip Grim, principal, and a Miss Rice, assistant. The salary of the principal was $28, and that of the assistant $14 per month. The first term of school began in June of that year. This building was used until 1862, when it was sold, the school board having purchased three lots on Jefferson street, on which a brick building was erected, which was completed in the latter year. It was a four-room structure, but was enlarged in 1868, and again during the "seventies." The steady growth of the town made a second building necessary and it was erected in 1884-1885, on Adams street. In 1891, it was again found necessary to increase the size of the school accommodations, and a four-room addition to the Adams street building was begun, and completed in the following year. The continued increase in population, and with it, a corresponding increase in the number of children of school age, has created a demand for a third building, and during the summer of 1899 the school board purchased two lots on Pinney street, on which a good brick building of modern design will shortly be erected. The town will then be provided with three substantial, well equipped brick buildings, located conveniently for the pupils in the various parts of the borough. The number of pupils enrolled is over nine hundred.

The High School department of the Rochester schools was established in 1890, under the principalship of W. F. Bliss. It was begun with a two-years' course of study, which was soon made a three-years' course, as it is at present. The attendance in the High School has constantly increased, until there is an enrolment of over sixty pupils, nearly equally divided between the three classes.

The teachers under the supervision of Prof. Darr are: S. C. Humes and Mary Stone (in the High School); and Mrs. E. C. McCoy, assistant principal; Mary Ewing, Kathryn Crane; Wilda Brown; Ada Spratly; Katie Gebhard; Kate Nannah; Kate Torrence; Martha McFetridge; Louise Taylor; Nannie Barto; Annie McCutcheon; Annie Lockhart; Fay Shanor; and Lillie Reno.

Prof. Darr married Louisa Kelley, a daughter of John Kelley, of St. Louis, and they have three children, namely: Sarah A.; John; and

Catharine D. Religiously, the Professor is a member and elder of the Presbyterian church. Socially, he belongs to the Masonic order.

———◆◆———

ROBERT M. BRYAN, the leading general merchant in the southwestern portion of Beaver county, is located at Hookstown, Green township, where he is one of the foremost business men. He is a son of James and Isabella (Miller) Bryan, and was born in Hookstown, Pa., November 14, 1850.

John Bryan, the grandfather of Robert M., was a farmer of Independence township, Beaver county, Pennsylvania. His son James, the father of the subject hereof, was born in that township, in 1806, and at an early age learned the trade of a hatter. In those days there were no shops, and he followed his trade at his own home in Hookstown most of his life, and in addition to that farmed quite extensively on land which he leased. He passed to his eternal reward at the age of eighty-two years. He was first joined in marriage with Margaret Veasy, and they had three children, as follows: Sarah, deceased; Mary, deceased; and Joseph, who is now a pilot on the lower Mississippi River. He formed a second alliance with Isabella Miller, a daughter of Col. Robert Miller, a soldier of the War of 1812, and a resident of Beaver county, and this union was blessed with seven children: Margaret, deceased; John, deceased, who served as adjutant in the

140th Reg., Pa. Vol. Inf., in the Civil War, and later practiced medicine in Kentucky and Missouri, dying in the latter state in 1874; Sarah (Smith), who lives in Arkansas City; Robert, the subject of this record; Mary, deceased; Jennie (Mercer), whose husband was formerly in partnership with Robert M. Bryan, and lives in New Wilmington, Pa.; Belle (Lawrence), who removed from Beaver county to Red Oak, Iowa, with her husband,—a physician of that place. Mrs. Bryan died in 1892, at the age of seventy-three years. Mr. Bryan was a Democrat in politics, and was a borough officeholder.

Robert M. Bryan obtained his education in the public schools of Hookstown, attending them until he was thirteen years old, after which he was a clerk for three years in a store at Shippingport, Beaver county,—thus early acquiring a knowledge of the business which he now follows. He then learned the trade of a carpenter, which he followed during the summer months for the succeeding fifteen years. In 1870, he went west to Missouri, and worked on a farm at his trade two years, but again returned to Beaver county and taught school for the next fifteen years. Subsequently he engaged as a clerk for A. G. Wilson, and served in that capacity for five years. Then, in company with Mr. Mercer, he bought a store at Hookstown, which they very successfully conducted for five years. In August, 1898, this partnership was dissolved, and Mr. Bryan became sole proprietor. He is a man of enterprise and has endeavored to please his patrons by stocking his store with

a comprehensive line of goods, including all articles in general use and for which there is a demand. He has been decidedly successful and his customers come from all over the surrounding country. Mr. Bryan owns considerable property, including a tract of forty-five acres of good farm land one mile from town, a house and lot in town, and six acres in the outskirts.

In 1874, he was married to Isabella Swaney, a daughter of Thomas and Isabella Swaney, both of whom are now dead. This marriage resulted in the birth of the following offspring: Mary, born in 1874, who lives at home; John, born in 1876; Thomas, born in 1878; Wallace, born in 1880; Joseph, born in 1883; Alfretta, born in 1886; Robert R., born in 1889; and Edward, born in 1896. Politically, Mr. Bryan is a Democrat, and served as postmaster during the administration of President Cleveland, and as justice of the peace for two terms. He was census taker of Independence township in 1882, and very satisfactorily performed his duty. He is also a member of the Beaver County Centennial Committee. Religiously, he is a faithful member of the United Presbyterian church.

———————

JAMES W. McKENZIE, of the firm of McKenzie Bros., leading contractors and builders in stone and brick, of Beaver, Beaver county, Pa., is a gentleman who has won the confidence and esteem of the citizens of that thriving borough. He is of Scotch ancestry, and was born near

Beaver, in Brighton township, October 1, 1850, being a son of Jonathan, and grandson of Joseph McKenzie.

Joseph McKenzie was born in Scotland, and came to America, settling with several other Scotchmen, in Vanport, which is just outside the corporate limits of Beaver. He bought a tract of land, which was almost entirely covered with timber, and, after clearing it, built a log house, and there reared his family. The farm is now owned by James Mitchell. Joseph McKenzie was a soldier of the War of 1812. He died at the age of eighty, and his wife also died about the same time. They were buried in the old cemetery, in Beaver. Their children were as follows: Maria, who married Alex Donald; Prestly; Hamilton; Sally, who married Robert McCabe; Jonathan; Hamilton; Joseph; Kirsley; Albert; Ellen, who married Ralph Russell; Emily, who married Oscar Conrod; and David. Emily is the only one now living, although the others grew to maturity,—the youngest of the family living until more than seventy-five years old.

Jonathan McKenzie, the father of James W., was born on the farm, and at the age of sixteen years was bound out to his brother-in-law, Alex Donald, to learn the tanning trade; the latter's tannery being the one subsequently owned by General U. S. Grant's father, in the Western Reserve, Ohio. After attaining manhood, Jonathan left this trade and went back to Vanport, where he manufactured lime, pottery and brick, and later began contracting for stone and brick build-

ings. Many of the buildings which he built are standing in Beaver at the present time, and show that the work was, for that time, of a high order. His sons, John and James, learned the trade with him, and he subsequently took them in as partners, the firm name being J. McKenzie & Sons. Mr. McKenzie met with a serious accident,—falling and breaking his hip,—which resulted in his death soon afterward, at the age of eighty-five. He married Ann McCurdy, a daughter of Andrew McCurdy, and she died at the age of seventy-eight. They were both faithful members of the M. E. church, and are buried in the cemetery at Beaver, Pennsylvania. Their children were: William, who died at the age of sixty-three years; Joseph, of Canton, Ohio; John, of Beaver; Mary, the wife of J. M. Graham; James W.; and George, of Beaver.

James W. McKenzie, whose name heads this sketch, assisted his father and became his partner, and after his father's death, he and his brother John conducted the business under the firm name of McKenzie Bros. Lately, Andrew G. McKenzie, a son of John, has also become one of the partners, and this firm is known to be the largest in their line, in Beaver. They have erected many modern and valuable houses, to the entire satisfaction of the owners. Among these houses are those of Rev. Dr. W. G. Taylor; Thomas F. Galey; John Snyder; J. B. Kirtz; J. I. Martin; J. Childs; Mrs. J. S. Rutan; D. A. Nelson; A. S. Moore; D. W. Miller; W. S. Moore; and others. The subject of this sketch built himself a fine residence on Raccoon street, which has every modern convenience. He married Mary French, a daughter of Captain Samuel B. French, of Beaver, and they have reared two children, the third child, Elsie, dying at the age of eighteen months. The others are Robert C., a graduate of Beaver College, and now a student in Effingham College, Effingham, Ill.; and Ralph, a student in the public school. Mr. McKenzie is a strong Republican, and has served six years as president of the board of education. The family are members of the M. E. church. The subject of these lines has many friends in the county, and is highly spoken of by all.

JONATHAN TAYLOR, a representative of the thrifty agricultural class of citizens of Beaver county, resides upon his fine farm in Chippewa township, where his family has lived for many years. He is a son of Jonathan and Elizabeth Taylor, and was born May 30, 1855.

His grandfather was Joseph Taylor, who was born in Oldham, England, where he followed farming, holding several life leases, and owning considerable property. He came to this country and purchased the farm which forms a portion of that owned by the subject of this record. This he improved greatly and built new barns on it, one of them being 40x60 feet, in dimensions. He raised stock and shipped to Fallston and Brighton, attaining good results in that line. He and his wife, Jane, reared six children, as follows:

Jonathan, Andrew, John, Sarah, Mary, and Ann.

Jonathan Taylor was born in Oldham, England, and after attending the public schools there for some years, worked in a coal mine until he came to America with his wife. He settled near Pittsburg and took up coal mining, which he followed for a period of two years. His father then came to this country with the rest of the Taylor family, purchasing the old Britain farm of one hundred and fifty acres in Chippewa township, and he assisted him in cultivating the farm. Upon his father's death, he received a one-third interest in the property, and later bought the entire place. He established an enviable reputation throughout the country as a stock raiser and prize winner; his animals, while being very heavy, also presented a fine appearance. This was attained mainly by the excellent care which they received, and, not as many thought who unsuccessfully tried it, by overfeeding. Many adopted his system, but never quite reached the same standard. One of his chief and most commendable characteristics was his systematic manner of doing everything, and his never-failing promptness,—it being a proud boast of his that no man was ever disappointed in an engagement made with him. He and his wife, Elizabeth, were the parents of seven children: Susanna (Rhodes), a native of England; Mary (Hooker); Joseph; J. H.; Jane (Smith); Elizabeth (Haley); and Jonathan, the subject of this biographical record. Politically, Mr. Taylor was a Republican and served as road commissioner of the

BOOK OF BIOGRAPHIES

township. Religiously, he was a devout Episcopalian. He died in 1886, at the age of seventy-four years.

Jonathan Taylor was born on the old homestead in Chippewa township, Beaver county, Pa., and obtained an elementary education in the district schools, after which he took up farming with his father. Upon the death of the latter, Jonathan inherited the farm with his brothers and sisters, but after the property had been leased for a year, he purchased it and began to improve the place. Like his father, he is a thrifty, energetic, and systematic man, and everything to which he sets his hand is done in the best fashion possible. He erected a new wagon house, and greatly enriched the soil and improved it in other ways; he has always carried on general farming and fruit raising, having a splendid orchard of goodly size. He is a man who is everywhere held in the highest esteem, and is one of the number who have done much to elevate the standard of the farming element of Pennsylvania.

The subject of this sketch was united in hymeneal bonds with Mary Reed, who was born and educated in Chippewa township, and they are the happy parents of four children, namely: Bertha M. (McGaffic); Carl Reed, who was born in 1883; Nellie B., born in 1888; and Lester D., born in 1895. In political views, he was formerly a Republican, but is now a stanch supporter of the People's party.

Mrs. Taylor is included in the membership of the United Presbyterian church.

RANKIN MARTIN, who efficiently served as district attorney from 1884 to 1890, is one of the leading practitioners of the legal profession in Beaver Falls, where he ranks as one of the borough's prominent citizens. He was born in Darlington township, Beaver county, January 14, 1852, and is a son of James P. and Mary C. Imbrie Martin, being of Scotch-Irish descent.

He was reared on the homestead farm in Darlington township; after receiving a preliminary training in the schools of his native township, he pursued advanced studies at Darlington Academy and then in Westminster College. He remained on the farm until 1876, when he was appointed deputy sheriff under his father, serving in that capacity for three years.

In 1879, he entered upon the study of law with Agnew & Buchanan, and after a careful preparation was admitted to practice, February 6, 1882. His success was immediate and in 1883 he was elected to the office of district attorney, and served with such satisfaction that he was re-elected upon the expiration of his term. He has been a constant student, increasing his vast store of knowledge in the science of law by study and practical experience, and today he ranks among the foremost of the county's attorneys.

In 1880, Mr. Martin was married to Anna Eakin, daughter of John R. Eakin, whose biography appears elsewhere in this work. They are the proud parents of three interesting children: Helen, Margaret and Mary. In religious attachments and fellowship, they

are devout members of the United Presbyterian church. Politically, our subject is a
stanch Republican.

———•◦•———

CHARLES W. WRIGHT, superintendent of the Aliquippa Steel Works, is
the youngest man in the country occupying a position of that kind in a plant of
such magnitude, and has established a reputation throughout Western Pennsylvania in
that capacity.

The Aliquippa Steel Company was organized in 1892, and has been the means of trans-
forming what was a small country way-sta-
tion into one of the most important manufacturing towns in Beaver county. Although
the town is but seven years old, it is now a
borough; it possesses excellent natural advantages, located, as it is, in the great Beaver
Valley. The officers of the company are as
follows: Joseph G. Vilsack, president; J. C.
Russell, vice president; C. A. Fagan, secretary and treasurer; Alexander Thomas, general manager; and Charles W. Wright, superintendent. The general offices are located at
No. 512-513 Times Building, Pittsburg, and
the plant covers fifteen acres of land at Aliquippa. They manufacture open hearth and
crucible steel, taking the pig iron and manufacturing the finished product; they make tool
steel for all purposes,—principally for circular
saws, disks and cross cut saws (surpassing in
this every other firm in the country), agricultural blades, and for round and hexagonal
tools. The plant consists of three buildings

and a boiler house, which is constructed of
corrugated steel, with seven immense boilers of the latest and most serviceable pattern,
which feed the 500 horse-power engine. The
dimensions of the three buildings are respectively as follows: 210 feet x 40, 230 x 40; and
160 x 40. The works employ three hundred and fifty men, and run all of the time, a
feature which is of material benefit to the borough. They have in use the six-ton steam
hammer, a machine of stupendous power,
which has revolutionized the manufacture of
steel. They also operate numerous heavy
shearing machines, punches, and several furnaces, using gas fuel from a well on the
grounds. The subject of this biography was
not yet thirty years of age when he was called
to assume the responsibilities of superintendent of these works, and having had a thorough training, he understands the business in
all of its phases. He has displayed wonderful ability in the manner of handling the large
force of men under his direction,—not only
getting their best efforts, but gaining their
good will, as well. He possesses the confidence of his employers to a marked degree,
and is held in the highest esteem by his employees. A young man of enterprise, he has
worked his way from the lowest step in the
business to his present enviable position, and
his future life presents a bright prospect.

Charles W. Wright was born in Pittsburg,
Pa., December 23, 1868, and was intellectually trained in the public schools of Pittsburg,
graduating from the high school with the
class of 1885. He at once went to work in

the mill of Park Bros., beginning at the bottom, and continued in their employ for eight years, as general mill clerk. He acquired a thorough knowledge of the business that made his services valuable, and then resigned to accept the position of assistant superintendent of the Aliquippa Steel Company. His efforts in that capacity met with such favor that, four years after, he was promoted to the general superintendency, which he now holds. He is gifted with the eye of an expert in judging the quality of steel,—deciding at a glance with as much accuracy as a chemical test would determine it,—thus saving time and expense. Mr. Wright resides in East End, Pittsburg, Pa., where he has many friends.

He was united in marriage with Catherine Clark, a daughter of Dr. H. H. Clark, the well-known physician, and they have two children: Bessie, born in 1893; and Catherine, born in 1897. Politically, he is a Republican, but is too busy to participate actively in partisan affairs. He is a member of the order of the Royal Arcanum.

———— • • ————

DANIEL R. CORBUS, postmaster and tax-collector of New Brighton, Pa., ranks among the most prominent and popular citizens of Beaver county. He was born in Beaver, September 29, 1839, and attended public schools until he attained the age of twelve years, when he was forced to work out as chore-boy on a farm, for several years. He afterwards entered the Lownsend

Wire Mills and learned wire-drawing, which he followed for forty-two years, with the exception of the time spent in actual service during the Civil War. In 1870, Mr. Corbus was elected coroner of Beaver county, and held that office until 1876. He was also elected tax-collector in 1894, and has been re-elected every year since; he is now serving his sixth year in that capacity. October 1, 1898, Mr. Corbus was appointed postmaster of New Brighton,—succeeding William Wallace. The office ranks in the second class, and its earliest record is the appointment of B. B. Chamberlain, as postmaster, March 12, 1849. He was succeeded by O. Waters, December 23, 1852; he was succeeded by C. H. Higby, July 7, 1853; he was succeeded by John Glass, April 16, 1857; he was succeeded by Isaac Covert, July 12, 1859; he was succeeded by John C. Boyle, March 13, 1861; he was succeeded by Mrs. E. B. Cuthbertson, January 24, 1869; she was succeeded by Walter S. Branden, March 1, 1886; he was succeeded in March, 1892, by A. J. Bingham, who was in turn succeeded by William Wallace.

Daniel R. Corbus was united in marriage with Cornelia Fairman, a daughter of Captain William Fairman, of Pittsburg. They have one son and one daughter, namely: William, and Thankful. William is a brakeman on the railroad, and makes his home in Perry, Iowa. He married Margaret Brown, and now has two children, Chester and Lucian. Thankful is her father's able assistant in the postoffice. The subject of this sketch is a son of John S. and Eliza (Reeves) Corbus, and a grandson of John and Betsey (Skillinger) Corbus. The original name of the family was Corbustria, and they descended from the early French Huguenots. John Corbus spent his early life in the state of Maryland, south of Baltimore. Later in life, he went west to Ohio, with Messrs. McIntyre and Zane, and assisted those gentlemen to survey and lay out the town of Zanesville, Ohio,—where he finally settled. He conducted a hotel there for many years, and the building which he occupied is still standing. Tradition says his hotel was famous for its clean floors and its good meals. In those days beds were almost unknown in country inns or hotels,—it being customary for each traveler to carry his own blanket and, wrapped therein, to sleep on the floor near the old fireplace. Mr. Corbus died when about the age of forty-two years. His wife was Betsey Skillinger, of George's Run, near Cumberland, Maryland. She bore him the following children: John S., Rosa, Tina, and Eliza. Some time after the death of Mr. Corbus, the widow contracted a second marriage. She became the wife of Mr. World, by whom she had several children.

John S. Corbus was born at Zanesville, Muskingum county, Ohio, and, while still a young man, went to Fallston, Beaver county, Pennsylvania. In 1824, he began learning the art of making scythes, under the instructions of a Mr. Blanchard. They were then made by hand, but several years afterwards machinery took the place of the hand-work, and then Mr. Corbus withdrew from the business, and learned the trade of wire-drawing

in the factory of Robert Lownsend, at Fallston. He followed the latter business during all of his active days. In 1836, or 1837, he purchased a lot on what is now the corner of Fourth avenue and Thirteenth street, and upon this site he built a substantial brick dwelling in which he spent the closing years of his life,—dying at the advanced age of eighty-five years. His remains lie buried in the Grove cemetery. His beloved wife, who was Eliza Reeves before her marriage, also attained a good old age, passing to the life beyond the grave, at the age of eighty-three years, and being buried by the side of her husband. Seven children were born to them; Mary J., wife of Hugh Irwin; John, of Beaver Falls; Thankful, wife of Dr. Louis Jack; Elizabeth, who came to her death by drowning in childhood; Margaret, wife of Richard Irwin; Daniel R., the subject of this sketch; and Jesse M., who resides at New Brighton.

April 17, 1861, Daniel R. Corbus enlisted in the New Brighton Rifle Company for a short time, but later re-enlisted as a private in the Ninth Pa. (Pittsburg) Rifles, and served in the battle of Dranesville, the Seven Days' Battle before Richmond, and the second Battle of Bull Run. Then sickness compelled him to enter the hospital; after recovering his usual health, he participated in the battles of Fredericksburg and Gettysburg, and was honorably discharged, May 4, 1864. He re-enlisted in the 17th Reg., Pa. Vol. Cavalry, and served until the successful termination of the war. Mr. Corbus is a member of the Union Veteran Legion, No. 1. He is a member and past grand, of I. O. O. F. lodge, and is past royal patriarch of the encampment, having also represented that body in the grand lodge of the state; he is also a member, and past commander, of the Knights of Pythias. He has taken a fitting and active interest in his borough, serving in the council for several years, and having charge of the fire department. In 1894, he was elected tax collector for a term of three years.

The subject of this memoir inherited a part of his father's lot on Fourth avenue, and erected a handsome brick residence upon it, which he now occupies. His political affiliations are with the Republican party, and he is universally esteemed by all who have the pleasure to know him. In business life Mr. Corbus is worthy and straightforward; in social circles, he is a true and firm friend; he has fulfilled the duties of his office with credit and honor,—having fine natural abilities adapting him to even a higher and more difficult position.

———◆◆◆———

WILLIAM H. FORBES is superintendent of the Keystone Axle Company, which is located at Morado, Beaver county, and the offices of this large plant are at No. 200 Telephone Building, Pittsburg, Pa. The method used in the making of axles by this company is called the rolling process, and it is the only company in the world that uses that method, all others using the hammer process. This process has attracted much attention throughout the world

and the subject of this sketch is to give an exhibition of the process to an audience of railroad and steel experts from Paris. Mr. Forbes was born at Warren, Pa., June 18, 1857, and is a son of William and Martha (Shaw) Forbes, both residents of Warren county, Pennsylvania.

He attended the public schools of Warren and then learned the trade of a carpenter, and later the millwright trade. He completed his mechanical trade at the Richmond Locomotive Works, at Richmond, Va., after which time he spent several months working in the round house of the Nickel Plate Railroad at Bellevue, Ohio. His next position was at Chicago, Ill., where he became foreman of the U. S. Rolling Stock Company; when that plant failed in 1890, he found employment in the large greenhouse of G. W. Miller, the largest florist of Chicago. In the spring of 1891 he was employed by the Standard Oil Company as fuel expert, being engaged in teaching the people how to burn fuel oil. January 1, 1892, Mr. Forbes became master mechanic of the Chambers & McKee Glass Works, at Jeannette, Westmoreland county, Pa., remaining with that company three years and three months. He then went into business on his own account as mechanical adviser, at No. 210 Bissell block, Pittsburg. After two years of this line of business, sickness compelled him to make a change, and after a year of recuperation, on February 22, 1897, he accepted a position as master mechanic of the company with which he is now connected. July 10, 1897, he again resumed his position with the Standard Oil Company as fuel expert, being assigned to the eastern states, and making a specialty of glass works. He returned to the Keystone Axle Works January 12, 1898, becoming superintendent of the works. The plant is 80 by 200 feet, and the company make railroad car-axles for the Pennsylvania Railroad and for many other railroads throughout the country. Although the rolling process is thought by many to be impossible, it has so far been pronounced by experts to be a decided success. Mr. Forbes is the third superintendent of this large plant, and is the only one who has made it successful.

Mr. Forbes was wedded to Miss Eva Randall, of Jamestown, N. Y., and six children have been born to them: Maude, Thomas, Francis, Alma, Edward, and Edna. The subject of this sketch is a member of the Latter Day Saints, of which sect he is an ardent supporter, and whose headquarters are at Lamoni, Iowa.

CHARLES A. TREIBER, the leading plumber and contractor of Beaver Falls, Beaver county, Pa., and an active member of the firm of Treiber & Co., has for many years been one of the most prominent men of the town, and is looked upon by all as a man of great worth and sterling business principles. In all business dealings he is honest and upright, as the large number of contracts which he receives goes to prove. He was born in Beaver Falls, in 1861; is a son of John Treiber, and grandson of Jacob Treiber.

Jacob Treiber was a native of Germany, and during all his active business life held an important position under the German government as inspector of forests, having a large territory under his supervision. John Treiber, the father of Charles A., was born in Germany in 1830, received his schooling in his native city, and graduated from one of the famous universities of the country. He came to America and followed the trade of paper bleaching, which he had learned in his native country. After working at this for many years in Latrobe, Pa., he was induced by the firm of Frazier & Metzger, to move to Beaver Falls, which he did in 1886. He was in the employ of this firm for twenty-five years. In 1852 he was united in marriage with Matilda Day, who was born in Beaver Falls in 1830, and received her schooling in that town. They reared four children, as follows: Charles A., the subject of this sketch; James, baggagemaster on the Fort Wayne R. R.; Catherine, now Mrs. Elliot, living in Pittsburg; and Jeannie, now Mrs. Couch, of Kent, Ohio. In politics Mr. Treiber was a Democrat. He belonged to the Lutheran church. Fraternally, he was identified with the I. O. O. F. and K. of P. His death occurred in 1889.

Charles A. Treiber received his schooling in Beaver Falls, and learned the trade of plumbing in the shops of Chandley Bros., and became an expert workman; the finest work in the shop was always given to him. He remained in the employ of this firm for twenty-five years, and in 1892 started in business for himself, under the firm name of C. A. Treiber & Co. His first store was located at 1404 Seventh avenue, and he then moved to temporary quarters on Fourteenth street. The store is now located on Seventh avenue, in handsome new quarters recently purchased by the firm. There is a fine display-room, sales-room, stock-room and work-shop. Some of the best and largest contracts in the county have been awarded to the firm, among them may be mentioned the buildings of John Elliot; Dr. Moon; F. H. Laird; J. Kurtz; Judge Wickham; the Doncaster house; McColl Tube Co.; Emerson, Smith & Co.; Glass Company; Mayer Pottery Co.; Enamel Sign Co.; H. M. Myers Co. The firm has also done a great deal of work for the P. & L. E. R. R. besides having numerous less important contracts. They do plumbing, gas, steam and hot water pipe fitting, and also do a large business in bath tubs. They are special agents in the county for the Champion beer pump, and Welsbach lights. They also deal extensively in gas stoves, and keep a large stock on hand. The firm can rightly be proud of their store, and feel that their efforts have been well rewarded.

The subject of this biography married Annie O. Connell, who was born and educated in Buffalo, New York. Mr. Treiber is an independent Democrat, is a school director; member of the R. A.; past chancellor, and grand lodge officer of the K. of P.; and a member of the I. O. O. F. He takes an active part in all political and social affairs, and is well known throughout the county.

C. McKIM,* a retired contractor and builder, is spending his declining years on his fine farm in Big Beaver township, Beaver county, Pa., and enjoying the fruits of a well-spent life. He was born December 17, 1834, is a son of William and Margaret (Gilkey) McKim, and a grandson of James and Hannah (Lewis) McKim.

James McKim was born in Ireland, in 1744. When twenty-two years of age, he came to America. Not many years after he sought a home in America, the Revolutionary War broke out. James joined the Washington Life Guards and served throughout that long and bloody struggle, as did his brother John, who was in the same regiment.

At the close of the war, James went to Northumberland county, where he found employment as a furnace man in the iron works. He left there eight years afterwards, and engaged in similar work in the Beaver Valley. About the year 1800 he bought a farm of wild land in Beaver county. After opening a small area, he built a log house and barn and engaged in clearing and cultivating the rest of the tract. He improved his place as rapidly as possible, and raised general farm products. He died at the good old age of eighty-eight. Hannah Lewis, also born and reared in Ireland, became his faithful wife and they reared six of their seven children. The names of their offspring are: Alexander; Thomas; John; William, the father of J. C.; Mary (Marshall); Hannah, who died aged eleven; and Elizabeth.

William McKim was born in Northumberland county, Pa., in 1790. When only ten years old, he accompanied his parents to Beaver county, where he attended school. After this he engaged in farming. When twenty-two years old, he enlisted in the army, and fought in the War of 1812, serving through that memorable contest. On the termination of the struggle he resumed work on the farm, assisting his father on the old homestead. At a period later in life, he purchased a farm of ninety-five acres, and upon this he built a two-story, hewed-log house, which was a very fine house, for those days. He cleared his land, raised a great deal of grain, and also devoted much time and attention to sheep-raising. He was a shoemaker, also, and followed that trade to a considerable extent during the winter months.

William McKim was twice married. In November, 1816, he was wedded to Letitia Miller, by whom he had four children, namely: Robert, Hannah, Lewis and James. Robert was born in 1818, was educated in the district schools, and was a teacher for fourteen years. He was a fine linguist; later in life, he devoted his attention to agricultural pursuits. Hannah (Cochran) was born in May, 1820; Lewis, was born January 7, 1823, and James was born July 14, 1825. Some time after the death of his first wife, Mr. McKim formed a second matrimonial alliance by wedding Margaret Gilkey, who was also born and schooled in Beaver county. This union resulted in five children, whose names are: T. W., a prominent educator; J. C., subject of this biography; William A., a successful

farmer in Kansas; Harvey M.; and Mary J. (Runyon). William McKim belonged to the Republican party. He served as school director, supervisor and collector. He was a consistent member of the United Presbyterian church, of which he was a deacon for many years. He died in 1856, and his widow survived him until 1879.

J. C. McKim was born on the old homestead, and was the recipient of a good practical education obtained in the district schools. He learned the carpenter's trade, and followed that line of work until 1861. He then enlisted in the Union army and served nine months in the Civil War. His brother, Harvey M., also enlisted, and served three years and a half. After the war, J. C. McKim formed a partnership with his brother, and worked at contracting and building, until 1868. He then bought his first farm, containing fifty-five acres. He carried on the double work of farming and contracting and was soon enabled to add forty acres to his original purchase. He then discontinued carpentering and devoted his time exclusively to farming. From time to time he has added to his land until he now owns one of the finest farms in Beaver county. It contains two hundred and fifty-nine acres and has two fine dwelling houses. One is an attractive brick residence and the other is a new frame, recently built by Mr. McKim from plans and specifications of his own design. It is a handsome structure and a model of beauty and convenience. It was built two years ago, and is now occupied by Mr. McKim as his home. The barns, sheds and out-buildings compare well with the house in the matter of modern design.

The subject hereof carries on general farming. He married Sabina Miller, a talented lady, who was born in 1840, and became Mr. McKim's wife, in 1864. She is a daughter of William and Margaret (Crawford) Miller, and a granddaughter of Robert and Catherine (Williams) Miller. Robert Miller was born at Northampton, and came to his death at the age of forty-five years,—while assisting in raising a barn. He married Catherine Williams, and they had ten children, namely: Aaron; William; Moses; Charles, who died at the age of eight years; Lettie (McKim); Jane (Crawford); Ellen (Shannon); Mary (McChesney); Sidney, who remained single; and Elizabeth, who was twice married. Her first husband's name was Eckels; her second was a Mr. Parker.

William Miller was born, in 1802, in Beaver county, where he was educated. He learned the shoemaker's trade, which he followed during the winters. When his services in this capacity were required he would go to the house where shoes were needed, and remain there until he had made shoes for the entire family, if so requested. During the summer he engaged in farming. He was joined in marriage with Margaret Crawford, a daughter of Robert and Martha (McClelland) Crawford. They reared six children, namely: Ellen, born in 1828; Robert, born in 1831; Martha (wife of F. W. McKim), born in 1834; Aaron, born in 1837; Sabina (J. C. McKim's wife), born in 1840; and Nevin, born in 1843.

To the subject of this biography and his worthy wife one son, William M. McKim, was born, in 1865. William M. McKim was a student at Bridgewater Academy, and is a fine scholar. He adopted, however, the peaceful, independent life of a farmer. He married Ironette Patterson and three bright children now bless their home. They are Mary R., born in 1894; John P., born in 1896; and Robert G., born in 1898.

Previous to his marriage with Miss Patterson, William M. assisted his father, who then gave him a place of his own, as a foundation for his future career. Mr. McKim has been an elder in the United Presbyterian church for several years. In politics he acknowledges his preference for the Republican party. He has served as school director, and in various township offices.

JOHN M. HUGHES,* who is highly esteemed as one of the leading citizens of Beaver Falls, Pa., is one of the most extensive contractors in this section of the state and has erected many industrial plants, and constructed a large number of railroads. He is a son of John A. and Elizabeth (Grubh) Hughes, and was born in Braddock, Pa., in 1860.

John A. Hughes, the father of John M., was born in Pine Creek, Allegheny county, Pa., in 1822, and in 1840 removed to Braddock, where he followed the business of general contracting for thirty years. In 1870, he built the Grant Mills on Clarion River, which he conducted until they were destroyed by fire. He then returned to Braddock, and started a steam saw-mill and a boat building yard. He bought the steamboat Kangaroo, of which he acted as captain for several years; in 1875, he moved to Beaver Falls, and engaged in general contracting. At a subsequent period he took in his sons as partners, as he preferred the river life, which he continued to follow until his death, on March 14, 1898. He married Elizabeth Grubb, and they became the parents of eight children: Mary (Sloss); Elizabeth (Beams); Margaret (Willets); Martha (Casner); James H., who was killed at Edgar Thompson's steel works; Olive L. (Willets); John M., the subject of this personal history; and E. O., who is also a contractor. Mr. Hughes was a Democrat in politics; he belonged to the Disciples' church. Fraternally, he is a member of the Odd Fellows order.

John M. Hughes obtained his primary education in the public schools of Braddock, and took an advanced course at Miss Bell's Institute, a private school. He moved with his family to Beaver Falls, and at once secured a position as office boy with the H. M. Myers Shovel Company; after a while he was transferred to the finishing and handle department. He was finally promoted to be inspector,—which speaks well for his ability and general knowledge of the business,—for that was a feature of the work which Mr. Myers had personally attended to for many years. Continuing thus for three years, he, in the meanwhile, took a course in civil engineering under the instruction of P. Kirkerwaugh. In 1878, he resigned and was taken into the partnership with his father, the firm name becoming John A. Hughes & Sons, with offices on Ninth street, between First and Second avenues. Their first work was to build the A. F. Wolf stove foundry, but as their reputation grew, their business increased, and they completed many large contracts,—including large coal works in West Virginia; the barns and houses of the Sewickley Dairy Company; the Newcastle Steel & Wire Nail Mills; the Beaver Falls Chemical Works; and the Bellevue school building. In 1888, John M. Hughes retired from the firm and started into business for himself, with offices at No. 1011 Seventh avenue. His first work was to erect a store room for J. T. Howarth, now the Farmers' National Bank, at the corner of Eleventh street and Seventh avenue. He then built a store adjoining this for John White, who occupied it with a five and ten cent store,—and he himself took offices over it. He then accepted a contract to build the Beaver & Ellwood Short Line R. R., and took options on a great deal of the property, selling it at handsome profits; this was his first important contract while in business for himself. He then went to Ellwood, while the railroad was in the course of construction, and drove the first stake, and put up the first building, in what is now one of the most prosperous towns in Lawrence county. He also built the tube works and the enamel factory, and later had charge of the entire property in the village. This was a very successful undertaking and in two years he made considerable money. In 1892, he returned to Beaver Falls and became interested in the street railways and other business ventures; he built the Shenango Valley Railway, from Sharon to Sharpsville, and also the pottery works. He then formed a special partnership with George C. Wareham, for the construction of the Pittsburg & Homestead Street Railway, which was completed in December, 1894, It might be stated here that owing to a lack of business ability, and the foolish and absurd actions of a few of the directors, this immense contract was almost a total loss, and was a severe blow to Mr. Hughes. Having once ascended the ladder to the top round, he was now forced to the ground, to begin anew. Everybody had the utmost confidence in him, and respected him for the scrupulous manner in which he met every obligation. In 1895, he went to West Virginia and built the Moundsville, Benwood & Wheeling R. R., but here again ill luck seemed to follow him, for it was not until after three years of litigation, that he was able to procure his money. In 1897, he returned to Beaver Falls, and made the plans and specifications for the Titusville, Hydetown & Pleasantville Ry., and a short time afterward became a promoter and builder of the Riverview Street Railway. He employs a large force of men, the number ranging between seventy-five and three hundred,—over whom he exercises personal supervision.

He was united in marriage with Ida L. Littlefield, a descendant of two of America's most distinguished families, and a daughter of Dr. Littlefield, of North Adams, Mass. She was born in Sterling, Ill., and after completing her education in Edwards Seminary, taught in the Sterling High School. Her union with Mr. Hughes has been blessed by the birth of two children: Homer L., who was born in November, 1892; and J. Mitchell, born in June, 1895. Politically, Mr. Hughes is a stanch Republican, but has accepted but one office,—that of postmaster of Ellwood. Religiously, he is a liberal supporter of the Presbyterian church.

———— • • ————

REV. ROBERT WILSON KIDD* is the beloved pastor of the United Presbyterian church at Beaver Falls, Pa., which charge he has had since the year 1892. He is a man of great strength of will and force of character, with brilliant mind and self-reliance, and by his courteous manners and winning address, he has not only won the esteem and affection of the members of his congregation, but also the cordial regard of the citizens of the borough. Mr. Kidd is a son of James and Sarah (Middagh) Kidd, and was born in 1848, in Juniata county, Pennsylvania.

James Kidd was born in Ireland, and came to this country in 1819; upon arriving he located in Juniata county, Pa., where he bought a large farm and followed agricultural pursuits the rest of his life. He was a strong anti-slavery man, and always voted the Republican ticket. As a result of his union with

Sarah Middagh, seven children were born.

Rev. Mr. Kidd received his preliminary education in the public schools, and afterwards pursued a course at Westminster College at New Wilmington; in the meantime having decided upon entering the ministry, he began his studies in the theological seminary at Newburg, N. Y., in 1873, and completed them in 1876,—when he was at once ordained to the ministry. A very prominent charge was assigned to him,—the Seventh Avenue United Presbyterian Church of New York City, and he continued to occupy the pulpit of that church until 1892. In that year, he accepted his present pastorate in Beaver Falls, which has ever since continued to flourish. The present edifice was erected, in 1893, at a cost of $17,000, and it is one of the most handsome churches in the county; the large liability thereby incurred has been very nearly cleared, through the untiring efforts of Rev. Mr. Kidd. When the subject of this sketch assumed his present position, the membership numbered only 224, which number has since been increased to about four hundred. The Sabbath school has about 300 members, and all the departments of the church are in a flourishing condition; these are the Young People's Church Union,—the Junior Society,—the Ladies' Aid Society, the Women's Missionary Society, and the Young Women's Missionary Society. Rev. Mr. Kidd is an earnest Christian, a messenger of peace and good will, and manifests those traits of character which gain for him the esteem and respect of all who know him.

Politically, Rev. Mr. Kidd is a strong Prohibitionist and interests himself in the cause of good government. He was united in the bonds of matrimony with Amanda Harper, a daughter of Dr. James Harper, now of Xenia Theological Seminary, in Ohio. This union was blessed by the birth of four children, namely: Robert Wallace; Chester Buchanan; Howard Carson; and Gladys Harper.

————————

SAMUEL J. CROSS, Jr.,* a prosperous citizen and well-known business man of Rochester, Beaver county, Pa., is agent for H. T. Morris of Pittsburg, with whom he has been identified for more than eleven years. He was born February 5, 1865, at Rochester, Beaver county, Pa., and is a son of Samuel J., Sr., a grandson of Joseph, great-grandson of Samuel, and great-great-grandson of Samuel.

Samuel J. Cross, Sr., the father of the subject hereof, was born in Charlestown, Washington county, R. I., January 6, 1828, and was a pupil of Greenwich Academy at Greenwich, R. I. He was subsequently engaged in teaching, which he continued until he became bookkeeper for Roland G. Hazzard at Peacedale, R. I. In 1855, he removed with his wife to Rochester, Pa., where he opened a general store on Water street, with E. S. Gardner, under the firm name of Cross & Gardner. At a later period he built the block where Mr. Thomas conducts a clothing store, and engaged in business alone, but the firm name finally became S. J. Cross & Co. It was the leading store in the borough and was extensively patronized. Mr. Cross was one of the most energetic business men, who have ever made their homes at Rochester, and his success was due solely to his own enterprise. He took an earnest interest in public affairs, and was connected with many business ventures as promoter and stockholder. He became agent of the Rochester Land Company for Samuel Signes, a company reported on the verge of failure. But his keen eye for business and rare foresight pointed out the way to success in that line, and the firm soon became a prosperous and influential one. He was a man of excellent standing in the community, and his advice, often sought, was freely given. He built a fine residence, known now as the Vandersliel estate. Politically, he was a stanch Republican and served in the state legislature in 1873-1874. He served as school director many years, and was instrumental in the establishment of first-class schools in the borough. Religiously, he was a Baptist and was a trustee and one of the founders of the church. His wife, whose maiden name was Frances Elizabeth Wells, is still living. They had the following issue: Julia F., the wife of B. T. Dimson; Mary E., who died in infancy; Samuel J., the subject of this personal history; Emma W., the wife of C. L. Blazier; George H., a grocer, of Rochester; and Thomas W., who also resides at Rochester. Mr. Cross died September 27, 1875.

Samuel J. Cross, Jr., attended the public schools, and after obtaining a good prelimi-

nary training took a course of study in Beaver College. He then attended the Iron City Business College, after which he entered the employ of his father, with whom he remained until January 1, 1880, when he became connected with the People's Institute, of Pittsburg, as clerk and agent. He continued in their employ until eight years later, when he became identified with H. T. Morris of Pittsburg. He is a thorough business man, quick to grasp an opportunity for advancement, and one in whom everybody has the greatest confidence. He has always resided at Rochester and, in 1895, erected a handsome home on Vermont street, where he now lives.

Mr. Cross was joined in hymeneal bonds with Effie Jenkins, a daughter of Oscar F. Jenkins of Wellsville, Ohio, and they have had five children: Oscar Joseph, who died in infancy; Mary B., who died in infancy; Alpheus Jenkins; Samuel Joseph, who died in childhood; and Effie Letitia. Religiously, he is a member of the Baptist church, while his wife is a faithful member of the Episcopal church.

---·•·---

T HOMAS E. CRAVEN* is a large stockholder in, and superintendent of, the American Porcelain Manufacturing Company of New Brighton, Pa., and he is the inventor of a composition, which is used in the making of pottery, that surpasses all other preparations used in the making of such wares. He was born in New Brighton June 3, 1856, and is the only child of John Craven, Jr., and grandson of John Craven, Sr.

The grandfather of Thomas E. was of English extraction and spent the greater part of his life in Beaver county, Pennsylvania. In 1830, he began the manufacture of threshing machines at Fallston, in this county, and after several years of success, his establishment was burned down, and he sustained a severe loss. He then applied himself to contracting in New Brighton, and followed that line of business until his death, which occurred at the age of seventy-eight years. His wife, Catherine, died when ninety-four years old, and they are buried in the Grove cemetery. They reared a family of children, all of whom grew to maturity; their names are: James, Sarah, Benjamin, Matilda, Isabella, John, William, Minerva, Charles, and Madison. The father of Thomas E. was a carpenter by trade; he died in the prime of life.

The subject of this memoir was reared by his grandfather, and the day before he was twelve years of age, he entered the pottery works as an apprentice; he worked in all the departments, and became a master of the trade. His inventive turn of mind led to the making of an enamel superior to pottery, and his secret process was not revealed until the organizing of the American Porcelain Manufacturing Company, of which he is superintendent, and a stockholder. This company was organized November 24, 1894; they purchased the tile factory of Scott Brothers, located on Allegheny street, and their kilns, engine house, storage and ware house, and shipping house cover three acres of ground. Thirty skilled hands are employed by this company, who turn out a fine grade of porcelain ware, which consists mostly of porcelain tubs, sinks, and kitchen and pantry utensils; they also have many orders for specialties in the porcelain line. Much of the success of this company is due to the untiring energy of the subject hereof, who is not only thoroughly acquainted with this line of business but is a man of good business ability. He is popularly known throughout the county and possesses many warm friends.

Mr. Craven erected, and lived in, the residence now owned by E. Liddell, on Fourteenth street; he now resides at No. 120, Tenth avenue. Mr. Craven first wedded Flora Hoagland, a daughter of John Hoagland, of Rochester; she died aged twenty-two years, leaving one child, Elva May. His second union was with Alice Thompson Foster, a daughter of Harry S. Foster, of Beaver Falls, and their home has been blessed by the birth of six children: Nellie Luzetta; Alice Verna; Luverne Eugene; Harry; Thomas H.; and a son who died early in life.

—— ·——· · ·——·——

E. L. HUTCHINSON*, a progressive business man, and highly respected citizen, of Beaver Falls, Beaver county, Pa., is secretary of the Emerson, Smith & Co. Saw Works, an extensive plant covering three acres of ground and situated on Fourteenth street, which ships its product to all parts of the world. He is a son of William and Sarah (Lowrey) Hutchinson, and was born in Pittsburg, Pa., August 28, 1852.

His grandfather was William Hutchinson, who was born in Ireland, and was of Scotch-Irish descent. He attended the local public schools and afterwards came to America, settling in Pittsburg, Pa., where he followed the trade of a mechanic throughout his life. Politically, he was a Whig and subsequently a Republican, but never sought office. In a religious sphere, he was a member of the Reformed Presbyterian church. He was the father of five children, whose names are as follows: William; Samuel, a patternmaker by trade; Robert, who followed the occupation of a machinist; Eliza J. (Armstrong), who was for many years a director of public works; and James, a machinist.

William Hutchinson, father of the subject of this sketch, was born in Ireland, and after receiving a good intellectual training in the public schools, was brought to this country by his parents. It was but natural that he should take up the occupation at which his father had been so successful. He became a machinist and engine builder, and was one of the finest workmen in Pittsburg. He was a member of the firm of Hartup & Co., and subsequently, of the firm of Robinson, Minnis & Miller, the well known manufacturers of marine and stationary engines. In connection with his brother Robert, William Hutchinson has the distinction of having built the first steam-power fire engine ever made in this country, which was tested in Cincinnati, in 1854, and was a pronounced success. It was while testing this engine that he contracted a severe cold, which shortly afterwards resulted in his death, in the year 1855. He was united in marriage with Sarah Lowrey, who was born and schooled in Ireland, and they were the parents of three children: William, a mechanic by trade; E. L., the subject hereof; and Clifford, who was cashier of the Allegheny National Bank up to the time of his death. In political affiliations, he was a Whig. He was a member of the Reformed Presbyterian church. Mrs. Hutchinson survived her husband six years, dying in the year 1861.

E. L. Hutchinson was left an orphan at an early age, and attended the public schools but a short time, when he entered the employ of J. H. Ellerman, the hatter. He subsequently became a clerk in the cashier's office of the Pennsylvania Railroad, and continued there for seven years, when he removed to Beaver Falls to accept a position as bookkeeper for the Emerson, Smith & Co. Saw Works. He continued in that capacity for about six years, when he was taken into the firm, and was elected secretary. He is also vice-president.— Julius F. Kurtz being president. He has served in that position without a break since his first incumbency, and has become one of the leading business men of the town. He possesses good business qualifications and manifests tact and enterprise in all of his transactions. The plant is located on Fourteenth street, and covers an area of three acres. It is a large stone building, and in addition, are the engine rooms and office buildings. They turn out saws, knives and all other edged tools, which are placed upon the market in all parts of the world. They employ a force of ninety men.

In 1881, Mr. Hutchinson was united in marriage with Clara Perrott, who was born in Fallston, Beaver county, and attended school in Beaver Falls; they have two children: Juliet, who was born in 1885; and Lucille, born in 1890. Politically, Mr. Hutchinson is a Republican. He is a trustee of the Presbyterian church.

INDEX.

Biographical.

INDEX.

Portraits.

www.ingramcontent.com/pod-product-compliance
Lightning Source LLC
Chambersburg PA
CBHW030951110726
47900CB00004B/1225